INVINCIBILIS

A William Occam Mystery

MICHAEL HARMON

This book is a work of historical fiction. Most of the characters depicted in *Invincibilis* actually existed, although their participation in the historical events described here is the product of the author's imagination. Other characters are wholly fictional, and any resemblance to real people, living or dead, is coincidental.

About the Author

Michael Harmon is Professor Emeritus of Public Administration and Policy at the George Washington University. He taught at GW for more than forty years, specializing in organizational theory, government ethics, and Pragmatist philosophy. He is the author or co-author of numerous scholarly articles and five books, including *Responsibility as Paradox* and (with O. C. McSwite) *Whenever Two or More Are Gathered.* He is currently working on a sequel to *Invincibilis* in which Friar William and Lady Eleanor may meet again.

Power . . . comes not from above but from below,

from the representatives of the people,

including laity, both men and women.

William Occam[i]

Cast of Characters
(* designates a fictional figure)

William Occam: Franciscan friar (aka Greyfriar)

Eleanor de Clare: Eldest niece of King Edward II; wife of Hugh le Despenser the Younger; formerly principal lady-in-waiting to Queen Isabella

Edward II: King of England, 1308-1326; son of Edward I ("Longshanks")

Isabella: Edward II's queen and sister of the French King Charles IV; ally of Roger Mortimer, with whom she later acts as regent for her son, Edward III

Hugh le Despenser the Younger: King Edward's court favorite; husband of Eleanor de Clare

John de Berkhamsted: Lady Eleanor's chamberlain

Charles IV: King of France, 1322-1328; son of King Philip IV (Philip the Fair); brother of Queen Isabella

Roger Mortimer of Wigmore: First Earl of March; English nobleman and enemy of Edward II; ally and purported lover of Queen Isabella

Adam Wodeham: Franciscan friar; Occam's friend and protégé in London

Manuele Fieschi: Genoese priest; aide to Pope John XXII

* *Brother Gerardo*: Young Franciscan friar in Avignon; Occam's apprentice and scribe

John XXII (nee Jacques Duèze): Second Avignon pope

Walter Burley: Dominican cleric and scholar; clerical courtier between Avignon and England

John Lutterell: Dominican monk; former chancellor of Oxford; member of the papal commission investigating Occam in Avignon

Richard de Bury: English secular priest; supporter of Isabella and Mortimer; tutor to Edward of Windsor (later King Edward III)

Durand of Saint-Pourçain: Dominican philosopher and theologian; member of the papal commission investigating Occam in Avignon

Stephen Dunheved: Edward II's bodyguard; pirate in league with Hugh le Despenser

Thomas Dunheved: Stephen's younger brother; Dominican monk; King Edward's confessor and private emissary

John of Reading: Franciscan friar in Avignon; former regent master at Oxford

* *Thierry of Narbonne*: Abbot of the Franciscan convent in Avignon

Francesco Petrarca (Petrarch): Italian poet and scholar

Michael of Cesena: Minister General of the Franciscan Order

* *Guarin*: A condemned Spiritual Franciscan

* *Joyeuse*: Novice at the Carmelite convent in Avignon

Gerard D'Alspaye: Sub-Lieutenant of the Tower of London; ally of
    Roger Mortimer

Bernard Gui: Dominican monk; Pope John's chief inquisitor

Bonagratia of Bergamo: Franciscan friar; doctor of civil and canon
    law

* *Brother Estienne*: Benedictine monk; official at the Avignon
    leprosarium

* *Véronique*: Abbess of the Carmelite convent in Digne

* *Verdun*: Officer of the Papal Guard

* *Clario of Parma*: Abbot of the Benedictine Abbey in the Piedmont

* *Prince Rupert*: Louis of Bavaria's nephew and spymaster

* *Berengar*: Agent of Prince Rupert

Marsilius of Padua: Italian philosopher in league with the
    Franciscans

* *William of Baskerville*: Franciscan friar; Occam's mentor at
    Oxford

PROLOGUE

AVIGNON

May 13, 1328 — The Piazza Steps and Greyfriars Convent

THE ASSASSIN'S BUSINESS was not yet finished. He had intended to deposit the victim in the palace's cistern, twenty paces from where the passageway branched off from the steps to the piazza. On descending to the murky bottom the body would escape notice until, days later, a sweetly noxious odor greeted the nostrils of a passerby. Which seemed like a sensible plan until, in a furious pirouette, the victim struck the assassin's chin with his elbow, driving his skull against the limestone wall behind him. It was the victim's final, instinctive act of defiance, coinciding with the thrust of a dagger between his ribs. He slumped to the base of the passageway, still a fair distance from the cistern.

A quarter-mile away the great iron bell of *Notre-Dame des Doms* pealed its summons to Avignon's faithful. Partly muted by wind and rain, the bell's incessant clanging confounded the assassin's senses. As he braced against the wall, claps of thunder made his ears ring, blood oozing from his brow clouded his vision, and bile surging in his throat made him fear he would vomit. A scarlet pool swirled lazily at his feet before vanishing through a crevice between the flagstones. He thought it beautiful but wasn't sure why.

Perhaps his time had run out. After all, hardened members of his brotherhood were often fully spent by his age. And what would his master say on learning of the mess he had made of his assignment? Left where it was, the body would be discovered within hours, even minutes, rather than days. But he had to escape, now, before curious intruders negotiated the piazza steps and discovered him. He would deal with his master's recriminations later.

* * *

The cathedral bell had stopped pealing. Except for the spattering of raindrops, the victim heard only silence—a loud silence in total darkness until his eyes fluttered open. He was now alone in the passageway. With terrifying clarity the memory of the assault flooded back. His head throbbed; every bone, muscle, and sinew hurt. But he must not rest, for if he did, time would surely kill him.

He willed his fingers to grasp the edge of a flagstone. Haltingly at first, then with desperate purpose, the victim dragged his body toward the steps.

* * *

Friar William Occam had also heard the cathedral bell in the distance as he penned another rebuttal to his accusers' slanders and calumnies. Outside the scriptorium that occupied most of the convent's second floor, wind-tossed branches of an olive tree scratched a baleful premonition against the crumbling stucco façade. The Feast of the

Annunciation had come and gone—almost two months ago—and William's reprieve was running out.

As darkness fell on Avignon, the rain conspired with the wind, pelting the leaky roof and forming puddles that threatened to soak the manuscripts littered beneath his desk. There weren't enough buckets and spare wine casks to catch all the rainwater seeping through the roof's sagging timbers.

When William stooped to retrieve the manuscripts his spectacles fell to the floor. "Damnation!" he muttered as he groped for them, bumping his head on the underside of his desk. Should a merciful God see fit one day to restore his youthful vision, he would celebrate by getting rid of that "wondrous device" Baskerville had given him years earlier. The old friar had advised William that the two glass ovals attached to a forked metal pin would help him see better, especially after sunset. No doubt Baskerville had meant well, but ever since, William suffered their habit of toppling from the bridge of his thin nose just as a keen insight poised at his quill.

William gathered up the manuscripts, adjusted his spectacles and resumed writing by the light of his last two candles. The odor of rancid beeswax conjured sour reminiscences of his first years at the seminary in London: exams labored over late into the night, nocturnal punishments for petty infractions, chanting before dawn while half-asleep the psalms and canticles he scarcely understood.

Not all of his early memories were disagreeable, although the happier ones were scenes of the English summer when the sun still shone long after Compline. Solitary pleasures like cooling his feet in a secluded inlet of the Thames that only he knew about; gazing at cows and sheep meditating in the lush meadows of that green and pleasant land; learning various names for the same flower on his treks between London and Oxford—and wondering which of the names, if any, Eve had whispered to Adam during a sublime interlude in the garden.

Spectacles and candles were the least of his cares. In a matter of days the inquisitors would decide his future. They might have already sealed their verdict, which meant it was up to Duèze—Pope John XXII, as he presumed to call himself—to accept or reject it. Not that William doubted the outcome, for he had long since ceded any hope his accusers would tolerate his blasphemies. And "His Holiness" had not taken lightly William's charging *him* with seven heresies and seventy doctrinal errors. Nor, he assumed, had the pope smiled on learning that William had called him an idiot. But William pressed on, if only to reaffirm to himself the divine justice of his cause.

𝔭𝔞𝔯𝔱 𝔬𝔫𝔢

PARIS AND OCCAM, SURREY

September 18 – November 7, 1314
(Fourteen years earlier)

MICHAEL HARMON

Chapter 1

September 18, 1314 — The Palais de la Cité

PARISIANS ESTEEMED SAINTE GENEVIÈVE so highly they named a mountain and a school after her. These accolades were but two among many she received in the millennium following her canonization as Paris's patron saint.

Since his arrival from Oxford eighteen months earlier, William Occam had taught and studied at Geneviève's school and slept in a boarding house atop her mountain. La Montagne Sainte-Geneviève was actually a small hill, which Parisians called "The Mount." In public forums William would opine on why the sermons regularly preached on The Mount failed to measure up to the original. He did so with an unmodulated gusto that raised eyebrows among the sober and cultivated Dominicans who ran the *School* of Sainte-Geneviève, the most prestigious of several institutions that loosely comprised the Sorbonne.

Near the end of William's stay in Paris, England's Queen Isabella made a brief trip across the Channel to visit her ailing father, France's King Philip IV—Philip the Fair, as he was known. Isabella was accompanied by her principal lady-in-waiting, Eleanor de Clare, who was given great latitude to do as she pleased during much of the queen's visit. At her chamberlain's suggestion Lady Eleanor attended a debate, or quodlibet as the friars called it, between Walter Burley and the young Franciscan from Oxford. Burley had also been a fellow at Oxford and later went to Paris where he had just completed his lectures on Peter Lombard's *Book of Sentences*. This was a work that William, like all Franciscan[ii] scholars, knew well.

Burley was acquainted with William's ideas and took vigorous exception to many of them. He would soon learn that vigor was no match for William's logic and erudition. The upstart Greyfriar decimated virtually all of Burley's arguments, but afterward William felt slightly ashamed of his keen satisfaction. Yet again his vanity had gotten the better of him.

The day after the debate Lady Eleanor sent word to his boarding house on the rue Coupe-Gueule requesting that William hear her confession. He was not completely surprised by her summons. Better educated, Greyfriars could minister the Sacrament of Penance with greater sensitivity and flexibility than the secular priests, many of whom were known to accept bribes to betray the confidentiality of the confessional. As mendicant preachers, Greyfriars seldom remained in one place long enough to fall under such suspicions. In the years after her marriage to England's King Edward, a pious and grateful Isabella had given them generous gifts of building materials, livestock, and other supplies. The friars returned the favor by hearing the sins, and also the lies, told by the queen and her attendants and kept quiet about what they heard.

William trudged three miles through muddy streets to the Royal Palace at the western tip of the Ile de la Cité. Here the kings of France prayed in their diminutive sanctuary, la Sainte Chapelle, surrounded by sacred reminders of the Crucifixion: the Crown of Thorns, a fragment of the True Cross, and other relics mentioned in the Bible. William planned to inspect them when they were exhibited to the faithful on Good Friday—and contemplate the rumors they were fakes. He would also marvel again at the slender piers that, in defiance of nature's known laws, suspended the chapel's steeply vaulted ceiling.

He felt mildly disappointed when he was escorted to the palace itself rather than to Sainte Chapelle's nave where confessionals were located. The queen's attendants lodged in the palace apartments during her visit, and it was there he and Isabella's companion would meet. His curiosity mounted as he climbed a long stairway to the palace's second tier. As requested, he arrived at the entrance to her apartment at ten o'clock.

At Lady Eleanor's design they met in full view of each other in what, to his embarrassment, he realized was a bedroom. She perched on a large canopied bed across from a lushly upholstered settee on which she directed him to sit. William twitched uncomfortably in this luxurious surround, the likes of which he had never seen.

Her appearance was not what he expected. Perhaps she had slept late, which could explain why she hadn't yet plaited her hair and wound it into the elaborate coiffure customary among noble ladies. The tangle of her uncovered red tresses sprouted in various directions, as if she had recently awakened from fitful sleep or had just witnessed a startling event. As modesty required, her limbs were fully covered, but only by a sheer beige linen gown (which may have been an undergarment of some sort) revealing the contours of her figure. He pretended not to notice, willing himself to look upward at Eleanor's wide-set dark hazel eyes, which at first met his only fleetingly.

William reminded himself that the nobles often took casual liberties in dealing with the clergy, which may have explained this morning's breach of decorum. As he sat across from her on the settee, he found himself less scandalized than curious, though also slightly irked. This was supposed to be a Sacrament of Penance!

Eleanor's sins at first seemed ordinary, leading William to believe he could assign penance and grant absolution as prescribed by one of the standard confession manuals. But as she continued, her reasons for confessing were unclear, and he began to wonder why she sent for him. The manual would be of little use after all.

Half consciously, William filtered what Eleanor said through the prism of her gestures and shifting postures. Considering the revealing garment she wore, he couldn't help himself. He averted his gaze from Eleanor's conspicuous display of her bosom with only intermittent success. Perhaps there were more good reasons for the barrier between confessor and penitent than he had been told.

His first teachers had warned him to be ever alert to the temptations women presented. By their nature sexual, women were lascivious, even disgusting, and therefore dangerous to men. His suspicion that this was nonsense was later confirmed when his mentor and great friend William of Baskerville explained to him that women couldn't possibly be the foul creatures most of their fellow clergy believed them to be, that God must have endowed them with great virtues. Why else, Baskerville asked, had God created woman in paradise from noble human matter rather than, like Adam, from the baseness of mud? And why had the Lord dwelled in a woman's womb rather than becoming miraculously incarnate in some other way?

Although William believed that Eve's daughters' virtues were the equal of men's, he wasn't entirely sure what those virtues were. Might Eleanor be toying with him, enjoying his hopeless efforts to conceal his attraction? He now felt self-conscious about his appearance: neither handsome nor ugly, he assumed, but might his deep-set grey eyes and sharp nose convey to Eleanor the impression of emotional distance or harsh judgment?

Even if she felt this, it was no reason to be angry with her. And then he remembered this was the very point of Baskerville's counsel: Just as women were by nature neither evil nor dangerous, so also should men—not least, friars like William himself—feel neither anger nor shame at being drawn to them.

He briefly entertained the hope that Eleanor was also drawn to *him*. It wasn't unheard of for penitents to become infatuated with their confessors; from awkward experience he knew this to be the case. Aware that wishful thinking may have led him to think so now, he pushed his hope aside. She had been hesitant and cautious, as if testing the waters to see if William might be someone she could confide in. More than just confide, for he sensed she was worried less that he might betray her secrets than whether he possessed the wit to help her with her predicament, whatever it might be.

As the time quickly passed, he must have done something right, because Eleanor became more and more forthcoming. His memory had since become hazy about many details of what she told him in Paris and of what he had said in reply. He would later recall that she revealed little about her present troubles and instead hinted at future, unnamed perils. She needed someone—perhaps William himself—to be her ally in facing what lay ahead. He then felt uneasy on realizing that that was what he wished for when he forgave Lady Eleanor de Clare her sins, admonishing her: "Give thanks to the Lord, for He is good."

With an air of priestly solemnity befitting the occasion, William rose slowly from the settee, squared his shoulders, and in steps soft as velvet padded to the bedroom door. Before reaching it he tripped over a small carpet and almost pitched headfirst onto the floor. *Shit*! From the corner of his eye he saw Eleanor reflexively place a hand over her mouth, partially concealing a smile.

* * *

His exit took him down a curved staircase from the mezzanine to the palace's main gallery. The flagstone floor was lined on one side by furniture covered with tattered draperies and on the other side by tables on which dozens of buckets were neatly arranged. The buckets smelled of paint, which explained the huge scaffolding that climbed to the uppermost reaches of the gallery's arched ceiling. Half the ceiling had been painted a bright azure blue—a fanciful rendering, William assumed, of Paris's grey, soot-filled sky.

The palace's interior was a work still in progress, which Isabella's father, King Philip, was known to supervise with an exacting eye on his better days. Today may not have been one of them, or so William guessed on noticing two anxious-looking men carrying apothecary's satchels rush past him. They had just come out of what he had been told was the king's private chamber.

Lady Eleanor's chamberlain, a tall and gaunt young man named Berkhamsted, spoke little as he led William briskly toward the building's main entrance. The ornately carved oak door was propped open, allowing workmen and members of the king's household to move freely in and out. Berkhamsted appeared intent on ushering William out as quickly as possible.

Before they reached the door a woman's voice announced with an icy laugh, "I expected him to be more handsome."

William jerked his head to the right upon halting. The voice belonged to a modestly dressed woman not yet twenty—blond, blue-eyed, and beautiful. He had never seen her before but knew at once it was Queen Isabella, Lady Eleanor's mistress. The queen was speaking about *him*. She stood near the base of an opposite staircase flanked on either side by two other women. They giggled as William's cheeks flushed. Behind them stood another grey-robed friar, probably the queen's personal confessor.

William's throat tightened when he couldn't recall the protocol for greeting royal personages. Forced to rely on his wits, he bowed slowly to the queen in order to buy extra seconds to think. But as a man of God he shouldn't bow *too* low lest he seem to grovel before secular authority. This involved a delicate calculation.

As he rose from his semi-recumbent posture, instinct told him that levity might defuse the queen's jibe. So, in the most affable tone he could muster, he said, "As My Lady Queen surely knows, God lodges beauty in the soul rather than worldly guises. Perhaps for that reason He makes those of us who serve Him ugly." The best he could come up with on the spur of the moment.

"Beneath your faux modesty, friar, do I detect a hint of rebuke? Or is it mockery? Whichever the case, remember who you are speaking to."

Groveling was now called for.

"I most humbly beg My Lady's forgiveness. Any offense I may have given was most certainly . . . unintended."

Isabella arched a skeptical royal eyebrow. Could his tone have struck her as cheeky rather than contrite? Or was it his slight pause before *unintended*?

"Yesterday my dear companion told me of your cleverness in debate; but later I wondered if other, less-than-godly reasons might explain her effusive praise." She paused briefly as she eyed him up and down and then said with a smirk, "It appears I was mistaken."

His cheeks turned a deeper red. "Might My Lady's companion feel flattered by such an admission? Overlooking my homeliness would appear to bring her great credit."

"That is surely for *me* to judge," the queen said as her nostrils flared. "As for yourself, you would be well advised to reflect upon the price of insolence," at which she turned away and, with her small entourage trailing behind, marched back up the staircase.

As they disappeared from view, William felt relieved that protocol no longer mattered; he wouldn't have to bow again. A fleeting comfort, for in less than a minute's time he had managed to offend the most powerful woman in England. Berkhamsted evidently knew it too.

"I suggest that you leave—now!" was all he said as he turned and stalked back toward the stairway to the mezzanine.

William watched Berkhamsted leave and then hurried out of the palace into the courtyard. From there he walked as quickly as his wobbly legs would carry him across a rickety bridge connecting the Ile de la Cité with the Left Bank.

He collected his thoughts on his way back to the boarding house. Had something Lady Eleanor reported after yesterday's quodlibet raised Isabella's suspicions about what her lady-in-waiting might reveal to William in confession? Or had the queen imagined that William, someone she did not know and had no reason to trust, might betray royal secrets and had thus contrived their meeting to take his measure?

William had also begun to take the queen's measure. In England he had scoffed at Isabella's nickname—the "She-Wolf of France"— as exhibiting little more than lingering Saxon resentment over the Gallic Conqueror's invasion three centuries earlier. Now he felt less sure of that.

The queen was more beautiful than Lady Eleanor, but Isabella's beauty was wasted on the feckless Edward II, a husband whose amorous attentions were rumored to point in another direction. Two years had passed since Edward's favorite, the late Piers Gaveston, lost his head after the barons protested his receipt of lavish royal patronage and other extravagances they could no longer tolerate. But the barons might have indulged these offenses were it not for their revulsion at Edward's public fawning caresses of his court favorite. Bitterly, his young queen must have noticed them too. If Isabella was indeed a "she-wolf" as the gossips claimed, William could understand her reasons.

Those reasons gave him small comfort. By his impertinence he may have made himself the queen's enemy, though she may have regarded him as just a soon-to-be-forgotten pest. He hoped that was the case, but in the future it would be best to steer clear of the palace.

As he approached the boarding house he had resided in for more than a year, his nerves began to settle. A bath, some hot porridge, and a goblet or two of the neighboring Dominican's excellent wine would settle them further.

Chapter 2

September 19, 1314 — La Montagne Sainte-Geneviève

WILLIAM HURRIED ALONG the rue Coupe-Gueule linking the boarding house with the school. He had misplaced his copy of Peter Lombard's *Book of Sentences*, which, along with his Bible, he usually stowed beneath his cot each evening before retiring. He had it at the quodlibet with Burley two days earlier and thought he took it with him afterwards. Maybe he left it in his carrel at Sainte-Geneviève's, though he rarely did so.

Losing any book was no small matter, but the *Sentences* was especially valuable and hard to replace. He had grown fond of his old and tattered copy, whose tanned leather cover was originally dyed a deep red but had faded by age and use to a mottled brown and grey. No one would steal it for its beauty. William's copy also included copious notes distilling almost a decade of study and reflection, which would make its loss more painful still. Perhaps even dangerous; taken together, his many notations portrayed a critique of the *Sentences* the Sorbonne's Dominicans would find highly offensive were they to read them. Lombard's magnum opus was second only to the Bible as the authoritative source of Church doctrine, and dissenters from the master's teachings had been hauled before the Inquisition for views less radical than William's. His more immediate concern was that without his book in hand he would be barred from attending lectures in the two courses in which he was now a student. He had not yet satisfied all the requirements for his degree at Oxford and planned to complete his coursework here at the Sorbonne while teaching classes of his own.

William climbed the stairs to his carrel on the school's second floor and found the small space occupied by a young Dane whose name he recalled as Bendt. Unfamiliar books and scraps of parchment were strewn across the desk, and the delicately carved Crucifix that hung above the desk wasn't William's. His own books were stacked on the floor.

Bendt read William's expression of surprise. "I assumed you were told," he said with a slight stammer.

"Told what?"

"Er . . . that this carrel was now available for the Danish students to use. We complained for weeks about the shortage of study space, so I suppose Brother Émile finally took our complaints to heart. As luck had it, I drew the long straw," he said with an apologetic shrug. "I don't know what else I can tell you."

William quickly examined the stack of books on the floor and didn't see his copy of the *Sentences*. He turned and rushed down the hallway toward the stairs leading to Brother Emile's chamber on the ground floor. As Sainte Geneviève's subrector, Émile supervised the school's day-to-day operations, which allowed him to dispense and withhold privileges that could make students' and faculty's lives pleasant or miserable.

This morning the anteroom to the subrector's chamber was more crowded than usual. William fidgeted for several minutes, waiting his turn in the queue as men clad in black and white habits entered and exited. Few of them offered so much as a perfunctory greeting, and many averted their eyes on recognizing him. He had not expected hearty congratulations on his thrashing of Walter Burley at the quodlibet two days earlier but still found his cool reception unsettling. Although the pompous Burley was widely disliked, his stature was such that few of Sainte Geneviève's other faculty dared cross him. Like most of them, he was a Dominican, and Dominicans stuck together. With one voice they controlled the Sorbonne's curriculum and much more: As the chief defenders of Thomas Aquinas, the Dominicans of Paris had become the theological arbiters of Europe.

His patience finally spent, William barged past the young monk guarding entry to the subrector's sanctum and found Brother Émile sitting behind a large desk. He was sorting documents into neat stacks.

"Ah, Brother Occam, I believe," the subrector said with eyebrows raised, feigning momentary uncertainty about his intruder's identity. He glanced up only briefly before returning his gaze to his documents. "And to what do I owe this . . . unexpected visit?"

"Unexpected, my ass! You know perfectly well why I'm here."

Brother Émile didn't blanch at this ungenteel outburst. (What else should one expect from an uncouth *Saxon*?) "One of my responsibilities is to ensure the optimal allocation of the school's limited space. As you might appreciate, this often involves . . ."

"I'm a *teacher* at Sainte Geneviève's!" William interrupted. "Since when did you deem it *optimal* to evict a faculty member from his carrel and give it to a first-year student?"

"*Evict* is a bit harsh," the subrector said with irritating calmness. "But of greater moment, I should think, are questions about your qualifications to teach at Sainte Geneviève's. I am aware, of course, that the chancellor hasn't yet granted you a teaching license."

"I was told I didn't *need* the license so long as I made progress toward my degree. That was agreed to before I left England."

"Regrettably, circumstances sometimes require us to revisit such agreements."

"*Revisit*? Are you saying I've been terminated?" William could scarcely believe what he had just heard. The loss of his book was now the last thing on his mind.

"Don't draw too hasty a conclusion," Émile cautioned, although his tone was not reassuring. "At the moment, the chancellor is reviewing the status of *several* non-licensed teachers. Along with the others, you'll be told of his decision in due course."

"Until then, what am I supposed to do? The term isn't over, and I have exams to sit for and classes to teach."

"I sympathize, of course. Quite obviously, you face some difficult choices. It isn't for me to point you in one direction or another—except to recommend that in the coming days you pray for God's loving guidance."

"You might urge the chancellor to do the same—instead of seeking *his* guidance from Walter Burley. Don't pretend I don't know who's behind this."

The subrector's response was as noncommittal as it was dismissive. "Assuming we understand each other more fully, I believe our business is concluded. May God grant you a blessed day!" he said as he resumed sorting his documents.

* * *

William spent the rest of the day stewing over his choices. He had little else to do. Without his copy of the *Sentences* he couldn't attend the class he was taking on Aristotle's theory of forms. It would be a waste of time anyway. He knew more about the Philosopher's theories than the instructor did and often bit his tongue so as not to show him up in front of the other students. Today would have been no different. But more worrisome was his growing certainty that the disappearance of his book must be somehow connected to his likely eviction from Sainte Genevieve's.

With no path in mind, he meandered through the Left Bank's warren of crooked streets across the river from the Ile de la Cité. He took care not to stray too close to the bridge leading to the palace lest one of Isabella's agents spot him. He then chided himself for his foolishness in believing she gave him a passing thought.

Partly concealed by the shade of a black locust tree, he saw two Dominicans in animated conversation walking toward the bridge. He didn't know the taller man, but the shorter, stockier man he immediately recognized as Walter Burley. His swift, purposeful stride suggested that he was not on his way to la Sainte Chapelle to admire its slender piers or inspect its relics. His taller companion struggled to keep pace.

William reversed course and walked a short distance to the south. He looked across the river at the palace's southeastern wall, hoping to locate the window that welcomed the morning sun into Lady Eleanor's apartment. He couldn't tell which window it was, so he picked one at random and gazed at it for several minutes.

This was a temporary respite from his troubles. Without telling him in so many words, the subrector had made it clear his service at Sainte Geneviève's was no longer needed. He had annoyed the Dominicans long enough, and Burley was merely the last straw. How much longer could he stay before they threw him out?

This question occupied his thoughts as he returned to the boarding house where, like him, most Greyfriars studying in Paris ate and slept. Darkness approached, but six or seven of his brothers had not yet gone to bed after returning from evening prayers. Huddled together on the stoop fronting on the rue Coupe-Gueule, they were engaged in lively conversation interspersed with occasional laughter. Greyfriars appreciated a well-told joke.

On other evenings William would have joined them. He was the most famous Franciscan at the Sorbonne—or the most notorious, depending on whom you asked. The other friars were always eager to hear his opinions and share his company. He often obliged, but on this hot autumn evening he kept his own company.

He was about to enter the boarding house when a voice startled him. "Might I have a word, Brother Occam?"

Pivoting about, he recognized the tall Blackfriar silhouetted against the fading sunlight. It was Durand of Saint-Pourçain, one of the few Dominicans at Sainte Geneviève's who hadn't shunned him. When they first met months before, William had noted Durand's striking resemblance to his mentor Baskerville—tall and thin, though younger by ten or fifteen years, so his dark brown hair hadn't yet turned the older man's iron grey. They shared the same narrow chin and hooded eyes, but, and unlike Baskerville's, Durand's face possessed a soft, almost feminine quality.

"As many as you like," William answered. "But forgive my surprise; most of your brethren wouldn't have asked for a syllable."

Durand smiled wryly and said, "I assumed you would know that the Blackfriars of Paris don't like it when outsiders expose them as fools."

"By 'outsiders' you mean Greyfriars like me? Or foreigners in general?"

"Either, and in your case, both."

After considering this for a moment, William said, "You spoke of Paris's Blackfriars as 'them.' I thought you were one of them."

"Perhaps because we all wear the same uniform," he said as he briefly inspected the black cappa covering his white scapular. "As you know, we Nominalists at the Sorbonne are regarded as rather eccentric."

Durand must have known that the notorious Occam shared some of his eccentric views. And William knew that Durand was now being investigated by his own order for taking issue with Aquinas, whose Realist orthodoxy most Dominicans in Paris defended with fervor.[iii]

"Aren't you worried? Everyone knows of the trouble you've gotten yourself into."

"Less than you might suppose," Durand shrugged. "Dominicans eventually get around to forgiving their errant brethren. They'll be satisfied if I confess to a few errors and then apologize for the grief I've caused them."

"So, as an outsider, I'm *less* likely to be forgiven?" It was as much a surmise as a question.

Durand drew William a few steps farther down the street from the boarding house stoop, safely out of earshot of the young friars. The Dominican's voice lowered to a conspiratorial pitch. "Which is why I came looking for you. Against my better judgment perhaps, I thought I ought to warn you that Burley won't be satisfied with merely taking your carrel from you."

William was surprised at this. "He's *that* thin-skinned?"

"You've tarnished his reputation more than you might realize. The thrashing you gave him exposed just how fragile it was. He fully expected to use you as an object lesson in his crusade to cleanse the

Church of dangerous notions. What better way to do that than by ferreting out radicals like you? A *Franciscan* radical, to boot!"

William shook his head, recalling the absurdity of Burley's arguments at the quodlibet. "He may be a fool, but he didn't strike me as a zealot."

Durand laughed. "He's anything *but*. Burley is a politician who wants his voice heard in the highest reaches of the Church. His 'crusading' is sheer pretense."

"Pretense or not, wouldn't his voice require a pope in Avignon to listen to it? Clement has been dead for going on six months now, and the cardinals still haven't agreed on a successor. So far, there's been only black smoke."

"They're in no hurry," Durand said as he again lowered his voice. "The Inquisition, such as it is, can muddle along *without* a pope, at least for the time being. In fact, the powers at the Sorbonne prefer it that way. It provides us Dominicans protection from Clement's minions still left in the curia. As things stand, they can't do much of anything until King Philip makes up his mind about who he wants to succeed Clement."

"And how does Burley figure in all of this?"

Durand waited before answering as two of his brother Blackfriars passed by, headed in the direction of the school. "As I said, Burley is a politician. He's recently insinuated himself between Philip and the cardinals—strictly behind the scenes, of course. I'm not privy to many details, but rumor has it he's advising Philip to back Avignon's bishop as the next pope, a man named Jacques Duèze."

Which would save on moving expenses. Duèze already occupied the bishop's residence, which would serve as Avignon's papal palace until a new, grander edifice was constructed. William knew nothing else about him except that he was old.

"But Burley is English. Hasn't he any ties to Westminster?"

Durand scoffed at the question. "Certainly not to King Edward. Like most everyone else in Paris, Burley regards him with contempt. But his queen, Isabella, is another matter. When Burley advises Philip, his daughter eventually hears of it and isn't shy about voicing her opinions. Better that Philip listened to *her* than his three idiot sons. Incidentally, I don't know if you've heard, but she's now in Paris for what could well be a final visit. It seems her father is fading fast."

William simply nodded at this.

"Even at her tender age," Durand added as an afterthought, "she's a force to reckon with."

"I should expect so," William agreed.

His thoughts drifted back to the events of the past three days, and he was nagged by the fear he had forgotten something—something more damning than the loss of his carrel or his copy of the *Sentences*. Durand noticed his changed mood as they stood without speaking, watching the last rays of sunlight vanish in the west. A breeze had sprung up suddenly, cooling the streets crisscrossing La Montagne Sainte-Geneviève.

As if taking the breeze as his cue, Durand said, "It's getting late, so I should best be on my way." He then paused and, before turning away, said to William, "May the Lord protect you!"

A few seconds passed before William gathered the wit to reply. "And you, as well," he called out. But it was too late for Durand to hear as he disappeared around the corner, the hem of his cappa fluttering in the breeze. Durand had meant his terse valediction in dead earnest.

Now alone on the dark street, William took just two steps toward the boarding house entrance when he halted, stunned by the realization of what he had forgotten. It was his "manifesto," as he had whimsically chosen to call it, which he had tucked for safekeeping between two quires of his copy of the *Sentences*. The manifesto: William Occam's brief draft of his private heresy in which he advocated that all Christian believers, including *women*, were fully equal to the clergy in their spiritual authority and thus within their moral rights to depose the pope for his sins.

How could he have been so stupid? He should have taken Baskerville's advice and burned the cursed thing, which he knew by heart anyway. By trying to hide it, especially in so obvious a place, he had invited its discovery. Stupidity born of his arrogance! If the manifesto, too, had fallen into others' hands, he would need more than the Lord's protection.

William waited a few moments before entering the boarding house and climbing the two flights of stairs to his tiny room. He was too tired and too shaken to light a candle, so he knelt to pray in almost total darkness. A narrow beam of moonlight spilled through the opened window, just enough light to reveal a folded and sealed sheet of parchment someone had placed on his cot. A message of some sort, probably from the resident master reminding him that he hadn't disposed of the scraps left over from the morning's breakfast. He considered laying it aside to read later, but curiosity got the better of him. After fumbling in the dark, he found his flints and lit a candle. In the flickering light he could see that the parchment was smooth and soft, and the seal's wax impression finely rendered—unlikely to belong to anyone at the boarding house or even Sainte-Geneviève's.

He broke the seal and started to read, rapidly at first and then slowly. It was probably her chamberlain, Berkhamsted, who had delivered her message. He stared at it for almost a minute before carefully refolding it, deciding at that moment to leave Paris the next morning—without his *Book of Sentences* and his manifesto—before the sun shone through the window of Lady Eleanor's apartment.

Chapter 3

October 2 - November 7, 1314 — Dover to Occam

ACH RECOLLECTION of the miserable voyage across the Channel renewed the profound relief William felt on reaching his native soil. The crossing from Calais should have taken less than a day. His had taken five. A southwesterly autumn gale pushed the single-masted cog on which he had begged passage halfway to Belgium before the storm blew itself out. On the third day a fair wind backed from the southeast, taking the cog safely to Dover.

Five days was hardly a record. The irate King John of France took *eleven* days to cross, whereupon he exacted revenge against the Channel's roiling waters by executing his ship's master and half her crew. William took meager consolation from this story, being otherwise occupied with heaving his guts over the groaning vessel's railings. (He had the presence of mind to do so on the leeward side lest the wind cast the residue of his dinner back in his face.)

Now thinner since his crossing, William trudged northwesterly from Dover, though keeping to the south of London. For protection against highwaymen he often joined with other friars and itinerant tradesmen and peddlers. The few women he encountered, mainly nuns from nearby convents, traveled in groups of five or more.

Twice he met bands of pilgrims making their way to distant shrines. By enduring the privations of their long journeys, the pilgrims hoped the chances of having their sins forgiven would multiply many-fold, as would the curing of their illnesses by the healing potions and special blessings dispensed on their arrival.

William was bound for Oxford where he could resume his studies and perhaps teach a class or two if the regent masters permitted it. But first, it wouldn't be far out of his way to stop at his birthplace, which he had not seen in nearly twenty years. Finding the tiny village of Occam was difficult. Most of his fellow travelers who might have known the shortest route eventually headed off for other destinations, either north toward London or southwest toward Winchester, Southampton, or Chichester. So, during the last stages of his trip he traveled mostly alone, stopping some nights for a hot meal and a warm cot at monasteries, convents, and hospitals along the network of old Roman roads. On other nights he huddled in crude shelters or in the open air before a small fire, armed only with his quarterstaff for protection.

William credited his unfriar-like martial prowess with his staff to ballads he heard in his youth celebrating the outlaw Robin Hood and his band of merry men. His favorite ballad sang of Friar Tuck who, with *his* staff, bested the great Robin himself in playful combat. William could still recite the minstrels' lilting chronicle and mused about the corpulent friar's successes whenever he practiced the manly art of staff-fighting.

His staff also served a more mundane purpose. He had been cursed with a right leg almost two inches shorter than his left, which caused him to limp unsteadily as he walked. With the aid of his staff he could trek long distances without tiring unduly but often struggled to keep pace with his abler companions. As a youth, his limp made him an easy target of taunting and bullying, which the young William pledged not to let pass if he could help it. He would usually obey Jesus' admonishment to turn the other cheek, but there were limits to what he would endure.

Three days from the village of Occam he came across two young workmen from a nearby mill sitting by the wooded roadside eating their midday meal. Thirsty and hungry, William eyed their jug of ale and a skinned hare roasting over a small fire. Next to the fire was a steaming iron pot that smelled like oatmeal pottage laced with onions. Befitting the custom among begging friars, he was about to ask for a share of the workmen's food in return for which he would impart to them lessons from the Holy Scriptures. But from experience he knew that not everyone wanted to hear them. Parish priests routinely warned their flocks to be wary of mendicant preachers like William, and poets often made them the butt of jokes to expose their wiles and trickery.

"May the Lord be with you on this fine day," he said with practiced affability as he approached the workmen.

The slighter of the two men looked up and, on noticing William's grey habit, said with a smirk, "Hmm, I wager he wants our vittles. Wonder what he's willin' to trade for 'em."

"Christ's blood! Not the Lord's message again," the stouter man exclaimed. "Already heard it, an' see where it got me." He spat into the fire to clarify his meaning.

The first man added with a harsh laugh, "With robes like his, maybe *we* could fill up our stomachs without dirtyin' our hands with honest toil." He rose slowly from the log he sat on and, with a wink and a thrust of his chin, signaled his companion to do the same.

This encounter wasn't going well, so William thought it prudent to try his luck farther down the road. Better a gnawing appetite than a clout upside the head—or worse.

"Perhaps I should wish you a blessed day and continue on my way," William said in an even tone he hoped didn't betray the mounting tension he felt. But as he started to pass by, the slighter man edged sideways to block his path, while the stouter man sidled slowly behind him. William halted, swiveling his head rapidly to the left and then to the right to keep each of them in view. His muscles tightened as he readjusted his grip on his staff: his right hand's palm facing up at its center and his left palm down near the butt end.

"Maybe he thinks we'll take pity on account of his gimpy leg," the stouter man said with gleeful sarcasm as he hopped on one leg and then the other, crudely mimicking William's limping gait.

"Likely a few coins in his purse from the fools that *did* pity him," his companion said as he started to reach toward the hemp cord strung loosely around William's neck.

His staff now at a ready, upright position, William whirled counter-clockwise on his left (good) leg, while in the same motion rotating his staff to a horizontal position and sweeping it with all his might across his tormentor's knees. The man screamed in pain and fell to the ground as William thrust his staff into the second man's midsection. He doubled over and exhaled a loud "ooph" as he fell to the ground. Had the staff been sharply pointed, the man would have been impaled rather than bruised and gasping for breath.

In seconds it was over. His chest heaving, William braced himself with his staff as he glared at his assailants. Both were on their knees as if preparing to pray. He considered leaving them with a fitting scriptural aphorism to reflect upon—maybe one about the wages of sin or the meek inheriting the earth—but each aphorism that occurred to him at that moment felt trite and heavy-handed. Earthier admonishments also sprang to mind, but he refrained from issuing these, too, recalling the frequent scoldings he received at the seminary for his salty language. He eyed once again the food and drink a few feet away but resisted the temptation to partake of them. Still hungry and thirsty, he resumed his journey down the road toward Occam.

* * *

During these solitary legs of his trip William often reread the cryptic message Eleanor sent him the day before he left Paris: "Pray forgive me for the trouble I have brought you," she had written. "You had best not come again. E." Nothing more than these brief words, so all he had were surmises about their meaning. She had included no salutation or valediction—unusual for an educated lady of Edward's court who surely knew her manners. From her hurried scrawl and the ink smudges on the parchment, she had written hastily with little time to spare. But this, too, was just a surmise.

As he drew closer to Occam, his thoughts of Eleanor receded, replaced by a feeling of urgency—his fear of getting there too late. Such feelings were nothing new. For as long as he could remember he had been afraid of being late. It explained much of what stimulated him, *drove* him, to answer this scriptural question or dissolve that metaphysical puzzle before anyone else did—and better than anyone else could. William also knew, or thought he knew, the root of his fear.

He had almost reached the age of five. As he and his elder sister Matilda went to sleep each evening in the bed they shared, their mother serenaded them from her stool by the fire in their cottage. She sang song after song, some about love and others of adventure and heroic deeds. But mostly she sang songs of God's blessings. The God of those songs, *her* God, was always merciful, unlike the stern and vindictive God of Father Julian, the dour old priest who presided over Occam's—Oak Hamlet's—parish.

He was astonished by how many songs his mother knew. During any evening she never repeated one, which made him wonder if she knew all the songs there were. But that was unlikely because Occam was such a small place. Other, distant places probably had songs, too, and he saw no reason to suppose they were the same ones, although they might have been. Could there, in fact, be songs out there, somewhere, that no one yet knew, either in Occam or those distant places?

This question raised others: How did people find songs? How, and where, could he find those songs no one else knew? And if he found them—just one song would do for a start—how could he remember them so that he might pass them on to his mother? He knew she would want to have them.

Because William's memory wasn't as good as his mother's, he would have to write down the songs once he found them; otherwise they might vanish. His problem, however, was that he couldn't read and write, although he now had a reason to learn as quickly as he could. But that could take many days, which made him worry that by the time he *did* learn, someone else would already have found all of the songs, all of the good ones at least. Then it would be too late.

When at Father Julian's urging he departed Occam for London four years later, his last memory was of his mother weeping. Wretchedly, he felt she wouldn't have wept had he given her a song before he left, one she hadn't heard before. So he vowed when next he saw her to give her a new song to atone for his failure. That day would be long in coming, as he learned on arriving at Greyfriars seminary to begin his studies. Novitiates were prohibited from visiting their families and were discouraged from doing so even after taking their final vows.

If he couldn't find a song to give to his mother, he owed her an explanation of why he couldn't. That would have to be enough. Finding the right moment, however, proved difficult because he was always busy: with his stacks of incomplete manuscripts, his lectures and debates in Oxford and London, his travels abroad—most recently to Paris. Doctor Invincibilis,[iv] as William's admirers would later call him, was much in demand.

Now, after years of delay, he decided that right moments, like songs, couldn't be found; they had to be made. This was why, on returning to England from Paris in the autumn of 1314, he took a short detour through Occam on his way to Oxford.

But when he reached Occam no one was there. The cottages and shops, even the church, were empty and decaying. Once generous in their bounty, the surrounding fields lay fallow and overgrown with weeds choking the remnants of rotting barley and wheat stalks.

Only the churchyard cemetery was crowded. The newest graves were marked with simple wooden crosses rather than the sturdy headstones that guarded the remains of the earlier departed. The crosses were scattered haphazardly around the cemetery's periphery as if barred admittance to the holy ground at the center. William bleakly imagined the crosses as crude, oversized daggers that impaled those buried beneath, proclaiming their misfortune of having lived, and then dying, in the first year of England's great famine.

From a passing stranger he learned that the only survivors were those strong enough to bury the dead before they themselves left Occam. The elderly and the very young had all perished. The man who told him this said he was a peddler, although his ragged clothes and lack of wares to sell or barter said otherwise. Unlike William, who begged by choice in emulation of his Savior, the stranger begged because he had to. Perhaps he felt ashamed of being down on his luck.

As the stranger shambled off, William resisted the urge to flee the desolation before him. He scanned once more the score of unmarked crosses and wondered which of them his mother lay beneath. Her name also was Eleanor, though no one in Occam called her that. Except for William and Matilda, everyone knew her as Nelly. And what of Matilda? Was she buried there too?

Sad minutes crept like hours as he continued to stare at the crosses. His thoughts had drifted to the Apostle John's story of Jesus raising Lazarus from the dead, and he wondered if his faith could spark a similar miracle. He quickly reproached himself for this fantasy, which of course had nothing to do with faith. It was merely hubris to mask the certainty he would never give his mother the explanation he owed her.

As the afternoon sun started its descent, William rose from the tree stump he had sat upon to resume his journey to Oxford. Dry oak leaves swirled and danced in the gusty late-autumn wind as he hobbled briskly to the northwest. He was in a hurry. He mustn't be late.

MICHAEL HARMON

PART TWO

LONDON

February 25 – March 3, 1324
(Ten years later)

MICHAEL HARMON

Chapter 4

February 25, 1324 — Greyfriars Church

A DECADE HAD PASSED since William slinked out of Paris in the dead of night. In the days just before his ignominious exit he had offended the Queen of England, incurred the Dominicans' extreme displeasure, and made himself a fool in front of the queen's closest companion. Each memory was still fresh, especially the last. And now Eleanor de Clare was back, having summoned him again to hear her confession. She was due to arrive at Greyfriars Church at three o'clock that afternoon.

William felt apprehensive as he entered the makeshift confessional near the entrance to All Hallows Chapel. The marble and sandstone dust made him cough, and the sporadic tapping of the stone carvers' mallets annoyed him. Minutes later Eleanor slipped in from the other side and drew the curtain closed. His heart started to pound when he heard the rustle of her gown as she shifted her weight before speaking.

Because the carpenters had yet to install the confessional's kneeler, she sat on a small stool. Other friars thought it scandalous, but William preferred this arrangement, which allowed him to counsel his penitents rather than dispense ritual absolution of their sins. But more than that, he hated the thought of anyone kneeling in submission before him. Another reason his brother friars thought him odd.

Almost inaudibly, Eleanor began, "Bless me, Father, for I have sinned. It's been months since my last confession, though I've told my husband and the king I confess often."

She had spoken the penitent's usual opening words, which sounded oddly rehearsed in view of their earlier encounter in Paris. He found this puzzling.

"So why haven't you?"

"God forgive me, but who can I trust? Surely not the drunkards and debauchers who pass for parish priests. I might just as well proclaim my sins to everyone in the king's court."

"Other friars were also available." Indiscreet of him to mention this, but recalling their meeting ten years ago, he wondered why she had risked asking for him again.

She slid back the lattice screen that separated confessor from penitent. On seeing her again William was taken aback. Errant wisps of flaming red hair sprouted from beneath her wimple, and he still found her quite beautiful. But she was now thinner despite giving birth to three more children since their first meeting, and her face was pale and creased by lines of worry.

"You probably weren't told," she said as she turned to face him, "that I often asked Brother Andrew if you could hear my confession. But he said when you returned from France you went directly to Oxford. My chamberlain Berkhamsted—he remembered you, by the way—told me just yesterday you've been here for more than a year." Eleanor paused as if to summon her courage: "But I haven't answered your question, have I? Perhaps I shouldn't say it, but in Paris I felt free to say whatever was in my heart. I had never confessed like that before. I also wondered if you had forgiven me."

William detected a faint smile and suppressed a smile of his own. Lady Eleanor's confession, if it could still be called that, tested even the friars' relaxed limits on what could qualify as a Sacrament of Penance. Almost a decade earlier she had taken similar liberties in Paris, so he could hardly reproach her now. But he was skirting forbidden territory. An artful segue was called for.

"Subjects, perhaps, for another time and another setting. But I assume more urgent matters have brought you here."

"I'm not sure where to begin," she resumed with a deep sigh, "but perhaps with the stories you've no doubt heard about Sir Hugh and my uncle."

William made a mental note of Eleanor's reference to her husband as "Sir Hugh," in contrast to the more intimate mention of her uncle, King Edward. "Friaries are dens of gossip no less than the king's court," he said. "How much of it one should believe is another matter."

"If you still don't know, what you've heard is true. At first I felt humiliated and betrayed, but now I'm just afraid."

"And who are you afraid of? Your husband? The king? The queen?"

Eleanor bit her lip as she considered her answer. "All three, I admit, though for different reasons. And not just them! The barons and other hangers-on at court know how awkward my situation is and are scheming to exploit it even if sacrificing me suits their purpose. Some of them, I'd wager, would take pleasure in it. Edward, bless him, does his best to protect me, but that's cold comfort when he's not in London, which nowadays is most of the time."

"Bless him? A generous sentiment about a man who's replaced you in your husband's bed." William was surprised by his bluntness.

"In truth, *Edward's* bed and almost anywhere else from what I've been told. But never mind that. You may find it hard to believe, but I can't hate Edward or even be angry with him for long. Ever since his affair with Piers Gaveston, I've known someday he'd find another man. The queen must have known too. Looking back, I shouldn't have been surprised it was Hugh and even less surprised that Hugh took advantage of Edward's infatuation with him."

"Took advantage, or," William fumbled for the right word, "succumbed?"

"Hah! Hugh le Despenser doesn't succumb," she said with a bitter laugh. "Don't be fooled by all the children we've had. Hugh is in love with power, a subject the good friars may not have taught you at Oxford."

"Only in the advanced courses," he said as his face reddened. He didn't like being condescended to, especially by Eleanor.

"Forgive me; that was uncalled for," she said. "If the barons ever get their claws into Hugh, merely beheading him without some gruesome preliminaries would be an act of mercy."

William squirmed as he contemplated the gruesome preliminary of disembowelment and now wanted to change the subject. He was also aware that the cold draft seeping through the confessional's doors made both of them shiver. Eleanor had had the good sense to bring a small woolen blanket to wrap around her feet, and William wished he had done the same.

"You've said little about the queen," he said as he rubbed his hands together for warmth. "I assume she's more intimate with you than anyone else—any other woman, that is."

"She once was, but when Edward asked me to be her companion, we were both very young. Isabella was barely twelve, and when she arrived in England, she didn't know anyone, so she had to rely on my advice about almost everything, even what to eat and wear. But she was stubbornly independent too. From her first days at Westminster she made outlandish demands so no one would doubt she was queen. She did herself no favors, though, by flaunting her Frenchness to show up her new countrymen as bumpkins and fools. Correcting our pronunciation, I recall, didn't endear her to anyone." Eleanor smiled without joy at the memory.

"And now?"

"I see what you're thinking, but no, we're further apart than we ever were. When her marriage collapsed, Isabella needed someone to blame. She let it be known that my failings as a wife made Hugh 'succumb' to Edward, as you put it."

"But no mention of her own failings?"

"No, though not that I blame her. She has more to lose than I do. Indeed, she already has."

As everyone at the Westminster court knew, the king and queen now lived apart, with Isabella held virtual prisoner in her small and heavily guarded cloister. William then mentioned the rumor that at Hugh le Despenser's urging Edward was about to ask the pope to annul his marriage to Isabella.

Eleanor scoffed at this. "Edward is often rash, but he's not the besotted fool the barons make him out to be. Annulling his marriage to Isabella would make all their children bastards. He won't sacrifice young Edward, whom he adores, just to please Hugh or anyone else. But he also needs the queen's help in keeping peace with Charles. Yes, I know we're officially at war, but they're not actually fighting because Edward can't persuade the barons to pay for another army."[v]

"Would Edward trust the queen to do his bidding?" He had lowered his voice again on hearing the footsteps of someone passing by the confessional. Eleanor must have heard them, too, and waited a few moments before replying as the sound of the footsteps receded.

"He hasn't any choice," she resumed. "And whether Isabella feels loyal to him is neither here nor there. She wants to remain queen but on her own terms. For her the question is how to use whatever influence she has to keep her crown."

"But other than the king's needing her as a go-between with Charles, what influence *does* she have?"

"I can't say for certain, but you shouldn't underestimate her. Nor should the king and Hugh, for that matter. Some of the barons, I've learned, imagine her as a possible ally against Edward. That's sheer fantasy, but she might play on their hopes if she can use them against Hugh. And Isabella's ties to the Church—to the pope—are far stronger than Edward's. She may still confess to Greyfriars, but the priests I've seen skulking about her cloister don't wear the same color habits you do. They wear black ones, and I shouldn't be surprised if they were made in Avignon."

Even by William's flexible standards, Eleanor's disquisition on court politics was more fit for discussion outside the confessional. He was also suddenly aware that *he* had crossed the line from confessor to gossip. "You seem more concerned with protecting yourself from the sins of others than atoning for your own," he awkwardly suggested.

Eleanor didn't take the hint. "I'm not as calculating as you believe. But yes, I do have my own interests to worry about. If Edward is deposed, the best I can hope for is to be stuck in a convent somewhere—or, God help and protect me, in the Tower. And who knows what would become of the children?"

"And what of your husband?" he asked, knowing that his motives in asking were mainly to satisfy his guilty curiosity. He wondered if Eleanor suspected this.

"Edward's only chance to keep his crown is to reconcile with the queen. Which means, of course, that Hugh would have to go. But Hugh is doomed no matter what happens, so he'd be wise to get as far away from England as soon as he can. I'm sorry for the children, but as they grow older they'll learn what a swine their father was. I'd never say this to anyone else, but that's how I feel about him."

Now resigned to serving as Eleanor's temporal advisor, William said, "From what you've told me, I wonder what you believe you can do. What do you want to achieve?"

"To save Edward from himself!" Eleanor said, raising her voice. "That was hard enough earlier, but he made it harder when he asked me to spy on Isabella. He was quite blunt about it, and I couldn't refuse. Most of what he tries to pry out of me are rumors of Isabella's treachery, which, if true, would make him even more determined to shut her off and draw him closer to Hugh. So the more I tell him what he wants to hear, the weaker he becomes. He just doesn't understand that—or doesn't want to."

"So you came to me for advice?"

"I suppose you could put it that way," Eleanor conceded after a brief pause.

"My advice won't be exactly, um, priestly."

"I assume," she said with another faint smile, "you're not surprised that's what I hoped for."

William wasn't surprised, but he was also unsure of what kind of advice he ought to give her. He drummed his fingers on his knee for several seconds before replying. "You might first consider what *not* to do," he began hesitantly, "such as not telling the king anything important, especially if it might risk his coming to his senses about the queen and your husband. If you must tell him something, make sure it's trivial, a bit of gossip he's already heard or may suspect, or that he'd likely learn later from someone else. Otherwise, there's probably little you can do. On occasion you might offer to help him so as to stay in his good graces and perhaps even try to regain the queen's confidence. That's unlikely, but at least don't antagonize her further." His own confidence growing, he added, "Finally—and I'm sure you've thought of this—stay away from the barons. They can use you better than you can use them. So don't delude yourself by plotting some misguided intrigue."

Eleanor thought for a few moments. "That's all very well, but things keep changing and I'm still at a loss about what to do."

"Apt punishment, I should think, for not confessing regularly," William reminded her.

"Yes, Father—and my penance?"

"Hmm, confessing more often would be a first step. Shall we say in a week's time?"

When William prepared to dismiss her, it occurred to him that Eleanor's penance was as much for his benefit as for hers. But she interrupted his thought: "Oh, I meant to tell you. One of the black-robed priests I told you about is your old friend from Paris, Walter Burley. A few days ago I saw him huddled in conversation with Isabella's chamberlain. He looked even more furtive than usual," she said slyly. "I thought you might want to know."

He was still digesting this last item as he mumbled the closing words to the Sacrament. When Lady Eleanor left the confessional, he sat alone, staring at the lattice screen she had removed. What had he gotten himself into? Eleanor de Clare was a woman in deep trouble, and she had asked him—or had *he* volunteered?—to get her out of it. God knew he had enough troubles of his own, but now he had added to them by conspiring with Edward II's favorite niece, the spurned wife of Hugh le Despenser.

William was late again for Vespers, he realized with a start. He could hear his brothers chanting as they plodded in double file toward the Chapel of Saint Francis: *Deus, in adiutorium meum intende. Domine, ad adiuvandum me festina. . . .*[vi]

* * *

William waited, giving Lady Eleanor time to make her exit. A minute later he stepped out of the confessional and saw his brothers streaming into the church. He expected to catch a glimpse of her passing by them on her way out; but because the sun had begun to set, the church's interior was growing dark, making it hard to see. He walked toward the main door beneath the choir at the church's west end and then halted on noticing that a small, south-facing side door was open. In the faint sunlight he saw her approach a tall, lanky man wearing a green cape and a floppy black hat.

He recognized the man from ten years earlier; it was her chamberlain, Berkhamsted, who ushered William out of the royal palace in Paris after her first confession. Eleanor spoke with him briefly, and then they exited the church into the friary's flower and herb gardens fronting on Newgate Street. William had intended to join his brothers in the Chapel of Saint Francis but on impulse decided to follow Eleanor and Berkhamsted. He ignored the reproving stare of the friary's abbot, Andrew, who led the friars' procession.

As William entered the gardens, he saw Eleanor and her chamberlain pass through a small opened gate and climb aboard an ornate and brightly painted carriage drawn by a team of two horses. A driver clad in the familiar blue and gold livery of the King's guard would take them, William assumed, along Newgate Street and then the Strand to Westminster. An extravagant means of transportation for a two-mile journey, but Eleanor de Clare was the king's favorite niece and could probably demand any transport she wished.

Out of the corner of his eye William noticed another man, short and in inconspicuous civilian attire, partly concealed behind a hedge of shrubbery. The man walked to the gate and, as if signaling to someone, pointed toward the stalls of Newgate Market and then to the carriage. Seconds later two horsemen passed by the opened gate. Their mounts trotted at a pace slow enough to maintain a calculated distance behind the carriage. William decided that the horsemen's purpose had nothing to do with assuring Eleanor de Clare's safe return. Puzzled about what he just witnessed, he reentered the church and joined his brothers in the Chapel of Saint Francis.

Chapter 5

February 27, 1324 — Greyfriars Church

THE LEAST TAXING of William's daily chores was tending the communal garden on the east side of Stinking Lane just across from Greyfriars. In winter there was little to do but repair the occasional damage to dormant crops inflicted by rats and feral dogs. Fancifully, William imagined the uprooted plants as victims of the ghosts of cattle, pigs, and sheep once butchered in the Shambles. A great open-air slaughterhouse, the Shambles had been bought a century earlier as the site for the new Franciscan friary. Perhaps the ghosts had taken belated revenge against their assassins.

Such were his idle thoughts as he completed his chores and started back to the friary. He passed by the lavatory abutting the church on the other side of the lane, then across the grassy cloister toward the library where, he'd been told, a new shipment of parchment awaited. Once plentiful, parchment and other supplies were now hard to come by, no doubt the result of the queen's isolation. Could Isabella no longer afford her earlier generosity, or had she more pressing matters to attend to? Whatever the reason, William had to vie with his brother friars for limited resources and incurred their resentment when they believed he had inveigled more than his fair share.

His walk was interrupted by the abbot, Andrew, a plump and impatient man who had just stepped out of the refectory into the fading afternoon sunlight.

"I've been looking for you," he said in what sounded like an accusation. "A visitor from Avignon wants a word with you. He's in a testy mood, so you'd be wise not to offend him. Perhaps he expected lamb, truffles, and a fine claret instead of our humble beans and beer."

As Andrew waddled off toward the chapter house, William suspected the abbot's weak joke conveyed a warning he shouldn't take lightly. He was also certain Andrew knew more than he had told him.

As he approached the cloister's west arcade, a lone black-robed priest exited the refectory amid a sea of grey habits. He was thin and balding, immaculately tailored, and otherwise forgettable in appearance—the sort who could blend in with any group, place, or circumstance and not be missed when he left. He carried a sleek leather satchel under his left arm. Because William doubted the visitor would know him by sight, he introduced himself.

"I'm William Occam. I'm told you wanted to speak with me."

"Ah, yes, Brother William. My name is Fieschi," he said in an Italian-accented French that took William's ears a moment to adjust to. "Please pardon my so abruptly announcing the purpose of my visit. I arrived in London only recently, and serve, one might say, as the pope's messenger. His Holiness sends his sincere greetings and hopes you are healthy in body and spirit. He also trusts that your thoughts and prayers are consonant with those of the Lord Jesus." As

Fieschi ended his preamble, William wondered how long he had taken to rehearse it.

"Indeed they are," he replied with extreme heartiness. "And I trust his are too."

Whether he was deaf to the edge in William's remark or decided to let it pass, Fieschi continued. "Pope John is most interested in—and yes, deeply grieved by—reports concerning some of your views. Accordingly, he has instructed me to relay his invitation to discuss them before a curial commission in Avignon."

"Hmm, 'an invitation to discuss,' you say—and before a *commission*! Should I assume the inquisitors have now been banished from the palace? Or perhaps they're enjoying an extended holiday to refresh their appetites for burning heretics and witches. The last I knew, they didn't issue invitations, at least the sort one can politely decline. Nor, for that matter, does Pope John, as you call him."

Fieschi's chin snapped slightly upward in disapproval at William's barb. "You would be correct in assuming the invitation isn't made casually but incorrect if you believe the discussion the Holy Father envisions shall be anything but open and genuine. Pope *John*"—Fieschi spoke the name with pointed emphasis—"has no wish to offend, much less suppress, the Franciscans but hopes to bring about a lasting reconciliation of his views and yours. And at the risk of appealing too cravenly to your vanity, who better to represent the Greyfriars' views than Doctor Invincibilis himself?"

Wincing at Fieschi's mention of his nickname, William said, "I can hardly claim to *represent* the order. Franciscans don't speak with a single voice, and anyone who doubts that should attend one of our frequent quodlibets. They're open to other clergy as well as the laity, and seating is almost always available. You would find, as but one example, the ongoing arguments between the Nominalists and Realists here at Greyfriars to be especially contentious."

"I suspect such rarefied philosophical disputes will be of less interest to the commission than items on which most of you appear to agree," Fieschi said. William guessed he was referring to such issues as apostolic poverty, papal authority over secular politics, and the pope's meddling in royal marriages.

"Should I understand that the Order of Saint Francis will *collectively* stand trial rather than just myself?"

"*Trial* is your word, not mine," Fieschi replied icily, for the moment sidestepping the question. "It is your own views that will be subject to scrutiny, no one else's. But let us say that your reputation makes whatever conclusions the commission may reach of wider interest than usual."

"Forgive me for being less than grateful for the compliment."

"Your gratitude may be too much to expect, but the Holy Father does expect your presence, as well as your willingness to engage in—how shall I put it?—spirited dialogue. And as a gesture of his goodwill he has secured an invitation from the Greyfriars in Avignon for you to serve as a visiting scholar during your stay. The pace of the commission's deliberations is quite relaxed, which will leave you ample time to pursue your studies. I should also tell you that the pope's request required no arm-twisting. The friars' enthusiasm about the prospect of your joining them is considerable. As an added inducement," Fieschi said with a practiced chuckle, "I might mention that the food and drink are better there than they are here."

They spoke while walking slowly from the refectory north toward the library, stopping occasionally in the relative warmth of the cloister's sunlit patches. William noticed other friars exiting the library, a few of them carrying bound bundles of the parchment he would no longer need.

"Because the commission expects you to arrive no later than the end of summer," Fieschi continued, "funds have been set aside in order to speed your journey. So that you might accept them, your minister general has been asked to grant a temporary dispensation from your vows. The journey to Avignon isn't merely long and arduous, it can be dangerous as well. As I assume you know, the crossing to Calais can be as hazardous in the spring as it is in winter."

"*If* I accept the commission's 'invitation,' please assure them I can manage without their help—or Cesena's." He felt slightly fraudulent in refusing the offer of money on principle and didn't care if Fieschi knew it. William's vows obliged him to beg for food, shelter, and any transport he would require, lengthening the trip by many weeks. But Fieschi could probably guess his reasons: William wasn't in any hurry, nor did he wish to incur the appearance of a debt of gratitude to the whoresons in Avignon who presumed to judge him. And to accept Fieschi's offer would signal at that moment his consent to Duèze's summons. Better for the present to keep him guessing.

As these thoughts coursed through his mind, he briefly lost track of what Fieschi was saying. ". . . won't try to compel you to accept them, although the commission's patience isn't unlimited. And as you make your plans, bear in mind that my stay in London should last no more than a week or two. Upon completing my other errands, I shall leave for Dover. In the meantime, I have been instructed to give you these documents so that you might prepare for your . . . discussion."

He said this as he reached into his satchel and handed William a thick packet of vellum. The packet was sealed by a dollop of red wax stamped with the papal coat of arms. Although the waxen image appeared smudged, in the waning daylight William could make out the crossed keys to the office of Saint Peter—the keys of heaven entrusted to each pope—beneath a three-tiered tiara. That Duèze presumed to hold those keys made William livid, but he took comfort in knowing that the impostor known as Pope John XXII would one day learn to his eternal chagrin that he had never held them.

"If I might offer some informal advice," Fieschi said, now in a less officious tone, "our paths will no doubt cross in Avignon from time to time, and when they do, you would be wise not to assume I am your enemy—nor to *make* me your enemy." After waiting to see that his message had registered, he turned and strode silently away.

William watched as Fieschi disappeared through the friary's main gate. His right leg ached from having been outdoors too long in the winter chill, so he found a sunlit bench next to the library and began to digest his meeting with the pope's messenger.

Grudgingly, he had to admire Fieschi's artful blend of carrots and sticks, which only made it harder to imagine how he could defy Jacques Duèze's summons. Did he have any choice but to leave England and perhaps never return? Beneath his flattery and promises, Fieschi made it clear, as far as the pope was concerned, that William had no choice. He had made enough enemies among the English Greyfriars to know they would not unite around him. Nor would they hide or protect him if he refused to leave. And even if they all liked him, which he knew they didn't, their internal doctrinal disputes alone would prevent them from rallying around him or anyone else as their standard bearer.

Most demoralizing of all was William's conviction that even those of his brothers who agreed with him were too cowardly to come to his aid. But what right had he to complain about the cowardice of others? For all his bravado in sparring with Fieschi, William was afraid. Could he, if it came to that, face immolation—along with the Jews and the heretics—on the inquisitors' pyre? Or would he in the end cave in to their threats and blandishments? He was terrified by the first possibility and revolted by the second.

William still bristled at the memory of his summons the year before to defend his commentary on Lombard's *Book of Sentences* at the Franciscan chapter meeting in Cambridge. In the main his ideas were not well received. Nor were his caustic asides about the current regime in Avignon. Because the meeting's large gathering may have included a few secular clergy disguised in grey, he wasn't surprised that word of his views had reached the papal palace. He was more than a little curious to know who the informer was and what his motives were—and whether the Cambridge meeting was in fact the source of the reports that "deeply grieved" Duèze. He had considered pressing Fieschi to tell him who had lodged the charges but thought better of it. Fieschi probably didn't know and wouldn't have told him even if he did.

William was too cold and too addled to focus on the meaning of Fieschi's "informal" advice. He needed someone to talk to. He had many admirers in addition to his enemies, but he knew only two men he could confide in and hope to hear anything sensible in return. One was Baskerville, who the last he had heard was somewhere on the Continent, possibly in Bavaria. The other was Adam Wodeham. Yes, he would seek out Adam tomorrow morning after Terce. Until then he would try to collect his thoughts, most of which now were of Eleanor de Clare.

Chapter 6

February 28, 1324 — The Elms of Smithfield

THE NEXT MORNING William rushed to catch up with Adam Wodeham. Adam had just exited the friary's gatehouse and was strolling westward toward Newgate, one of seven gates guarding the old Roman Wall encircling the City of London. He wasn't hard to recognize even at a distance. William had never known a fat friar, but one day Adam would likely fit that description. He stood almost six feet tall, which for the present allowed him comfortably to carry upwards of fourteen stone. He was still a young man, eight or ten years younger than William, so his muscle hadn't yet softened and turned to flab. The joke around Greyfriars had it that he took his task of procuring the friary's weekly pittances of meat and fowl so seriously he felt obliged to sample them, generously and often, to make certain they were palatable and untainted. The joke wasn't always meant kindly, but Adam didn't mind. Those who told it knew he was an astute judge of livestock and poultry as well as a shrewd bargainer who could cajole the Smithfield vendors into accepting the most minimal compensation. These were valued talents now that the queen's largesse was drying up.

Heading north on Giltspur Street toward Smithfield, they swapped the curt pleasantries that pass between close friends. They made an odd-looking pair: the much taller Adam and William—even shorter owing to his limp. Within minutes Adam saved William the trouble of having to broach the awkward subject he wanted to talk about.

"Should I assume you've been asked to advise Duèze on some baffling scriptural questions? Or possibly he wants to assess your qualifications for sainthood, although it's a bit premature to send someone all the way from Avignon for that. You don't appear to be dead yet, which as I recall is a key requirement."

"So you're curious about my meeting yesterday," William replied. "But I assumed you already knew. Our esteemed abbot tells everyone else more than he tells me. Word spreads quickly here."

"Quickly, but not as accurately as you might think. Andrew pretends to know more than he does. His lofty station permits him to spread curial gossip even if it's filtered through his overworked imagination. But this Italian," Adam asked, changing the subject. "What was his name? Fleshy?"

"Fieschi." William pronounced the name slowly.

". . . Fieschi—seemed a circumspect sort and a bit, um, oily, which considering where he hails from shouldn't come as a surprise."

"When the throne returns to Rome, I'll make a point of reminding you not to seek an audience with the new pope. Who knows what atrocities you might blurt out. And in case you've forgotten, our beloved Francis didn't hail from Yorkshire."

"Rules have exceptions," Adam said.

They drew closer to Smithfield Market, dodging scores of carts heaped with the meat, fruit, and vegetables that would fill the stomachs of London's exploding population. Their conversation turned serious as William recounted his meeting with Fieschi, including a description of the contents of the packet he had received.

"Fifty-one 'items for discussion'!" William said. "The commissioners—bishops, most of them—are nothing if not thorough. So perhaps I should feel relieved they called them 'items' rather than 'charges.'"

"Charges" might augur a trial for heresy, so he hoped they had in mind some lesser offense. Even by Duèze's lights, excommunication, not to mention what *that* might lead to, was excessive for yet another commentary on Lombard's *Book of Sentences*, even one as unorthodox as his.

"I should think they have more pressing matters to deal with. Just think of all the witches, Jews, and lepers they haven't yet consigned to the pyre."

"At least two possibilities," Adam said. "Either the bishops have inflated philosophical pretensions *or* they plan to use your quarrel with Lombard as a ploy to confront you later on the poverty question. That's what really matters to them. Otherwise, you might sneak off to Bavaria."

"Those possibilities aren't unrelated."

"But that just shows how dangerous your situation could be. You probably won't know *how* dangerous until months, even *years* after you arrive there. You might make some informed guesses, though, if you knew who your accuser was."

"I've already thought of a few candidates: Lutterell, Reading, Chatton, and Burley. Of the four, Lutterell seems most likely. He still blames me for ruining his chancellorship, even though his grudge is misplaced. Almost all the regent masters at Oxford hated him, and they're the ones who forced him out."

"Even so, Lutterell may have blamed you as much as he blamed the masters. He also had a chance to cause you mischief after he left for Avignon last year. No doubt he was eager to ingratiate himself with Duèze and his minions as soon as he got there. What better way for the Dominicans to give us self-righteous Franciscans our comeuppance than pillory our most obnoxious spokesman?"

"I see," William said blandly.

As they neared Smithfield market, Adam's pace slowed as he scanned the covered stalls along their route. Vendors proclaimed the excellence of their goods, and Adam scoffed at their promises, made only to a Lord's servant such as himself, of prices well below what they had paid for them.

"Obnoxious to *them* is what I meant, the Blackfriars versus the Grey and all that," Adam said with a slight grin as he turned back to William. "And speaking of Greyfriars, what about Reading?" As both Adam and William knew, John of Reading was Lutterell's last remaining ally before he left Oxford the year before Lutterell's ouster.

"Reading now teaches at Greyfriars in Avignon, which means we'd be colleagues there. So he's had a year longer than Lutterell to prepare a case against me. And because Reading is much the smarter of the two, the bishops would be more likely to take him seriously."

"Mm, perhaps," Adam said, "but not as seriously as Chatton. He's smarter than Reading."

"Maybe, but Walter's never been away from England and, as far as I know, has no plans to leave."

"You may be right, but don't eliminate him just yet. He didn't need to *be* in Avignon to level the complaints against you. I've also heard the rumor he's being groomed for some sort of advisory position to Duèze, although on *what* I have no idea." Adam paused before nudging William to complete his list. "You also mentioned Burley."

William sighed and shook his head. "He's borne a grudge ever since the drubbing I gave him in Paris—not that his stature was luminous to begin with. He'd have even less standing in Avignon than Lutterell."

"Your accuser's reputation shouldn't matter," Adam said while stopping briefly to inspect a brace of pheasants on display at one of the stalls. "If Duèze simply wants an excuse to bring you to Avignon, why would he care? And maybe Burley's been biding his time, waiting for the chance to make his move. Since your 'performance' in Cambridge last year, his allies have been multiplying by the moment. I've told you before, Willie, you really must learn to guard your tongue! Do you believe it's just a coincidence Burley and Fieschi showed up in London at the same time?"

William shook his head. "I doubt their arrivals here are related. Fieschi told me he has several matters to attend to, and I should think Burley has bigger fish to fry than an obnoxious Greyfriar. From what I've heard, he's been busy conspiring with the queen's chamberlain in addition to whatever else brought him here. And if Burley *were* my accuser, I can't see how his travelling all the way from Paris could have anything to do with me unless he found the temptation to gloat too delicious to resist."

* * *

They talked while navigating between rotting carcasses and mounds of animal shit strewn along the busy lanes. William's sandals and the hem of his habit were soiled, and he almost gagged on the foul odors wafting from the butchers' stalls. While Adam appeared cheerfully oblivious to the smells and filth, William felt his affinity for gardening reaffirmed. Better to leave Adam to go about his chores and seek a bit of privacy in a less noisome locale.

Smithfield was more than a livestock and poultry market. A flat, grassy expanse situated north of the old city wall, the larger area of Smithfield extended nearly two miles in width to the eastern bank of the River Fleet—in fact, little more than a stream except during the spring floods—which emptied into the Thames a short distance to the south. Once called Smooth Field, the area had for more than two centuries been a favorite site for gatherings of all sorts, including archery and jousting tournaments for the nobles and other, humbler amusements for the common folk.

Although the two classes mingled infrequently, they would unite on the occasion of public executions at the Elms at Smithfield, the oldest gallows in London. The administration of final justice to dissidents, witches, heretics, ordinary felons, and especially captured foreign enemies provided entertainment everyone could enjoy. Preferred seating on balconies and rooftops was reserved for those few who could afford it, and the cost of admission varied according to the degree of infamy of the condemned. Residents took pride in the Elms as a distinguished local landmark, rivaled in prestige as a tourist attraction only by the gallows at Tyburn and the Tower of London.

In August of 1305, a year before his ordination as subdeacon, William and a few other novitiates sneaked out of

the seminary to witness the Scottish nobleman William
Wallace's execution for treason. Wallace had been a thorn in
the side of King Edward I ever since he and his ally Andrew
Moray defeated the English, against overwhelming odds, in
the Battle of Stirling Bridge. A Scottish knight loyal to the
aging king caught up with Wallace eight years later near
Glasgow and turned him over to English soldiers who
transported him to the Tower of London. After three weeks
of intense contemplation of his ignominy, the naked Wallace
was dragged through the streets of the city to the Elms where
he received the full gamut of punishments that were a
traitor's due. These included being half-hanged by the neck
and then, while barely alive and conscious, forced to gaze
upon the evidence of his emasculation and disembowelment.
And finally, beheaded, with the remainder of his corpse hewn
into quarters.

William had felt relieved that the enormous crowd
obstructed his view of the proceedings, although he still
could hear Wallace's horrific screams until the spectators'
cheers drowned them out. William was physically sickened
by the raucous crowd's enthusiasm for the spectacle. Might
the soul of the Scottish renegade stand a better chance of
redemption than the citizens of England who celebrated his
torture?

The king was the father of Edward of Caernarfon, Prince
of Wales, who would succeed him, as Edward II, upon his
death two years later. Edward I, "Longshanks" as he was
called owing to his tall and lanky physique, attended the
execution in the company of his son. By chance, William's
view of the two Edwards was clearer than that of the

unfortunate Wallace. Despite his drooping eyelid and slight stammer, the elder Edward appeared regal and solemn, while the twenty-one-year-old prince smiled and winked at the assembled spectators, eager to show that he enjoyed the event as much as they did. Where Longshanks commanded respect by virtue of past deeds and the gravity of his presence, his son appeared to beseech the crowd to take notice of him.

William was jolted back to the present by a commotion behind him. He turned and saw that many of the tradesmen and merchants who moments earlier were going about their business had scattered to make way for a phalanx of armed men, about twenty in all, approaching the gallows from the west. A few rode on horseback while the rest marched behind and to either side.

At the front and center of the group rode King Edward II, flanked on his left by Hugh le Despenser. William recognized them both despite the bulky fur outer garments protecting them against the winter cold and the floppy, ornately decorated velvet hats that partially concealed their faces. Like many Londoners, William had seen them before, sometimes alone and at other times together.

The two of them made an imposing pair. Though slightly shorter than his father, the king was undeniably more handsome and blessed with thick blond hair that fell to his shoulders. Almost as tall as Edward, the black-haired Despenser exuded menace, owing in part to heavily hooded eyes that shone as dark as his hair. His wide, full mouth curled down on one side and up on the other, giving the unsettling impression of a man who snarled and smiled at the same time. On seeing him again, William wondered fleetingly if Eleanor found her future husband's looks appealing when they first met. Not that she had had any choice in marrying him. It was he, albeit with Edward's blessing, who made *that* decision.

The king and Despenser were protected by a formidable array of weaponry—spears, maces, pikes, and crossbows—borne by the guards who surrounded them. The guards were prepared for any contingency should the crowd become unruly. After halting their mounts, Edward and Despenser chatted as they examined the scaffold, perhaps noting defects in need of repair before its next scheduled use. Or were they just reminiscing about past enjoyments at the Elms?

While the king focused his attention on the gallows, Despenser's eyes darted about, alert to possible trouble. He gave no hint of being nervous and seemed to relish the fact that the onlookers had meekly cleared a path for them. His expression hardened on hearing the jeers and catcalls of those who wisely retreated a safe distance away. Edward was an unpopular king, especially in London, where citizens felt free to hurl their scorn at him so long as they couldn't be identified and caught.

Those who had not withdrawn either turned away or sullenly cast their eyes downward to avoid staring at the king and his protectors. The lone exception was William. Conspicuous in his grey habit, he stood just twenty feet from where Edward sat astride his magnificent black charger. As he watched the king with rapt interest, his attention was diverted when he noticed one of the other horsemen tugging at Despenser's sleeve and nodding in his direction. He thought he recognized the man—a scar on his brow and stringy blond hair—but he couldn't be certain. As the two of them talked, Despenser stared straight at William. Laughing, he then spoke so that all who were still gathered about could hear: "I take it, friar, you believe you can save the souls even of the depraved folk here at the Elms."

"All the more reason to come, M'lord," William shot back as he edged closer. "But do you have in mind the unlucky ones dragged here against their will or those, like yourself, who show up for the entertainment? And in case you have forgotten, Greyfriars don't hide in our cloisters waiting for the sinners to come to us. We take them where we find them."

"Not *all* of the sinners," Despenser smirked, stealing a glance at his aide. "Or so I've recently heard."

William froze. The time for clever ripostes had passed. He didn't dare press Eleanor's husband about what he had "recently heard," although he was anxious to learn. But before he could recover his wits the king signaled his men to move on. His brief business at the Elms, whatever it was, was finished.

William stared at the scaffold, cursing his impertinence. Adam was right: He should learn to guard his tongue. His habit might offer *some* protection against Despenser, but not a lot. The king's favorite was unlikely to tolerate any slight for long—even, perhaps especially, by someone such as William who presumed the divine authority to cure his soul.

His mind buzzed with questions: How much did Despenser know, or care, about his wife's comings and goings? Had William recognized his aide? If so, had he seen him at the friary around the time of Eleanor's confession? Did Despenser know who William was? Or was he just one more sanctimonious crophead, indistinguishable from all the rest, whose sheer presence provoked his taunts?

He should assume the worst: that Despenser knew about Eleanor's confession and thus posed a greater threat to her safety than she believed. And danger for Eleanor could also mean danger for William—but just how much or what kind, he couldn't tell. He needed to be alone, so he decided to return to the friary without Adam's company, relieved of the burden of keeping pace with the younger man's longer stride.

* * *

As he set off toward the friary, William's thoughts drifted and his nerves calmed. He reflected again on the follies of Boniface VIII, who, in the year 1300, appeared before a huge throng in Rome for the first Christian Jubilee. He brought with him two swords for the occasion, the first symbolizing the spiritual authority of the Church and the second, temporal authority in Christendom. "One sword ought to be under the other," he brazenly proclaimed, "with temporal authority subjected to the spiritual."

The English King Edward I and the French King Philip IV were not amused. Already chafing under the barons' restrictions on his authority, Longshanks refused to tolerate this new papal incursion into his already diminished powers. Nor did Philip the Fair, who prepared a list of twenty-nine charges of murder, simony, and immorality against the pope. Boniface promptly excommunicated Philip, setting in motion a chain of events culminating in the transfer of the papal throne from Rome to Avignon. By then, Boniface had died unaware of the calamity his actions had wrought for the Vatican.[vii]

Boniface was not the first pope to over-assert the Church's authority, nor would he be the last. The current claimant to the keys of Saint Peter, the so-called John XXII, was now moving in the same direction. The French popes were no better than the Italians at curbing their lust for power.

As he approached the friary's gatehouse, William wondered why his thoughts had strayed to the symbolism of Boniface's swords. And now it occurred to him that in the brief span of two days, both swords converged—and pointed at him.

Chapter 7

February 29, 1324 — Newgate Market

"FOR THE LOVE OF GOD, WILLIE," Adam fumed the following afternoon as they passed through the friary's gatehouse, "when will you learn to keep your mouth shut? It doesn't matter if Despenser knew who you were. If he didn't know at the Elms, he could easily find out—and probably will. And don't think your tonsure and habit can protect you. If he has no compunction about lopping off the head of an occasional baron, he won't think twice before going after a cheeky friar."

"I hate to spoil an insufferable scold's pleasure," William said as they turned left into the bustle of Newgate Market, "but if I hadn't said what I did I couldn't have known he might pose a danger to Eleanor. Now, at least, she won't be caught completely off her guard. And even if Despenser learned that I confessed her, there's nothing so remarkable in that. He knows—at least he *thinks*—she confesses regularly, and this time she happened to end up with me."

Adam shook his head. "I'm confused. First you say she's in danger from her husband and next you tell me he has no reason to suspect anything."

"That's my problem. I don't know *which* is true," William said as he swatted away a fly, "so I have to prepare for either possibility."

"Yes, but now he'll suspect that *you* might suspect something, which gives him the advantage—as if he didn't already have it. He does work for the king, you know."

"But does Despenser suspect that *I* suspect *he* suspects?" Both couldn't help laughing about suspicion's infinite regress.

"And I noticed you spoke of 'Eleanor' rather than '*Lady* Eleanor,'" Adam said as he raised a curious eyebrow. "It appears the two of you have become close friends."

William gave him a withering look but said nothing.

"Look, you know I'm not a prude, William. But I wonder why you're so concerned about *Eleanor's* welfare. It's obvious you're worried about more than the destination of her soul. Mind you, I'd be the last to chide you or anyone else on that account; God knows I've been there a few times myself. I do wonder, though, how clear you are about your reasons and whether you've thought about the consequences of whatever it is you plan to do."

"I don't *have* a plan yet, at least the details of it," William said. "And there are limits to what I can say without betraying *Lady* Eleanor's confidences more than I already have. The meeting with Fieschi changed everything. But I can tell you that I may ask you a few favors."

"Favors? You still haven't said whether you've decided to go to Avignon."

"At the moment I can't see how to avoid it."

"Nonsense! There's always Bavaria. Baskerville and Marsilius are already there, along with several of the others."

"And never return to England?" William said, shaking his head. "No, that's a bridge I refuse to burn."

"I thought you'd say that, but I had to raise the possibility. So," Adam said after hesitating, "when do you plan to leave?"

"Just over a month from now, after the feast of the Annunciation. I promised to help Andrew prepare for it, so I don't want to fall out of his good graces by leaving before then."

As the two friars wended their way through the market's maze of stalls, Adam sampled an occasional onion, shallot, and sprig of parsley. He hinted to the skeptical vendors that the Greyfriars' cellarer might be inclined to purchase substantial quantities should their produce measure up to the friary's high standards. He obviously relished this activity, but William believed his friend's mood was brightened mainly by the tongue-lashing he had meted out.

Neither friar was in a hurry. The lengthening days meant the sun wouldn't set before evening prayers ended, but otherwise there were few visible signs of spring's coming. The dignified elms—"trees of justice," the Normans had called them—were still barren of leaves. And the new season's first flowers—daffodils, dog's mercury, primroses, and sweet violets—had yet to bloom. Hardy robins and finches continued their year-round patrol of London's skies, awaiting the arrival of waxwings and swallows, their delicate constitutions renewed by an annual southern holiday.

The only other hint of winter's passing was an unseasonably warm breeze. But rather than cheering William, the milder weather reminded him of the moist and sticky climate he could expect in the south of France. The English spring he so looked forward to would barely have begun by the time he had to leave.

William had not been entirely candid with Adam. He had already started to formulate a plan, which would require his friend to serve as intermediary in forging a possibly dangerous bond with Eleanor. William still wasn't sure what he wanted that bond to consist of, and whether he was justified in asking her to agree. And long ago he had given up believing he could know what God did or did not approve of, which meant it was up to him to decide. But the decision wasn't only his to make, he reminded himself. It was Eleanor's too.

As they walked back to the friary, Adam asked, "And what about those favors you mentioned? I know you haven't yet told me everything."

William exhaled heavily before replying. "When I leave, Lady Eleanor will need a new confessor."

Chapter 8

March 2, 1324 — Greyfriars Church

MARCH'S LION HAD ROARED in with a vengeance. Eleanor was dressed for it: a grey fur-lined cape pulled tight over her gown and the same woolen blanket she had wrapped around her feet a week earlier. As she sat beside William in an alcove next to All Hallows Chapel, a few flakes of snow still covered her shoulders and the crown of the wimple framing her face. An unhappy face, since William had just told her of his meeting with the pope's messenger. Her confessor would be leaving for Avignon within the month. The more immediate cause of Eleanor's distress, however, was William's report of his encounter with her husband at the Smithfield gallows.

"I blame myself," she said. "I should never have drawn you into this. And I should have known Hugh would have me followed."

"Nonsense! You asked me to hear your confession, and that's what I did. That's what I'm *obliged* to do, which I assume your husband knows full well."

"Father—Brother William, if I may—you couldn't have known, but Hugh already knew about you," she said, taking a deep breath. "Years ago I told him about my confession in Paris. When our life together was happier, we shared all sorts of intimacies. That's what married people do, and at the time I thought nothing of it."

"Even so," William said, "I'm at a loss to know why he, or Edward, should give my existence a passing thought. I have my own reasons for wanting the king to keep his crown. What I object to is Pope John's poking his nose where it doesn't belong. So, if I pose a danger to anyone—a laughable thought to begin with—it's to him, not the King of England."

William left unsaid that King Edward was his "friend" only because he was his enemy's enemy. He was contemptuous of the king, whom he regarded as both feckless and devious. Edward waged expensive wars he couldn't win, mainly against the Scots led by his distant cousin Robert the Bruce. And he was forever at odds with the English barons, who succeeded in placing limits on his authority to levy taxes, raise armies, and enter into agreements with foreign powers. Magna Carta, they reminded him at every turn, supported their side, not his.

"To Hugh," Eleanor said, "your argument with Pope John is tedious hair-splitting by men in robes with nothing better to do. Hugh knows nothing about the Scriptures and cares even less. He does know you're a Franciscan—an impertinent one, at that—and here in England Greyfriars are loyal to Isabella, not the king. That's reason enough for him to regard you as a threat."

"A compensation, I suppose, for going to Avignon," William said with a forced laugh. "It's a safe distance away from him and his henchmen. Speaking of which, do you know who his aide was, the man who pointed me out to him at the Elms? He appeared to be about thirty, short and compact, with long, stringy blond hair and bushy eyebrows—altogether, not very pleasant looking. As I recall, he had a scar on his forehead above his left eye."

"Dunheved! *Stephen* Dunheved, that is, not his brother Thomas, though the two of them are equally vile. I could have guessed it was Stephen before you described him. He and his brother are fanatically loyal to Edward. Stephen once served as Edward's 'valet,' although 'bodyguard,' or something worse, would be closer to the mark. He now spends his time running unsavory errands for Hugh."

"Such as?"

Eleanor pursed her lips as she searched her memory. "When the barons forced Edward to exile Hugh and his father—when was it, three years ago?—Hugh took up piracy, of all things, preying on French and Dutch merchant ships in the Channel. Stephen was Hugh's first mate. He knows nothing about seamanship but knows all about killing."

"Wasn't it Stephen who foiled Mortimer's attempt to kill your husband last year?" William recalled a rumor to that effect, but he might have been misinformed or confused. He did know that Mortimer and Despenser despised each other.

"I can see why you would think so, but it's more likely it was his brother Thomas. Stephen was in France, on Hugh's order, trying to kill *Mortimer*! I couldn't swear to it, and in any case he didn't succeed."

William paused before replying as two leering stone carvers swapped remarks about Eleanor as they passed by. He glowered at them but bit his tongue. "What of Thomas? I know only that he's a Dominican with—how should I put it?—a questionable reputation."

"Thomas sometimes confesses Edward, but he mainly acts as his private agent in dealing with the Dominicans when Edward wants no one to know. He would have been banished from the order years ago if not for the king's gifts he sends their way. He survives because he's useful to both sides."

"Should I worry about him too? I'll recognize Stephen if I see him again, but not his brother. I'm quite certain I've never seen him."

"He'd be easy to recognize," Eleanor said. "Thomas closely resembles his brother. They're not twins but look as if they could be. Imagine a slightly younger Stephen without the scar on his face, and perhaps a bit taller. Word also has it that Thomas isn't as violent as Stephen, but craftier."

William stored away Eleanor's description of Thomas Dunheved, vaguely sensing that the wayward Dominican and his violent brother would one day return to haunt him.

The stone carvers resumed the annoying tapping of their mallets and chisels at the far end of the church, next to the choir just above the church's main entrance. Eleanor shivered in the cold as she inched nearer to him, making the faint scent of her perfume more noticeable. She smelled of lilacs, which William had not especially favored until now.

"And what about Mortimer?" he asked, willing himself to concentrate.

Mortimer! With the Earl of Lancaster dead—executed two years earlier following his failed attempt to kill Despenser—Roger Mortimer, the First Earl of March, assumed the mantel of leadership in the barons' stalled rebellion against the king and his favorite. Not that he was in any position to act, having surrendered to the king at Shrewsbury and imprisoned in the Tower of London in January of 1322. Unlike Lancaster, Mortimer was spared an appointment with the gallows, instead residing in a spacious, well-appointed cell with an excellent view of the Thames.

With ample provisions supplied by relaxed and sympathetic jailers, he enjoyed comforts denied the occupants of the Tower's less sumptuous quarters.

His escape eighteen months afterward became an instant legend throughout England, especially in London where Edward's popularity had sunk to new depths. The local townsfolk delighted in recounting, and often embellishing, the now-infamous feat, accomplished only once before in the Tower's history more than two centuries earlier.

The date was August 1, 1323, Mortimer's birthday and the feast day of the Tower garrison's patron saint, Saint Peter *ad Vincula*—Saint Peter "in chains." William wryly contemplated this particular choice of a patron saint. The Apostle Peter, he remembered from his earliest days as a novitiate, was imprisoned by King Herod but freed by an angel the night before his trial. In choosing Saint Peter as their patron, had the garrison's hierarchs intended a cruel irony to mock the futility of the prisoners' hopes of escape or pardon? Where was *their* angel?

Details in the escape's frequent retelling varied, but the consensus view had it that Mortimer enlisted as an ally the Tower's sub-lieutenant, Gerard d'Alspaye. D'Alspaye, who hated Despenser, brought Mortimer an iron chisel he used over a period of several weeks to bore a concealed hole in the wall of his cell, setting up the first leg of his exit. On the appointed evening, and again with d'Alspaye's aid, Mortimer hosted a lavish party for the Tower's Constable and his guards, drugging their wine and ale to render them comatose. He and his accomplice then slipped through the hole in the cell's wall, landing them in the king's kitchen, after which they climbed up a huge chimney to the roof of the Hall Tower. Crossing over to Saint Thomas's Tower, they scaled down the outer bailey's wall to the wharf using a rope ladder. A waiting boat then ferried them across to the south bank of the Thames. Once ashore they were provided horses by some of Mortimer's friends and rode overnight to the Hampshire coast. From there they sailed across the Channel to Normandy and made their way to Paris where Isabella's brother King Charles IV greeted them with great fanfare.

"Wouldn't the queen have had a hand in getting him out?"

"Unlikely," Eleanor answered, shaking her head. "She comforted *Lady* Mortimer when her husband went to the Tower, although they've always been on friendly terms. They're also cousins. And even if Isabella were tempted to help with Mortimer's escape, I don't know how she could have, especially after Edward locked her away in Westminster."

"Perhaps by encouraging her brother Charles."

"*That* ninny?" Eleanor scoffed, instantly confirming what William had heard about the recently anointed French king, Charles IV. Charles was the last of Philip the Fair's three foolish sons to succeed him. "I can't see how she could have. Remember, as Isabella's 'housekeeper' I've read her mail for more than a year, letters written *to* her as well as *by* her."

"All of them? She still has allies, as you said before, including clergy who pass freely in and out of her quarters." William had Walter Burley in mind but felt no need to raise his name again with Eleanor. "They could easily smuggle out her letters to Charles or anyone else. Surely King Edward wouldn't offend the pope more than he already has by ordering his guards to search them. But setting aside the queen's involvement, what about her brother?"

"Even with Isabella's help, I doubt Charles could have plotted with Mortimer while he was still in the Tower. But protecting him after he landed in France is another matter."

"I'm still not convinced the queen wasn't involved with Mortimer," William said, pressing the issue further. "If she hadn't intervened on his behalf, wouldn't the king have executed him along with Lancaster?"

"But if Isabella did plead with Edward to spare him," Eleanor said impatiently, "it was more out of sympathy for Lady Mortimer than loyalty to her husband. And Mortimer had enough supporters in England without needing Isabella."

William was in no position to dispute Eleanor's account. She seemed too eager, however, to deny Isabella's complicity with Mortimer, and so he took her claim about the queen's innocence with a grain of salt.

Neither of them spoke for what seemed like minutes but was just a few long seconds. A shaft of sunlight slanting through a newly installed stained-glass window above the nave basked Eleanor's cloak in refracted shades of red, yellow, amber, and green. Both of them gazed at the window's serene depiction of Saint Francis caressing a fawn as six white doves fluttered above him, freed by his serenade. It was a peaceful scene, much at odds with Eleanor's now somber mood and anxious voice.

"Brother William, I haven't yet told you what most troubles me."

"Which is," he ventured an awkward guess, "who might hear your confession when I leave?"

"No, not that," she said with a nervous laugh that failed to mask the tremor in her voice. "Although I did wonder after you told me you would soon leave England. Please forgive me—I've already crossed boundaries I shouldn't—but I fear you will forget...." Eleanor stopped speaking and looked away.

William clasped his hands tightly together and stared down at his feet. He imagined how he wanted her sentence to end and then began to brood over the perilous terrain he had just entered.

MICHAEL HARMON

₱ART THREE

AVIGNON

February 14, 1325 – December 4, 1325
(One year later)

MICHAEL HARMON

Chapter 9

February 14, 1325 — The Papal Enclave

THE SAINT BÉNÉZET BRIDGE spanned a thousand yards across the Rhône, linking Villeneuve-lès-Avignon on the west with the city of Avignon and the papal palace on the east. The bridge's twenty-two stone arches made for a magnificent sight, although its grandeur was tarnished by the arches' frequent collapse from the floods that lashed at them each spring. The Saint Bénézet was under almost constant repair, a task of great urgency considering its commercial importance to the region. It also stood at the midpoint of the main pilgrimage route between Italy and Spain. Merchants and the faithful depended on the bridge in equal measure.

No other means of crossing the river, except by boat, existed between Lyon and the Mediterranean Sea, as William learned during the final stage of his journey. Starting at Lyon he obtained passage on three shallow-draft barges, in return for which he would dispense spiritual guidance to their pilots and crews. The bargemen, however, were singularly uninspired by his counsel, so he promised to keep silent and help with the poling and oaring. Perhaps his strange accent accounted for his meager success in enlightening them, but by then he didn't care; he was tired, and his right leg, weaker and shorter than his left, ached worse than ever.

Now, seven months later, William knew the bridge well, at least the portion of it the terms of his parole permitted him to cross. That was not far, only to the Saint Nicholas Chapel, which perched atop the bridge's second pier, connecting the second and third arches from the Avignon side. Built as a devotional site for the Rhône's boatmen, the chapel attracted many of Avignon's clergy and laity, if for no other reason than to escape the city's stench.

William had other reasons for coming, chief among them that the Chapel of Saint Nicholas displayed none of the ostentatious ornamentation that defiled the chapels and other buildings in the papal enclave. The murals, tapestries, paintings, and sculpture that so impressed popes and cardinals offended the austere sensibility the Franciscans ingrained in William during his years at the seminary.

Here at Saint Nicholas's he could imagine Jesus praying. The clean sandstone walls were barren of artifacts, and the small apse contained only the Crucifix. Beneath it William could kneel in prayer without visible reminders of the Church's corruption. Except for a single small window stained with an image of the Virgin, the other windows were clear, ushering in the sunlight. On especially fine days the river's shimmering reflection brightened the chapel's interior.

At times other than his short pilgrimages to the chapel, William didn't mind Brother Gerardo's constant company. Within a month or two of his arrival in Avignon he got used to the fact that his apprentice and scribe was also his overseer, monitoring his movements while catering to his needs. Thierry of Narbonne, the abbot of Greyfriars convent, explained to William the delicate nature of Gerardo's assignment. He did so in vague and cryptic terms, but there was no mistaking that the young friar had been instructed to spy on the notorious Englishman. Among his other duties, Gerardo would restrict William's travels to the city, with occasional exceptions permitted under escort by the pope's guard. If other conditions were attached to Gerardo's role, the abbot hadn't told William what they were.

The compliant abbot was acting on Pope John's instructions (transmitted through Manuele Fieschi), which allowed William to teach and write at the convent while the papal commission's investigation proceeded at a snail's pace. The abbot was firmly under the pope's thumb, which Fieschi neglected to tell William at their first meeting in London. Nor had he bothered to mention that the pope and Thierry shared a common ancestor, which may have explained the alacrity with which Thierry carried out the pope's instructions.

William often wondered how long he would have to tolerate the abbot's supervision, for he was nearing the end of his days. He was often seized by fits of coughing and walked in slow, halting steps. William surmised soon after arriving in Avignon that the thick silvery hair encircling Abbé Thierry's head like an incandescent halo had been his sole recommendation for election as the convent's leader.

Thierry seldom interfered directly with William's activities but kept a watchful eye from a distance. The old abbot focused his attention instead on the brotherhood's other friars, finding them more amenable to his supervision than the cantankerous Doctor Invincibilis.

William's dual status as guest and prisoner bothered him less than it bothered Brother Gerardo, who took his final vows just the year before. The young Genoese friar showed unfailing deference, as if he were too eager to accommodate William's every wish. Outwardly, at least, Gerardo was earnest and guileless, an impression perhaps falsely conveyed by his wide, gap-toothed smile. Even after many weeks of their acquaintance, William had to remind himself that the wide space between his apprentice's two front teeth, coupled with his wild, curly red hair, weren't conclusive evidence of youthful naiveté. Nor was he physically imposing, roughly the same height and girth as William himself. William could not yet tell whether Gerardo's deference stemmed more from genuine discomfort over his assignment as Duèze's informant or from a calculated effort to ingratiate himself with William in order to extract damaging information about him.

In addition to his assigned duties, Gerardo assumed the task of serving as William's tour guide, escorting him around the city and pointing out which sections were safe and which to avoid. Today Gerardo took him through the streets of Saint-Étienne parish, Avignon's crown jewel housing the pope's palace and much of the papal enclave. The city's wealthiest residents lived here, and rich visitors would lodge at its most elegant inns: The Red Hat, the Black Peacock, the Griffon, and the Golden Bowl.

Saint-Étienne's streets were carefully maintained; and at the pope's direction, city officials regularly inspected, cleaned, and repaired the parish's fountains, aqueducts, and sewers to discourage littering and the disposing of dead animals in any place other than the Rhône. During his first months in Avignon, William had noticed that the other parishes, especially those on the city's poorer outskirts, received considerably less official attention. Which must have explained their noxious odors and the charred remains from the frequent fires that plagued the city.

They had just passed by the Golden Bowl Inn on their return to the convent when Gerardo said, "I have news about the new members His Holiness will appoint to the commission, Brother William. You should hear officially no more than two or three days from now. I expect you'll be pleased with one of them but not the other."

"Start with the *bad* news."

Gerardo hesitated before answering. "Lutterell."

"Hah!" William snorted. "I'm surprised he wasn't named earlier. Why the pope appointed Raimondo I've never been able to fathom." In Gerardo's presence William made a point of referring, neutrally, to *the pope*, avoiding the impertinent *Duèze*. He cringed, however, at the thought of uttering the sublime honorific *His Holiness* except in ironic moments. "It was obvious months ago Raimondo was on his last legs. You should have seen him at my first session with the commission. He had to be carted into the chamber by two of the palace guards and soon afterward fell asleep. But getting back to Lutterell, I suppose you know he set all this in motion."

"I couldn't say; but since he was already here in Avignon, his appointment was convenient, if nothing else."

"And what of the second?" William asked, abandoning for the moment his hope that Gerardo would confirm his accuser's identity.

"To everyone's surprise, the Holy Father has appointed Durand."

William gave Gerardo a startled look. "That *is* welcome news."

Like William, Gerardo knew that Durand of Saint-Pourçain was a Dominican trained in Paris. But unlike most members of his order, Durand shared many of William's radical views. They had met in Paris several years earlier, not long after Durand got into trouble when he took issue with Thomas Aquinas, of whom William himself was critical. After Durand made a few modest concessions to mollify his critics, his Dominican superiors relented and let him back into the fold.

"I believe you'll find, Brother William, that Pope John is more fair-minded than you suppose," Gerardo said with great earnestness. "He *is* serious about the open exchange of ideas and probably believes Durand's presence on the commission will contribute to that. And despite Durand's sometimes unorthodox views, he's always submitted to the pope's corrective prerogative—first Clement's and now his own—which His Holiness prizes highly."

"Oh, I have no doubt of it!" William laughed. "Perhaps the pope hopes I'll emulate Durand and decided to appoint him for *that* reason." He found it hard to disguise his disdain for his apprentice's callowness. Because Gerardo had only recently taken his vows, his presuming to know Duèze's inner thoughts must have been gleaned from something Abbé Thierry passed on to him.

Gerardo blushed at William's rebuke and changed the subject. "When we reach the convent, you'll find a packet from London addressed to you. It arrived last evening in the palace's mail pouch."

"Mm, news about the consecration of Greyfriars Church, I should think. The final stages of construction should be complete by now." William shrugged, feigning indifference to what Gerardo had just told him. He assumed that Adam Wodeham sent the packet according to the agreement they made just before William left London. Sending mail via the pope's couriers risked exposure to prying eyes. But it was faster than entrusting delivery to his brother friars, whose treks to Avignon, as William knew from firsthand experience, could take several months. Mail carried by the friars was also apt to be lost or stolen en route.

William dismissed Gerardo just before entering an alcove inside the convent's main entrance where mail was held. Almost a year had passed since he left London, and during that time he heard nothing from either Adam or Eleanor. Eagerly, he retrieved the packet and hurried off to the privacy of his cell.

The packet contained two letters addressed by different hands but stamped with the same familiar Greyfriars seal: the waxen image of Jesus' bare arm folded across the robed arm of Saint Francis. He examined both seals carefully and with relief determined that neither had been tampered with.

Before leaving London he suggested a precaution to Adam and Eleanor enabling him to detect evidence of tampering before he unsealed their letters. Sealing stamps could easily be stolen (and often *were*); and wax seals could be melted and removed, allowing letters to be opened, read, and then resealed using a stolen stamp. William could know if any of Adam's or Eleanor's letters had been intercepted and read by checking to see if a tiny notch was etched just below the upper right corner of the square-bordered Greyfriars seal. The notch, made while the wax was still warm and soft, would be unnoticeable to anyone not looking for it. This wouldn't, of course, prevent their letters from being stolen and then not delivered. To determine if any of their letters hadn't reached him, he asked Eleanor and Adam to number them. Any gaps in their numbering would tell him that an earlier letter had been stolen or lost. He was lucky this time: a notch was visible on each seal; and each letter, as he discovered upon opening it, contained a small numeral "1" in the lower left corner of its last page.

One of the letters was Adam's, which he opened first. He would save the letter he presumed was Eleanor's to read afterward. Adam's letter was something of a disappointment. It was full of news, much of it gossip about the friary's internal politics, which William no longer cared about. Adam also relayed items William learned after arriving in Avignon. The pope, he confirmed, excommunicated the German King Louis—"Louis the Bavarian." Louis and Duèze had crossed swords over the years on many issues, including Louis' standing offer of protection to dissident Greyfriars. Few were surprised at Louis' fall from ecclesiastical grace.

William was struck more by the tone of Adam's letter than its content. Loquacious in conversation, he was cautious and restrained in this, his first letter. In enlisting his protégé as Eleanor's confessor and asking him to safeguard the transmission of her letters, William feared he had placed Adam in harm's way. To persuade him William appealed to their shared hatred of Duèze's regime. But he knew that Adam agreed to act as intermediary between himself and Eleanor out of friendship and, possibly, the prospect of vicarious adventure. He was a devoted and disciplined scholar but chafed under the often-tedious regimen of day-to-day life imposed by the Franciscan Order—even to the point of provoking whispers of doubt about his piety.

Adam made no explicit mention of Eleanor in his letter, a sensible precaution to protect himself and to prevent exposure of her participation in what her husband would surely construe as intrigue against the king. He did make a veiled reference or two to the counsel he had given "our mutual friend," no doubt to reassure William that he continued to confess Eleanor.

After setting aside Adam's letter, William broke the seal of Eleanor's and unfolded the parchment on which she had written. He winced on noticing her salutation's ornate flummery, but his mild irritation quickly passed. He had waited almost a year to receive her first letter.

Eleanor Despenser, lady of Glamorgan, to our beloved and
most faithful Brother William, our confessor, greetings in
God. I trust that you are safe and well, and pray that the Lord
is always with you.

In the months since you left London, I have become less
and less certain He is with me. But before explaining my
lament, I should tell you of my reasons for not writing
earlier. Be assured it was not out of indifference. Nor is
Brother Adam at fault, although events at the palace have
made it hard for us to meet without arousing suspicion. On
the few occasions we have met, he has proved wise and
steadfast and, as you won't be surprised to learn, raised my
spirits if only for a short while.

The court gossips would no doubt scoff at my
complaints. In their eyes I have replaced Isabella as the
loftiest lady in the land. Edward makes a great public display
of showering me with compliments and gifts, and has even
dubbed a ship in my name. Hugh bites his tongue and
pretends not to notice. He is warier than ever and suspects
everyone, including me. I'm surprised he still confides in me
at all, and when he does I can't be certain he tells the truth.

I have paid a price for Edward's attentions and have
even had to fend off his advances, including invitations to
share his bed. I'm sorry if that shocks you, but by now little
should surprise you about the goings-on at Westminster.

His attentions have also brought other burdens. I'm now
charged with caring for Isabella's son John, much to her
anger and sorrow. Despite her isolation from her children the
queen gives the outward appearance of being stoic. She even

manages to act civilly toward Hugh, whom of course she despises.

Her reasons are easy to understand. After Edmund's failure in Gascony, she knows she is the final card Edward can play in persuading Charles to return it to English control. In fact, Edward has decided to send Isabella to Paris as "ambassador extraordinary" to try to reclaim it, and only a few details remain to be sorted out before she leaves. Edward himself does not want to go because he fears for his own safety were he to set foot in France. I suspect also that he would feel humiliated by swearing fealty to Charles.

Everyone at court wants the queen to go to France— Hugh most of all. He does not want Edward to go for fear that, with the king out of the country and unable to protect him, the barons would take their revenge. Both Pope John and Isabella's allies have been urging Edward to send her. Isabella wants the assignment, which explains why she has been tolerably pleasant toward Hugh. Indeed, I suspect the mission to Paris was her idea, that behind the scenes she has been contriving the "requests" for her visit while convincing Edward that he had a real choice in the matter. If so, he may be sending the queen on a fool's errand but with himself the fool rather than her.

Once Isabella reaches Paris, Edward will have little control over her. She can disregard any of his instructions, very likely with the encouragement of her brother and also Mortimer, who is much in Charles's favor. That is hardly a surprise in view of Mortimer's offer last year to fight on France's side in Gascony. At least that is the rumor Berkhamsted told me a few months ago.

I fear your suspicions about an alliance between Isabella and Mortimer were nearer to the truth than I wanted to believe. Edward has long feared it to be so, but he now has no choice but to send Isabella to France and hope she will return to England with an acceptable agreement rather than an army of French soldiers to depose him. In his optimistic moments Edward expresses cheery confidence she will do as she has been told, while many at court roll their eyes and snigger behind his back.

I won't accompany the queen. My days as her companion and confidant are long past. And Edward knows she would refuse to leave London if my traveling with her were imposed as a condition. Besides, Edward claims to need me here, although his "need" grows out of his increasingly vain and suspicious nature.

I wish I were going to Paris, if only to escape the intrigues of the court here in London. I'm weary of being lied to and weary also of Edward's incessant demands on me. The more I'm seduced into his schemes, the lonelier and more vulnerable I feel. Edward's protection, if ever it was that, now appears to be an illusion. Perhaps that is why I am ashamed at my betrayal of the queen. Isabella is a hard woman to like, but I cannot begrudge her feeling abused by Edward and Hugh—and by me, not least of all.

Paris would also bring me nearer to Avignon and thus nearer to your counsel. Unlike so many others, you expect nothing from me in return. Please forgive me, Brother William, for saying more than I should and for being so mawkish in doing so. . . .

William squirmed on reading Eleanor's last few lines. Though it was true he expected nothing from her, what he *wished* for was another matter. But he could tell her none of this, for he feared she would scoff at *his* mawkish sentiments. So he kept these to himself, along with his bittersweet memories. In his reply to Eleanor he took pains to conceal them and concluded with bland assurances that her fortunes would soon improve.

Chapter 10

September 7, 1325 — The Papal Enclave

"I ASSUMED YOU KNEW," John of Reading said, surprised at William's ignorance. The two of them, the most eminent Franciscans residing in Avignon, resumed their weekly conversation after yet another of William's interrogations by the commission. Today's route took them over and around construction debris cluttering the papal enclave.

In view of their earlier disagreements at Oxford, their emerging friendship was an unlikely one, and William still guarded what he said to the former regent master. The amiable Reading, however, was never at a loss for words. The large man's face was wide and florid, and he was prone to making sweeping gestures with his long arms.

"Fieschi," he explained, "is the younger brother of Gerardo's father, Count Gabriele Fieschi. The Count heads an old Genoese banking family and for many years has had close ties to the English crown. Edward, in fact, is heavily in debt to him, as well as to several other Italian houses. Gerardo, I believe, is Count Fieschi's third, and youngest, son. I'm not sure it's widely known, but Fieschi—Manuele, that is—used his influence to secure his nephew's invitation to enter the Order four years ago. Gerardo had other ideas about what to do with his life and wasn't keen about the prospect of marrying Lady Poverty. But he eventually gave in to his father's wishes."

"Hmm, now I understand why I often see them together," William said, "and also why Gerardo cuts their meetings short whenever I appear. I doubt he'd have lied to me about it, but I also suspect he won't be pleased when he learns that I know. Not that it matters."

They stopped to rest on a bench at the eastern end of the piazza. William's leg was aching again. Reading, who frequently complained about the rheumatism in his knees, did not object.

"I doubt it matters to Fieschi, either, although he's never deigned to confide his innermost thoughts to me." Chuckling, Reading said, "In fact, I find it hard to imagine what they might be. He's the most opaque man I've met since coming to Avignon."

William remembered Fieschi's advice to him a year and a half before. "When we first met in London, he said I would make a mistake to assume he was my enemy. I'm still not sure what he meant or why he made a point of telling me."

Reading scratched his chin before replying. "He may have been referring to his connection with King Edward."

"And what connection is that?"

"My recollection is a bit vague, though I recall hearing that Fieschi is distantly related to Edward through his uncle Cardinal Luca Fieschi. I know little about their converging lineages; but as you know, family ties cross all sorts of boundaries, especially where the royals, aristocracy, and higher clergy are concerned. But back to my point: With Edward's help Fieschi was granted a benefice or two in England eight or ten years ago."

"Perhaps," William said, "but only if the benefices were small enough to be granted by an English bishop rather than the pope. Edward's influence with Pope John is almost nil. And if what you say about his and Fieschi's family connection is true, it explains something I learned years ago at Oxford: that the king once sided with Fieschi on some sort of doctrinal dispute. If he did, their kinship more likely accounts for Edward's support than his views on the Holy Scriptures. I doubt he has any. It's also possible Edward intervened on Fieschi's behalf in return for keeping at bay the Count's demands that Edward settle his debts."

"If so, Fieschi would be wise to exercise great care," Reading said. "I daresay the pope wouldn't be pleased if he knew of his sympathies toward Edward."

"No doubt. He'd be lucky to live out his remaining days sharpening quills and stomping grapes in a monastery somewhere off in the Pyrenees."

Reading laughed at this as the two of them stood and resumed their stroll. "Being careful is what he's most accomplished at. Fieschi is a careerist if ever there was one and would reconsider his loyalties, even to his 'cousin' Edward, if he found it expedient."

William stopped for a moment to reflect on this. "What you've just told me answers my question about whom Gerardo reports to at the palace. I've never believed, of course, that he deals directly with the pope. But Fieschi *does* and may well use what he hears from Gerardo to suit his own ends. Although, I have no idea what they might be."

"Nor do I," Reading said as William pondered whether to broach the question of who had brought charges against him to the pope's commission. Recalling Reading's alliance with Lutterell at Oxford, he thought better of the idea.

"I hope I'm not crossing a line I shouldn't," William said, "but I can't help asking why you've confided all this to me. I've never had any reason to doubt your allegiance to the pope."

"That I don't call him 'Duèze,' or 'Old Cahors,'doesn't make me his toady," Reading answered testily. "Give me that much. Yes, it's true I side with him on doctrinal matters more often than I side with you. And I think he's right, and that you and the other Spirituals are wrong on the poverty question—a subject, incidentally, you've been wise to avoid in your 'conversations' with the commission. But I must say I find the burning of heretics, not to mention Jews and witches, a horrible business that does grave damage to the Church's spiritual authority." Reading's voice gathered in intensity: "When the Lord died for our sins, I doubt He had *those* barbarisms in mind."

* * *

When he arrived in Avignon the year before, William learned that its first pope, Clement V, was content to live modestly in the nearby Dominican monastery. His successor John XXII had grander ideas, lavishly refurbishing and enlarging the Avignon bishop's residence as befitting its new status as the pope's palace. But John didn't have to move there, having served as Avignon's bishop before receiving the keys to Saint Peter's office. He could simply remain where he was.

The palace was the most imposing structure among several located at the base of *le Rocher les Doms*, a massive rocky outcrop dominating the northwest corner of the city. The palace overlooked not only the Rhône and the Saint Bénézet Bridge but also the Cathedral of Notre Dame, which stood next to it. *Notre-Dame des Doms* was an odd-looking Provençal Romanesque structure whose new bell tower, rather than adding to its grandeur, appeared to have been designed by a committee beset by confusion and dissension.

Incoherence in architectural design marred not only the cathedral but also the rest of the papal enclave and indeed the entire city. Flanked by ugly new warehouses, dozens of recently opened shops ("official suppliers to the pope," or so their proprietors advertised) offered for sale the most luxurious merchandise in the known world. The shops sprouted incongruously amid the proud new mansions of cardinals and burgesses. Rich merchants paraded about the enclave, wearing velvet, fur-lined surcoats and embroidered, pearl-studded shoes. These titans of commerce vied for public notice with dozens of cardinals who, like the preening boulevardiers William had seen in Paris, strutted through the palace piazza in their bright crimson robes. Some of the cardinals hired torchbearers to signal their approach while feigning indifference to the common folk's admiring glances.

Not far from the palace stood the Dominican monastery; the houses of other religious orders were scattered farther out on the enclave's periphery. Among the least impressive of these was the Franciscan convent, a nondescript two-story limestone building covered by a crumbling veneer of faded yellow stucco. Accommodating up to sixty resident friars, the convent housed only a single small chapel for solitary prayer, which meant the friars had to trudge to a nearby church to attend holy offices. William was grateful for his exemption from that requirement owing to his physical infirmity but also out of deference to the special circumstances of his presence in Avignon. He had to remain, on a moment's notice, at the commission's beck and call.

The upper floor of Greyfriars convent consisted mainly of an enormous sunlit room that served as both library and scriptorium.

William was disappointed by the convent's meager collection, only a fraction the size of the Greyfriars library in London. One of Duèze's few achievements William could applaud was tripling the number of volumes in the palace library's collection to more than two thousand. William, Reading, and a few other senior Greyfriars were given unlimited access, although William suspected that his "privilege" was granted in order to ease the papal guards' task of keeping track of him.

I'm due at a meeting with a few of the bishops to discuss how the library might acquire some beautifully illustrated volumes by Bede," Reading said, breaking the silence that had followed his outburst. "The Benedictines across the border in Italy now have them, but the monks there are none too eager to sell, at least to Pope John or his agents. The abbot and most of the elder monks are Italians who still haven't reconciled to the throne's removal from Rome. And the abbot—Abo, I believe he's called—guards his treasures with greater jealousy than the pope anticipated. But His Holiness keeps nudging us to press on with the matter. Which, I'm afraid, is an overlong explanation of why I have to take your leave."

As he started off in the direction of the palace, Reading halted and turned back toward William. "I know you've wanted to ask, so I'll save you the trouble. You're quite right in suspecting that Lutterell brought the charges against you. I doubt he'd mind my telling you, so I don't believe I'm betraying a confidence. In fact, he might even take perverse satisfaction in knowing that you know. I do find it curious that he did so with Walter Burley's encouragement. I still can't fathom what their connection is and I may have misheard what Lutterell told me." After pausing briefly: "But I ought to be on my way."

Lutterell and Burley. William would not have been surprised to learn that either one of them had brought the accusations against him. He had always believed Lutterell to be the more likely of the two, having just received his appointment to the papal commission. But why they might have conspired with each other puzzled William. As far as he knew, Lutterell had never been involved in the politics of the English court, while Burley was right in the thick of it and squarely on Isabella's side. And why had Reading been so forthcoming, even indiscreet, not only in telling him about Lutterell and Burley but also about Gerardo, Fieschi, and King Edward? Reading's distaste for the burning of heretics struck William as genuine, and his implication that the pope ought to stop meddling in secular politics was unmistakable—or so he thought.

But rather than feeling reassured by Reading's friendly disclosures, William still felt wary of him. Reading made no bones about wishing to be appointed palace librarian, a position Duèze directly controlled. Despite his obvious affection for his brother friars, the amiable Reading's fortunes depended on his unwavering fealty to the pope. He would never cross him.

Chapter 11

October 9, 1325 — The Papal Palace

BY WILLIAM'S COUNT this was his eleventh session before the commission. As Gregory of Lucca incanted his benediction, he reflected again on Adam Wodeham's parting advice.

"If nothing else, Willie, remember this: Dazzle the bishops with your erudition, but limit it to subjects they neither care about nor understand. And don't flatter yourself by believing you can change their minds. Just keep them stroking their chins and scratching their heads until you've exhausted them."

"Supposing I possessed such a gift, what good would it do?"

"Not to put too fine a point on it, but it could save your life. Erudition will confuse rather than enlighten them, unless they're keener than I predict. So long as they're confused, their attention will fix upon metaphysical nit-picking, a talent *you* possess in prodigious supply."

"I trust that's meant as a compliment."

"It *is*, and don't for a moment doubt my seriousness. However long your stay in Avignon lasts, you won't come away unscathed. At the very least, the pope's lackeys will have to end up censuring you for your 'errors.' They won't vindicate you fully, nor will Duèze himself. Otherwise, they'll have wasted their time. So the best you can hope for is a mild rebuke. And in order to limit the damage, stay away from disputes where the lines are already drawn. In particular, don't become trapped in the poverty question. Leave that to Cesena and the others. Where Duèze's power is at stake, your cleverness won't protect you."

For more than a year William only partly succeeded in following Adam's advice and often came close to ignoring it altogether. He had Durand of Saint-Pourçain to thank for hewing to it as closely as he had. Unlike the five Realist members of the commission, Durand, the commission's single Nominalist, refrained from taking sides and instead deftly changed the subject when William overplayed his hand. Or, Durand would come to his rescue by injecting irony and puns to soften the tenor of the proceedings. At other times he arched an eyebrow or cleared his throat, signaling William to temper his ire.

Other members were less restrained. Raymond Béquin, the Patriarch of Jerusalem, and Dominique Grenier, bishop elect of Pamiers, reminded William of mastiffs charging into bloody combat, only to emerge licking the wounds inflicted by his rebuttals. Each, however, would reenter the fray, ever hopeful of a happier outcome. John Paignote, the frail and diminutive Augustinian regent at the University of Paris, showed greater restraint, although William still couldn't tell whether his diffidence bespoke a mild temperament, apathy, or a fear the acerbic Greyfriar might thrash him in front of his peers.

Gregory of Lucca, just recently appointed as bishop of Belluno-Feltre, presided over the sessions and tried to steer the questioning. The items on which the commission was charged with examining William were supposed to be drawn solely from his commentaries on Lombard's *Book of Sentences*. But like many quodlibets William attended over the years, the commissioners' agendas were often discarded or construed so broadly as to be useless. The affable Lucca had to be content with nurturing an ambience of pious decorum. William ranked Lucca as the most astute member of the panel—except for Durand, who occupied a category unto himself. Not all the commission members were the dullards Adam had predicted. Even Grenier, despite his lack of subtlety and his coarse demeanor, revealed himself a formidable power for William to reckon with.

Finally, Lutterell. William was surprised at how little the erstwhile Oxford chancellor had spoken. He remained content to observe and listen, having already done his part by bringing to the pope's attention the original fifty-one charges. To Lutterell's dismay his colleagues discarded almost half of them as irrelevant or fatuous. Perhaps their rebuke accounted for the squat Dominican's constant scowl. The corners of his mouth turned downward as if he were trying to impress upon the others his capacity for deep thought and grave concern. He fooled no one, no more than he had fooled the regent masters at Oxford who deposed him two years earlier. Sensing the slight regard in which Lutterell was held, William found ways to play it to his advantage.

He was also pleased by the recent change of venue. Until renovations on the palace's upper tiers were completed, the first eight sessions were held in what were previously servant quarters.

The dozens of tallow candles stuffed into the sconces provided barely enough light and, making matters worse, gave off a foul odor. The large room looked and smelled like a dungeon, and upon entering William would instinctively scan its periphery for instruments of torture the commissioners could employ should he prove uncooperative.

Resembling ornate modest-sized thrones, the commissioners' chairs were aligned in a straight row, spaced precisely the same distance apart. Opposite them stood William's chair: straight-backed, unupholstered, and, like himself (he noticed), having one leg shorter than the others.

With the coming of spring the first stages of the palace renovations were almost finished, allowing the commission to occupy a smaller but more resplendently appointed chamber on the palace's second tier. The room's southern exposure ushered in ample light, which showed off to good effect the tapestries adorning its walls. But in William's opinion the hunting scenes they depicted had been shoddily executed. Perhaps the tapestries were hung there temporarily pending the arrival of more impressive specimens recently plundered from the Vatican.

Best of all, at least for William, was the new seating arrangement. All the chairs, including his, were of similar design and, at Durand's urging, arrayed in an almost perfect circle. Next to each chair was a small table on which were placed a Bible, the *Sentences*, and various documents the commissioners and William could refer to, which they often did.

The effect on the proceedings was immediate: William's interrogators now sparred with one another as often as they did with him. With some notable exceptions the discussion's give-and-take grew less combative, and its direction proved even harder for Lucca to control. The bishop of Belluno-Feltre accepted with equanimity this erosion of his authority, leaving only Lutterell in a worse mood than before. William suspected Lucca and his colleagues were grateful also that the new, airier atmosphere had lessened their chances of becoming tubercular.

* * *

"But, Brother Occam," Grenier asked, "is it necessary for God to do *anything*?"

"Nothing God does is necessary," William replied in a tone suggesting the answer should be obvious to a half-wit. "Because He acted freely, for example, in creating Adam and Eve—indeed *all* His earthly creatures—then, to be consistent in our reasoning, we would have to say also that He could have chosen *not* to. His freedom has to allow for the possibility of choosing either way. Otherwise He would not be free at all."

"Which means, does it not, that in the absence of any such necessity, God is free to do, to create, whatever He wishes?"

"It does," William replied, "unless it involved a contradiction."

"Pray indulge us with an example."

William was ready with one. "If God were free to do *anything*—that is, if He possessed unlimited power and imagination—He would be 'free,' let us say, to create a rock too heavy for Himself to lift. But if He is in fact all-powerful, then, of course, *no* rock, whatever its weight, *could* be too heavy for Him to lift, in which case His purported power to do that would involve a contradiction. Ergo, He wouldn't, *doesn't*, have such a power."

"That's easy enough to follow," the stout, grey-bearded Grenier said archly. "I'm sure all of us present learned about simple paradoxes long before your reminder. So, given His *otherwise* unlimited freedom and power, are we to assume that God can create all sorts of earthly objects and forces, as well as human experiences and abilities, that are in fact unnecessary?"

"Yes," William said, "but perhaps I haven't yet made it clear that *all* of what God created, or might create at some future time, is unnecessary. It isn't the case that only *some* of the objects He created are unnecessary, because that would imply others *are* necessary, when in fact none of them are."

"But," Grenier said, poised to expose the flaw in William's logic, "doesn't such a claim contradict your own maxim, one you asserted quite forcefully just one or two sessions ago, that we shouldn't multiply entities beyond necessity. And if *we* shouldn't, then why should, or would, *God* do so? Moreover, isn't it quite incongruous to believe God expressed His own perfection in creating the Earth and its creatures as he did while at the same time cluttering it with extraneous entities and forces? And should we not also infer from your reasoning that the Philosopher was in fact misguided in claiming 'God and nature do nothing that is pointless?'" Grenier asked these questions with eyebrows raised as he glanced around the room to see if the other commissioners grasped their perspicuity.

"What God may or may not regard as pointless, or indeed how He construes 'perfection,' is quite beyond our capacity to know," William said in a weary voice. "He alone is privy to the reasons guiding His decisions about what, and what not, to create, irrespective of whether those decisions issue from His infinite wisdom or merely His caprice. No earthly being, Aristotle included, can gainsay them. Moreover, 'pointless' and 'extraneous,' I should emphasize, are *not* synonyms for 'unnecessary.' 'Unnecessary' means only that God is free to act in whichever way He chooses, including changing His mind, so long as it doesn't involve a contradiction. And at the risk of appearing impolitic in saying so, your conflating the meanings of those words is one of the chief reasons for your confusion."

"Reluctance to appear impolitic hasn't held you back up to now," Lutterell muttered from across the circle. His scowl was deeper than usual.

Grenier ignored Lutterell's remark and pressed on with his questioning. "You still haven't explained why entities shouldn't be multiplied beyond necessity."

"I believe I *have*, at least by implication. But let me try again from a different vantage. When I urged that we not multiply *entities* beyond necessity, the entities I referred to pertain only to the elements of the theories we use to *explain* reality. I make no claim about the nature of reality itself, its degree of 'complexity' or 'simplicity,' for example, and certainly not about God's purpose in creating it as He did. For all we can know, He may have created many more things than He believed required to achieve His purposes. He needn't explain, much less justify, Himself to *us*, nor, indeed, to Himself."

Waving aside William's superfluous concluding comment, Grenier forged ahead: "But doesn't the complexity—or the simplicity, if you prefer—of any theory need to correspond in similar degree to the complexity of those features of the world—the reality—that the theory purports to describe or explain?"

"Most assuredly not," William replied, "because no such 'correspondence' can possibly be demonstrated. Although God might, in an idle moment, make His own assessments of the complexity or simplicity of the world He created, we aren't privy to those assessments and for the same reasons we aren't privy to knowledge of His purposes or His views about perfection.

"Nor, in *not* knowing," he continued before Grenier could interrupt him, "are *we* deprived of any useful information as we seek answers to practical questions. For such purposes we needn't be concerned with whether the *world* is simple or complex, for that is merely a metaphysical question of the sort we should get over rather than try to answer. And any speculation we might engage in about the matter will in any case reveal as much, indeed it will reveal far *more*, about ourselves than the 'reality' we seek to comprehend. Your question, if I might say so, commits the same old Realist error of confusing ontology, and metaphysics as well, with epistemology."

"Assuming you are correct about the profound character of our ignorance," Bishop Lucca interjected with a hint of irony, "are there, then, no guides to, nor any limitations on, what we can know with confidence or certainty? Or perhaps I *should* have asked: Are simple explanations—*parsimonious* ones, as you've called them on prior occasions—to be preferred in all instances? Is parsimony always the virtue you say it is?"

"*Confidence* in our knowledge is one thing and *certainty* about it quite another," William replied more affably than before. A cooling breeze wafting through the chamber's large open window had lightened his mood. "But setting that matter aside, I trust you'll be relieved to hear, Bishop, there *are* conditions under which departures from parsimony are not only permissible but indeed required: first, when reason demands it, which is to say, when the need for more complicated explanations can be logically inferred from premises no one disputes; *or* from indubitable experience; or, finally, from an infallible source of authority."

"And those infallible sources of authority you refer to . . . ?"

"It should surprise no one that I include here the Holy Scriptures, as well as the Saints, and, um, various ecclesiastical pronouncements."

"*Various*?" Lutterell exclaimed, pouncing on the opportunity. "And would you deign to include the pronouncements of Christ's *Vicar*? Or just those you happen to . . ."

Before Lutterell could finish his question, Durand deflected it. "No doubt we can all agree to such an obvious stipulation," he began vaguely. "But I have to ask, Brother Occam, whether the 'experience' you refer to in your second condition can ever be as indubitable as you seem to presume. How can I know, for example, that my own sense of 'indubitability' isn't a delusion, a product, say, of my weakness of mind or even madness? I'm certain at least a few of my detractors over these many years would fervently insist it that *is*. And who is to say," he shrugged with eyes twinkling, "they could be right."

"I very much doubt that," William replied, wincing at his fawning gesture to curry the friendly Dominican's favor. "But you nevertheless raise an interesting problem, one that surely invites further investigation. I might note, however, that even if we could exclude weak-mindedness and madness as possible contaminants, we should always view claims of indubitability with a skeptical eye, not only as we reflect upon our *own* experience but also upon the credibility of the claims others make. And if I could be permitted to venture a prediction, I think it likely that decades, perhaps *centuries*, from now scholars will still be grappling with this problem with great earnestness, no doubt deploying terminology and concepts none of us here could possibly foresee."[viii]

William was stalling for time, hoping someone other than Lutterell would interrupt him and change the subject. Béquin obliged, cutting off Lutterell again as he was about to reclaim the floor.

"Brother Occam, I assume your recitation of the conditions under which parsimony no longer applies are intended in part to reassure us that the foundations of truth remain secure," Béquin said as he leaned forward, squinting over his steepled fingers. "But I wonder just how sincere you have been in implying that reassurance. You have already agreed with Durand about the dubiety, as it were, of claims to 'indubitable' experience. And Lutterell, like some of the rest of us, has good reason to be apprehensive about the ambiguities and the contradictions you and your fellow Nominalists will no doubt winkle out of 'various' ecclesiastical pronouncements— especially in view of your previous arguments that all words can do is refer to other words, and so on and so forth. That is a position I still find hard to agree *or* disagree with, mainly for want of grasping it fully. Whether that reflects weak-mindedness on my part or muddle-headedness on *yours* remains an open question. Finally, are there indeed premises 'no one disputes'? And if there *are*, can we be confident that everyone who tries to reason from them will reach the same conclusions?"

"Your summary of those difficulties is quite accurate. But," William added heatedly, his shoulders tensed, "your doubts about my sincerity are not! I find myself puzzled as to whether you intend to disagree with me or to make my argument *for* me. That all three of the conditions I mentioned are often hard to satisfy provides no reason to throw up our hands. Indeed, it gives us even more reason to take them seriously. And one of the chief benefits of doing so, I might add, is to expose the hubris of those who arrogantly proclaim their fallible opinions as unassailable truth."

"Such vigilance is no doubt commendable," Béquin replied with undisguised sarcasm, "although from what you've said, I still fail to see any grounds for optimism about our getting closer to finding the truth—if, that is, we were to follow your advice."

"We won't get any 'closer,'" William responded, "and we should stop gnashing our teeth over our inability to do so!"

Sensing confusion about such a crucial term, Lucca interrupted Béquin's line of questioning: "Might a definition of *truth* be in order? Greater clarity about it could, among other things, help dissipate the present rancor."

William pursed his lips as he pondered his reply. "Consider this one: *Truth*, if one insists on using the word, is whatever God knows."

"But," Béquin shot back, "if, as you say, we cannot *know* what God knows, then the very idea of truth, at least insofar as *we* might try to discover it, is rendered utterly trivial!"

"With *that* I would heartily agree," William said, to the consternation and confusion of most of those present. He had just succeeded in following Wodeham's advice after all.

"I fear," the exasperated Lucca said, "that our discussion has reached something of an impasse and, in any event, shows signs of moving in a new and more contentious direction. That being the case, I propose that we close for the present and resume at a later date. It has also come to my attention that the vitality of at least one of our members has begun to wane," he noted dryly, looking in Paignote's direction as the Augustinian regent began to snore softly.

Chapter 12

November 11, 1325 — The Papal Infirmary

ILLIAM'S LEG ACHED, a sure sign winter was coming. He finally caved in to Gerardo's nagging him to visit the infirmary to see what magic its resident healer, Brother François, might perform. William was not optimistic. Nor was his mood lightened by their brief journey. Avignon's sky was grey and bleak, much like the visages of the beggars crowding the lane as William and Gerardo neared their destination. The beggars looked despondent, weary from the futility of beseeching passersby—always in Jesus' holy name—to deposit in their wooden bowls a small coin or two, or toss a crust of bread their way. Many of the passersby were clergy bustling to and from the palace, God's official servants who had other, pressing matters to attend to.

Sights such as this one made William wish *he* had carried a few coins, which he had no personal use for. And seeing these sights further hardened his contempt for the unholy church that had brought him to Avignon. He was in a foul humor, which Gerardo's advice did nothing to lift.

"Brother William, might I suggest, at least in his presence, that you not refer to Brother François as a *shaman*? He's a physician in the most scientific sense of the word and comes highly recommended by several of the bishops. They report that his herbals and salves have worked wonders for them."

"From what I've seen, most of them would be better off imbibing a strong claret."

"Perhaps you shouldn't confuse your personal tastes with sound medical practice," Gerardo needled him back. "I should remind you that François was once a student of the great de Villanova, who until his passing was a close friend and colleague of Pope John. And the Holy Father himself, you may recall, studied medicine as a young man before finding his true calling doing the Lord's work."

"De Villanova the alchemist? I can now guess how his *Holiness* whiles away his idle moments in the palace laboratory."

"Pope John is not an alchemist, at least not in the scurrilous sense you suggest. In fact, he's issued clear warnings against the charlatans who boast, among their other preposterous claims, of extracting gold from lead."

"That's hardly reassuring, especially if he puts his stock in a 'physician' who believed in the curative power of boiled cat entrails."

"Arguing with you is pointless," Gerardo said with an exasperated sigh. "You can either persist in complaining about your leg or *experiment* with one or two of Brother François's remedies— if, that is, you're the empiricist you say you are. I hate to sound petulant, but I urged you to come here out of concern for your well-being, not for the pleasure of hearing your complaints."

William shrugged in reply as they approached the infirmary. He had to admit that Gerardo had made a telling point, and he much preferred his apprentice's recent brashness to his usual obsequiousness. Perhaps there was hope for him yet.

Before entering the infirmary, they passed through a neatly groomed herb garden, which supplied the grist for the potions that passed for medicine in the papal enclave. His nostrils were immediately bombarded with the sweetly exotic aromas of cloves and aniseed. As he surveyed the multicolored array of plants—most still in bloom and others cut, dried, and neatly bundled and bound—William conceded the possible merit of some of Brother François's claims: that cloves might ease arthritic pain, that coriander might deter fevers, lavender cure headaches, and that cumin could remedy flatulence. He felt less confident that mint prevented infection in wounds or that ginger and rosemary warded off the plague.

Most absurd was the physician's contention that the lemon scent of melissa could cure melancholia. As a recent sufferer from that particular malady, William found himself pining for the soothing balm of the River Thames, most especially the view from his beloved Oxford. After almost two years of captivity in Avignon, only now could he start to grasp the river's deeper meaning: the invisible life beneath its surface that evoked the presence of an ineffable God and the river's calm, perpetual renewal of His still mysterious purpose in placing on the Earth men, women, and all the other creatures.

The Rhône summoned none of these thoughts, although William assumed that it must to the natives of southern France. The Rhône was *their* river, not his; so he concluded that melancholia must be another name for homesickness. The Thames of his native land ferried people and things from one point to another along its path, but its slowly winding currents also transported and then fused the unique communal spirit called England that he still longed to feel a part of.

William set aside his misgivings as he and Gerardo waited in the infirmary's anteroom. Others waited too. A young woman of perhaps eighteen sat quietly in a corner trying to conceal beneath her ragged, loose-fitting garments what William's experienced eye identified as an early stage of leprosy. Owing to an unspoken system of triage practiced by the resident healers, she would be the last to receive attention. There was nothing to be done—save exhorting her to pray for a miracle or, failing that, to beg the Lord's forgiveness for the sins that must have caused her affliction.

In need of urgent care was a young boy, no more than nine or ten, who tried without success to put a brave face on having broken his ankle from a fall while climbing a tree. Sitting beside him was his mother, cooing soft reassurances and shedding sympathetic tears.

A few clergy also waited, the more senior jostling for preferred positions in the queue, ignoring those whose ailments were more acute than their own. But these clergy were forgotten the moment two palace guards burst loudly through the entrance. They carried— dragged, rather—a chubby middle-aged priest, his habit torn and bloodied, his eyes glazed in shock. William didn't recognize his face but assumed he was someone of importance. This was confirmed by the appearance of Brother François, who, on hearing the guards call out the name *de Bury*, entered the anteroom and rushed to the wounded man's side. The others continued to wait. Except for William, who stomped out of infirmary in disgust, his leg still aching. Gerardo followed him.

* * *

𝔚idway along the path through the herb garden, William halted in his tracks. De Bury! And then he recalled items from a second letter he received from Eleanor two weeks earlier.

. . . Poor Edward! He sent Isabella dozens of affectionate letters, begging her to return to England. She didn't even bother to reply, so in desperation Edward wrote to Pope John, pleading with him to command King Charles to put a stop his sister's liaison with Mortimer. Against my advice, which he seldom listens to anyway, the king decided to send that vile toad Thomas Dunheved to Avignon to press his case further. (I can only pray he hasn't taken his brother with him.) Berkhamsted tells me that Thomas may also have been instructed to gather intelligence about schemes Mortimer's agents might be hatching there.

The pope is well aware that Edward won't go to Paris to confront the queen face-to-face. If he did, he would find it awkward to refuse to swear fealty to Charles as a condition for the return of Gascony. Edward loathes the prospect of abasing himself in this way. Knowing this, the pope urged Charles to recognize young Edward as the new Duke of Aquitaine. As duke, *he* can swear fealty to his uncle so his father won't have to. His father and Charles both agreed to this, and he has now left for Paris along with a gaggle of knights and servants.

I worry whether my dear young cousin fully appreciates the weight of his new responsibilities. Before his departure I heard him issue orders to those who would accompany him as if he fully understood his mission. I doubt that he does, but his brave performance was still endearing, if a bit unsettling.

> After all, he is just a boy, eager to reunite with his mother, uncle and cousins, and with his tutor Richard de Bury. . . .

So why, in heaven's name, was the prince's tutor here in Avignon and not in Paris at his royal pupil's side? More important, at least to de Bury: Why did someone in Avignon want to kill him? William wasn't sure why he wanted answers; de Bury's adventures had nothing to do with him. He was curious nevertheless and decided to return to the convent to give Eleanor's letter another reading.

The lane they walked along separated a nunnery, on their left, from a row of shops and covered stalls, on the right. Today was market day, and the lane was crowded. Vendors hawked their wares with crudely rhyming advertisements, while customers haggled over prices. Others ignored or scoffed at the vendors' imprecations as they hurried by.

During the quarter-mile trek back to Greyfriars, Gerardo affected grave concern over de Bury's assault, although William detected a trace of excitement in his apprentice's voice as he chattered about the chubby tutor's misfortune. William was only half-listening, his attention diverted by recollections of Eleanor's letter and the smells of pepper and cinnamon emanating from a spice shop. He walked more quickly than usual as his staff thumped rhythmically on the cobblestones.

From behind them, they heard a woman's voice shouting, "Thief! Stop him!"

William turned and saw a score of startled onlookers and several goats scatter to either side of the lane—parting, he imagined, like the Red Sea's waters—as a man raced in his direction. William and Gerardo had passed by him just a few moments earlier, and William noticed him eyeing the meat pies on display at a baker's stall.

William shoved Gerardo aside with his elbow, adjusted his grip on his staff, and in one fluid motion whirled clockwise, swinging his staff at knee-level into the fleeing man's path. The thief somersaulted and landed on his back in the middle of the lane. He writhed in pain as four small pies spilled from a sack he carried. The woman from the baker's stall rushed to the scene and bent to scoop the stolen goods into her apron.

Nearby witnesses, including Gerardo, gaped in astonishment at the lame friar's heroics. Some of them applauded his improbable feat. William squirmed in embarrassment while trying to conceal his satisfaction.

"I had no idea," Gerardo stammered in admiration. "Where . . . *how* did you learn to do that?"

William pondered a modest reply as he glanced back at the thief, now in the clutches of two onlookers. The man was weeping, and William thought he heard him say, ". . . my children, they haven't eaten in . . ."

His vanity punctured, William turned away and resumed his march to the convent.

Gerardo rushed to keep up with him. "Perhaps you could give me a few lessons . . ."

William ignored him as his staff thumped on the cobblestones.

Chapter 13

November 12, 1325 — The Palace Piazza

BY THE NEXT DAY, word of Richard de Bury's bloody encounter had spread through the enclave. No one of consequence among the higher clergy, aristocracy, and the royal families of England and France could be indifferent to the fate of the English throne. But on whose side was de Bury aligned? The answer might provide a clue as to the younger Edward's own allegiance—whether he now sided with his mother, Isabella, or with his father, the king. Indeed it was possible Edward of Windsor himself didn't know, that his filial affections were agonizingly divided.

If anyone in Avignon knew about de Bury's loyalties and thus knew of the motives behind the attempt on his life, it would be the cardinals and bishops ensconced in the higher reaches of the palace—and of course Pope John himself. Aware he was among the last to whom they would confide their secrets, William looked for answers elsewhere.

As he left the palace library, William brooded over his meager progress on the manuscript that consumed much of his recent energy. Distracted by his curiosity about de Bury, he hoped to find John of Reading hobnobbing, as he often did, with officials at the palace. When he failed to find Reading there, William redirected his search. But it wasn't Reading he found as he stepped through the building's south entrance into the sunlit piazza. Instead, he saw Manuele Fieschi engaged in what appeared from a distance to be an unpleasant conversation with a monk clad in a black woolen habit like those favored by English Dominicans. The monk's face was hidden by the middle pillar of one of the two small loggias directly beneath what William knew were the pope's private chambers. The Dominican's palms faced upward, as if imploring Fieschi to bestow a favor or grant a concession. Fieschi intermittently shook his head.

A few moments later Fieschi started to turn away, leaving the monk empty-handed. He then turned back to face the monk on hearing him bark something unintelligible while jabbing a threatening forefinger. Unmoved, Fieschi said nothing as he turned about once again and walked toward the palace's main entrance.

A minute passed before the monk emerged from behind the pillar and headed, with his fists clenched, in William's direction. William resisted the impulse to step aside and instead stood where he was, striking a casual, reflective pose.

A spark of recognition crossed his mind when the sleeve of the monk's tunic brushed his own as he strode by. Beneath the hood of his cowl protruded wisps of stringy blond hair partially obscuring the thick eyebrows above his small blue eyes. He was short and sturdily built, and his brow was smooth and unblemished.

This last feature—an absence rather than a presence—drew William's attention. What he had *not* seen on the monk's face was a scar: the scar he noticed, two years before, just above the left eye of Hugh le Despenser's aide, Stephen Dunheved. The monk he had just seen was his brother Thomas—looking just as Eleanor had described him in London.

* * *

William headed back toward the convent as he digested the scene he had just witnessed. As he approached, he spied Gerardo walking in his direction.

In recent months Gerardo had relaxed his deferential demeanor and showed little hesitation in questioning and even challenging William's opinions. He continued to perform his assigned tasks but now did so with brisk and detached efficiency rather than in the fawning hope his master might grace him with his approval. All of which was fine with William, who detested dealing with anyone from a position of authority. Each of them knew full well Gerardo wasn't yet his peer, but William didn't mind if he acted like one. In fact, he welcomed his newfound assertiveness.

William was pleased by his protégé's change in demeanor, but that didn't prevent him from exploiting opportunities their altered relationship had opened. He no longer felt constrained in pressing Gerardo for intelligence about palace intrigues that might affect him. Gerardo understood the tacit quid pro quo William imposed: *If you want me to treat you as a peer, Gerardo, stop beating about the bush and tell me what you know.*

"So, enlighten me about de Bury," William instructed him. They had just reentered Greyfriars and sat on a bench near the entrance to the convent's small chapel. No candles were lit inside the chapel, and only one burned in a hallway sconce, which lent an aura of secrecy to their conversation. "To begin with, is he alive?"

"Very much so." Judging from the normal volume of his voice, Gerardo was indifferent to secretive auras. "Not to minimize the trauma he must have suffered, but his wounds turned out to be less serious than they first appeared. Brother François's poultices stanched his bleeding and, as of yesterday, he was comfortably sedated by the herbals the infirmary prescribes in these cases."

William didn't ask what Gerardo meant by "these cases" and let pass his annoying advertisement for the shaman and his nostrums. "And what about today? Guards were posted outside the entrance yesterday, I suppose for his protection. Which means he wasn't a victim of a random assault. But late this morning the guards were gone, so I assume he's been taken elsewhere. Unless, of course, he died last evening."

"No, as I said, he *is* still among the living, and yes, he's no longer in the infirmary. I can't say much more than that—can't, that is, because I don't know. But I've heard a rumor he may already have left the city."

"Hmm. If so, he must have gotten help. Even if his wounds didn't slow him down, he'd still need friends to protect him. Which raises the question of whether the pope's guards or anyone else at the palace know who his assailant was. I take it no one's been arrested."

"Not yet, and neither the guards nor the local constables have come up with any suspects. Father de Bury was attacked from behind and knocked unconscious, so he couldn't identify his attacker. He doesn't even remember being stabbed and didn't know the nature of his wounds until he regained consciousness at the infirmary an hour or so afterward."

"Why didn't his attacker finish him off?

"Luckily, he was interrupted by Benedictine nuns, six or seven of them, on their way to the palace with baskets of eggs from the poultry farm their order tends. They took a shortcut through the alley leading to the palace where they sell their eggs to the pope's cook. Halfway to the top they rounded a bend and ran straight into de Bury seconds after the attack started. The sisters started to yell and scream, spilling their eggs and breaking most of them."

"The attacker fled?"

Gerardo nodded. "Down the alley in the same direction the nuns had just come from."

"You say there were six or seven of them. I assume at least some were able to describe him."

"Almost all of them did."

"And?"

"Two of the sisters said he was short, and others said he was tall. One of them described him as a *giant*, while another said she spotted horns poking out from under his hat and a tail through the rear of his cotehardie. But," Gerardo added with his gap-toothed grin, "she later admitted she wasn't sure about the last item."

William rolled his eyes. "I'm surprised no one saw him sprout wings and fly away."

He hadn't asked Gerardo about Thomas Dunheved. His apprentice could tell him nothing he didn't already know. Other than William, no one in the enclave knew the reasons for Dunheved's journey to the south of France. Not even Fieschi, despite his acrimonious conversation with King Edward's agent earlier that afternoon. Eleanor had told William the real purposes of Thomas's mission in her last letter, and he knew she had written to no one else.

* * *

He still wanted to speak with John of Reading, but he now had to wait, as shortly after Vespers the friars went to table in the convent's refectory. After solemnly filing in, they kept silent except to utter their Blessing prior to eating. The friars stood with heads bowed and hands folded beneath their scapulars as Abbé Thierry intoned his Benediction, which would finally, and mercifully, end with the pronouncement: *Edent pauperes*—"The poor shall eat." As Thierry droned on, he peered from under his silvery eyebrows, alert to possible mischief by the hungry novitiates waiting impatiently at the far end of the room. William himself had long since outgrown the puerile antics the abbot was ever vigilant to identify and punish. He wryly recalled meals when, on identical occasions, he and his young comrades at the seminary in London furtively swapped jokes in the "alphabet of fingers." Today, two novitiates would eat their supper sitting cross-legged on the floor at the base of the abbot's table. This was their punishment for a similar offense at the previous day's meal.

Compared to the richer religious houses in Avignon, the Greyfriars' refectory was small and humbly furnished. The forty-foot-square room doubled as the chapter meeting hall where, late each afternoon, the abbot conducted the convent's business. William seldom attended these meetings (and was often late when he *did* attend), which explained why, at mealtime, he was not invited to sit at the abbot's table alongside Reading, Brother Marcel the cellarer, and other senior friars. This prevented William from partaking of the better cuts of meat, but he did not complain. As Manuele Fieschi had told him in London, the food in Avignon was better than the diet of beans and beer common to English friaries. There, *any* kind of meat was deemed a rare delicacy and thus a cause for quiet rejoicing. Today's supper at Greyfriars consisted of roasted chicken, peas, and cabbage laced with aromatic herbs and spices not found in England. William especially appreciated the olive oil, rather than the congealed animal fat of his homeland, the convent's cook used to baste the chicken. He also preferred the single goblet of watery red wine dispensed at the friars' main meal to the weak beer he had tolerated in his native England.

* * *

"Perhaps we could talk while I run a small errand," Reading said on spotting William later in the corridor outside the refectory. Despite his considerable bulk, the grey-haired Franciscan moved with surprising agility, outpacing William as they left the convent and walked in the direction of the infirmary. Reading chattered idly about recent purchases for the palace library and herbal remedies for his rheumatism. He and William paused outside the infirmary where Reading briefly consulted with one of the resident herbalists about the comparative merits of ginger and frankincense. His knees were bothering him again. The herbalist had no firm opinion on the matter and advised Reading to try both remedies to see which worked better. The empiricist in William applauded this advice. Reading tucked his new medications into a fold in his cowl and turned the conversation to Richard de Bury. "I take it you knew him at Oxford."

"Along with everyone else there, of course, I knew *of* him. But we traveled in different circles. He left soon after his appointment as young Edward's tutor and, I assume, took lodgings in London close to Westminster."

"Yes," Reading confirmed, "after leaving Oxford he often appeared at court, though at Isabella's sufferance rather than the king's. The queen, as I understand it, is far more engaged with their son's education than is her husband. But lately de Bury has spent much of his time in France, funneling money—not very secretly, at least any longer—to Isabella and Mortimer."

Reading had just answered William's question as to whose side de Bury had taken. William leaned closer and asked quietly, "So what was he doing here in Avignon?"

"Apparently, Edward got wind of what de Bury was up to and sent his agents to France to track him down and eliminate him. So de Bury came to Avignon, probably to seek Pope John's protection, although I suspect he had other reasons as well. Edward's agents found out and came after him."

"I don't understand," William said as they neared the base of the piazza steps. "Why did de Bury leave Avignon in such a hurry? Wouldn't he have been safer remaining at the palace than fleeing to the countryside with Edward's men hot on his trail?"

"Once he got here he found he had no choice but to leave. The pope, I've heard, was offended on learning of Isabella's 'intimate' relationship with Mortimer. As you might imagine, His Holiness casts a jaundiced eye on adultery, especially among the royals, and has urged Charles to put a stop to his sister's indiscretions."

"So," William surmised, "de Bury found himself persona non grata owing to his alliance with Mortimer and Isabella."

They had just reached the top of the steps where Reading signaled with an outstretched forefinger to a pair of bishops from the palace to wait for him. So their conversation ended on that note as Reading turned and headed off to meet with his two associates. A flock of pigeons leapt from the branches of a stand of olive trees to announce his imminent arrival.

127

Chapter 14

November 14, 1325 — The Zoo and the Exchange

"I'M GOING TO THE ZOO," William announced, daring Gerardo to object. "I assume you can keep yourself usefully occupied while I'm gone."

Gerardo did not look up from his desk as he continued transcribing the manuscript William gave him the day before. "You'll need a pass from the zookeeper," he advised. "Otherwise, they won't let you in."

William felt relieved that his apprentice had not invited himself to join his excursion. After sixteen months in Avignon, he had wearied of Gerardo's chaperoning. Gerardo may also have wearied of it.

William was only mildly curious about the pope's zoo but had seized upon the spring-like break in the late autumn weather to wander, by himself, through parts of Avignon he seldom explored. Like the early morning hours he spent hoeing and pulling weeds in the Greyfrairs' garden, his occasional sightseeing gave him time to reflect on recent events. Three puzzled him: Richard de Bury's assault in the alley below the *Doms*, Thomas Dunheved's rancorous encounter with Manuele Fieschi, and John of Reading's gossipy analysis of de Bury's hurried departure.

His route took him from the Franciscans' Parish of Saint-Geniès, southwest toward the zoo in Saint-Didier Parish. On the way he passed through what was once the Jewish quarter where the residents had eked out an anxious subsistence until, three years ago, Pope John expelled them for their anti-papal conspiracies. Small shops, modest dwellings, and a cemetery now occupied the land the Jews had abandoned. Children shrieked as they played tag among the headstones. A cluster of old women chattered in a small vegetable garden next to a mausoleum. A baker hawked his aromatic pies from atop an earthen mound William imagined covered a mass grave. The dead and the living blithely shared a common space—as if doing so was in the ordinary nature of things.

A quarter-mile from the cemetery William passed by the Almshouse for the Poor, known locally as la Pignotte ("little bread"). Each day more than a thousand poor and hungry queued up for modest rations of bread and wine. In a courteous and businesslike fashion armed ushers monitored the potentially unruly crowd, thus burnishing the pope's reputation as a conscientious and efficient administrator. Whatever his faults—and they were many—Duèze took his charitable obligations seriously.

On leaving la Pignotte, William felt the midday sun warm his bare head as the windless sky intensified Avignon's stench. He wondered why the nighthawks soaring lazily overhead didn't fly off to the countryside where the air was pure.

He neared the zoo at Saint-Didier Parish's southern boundary where the smells of the city mingled with unfamiliar odors of exotic animals. As Gerardo warned him, William couldn't enter the main building without a zookeeper's pass. On noticing the expensive finery of those who entered and exited, he concluded that only the well-off could afford passes. Unless, like the priests he saw waiting in the queue, they had connections at the palace—which William didn't.

He wasn't sure he wanted to go inside anyway. It was rumored that a deep pit at the building's far end contained alarmingly large snakes, some of which slithered, while others, for God knew *what* reason, coiled around one another in groups. William hated snakes.

Also inside the building dwelled the zoo's prize possession: a lion recently arrived from Africa. A gift, so it was said, from a sultan hoping to dissuade the pope from launching a crusade to enlighten him and his subjects. William was curious to see what the lion looked like, but his curiosity ebbed on overhearing a well-dressed merchant complain to a companion: "A mangier, more desiccated beast I can scarcely conceive. My wife's *cat* is infinitely more terrifying."

A plaintive wail echoing from the building's interior confirmed the merchant's opinion. It seemed the poor animal had lost its will to roar.

Still, he was glad he had come. Along with the others without passes he saw two leopards through the bars of an open-air cage fronting the street running alongside the zoo. The muscular spotted cats lounged on large tree limbs as they discreetly eyed a half-dozen diminutive gazelles grazing in the adjoining cage. The prettiest one (a doe William decided to name *Giselle*) munched coyly on tufts of grass as she ignored the advances of a young buck. Her suitor quivered in anticipation as he sniffed Giselle's hindquarters.

This romance was interrupted when one of the leopards sprang from its perch and let out a piercing whine as it pawed at the bars of the cage. The gazelles froze and stared straight ahead as though, by appearing inanimate, they would be less appetizing. A minute later the disappointed leopard turned and crept back to its perch. Having short memories, the gazelles began to graze again as if nothing had happened. The amorous buck resumed his quivering and sniffing.

* * *

At other times William's imagination might have divined amusing lessons from the animals' behavior, but today he decided to give his imagination a rest. Besides, it was time to return to the convent where he still had work to do.

The safest and most direct route back was through the Exchange. Housing the important commercial institutions on which the Church depended, the Exchange was Avignon's most prosperous and least crime-ridden quarter. Traders and merchants of all sorts came there, transporting and selling wine and grain from Provence, dried fish from as far away as Brittany, tapestries from Bruges and Tournai, spices and silk from the distant reaches of Asia. Most conspicuous in the Exchange were the international merchant bankers who served as intermediaries between the Church and its debtors and benefactors. For scandalous fees the bankers, most of them Italians, administered the collection of taxes and tributes that stuffed the coffers of the Apostolic Camera—the papal treasury.

Infuriating William more than the bankers' presence in Avignon was the cynicism of the Church's policies that indulged them. Campaigns against usury waged by friars like Bernardino of Fèltre had shown modest success but only in curbing the practices of small-time lenders and pawnbrokers. The current pope applauded such censures as sparkling emulations of Jesus' casting out the moneychangers from the temple of God, while anointing the bankers "peculiarly beloved sons of the Church" and lining their purses with gold.

William sat on a bench on one side of the Exchange's main boulevard in the shadow of a wine merchant's shop. More than a mile in length, the boulevard bisected the quarter, running from the center of the city toward its southwestern border. Facing him stood a stolid two-story marble façade of one of the many banks built soon after the papacy's removal from Rome. It was a branch of the bank owned by Gerardo's father, Count Gabriele Fieschi, which his son meekly pointed out to William on one of their previous excursions. The count, however, seldom traveled to Avignon from Genoa, much to the relief of Gerardo, who now professed with great zeal Saint Francis's vow of poverty.

On his return to the convent he should apologize to Gerardo for having taken his dutiful service for granted and for often treating him badly. Not just for Gerardo's sake, but also for his own. Except for his weekly conversations with Reading, William felt isolated and vulnerable. He had few friends, and still fewer who could protect him even if they were inclined to. There was Eleanor, but she could do nothing other than send him encouragement and occasional warnings of danger. Wodeham and Baskerville, his firmest friends and confidants, were both vast distances away and, in Baskerville's case, in whereabouts unknown. Only Durand of Saint-Pourçain was here in Avignon, but as a minority of one on the commission he had been marginalized by his peers and was in no position to help him.

* * *

The sun was setting beneath a bank of rain clouds rolling in toward the city from the west. To escape the approaching downpour, William started back to the convent, sidestepping the pedestrians, handcarts, and horse-drawn carriages crowding the boulevard.

Passersby occasionally stared as he made his way northward. Perhaps his limp attracted their attention, but more likely it was the color of his habit. As mendicant preachers sworn to poverty, Greyfriars were seldom seen among the crush of traders, financiers, and prostitutes who frequented the Exchange.

To avoid the boulevard's congestion, he prepared to turn into a narrow lane branching off to his left. From an earlier trip he recalled that it led to an alternate, lightly traveled route to the convent. Glancing to his right before entering, William thought he recognized a familiar face, which caused his pulse to quicken. A passing handcart laden with pungent-smelling sausages momentarily blocked his view, but as the cart cleared he could make out the scarred brow of Hugh le Despenser's henchman, Stephen Dunheved. Thomas's elder brother had come with him to France!

As he started to turn away, William saw out of the corner of his eye that Dunheved was staring at him with a puzzled expression, which changed to a faint smile. William ducked into the lane—not too abruptly, he hoped—hugging the stalls and shops on the right for cover. After a dozen steps he realized he didn't know where he was, having mistaken the lane's entrance for another much like it. From this one there was no exit at the far end. He was in a cul de sac.

Dunheved's left forearm tightened across his throat from behind. His left leg collapsed as Dunheved's knee jammed into the back of his thigh. The tip of a dagger pierced his skin on the right side of his neck, just above the cowl loosely covering his shoulders. Blood trickled down toward his collarbone as his assailant shoved him into an alcove leading to the boarded-up door of a vacant shop. The pressure from Dunheved's arm eased, and William gasped for air.

"Listen well, crophead," Dunheved whispered with a raspy, high-pitched Midlands accent, "and thank Christ you're alive to hear this. At the Elms, my master wasn't pleased by your impertinence, nor by your attentions to that whore who calls herself his wife. So when next in London, I'll make sure to convey your sincere apologies," he said, savoring his heavy irony. "In the meantime, tend to your proper business of saving souls, or whatever it is you self-righteous bastards do. For the present, you're worth no more of my valuable time. But if you don't behave, our next visit won't be so pleasant. In fact, there'll *be* no 'visit'—if you take my meaning."

William pulled at Dunheved's left arm, trying without success to release the grip around his throat that again made breathing difficult. The staff he had carried lay at his feet, now useless. Dunheved saw the staff and kicked it a few feet away. He laughed at his victim's helplessness while slowly releasing his grip. In an exaggerated display of tidiness he wiped the blood from his dagger onto William's sleeve. He turned away and strolled back to the boulevard as William sank to the cobblestones paving the lane. Dust and cobwebs stirred up by their scuffle in the musty alcove wafted in the air before settling around him. Two rats, their curiosity satisfied, scampered off to inspect the stream of sewage running down the lane's kennel.

After several minutes William crawled to retrieve his staff, rose unsteadily to his feet, and inched out of the lane into the boulevard to return to the safe haven of the convent. As he headed northward, his terror receded, giving way to relief and then to anger.

His anger was not limited to Stephen Dunheved and Hugh le Despenser, but included the entire gamut of forces—people, events, and ideas—that conspired to bring him to Avignon. With a crash of thunder the heavens opened, washing the blood from his neck and the tears from his face.

Chapter 15

December 4, 1325 — Greyfriars Convent

ERARDO HAD BECOME irritatingly polite.

"If you need new quills, Brother William, the chandlery isn't far out of my way." "I've almost finished with your transcription; it should be ready tomorrow at the very latest." "How is your leg this morning?" Gerardo's newly solicitous attitude rang false to William's ears, and it also alternated with bouts of sullenness.

Which may have been William's fault. He had yet to apologize to Gerardo for his own irritability and taking for granted Gerardo's efficient performance of his tasks. William fully intended to apologize but was still reeling from his encounter in the Exchange three weeks earlier. He hadn't told Gerardo about Dunheved's assault and, when pressed, deflected his questions about the wound (which had since become a scar) on his neck. No need for Manuele Fieschi to get wind of it. Or Abbé Thierry. At least once William spied the nosy old abbot pulling Gerardo aside for a hushed consultation.

As his suspicions grew, William guarded more closely what he revealed to him. Gerardo had surely noticed, which would account for his sullenness and faux politeness. Things had come to a pretty pass between them.

Nor was William's mood cheered by his recent interrogations by the commission. The fifteenth session, held two days earlier, had been acrimonious and puzzling. His accuser, John Lutterell, was so emboldened as to challenge William on arcane points of interpretation of Lombard's *Book of Sentences*. William easily dispatched his arguments but was surprised that Lutterell knew enough about his opinions to raise them. And from Lutterell's smug expression William sensed he was holding something back, perhaps an unexpected and damaging line of argument.

It was now dark and the scriptorium was empty except for William, who sat at his desk fussing over a manuscript in the faint light of the candles he had just lit. The other friars were asleep in their cells. His concentration was keen during these rare moments of solitude, so he barely heard the approaching footsteps.

"I believe this belongs to you," Gerardo said as he plopped a book on the corner of William's desk. It made a loud thump that echoed in the large room. He said nothing more and headed toward his own desk. Puzzled, William watched as Gerardo walked away and then turned his attention to the book. The fiber cords laced through the quires had recently been replaced, and the edges of some of the sheets of parchment were trimmed.

The mottled brown and grey leather cover looked familiar. Indeed, it was unmistakable, he realized as he sat bolt upright. It was his copy of the *Sentences*, which Walter Burley stole from him a decade earlier in Paris. He quickly thumbed through the yellowed pages and noticed that the draft of the "manifesto" he hid years earlier between two of the book's folios was missing. This was the short document in which the young Friar Occam argued that the entire body of Christian believers had the moral right to depose the *pope*. Perhaps Burley simply discarded it without bothering to read it. He hoped that was the case, for his manifesto was surely a more brazen assault on the Church's authority than his quibbles with Peter Lombard.

With his book in hand William hurried over to Gerardo's desk. He was so stunned by his discovery that it didn't occur to him to thank Gerardo. Instead, he asked, "Where did you get it?"

"At the palace, if you must know." Gerardo didn't look up. His hands shook slightly, which belied the sullen indifference of his tone.

"That's not what I meant. Who gave it to you?"

"No one *gave* it to me; I took it."

"You *stole* it?"

Gerardo shrugged.

William glanced around the scriptorium to make certain no one could overhear them. His nerves had begun to settle, but only slightly. He had questions, which for the moment pushed aside his feelings of gratitude.

"Perhaps you could elaborate."

"Lutterell had it. I overheard him discussing it with one of the other commissioners—Grenier, I believe it was—just before your last session. At the time I didn't realize it was *your* copy, just that Lutterell was crowing about discovering some items in it that might prove embarrassing."

"But what were *you* doing there?"

"I thought you knew. I'd been instructed to prepare the chamber before each session—arranging the chairs, making sure refreshments were supplied, that sort of thing—and then afterward to gather up items any of you might leave behind. Two days ago, while waiting outside the chamber for the session to end, I saw all of you leave in something of a hurry."

"Mm, a commotion in the corridor," William said, recalling the event. "One of the elder cardinals had fallen, and we went to see what had happened. I think I saw you as we were leaving."

Gerardo nodded, and William saw that his hands no longer shook. "A large book lay on the table next to where Lutterell always sits. I thought it might be his copy of the *Sentences*, though it struck me as odd that a commissioner would have a copy so old and beat up. Out of curiosity I began to look through it."

"So how did you know it was mine?"

"Even though they were faded, your scrawled notes would be hard to mistake for anyone else's."

As he tapped his free hand against his thigh, William pieced together an explanation: Lutterell must have gotten the book from Walter Burley. Reading had told William that when Lutterell leveled his charges against him two years earlier, he did so with Burley's encouragement. This meant that Burley, or one of his minions, stole the book soon after their quodlibet at the Sorbonne and later gave it to Lutterell. From William's notes, Burley and Lutterell would have understood their radical implications. Armed with proof, they could shield the Dominicans' orthodoxy from William's blasphemies. The legacies of Aristotle and Aquinas would remain safe.

But even more dangerous would be their discovery of his "manifesto," which he had rashly scribbled a decade earlier and then, stupidly, hidden in his copy of the *Sentences*. In three brief pages he challenged the very edifice of the Church's authority by urging that the laity had the moral right to depose the pope for his sins. He again cursed himself for not burning it—for having, in effect, dared the Dominicans to find it. And if they now *had*, Lutterell could take sweet revenge against Doctor Invincibilis for ruining his chancellorship at Oxford, while Burley could avenge his drubbing at the Sorbonne.

"I'm sure you've thought of this, but you're going to be suspected of taking it," William said.

"But so will others. A few servants were also in the chamber cleaning up afterward. It's not unusual for them to steal items from the palace and sell them. Any bookseller in the city would jump at the chance to get a copy."

"I should think Lutterell is furious."

"I assume so, but he's a bit scatterbrained, always losing or forgetting things. So he may not know it was stolen, although he'll no doubt claim it was." Gerardo's voice, his demeanor, had changed. He was neither polite nor sullen.

"Surely you knew the risk you were taking."

"I didn't consider the risk, and at the time it didn't feel like stealing. Besides, Lutterell is an insufferable prick who deserves to have his things taken from him."

"Do you still believe that?"

"What, that he's an insufferable prick?"

William rephrased his question. "Do you still believe that's why you took it?"

"I'll say this just once," Gerardo answered with a weary sigh. "I wanted to make clear which side I'm on, where my loyalty lies. I've grown tired of your evasions, half-truths, and simply ignoring my presence except when you want something from me. It occurred to me only afterward that by taking the book and returning to you, I might finally make you understand that."

William could think of nothing to say.

"Mind you," Gerardo continued, "I don't expect your thanks. What I do expect, and believe I've *earned*, is your trust."

140

"It would appear, Gerardo, that I owe you an apology . . ."

"I don't want your apology, either," Gerardo interrupted. Nodding toward the *Sentences*, he said, "I'd be satisfied for the present if you stashed it somewhere safe. And then perhaps you could humor me by explaining how you got that scar on your neck."

MICHAEL HARMON

𝔓𝔞𝔯𝔱 𝔣𝔬𝔲𝔯

AVIGNON

March 4, 1327 — May 26, 1328
(Sixteen months later)

Chapter 16

March 4, 1327 — The Dominican Monastery

AFTER INTERROGATING WILLIAM for nearly three years, the commissioners appeared hopelessly divided. They had yet to agree on the errors he should be officially scolded for, and frequent absences caused the sessions to become sporadic. The pope sent Lucca and Grenier on missions away from Avignon for lengthy periods. Two others, Paignote and Durand of Saint-Pourçain, were in precarious health, so they, too, were often unavailable. Durand, however, still summoned the strength to meet with William privately, which neither advertised.

As the spring of 1327 approached, William settled into a routine far removed from the political storms raging about Edward and Isabella, Despenser and Mortimer, and the French King Charles IV. William found himself less and less interested, except as the reports he heard provided hints about Eleanor's circumstances. She hadn't written in over a year, and he wondered if he would ever hear from her again.

His meetings with Reading, his chief source of intelligence about recent events in Paris and London, were also less frequent, owing more to William's indifference than to his distrust of the garrulous Greyfriar. Stephen Dunheved's attack was still fresh in his memory, but he no longer dwelt on it. His fears had turned to anger, and his anger to a sturdy resolve to forge ahead with his work without fretting about events outside his control.

The past year had been among the most intense and productive of his life. He completed six long manuscripts, the first taking issue with Aristotle on ethics and cognition, and another with his longtime adversary in Oxford and London, Walter Chatton. As a metaphysical Realist, Chatton believed the world consisted of an invisible structure: that properties, numbers, causality, and even free will all existed as real, universal entities no different in principle from the ordinary physical objects people could see and touch. For Chatton "believing was seeing," while for William "seeing was believing." Yes, that was an apt summary of their opposing ways of knowing about earthly things.

William's grand project was to strip away all that was unnecessary—in philosophy, theology, and metaphysics—so the true nature of faith could be laid bare. If the existence of God could be proven by recourse to Chatton's metaphysical paraphernalia, then faith, the human impulse to believe in Him, would no longer be necessary. Such "proofs" as to His existence were therefore substitutes for faith rather than the justifications for it. Faith was not a matter of justification, and God Himself was the only necessary entity. His existence defied proof by human reason. The infinity of God and the immortality of the soul were instead knowable only by revelation.

He often spoke about these matters with Durand. The Dominican's failing health prevented him from venturing far or often from his monastery, where his frequent fits of coughing and almost constant wheezing now confined him. Durand seldom complained about his malady, however. Unlike the Greyfriars' spartan quarters, the monastery's leafy atrium afforded Durand a pleasant place to recline in comfort while engaging in long and spirited conversations. He also benefited from the medicinal qualities of the robust red wine the Dominicans managed to procure from far-off Burgundy. William also enjoyed the wine, which Durand dispensed whenever he visited.

"If God's freedom to create implies his freedom *not* to," William explained, "then, by the same measure, our own freedom consists in our choosing whether to believe or *not* believe in Him. Bad faith, as one might call it, replaces such freedom with fictitious necessities that could somehow *compel* belief rather than inspire it."

"I assume you're aware, Brother William, that the freedom you speak of, including in particular the freedom not to believe, makes you vulnerable to accusations of impiety. And worse, that you invite others to entertain similar doubts before they affirm, or don't affirm, *their* faith. So you should hardly be surprised if my brother commissioners charge you not just with impugning the authority of the Church, but questioning God's very existence."

"I know that, but as I've told you before, I accept only the authority of the Scriptures, not the authority of those who foist their interpretations on the rest of us."

"Be that as it may, you should realize this is an argument you can't win. So, my advice is the same as your friend Wodeham's: Don't ruffle the other commissioners' feathers more than you already have. You needn't worry about ruffling mine, though. I have few enough left as it is," Durand said with a rueful chuckle as he took another generous swallow of the wine. William noticed that both of their goblets were almost empty.

"I'll bear that in mind, but I may not always succeed in following it. And speaking of ruffled feathers, what about Duèze's—er, Pope John's?"

"At the moment," Durand said with a wink acknowledging William's intemperate slip of the tongue, "John is troubled more by the commission's sluggish pace and indecisiveness than by you. Just about the only thing we agree upon privately is that Lutterell is a total ass."

"Which is certainly a relief," William laughed. "If Lutterell had his way, I'd have been consigned to the pyre after the first session." William pushed his goblet an inch or so nearer to Durand's, signaling he'd be happy to have a refill. "But back to Pope John, dare I ask what he hopes the commission will decide?"

"He may no longer know," Durand said as he obliged William with another generous serving. "The commissioners' divided opinion troubles him because he wants a clear consensus, even if it falls short of strict unanimity, before he decides. He took longer than I expected to conclude that Lutterell's zeal exceeds his intellect by a wide margin. His charges were what brought you to Avignon to begin with, and I suspect that John may now have second thoughts about the entire matter."

"Be assured, I shall refrain from premature celebration."

"That would be wise," Durand agreed.

Chapter 17

March 17, 1327 — Greyfriars Convent

THE RUMORS REACHING AVIGNON had hardened into fact: Isabella and Mortimer had won, and Edward II no longer reigned as England's king.

In early 1326, Isabella refused to return to the arms of her husband so long as his chamberlain and favorite, Hugh le Despenser, remained at his side. Edward would not budge, dashing any hope of Isabella's return and that of their son, Edward of Windsor, who had joined her in Paris a few months previously. The king's intransigence thus sealed the queen's alliance with the leader of the rebellion, Roger Mortimer.

Isabella and Mortimer needed backing from sources outside of France. The queen's brother Charles IV caved to pressure from Pope John to distance himself from his adulterous sister. Faced with the French king's flagging support, the couple left Charles's court in Paris to seek allies elsewhere.

Their chief recruit was Count William of Hainault, in Flanders, who nursed grievances against Edward for failing to do justice to his courtiers robbed in England a few years before. But the count's chief inducement was Isabella's betrothal of her son, the fourteen-year-old Edward of Windsor, to his eleven-year-old daughter, Philippa, whom the young Edward was to marry within two years. In return, the count supplied Isabella and Mortimer with ships and a small band of mercenaries, all paid for out of Philippa's generous dowry.

On September 20, their tiny fleet set sail from the port of Brill, near Rotterdam, landing in Suffolk four days later on the north bank of the River Orwell. The usurpers were now within striking distance of London. Edward and Despenser knew from their spies the invasion was coming and also knew the landing's location. Expecting an army of thousands, they were relieved to learn that the invading forces numbered only a few boatloads of men, most of them foreigners and thus not, or so they believed, a serious threat.

Edward's relief was short-lived. Bad weather delayed not just the fleet's landing but, more crucially, elements of his army charged with killing or capturing the enemy forces as they disembarked. The landing site was situated within lands controlled by the Earl of Norfolk, who despised Despenser and his father, Hugh the Elder. The earl eagerly agreed to lodge and feed the invaders as they made ready for their trek inland, soon to be joined by many of Edward's own men who defected to the queen's side.

A few days after the landing Isabella and her son took temporary refuge in the abbey at Bury St Edmunds, while Mortimer, the Hainaulter mercenaries, and a growing army of disaffected Englishmen marched toward London. News of their advance spread quickly throughout the city, where the king's precarious authority collapsed as anarchy broke out. Just weeks earlier, Edward prepared the Tower of London for a siege by the invaders. The futility of his efforts became clear, however, as most of his panicked forces deserted him.

To meet the invasion Edward amassed a huge but scattered army, promising extravagant rewards for defending his crown. But his skeptical supporters doubted his ability to pay what he had promised, and Isabella's popularity, especially in London, ran high. Above all, hatred of Despenser was almost universal even among those still personally loyal to Edward. Knowing this, Mortimer spread the false rumor that his and Isabella's aim was *not* to depose Edward but merely to rid England of the odious Despenser who had ravaged and stolen their lands.

Realizing the hopelessness of their plans to hold London, the king and Despenser fled the city on October 1, making their way toward Bristol, in Wales. Edward clung to the hope that his few remaining supporters there would defend him or, failing that, aid in his evacuation by sea. Mortimer's army quickly routed Edward's crumbling forces, and, on October 29, the ship the king commandeered at Chepstow for his escape to Ireland was forced back to shore by contrary gales and currents. The king and his favorite remained at large for three more weeks but were tracked down and caught in the countryside near Llantrisant on the Welsh border with England. Despenser was then wrested from the distraught Edward's side and taken to Hereford, in the English Midlands.

There, as Eleanor predicted, her husband met the same gruesome end as William Wallace, the rebellious Scottish nobleman whose execution a youthful William Occam witnessed two decades earlier at the Smithfield gallows. Judged guilty as a thief, Despenser was sentenced to be hanged; for fomenting discord between the king and queen, both castrated and disemboweled; beheaded for returning to England illegally after being banished; and finally, as a traitor, drawn and quartered. On November 24, Isabella, Mortimer, and their allies beheld the spectacle of his execution, savoring each phase while consuming a sumptuous feast spread before them at the base of the fifty-foot-high scaffold erected for the occasion. Despenser's severed head would later garnish a pike at London Bridge as a public notice of tyranny's wages.

Against Mortimer's wishes, Isabella insisted that her husband's life be spared. Their powerful ally, Henry Earl of Lancaster, also protested the queen's plea for mercy but eventually relented and agreed to transport Edward to Kenilworth Castle, the earl's fortress in Warwickshire. It was there the deposed king was to live out his remaining years—or would it be months or even weeks?—in "honorable captivity." After some hesitation to make certain that legal niceties were respected, Isabella consented to Mortimer and the triumphant barons' demand that Edward abdicate the throne. He did so, dressed in black and weeping inconsolably, at Kenilworth Castle on January 21 of the following year—but with the understanding that his eldest son would succeed him. Henceforth the former king would be known as "Sir Edward of Caernarfon."

On February 1, 1327, Edward of Windsor was crowned King Edward III. Still only fifteen, the new king was too young to govern, leaving Isabella and Mortimer, though not officially his regents, effectively the rulers of England.

* * *

In March, Gerardo informed William that another letter had arrived from London. William didn't conceal his eagerness to read it and sent Gerardo on his way. He assumed the letter was from Adam Wodeham and might contain news of Eleanor.

In his cell at the convent William noticed the familiar square-bordered seal of the Franciscan order. The reassuring notch was visible in its upper right corner. He heard his own heartbeat as he smoothed the sheets of crude parchment and recognized Eleanor's handwriting.

> My dear Brother William [she began, now dispensing with a formal salutation]
>
> With each letter I write, I doubt more and more that my words will reach you. Brother Adam tells me you are still in Avignon, but that gives me scant assurance. I may be writing to the wind—but I write nevertheless, hoping you might hear my voice.
>
> You must have learned that Edward is no longer king and now spends his days—his life—imprisoned in disgrace at Kenilworth. In the wake of their triumph, the queen and Mortimer avenge themselves against their enemies. Alas, I am one of them, or so they decided.
>
> Since London fell to the mob, I have been held prisoner in the Tower, where earlier I dwelt in official custody of it at Edward's behest. I don't fear the same fate as Hugh's, but my loneliness is punishment enough. My beloved daughters Margaret, Nora, and Joan have been taken from me and sent to convents to become brides of Christ, never to marry or bear children. My sons Hugh, Edward, and Gilbert are gone too, though I'm not certain where they were taken. Still too young to grasp their father's perfidy, the children grieve deeply and are confused about why he was executed.
>
> I am now alone save for the blessed presence of baby Lizzie and my maid Gladys, who insisted on remaining with me when the other servants left. She is a sweet thing, who frets about my spirits and pretends to keep busy in the absence of the other children she so tenderly looked after.

One of my few consolations is Brother Adam's counsel, which to my surprise the queen allows. The guards in the Tower permit him to come and go as he pleases, and I often confess to him in the Chapel of Saint Peter *ad Vincula*, where I also pray each day. Adam, may God bless him, has again agreed to send you my letters and deliver yours to me should he receive them.

Soon after Hugh's execution, Isabella sent Mortimer's sergeant-at-arms, a coarse and vulgar brute fittingly named Ogle, to taunt me with the ghastly details. No doubt he was following her instructions to shock me out of my wits or drive me further to despair. I assume she also ordered him to gauge my reaction and report back what he observed. She and Mortimer must have been disappointed. Ogle had no way of knowing if I was indifferent to what he told me or too stunned to betray my feelings. He did have the decency, if I should call it that, to allow me to send the remaining children to an adjoining room to spare them the horror of his account. Dear Gladys, however, stayed at my side and wept the whole time.

A few days before Christmas, Isabella herself paid me a visit. She wore black robes of widowhood, which she donned in Paris last year when Edward made it clear he would never give up Hugh. At first she was reticent, which left me puzzled as to why she came. Indeed, when the turnkey announced her arrival, my first instinct was to believe she couldn't resist the pleasure of gloating in my presence over the agony of Hugh's final hours.

But from the questions she asked about Edward, I sensed different reasons for her coming. Isabella still cares about her husband—at least she pretends to. She told me of letters she and Edward exchanged since his capture, as well as gifts, such as warm fur robes, his favorite scents, and a caged songbird she recently gave him. She even asked my advice about future gifts, and with some embarrassment I suggested a few items that might make his ordeal easier to bear.

She then startled me by asking if I knew why she wore her weeds of mourning. I answered that I took it as a declaration of her independence, that she would soon be free to do as she pleased in matters of the heart. She laughed, saying she did mourn the loss of Edward, and hoped one day to shed her weeds and return to his arms. Her aim all along, or so she said, was to rid England of Hugh so she could resume her rightful duties as queen and reunite with Edward as his wife in more than name only.

She hadn't reckoned with the barons and bishops' refusal to rally to Edward's side after Hugh was brought to justice. With Mortimer she set in motion events she couldn't control once the invasion started. She claimed that Edward's deposition took her by surprise, forcing her to plead with Lancaster and the other barons to keep him alive. Even young Edward's coronation as the new king had not been the certainty she expected once his father was deposed.

Isabella said little about Mortimer, leading me to wonder why he agreed to spare Edward from the gallows. Might there be growing discord between them? Are they—indeed, were they ever—lovers as everyone at court says? Or, since joining forces in Paris, have they been allies united only by their loathing of Hugh? Together, Isabella and Mortimer now control England, but how content are they with each other?

And will their shared rule run smoothly in the coming months? Maybe Isabella is unsure herself.

And what of the new King Edward? Though only fifteen, he is strong-willed, like his grandfather Longshanks, and unlikely to sit by for long while Mortimer and his mother make decisions in his name and loot the royal treasury, which they will surely do. He sided with his mother upon arriving in France, but his affection for his father remains true—more so, I suspect, since Hugh's death.

Above all, I despair about what will become of my children while I am held prisoner in the Tower. And if one day I am set free, what then? So many questions. . . .

Eleanor closed with hurried apologies that baby Elizabeth cried for her mother's milk and that she was late for confession.

After rereading the letter William put it aside and weighed what he should write in reply. Six months had passed since he last wrote to her, and he had wondered if his letter was safely delivered. He could now assume it was. At the moment he had plenty of news from Avignon he could report and many questions he might ask; but in view of her captivity in the Tower he doubted she would find the news or his questions of interest. What troubled him most, however, was the tone his return letter might convey: that of the Lord's wise confessor, a sympathetic friend, or a moonstruck swain?

Sensing Saint Augustine's wagging finger of reproof, William ceased wallowing in this question and turned to others better suited to his temperament. To begin with, why had Isabella permitted Adam Wodeham free entry to the Tower, and what did her reason have to do with her strained relations with Mortimer? Perhaps she felt guilty for having taken Eleanor's children from her and hoped to renew their former bond around their shared relief at Despenser's execution. Or, in a more sinister vein, might Isabella have tried to induce Adam to act as her spy, suspicious that Eleanor still posed a threat to her? If so, she would be disappointed. Whatever the cost, Adam would guard Eleanor's secrets. The simplest and most likely explanation, William concluded, was that Isabella had nothing to lose and thus agreed out of indifference.

And what should he make of Eleanor's conclusion about Isabella's alliance with Mortimer? That they "conspired" but hadn't "kissed" and that the queen had hoped Edward would retain his crown. Recalling her first two letters, William suspected that Eleanor's views about the queen's motives were naively generous. The consensus opinion was probably closer to the mark, namely, that Isabella, no less than Mortimer, wished England rid of both the hated Despenser *and* her feckless husband. The promiscuous Isabella was just as cunning and ruthless as Mortimer, and her aims all along included avenging Edward's vile treatment of her and seeing to it that her son would replace him as England's king.

How, then, to explain Isabella's gifts and letters to Edward since the start of his captivity? Politically she had nothing to gain by sending them, nor indeed anything to gain by lying about them to Eleanor. Perhaps Eleanor exaggerated their significance, but it was also possible the queen was having second thoughts about her future with Mortimer. It wouldn't be the first time conspirators had fallen out while dividing the spoils of war.

William prepared to stow the letter beneath the straw matting of his cot, then paused and reopened it. Eleanor had tucked a small numeral *3* at the bottom left corner of its last page. He then refolded the pages and placed them next to her first and second letters.

After gathering his thoughts, he retrieved a fresh sheet of parchment, lit another candle, and began his reply. He was not sure what he should write—other than assuring Eleanor that she hadn't written to the wind. Perhaps it was all he needed to tell her.

Chapter 18

June 4, 1327 — The Church of Sainte Claire

"PLEASE, BROTHER WILLIAM, it's *Petrarca*," Francesco insisted, melodically drawing out the three syllables, "not *Petrarch*! You English show no appreciation of language's lyricism, how tone conveys meaning as well as mood."

Francesco corrected William's pronunciation as they made their way along a winding lane to the Imbert Gate at the southeast corner of Avignon's protective wall.

"Hah! Do you believe I don't know *Petrarca* isn't really Italian, that it's just a corruption of *Petracco*?" William asked, pronouncing Francesco's actual surname in an *un*melodic, staccato cadence. He was starting to tire of Francesco's complaining about how the English abused his native tongue.

"A *corruption*, you say! Mm, perhaps, but *we* know when to take liberties pleasing to the ear. Your own deficiency in that regard no doubt explains why your drab little country has yet to produce a great poet."

"How would you know? You can't speak the language."

"And why should I trouble myself to learn it? To confabulate with *peasants*? England will never amount to anything until the people of consequence speak in their *own* tongue instead of imitating their 'betters' across the Channel."

Their excursion took William and Francesco farther afield than usual on this sticky spring afternoon. A few months earlier, and quite out of the blue, the handsome young poet had come to William for confession. It soon became clear that he sought out the notorious Greyfriar more for mental stimulation than to beg forgiveness for his sins. Francesco harbored few concerns about his soul's destination, and to him the Lord's commandments were more like recommendations that ought to be followed, or not, as the circumstance warranted.

As one example, fidelity to marital vows ranked low in his priorities, and his several other lapses would elicit stern rebuke from a less indulgent man of the cloth than William. Francesco would regale him with novel opinions on art, politics, poetry, architecture, philosophy, the Holy Scriptures, and, above all, love. In return William shared some of his own opinions, except on the last of these subjects, about which he had little experience and even less inclination to confide. Hearing Francesco's kind of confession, however, wasn't new to William. With Eleanor de Clare he had blurred and then obliterated altogether the distinction between confessor and penitent, though he still felt guilty about it. He felt no such guilt with Francesco, who, after all, wasn't a woman.

For weeks Francesco beseeched William to accompany him a half-mile beyond the city's giant protective wall to the rue des Teinturiers. He wanted to show William the church of Sainte Claire where his inamorata Laura de Noves first greeted his eyes. William finally agreed, though mainly to annoy the pope's guards tasked with tailing him whenever he ventured beyond the city's gates.

On reaching their destination Francesco waxed rapturously about the moment he first saw Laura emerge through the pointed arch of the tiny church's entrance. "The rays of the morning sun," he swooned, "basked her delicate features in a radiant glow, and. . . ."

William's eyes glazed over, dreading that Francesco's mood would spawn a soliloquy on his sublime torment about Laura's recent marriage to another man. Or worse, he might recite one of his treacly sonnets. William preempted these possibilities with a disquisition on the many flaws he detected in the church's design and construction. Francesco grudgingly took the hint, and soon afterward they began their return to the city's interior. William hadn't spotted the guards who were supposed to be following him, but he assumed they were somewhere close by.

"I thought you came to me to confess, Francesco, and instead you rave on about my country's shortcomings," William said as he felt a few raindrops spatter his head. They were still a mile from the convent, and he wondered if they would arrive there before the dense dark clouds opened.

"Ah, but you pride yourself on your *expansive* view of the confessor's role. The others expect me to beg forgiveness for habits of the heart that shouldn't need to be forgiven. I trust *you* don't believe God reproaches me for adoring the divine Laura!"

"As I recall, she *is* a married woman, which in itself would likely give Him pause—setting aside the question of how her husband might feel about it. And surely I needn't remind you of His commandment about coveting your neighbor's wife."

"But I live *outside* Avignon in Carpentras, so we're, um, not exactly neighbors," Francesco deadpanned. "But that may be just an esoteric quibble my prior legal training inclines me to point out."

William gazed back at him with a stony expression. "All the more reason to applaud your giving up the law. Sooner or later it would have given up on you."

"Hmm, I'm sure you're right. But seriously, Brother William, do you believe God will punish me for my thoughts as well as my deeds? 'Coveting,' I assume, is a *thought*, isn't it?"

"I should think sending her sonnets lavishly declaring your affections qualifies as a deed—twenty-two of them at last count, or so you told me. But as I'm sure you're aware, that's quite beside the point. It is your thoughts—or, in this instance, your *emotions*—that matter here. God doesn't *reproach* you, to use your word, just for *having* them . . ."

"So," Francesco interrupted, "if I *thought* the sonnets but didn't write them down I'd have nothing to worry about?"

"Indeed you would have a great deal to worry about," William replied testily, "for reasons I'll explain if you'll keep quiet."

"Do go on, then," Francesco allowed.

"The experience of emotions—temptations, say, provoked by unwanted images or impulses—is purely involuntary," William lectured him. As he did so, he was uncomfortably aware he was merely rehearsing lessons from his youth he had learned at Greyfriars seminary in London. He proceeded nevertheless. "You can't will yourself not to have them, which of course God knows. But, while having those unwanted emotions can't be helped, He looks more deeply, at more than a transitory image, to see whether they're contrary to what you truly believe. Put another way, a temptation does not become a sin unless you *wallow* in it. And to discourage you from doing that, He admonishes you not to fill your mind with ungodly, blasphemous thoughts that could then produce that temptation."

"Mm, I understand the distinction," Francesco said as he ostentatiously scratched his head, "but I can't see how it helps me with my predicament. My feelings about Laura are neither unwanted nor transitory. Even if I tried, I couldn't will myself not to 'wallow' in them, which is what, in *your* word, my sonnet-writing amounts to. Despite what Augustine says, I can't will my own will, especially when it comes to my feelings. Yes, I suppose I *could* stop composing the sonnets, but those feelings wouldn't change."

A heavy rain forced them to take cover, just in time, beneath the awning of a fishmonger's stall at the northern end of the Exchange. They were still a fair distance from their destination, and William wanted to end their conversation. He knew he was treading on shaky ground. Any judgment he might—in fact, *should*—make regarding Francesco would, given his own feelings toward Eleanor, apply equally to him. Although he hadn't made his feelings known to her, William was no less sinful than his young penitent. Lustful thoughts were just as sinful as carnal deeds; it was a distinction without a moral difference—or so he had been taught. He could contrive a facile argument as to why his own sins were less egregious than Francesco's, but that would be self-serving, and both he and God would know it.

Moments later Francesco resumed. "I have a syllogism for you to ponder, Brother William. If sinful thoughts and sinful deeds are morally equivalent in God's eyes, and if, owing to the depraved state of my soul, I'm helpless to curb my sinful thoughts, it then follows that I would have nothing *further* to lose by acting on them. I might just as well continue to send Laura my sonnets and even seduce her should the opportunity present itself."

"If God thought only in syllogisms, Francesco, He might agree with you. His cognitive repertoire, however, infinitely surpasses your clever exercises in logic. As I assume you know, He searches the depths of our hearts in addition to the contents of our minds and would thus take grievous exception to your *mocking* Him!"

William had tired of bantering—but also, it now dawned on him, of presuming to read God's mind.

Chapter 19

August 7, 1327 — The Infirmary and the Bank of the Rhône

WHENEVER WILLIAM PASSED by the infirmary he recalled his truncated visit two years before. Gerardo had persuaded him to ask Brother François to treat his aching leg and accompanied William to make sure he would not change his mind. The visit didn't end well. Palace guards interrupted his long wait in the anteroom by dragging the bloodied Richard de Bury through the entrance. William's patience at the long wait had worn thin before de Bury's sudden appearance, and after the turmoil subsided, he left and vowed not to return.

His leg was aching again, and he decided to pay another visit. As an empiricist—an experimenter—he should give Brother François another chance to prove himself. But on reaching the infirmary's herb garden, he heard an unfamiliar voice ask, "Friar Occam, is it not?"

He turned and saw a lithe young man, not yet thirty, with close-cropped blond hair and a thick reddish-brown beard. He was of medium height but seemed taller owing to his severely erect posture. His appearance announced that he represented a personage or institution of stature.

"And who are you?"

"My name is not important," the man said in a heavy German accent.

From the man's steely-eyed gaze, William concluded that this was not a confession of modesty. He began to feel testy. "Perhaps not, but who sent you *is* important. And how did you identify me?"

"I was told you were of middle age, carried a staff, and walked with a limp. I waited outside your convent and followed you here." The man paused and glanced about as if wary of being overheard. He offered a hint of a smile. "Perhaps we could speak somewhere more private." He led William to a shaded bench surrounded by rows of mint and rosemary plants. He positioned himself for a clear view of the garden and carefully eyed those who lingered more than a few moments. "I have been instructed to deliver a letter," he said as he turned to face William, "but first I need to be certain you are who you appear to be."

William smiled inwardly at the suggestion anyone might be mistaken for him. He nodded that he didn't object to his visitor's precautions.

"I was told I could confirm Friar Occam's identity by asking who would describe him as, er," the German uttered a slight cough, "'all head and no heart.'" From his bland expression, the man evidently saw no humor or irony in that description.

"Baskerville!" William immediately replied. His mentor would have known William would remember his not-so-friendly barb years earlier.

Satisfied, the German again scanned the garden for prying eyes as he slid a sealed packet across to William. "I advise you to open it later, alone."

William saw that the packet was stamped with the Greyfriars seal. "But why did he send *you*? And where is he now?" The last he had heard, Baskerville was in northern Italy, having gone there from the Emperor Louis' protective sanctuary in Bavaria.

"I am not at liberty to say." Then, without so much as an adieu, the young man stood, scanned the premises again, and disappeared into the crowded lane.

William watched him leave as he sat and massaged his leg. He could tolerate the ache a while longer, so Brother François would again be spared the opportunity to prove himself. He grasped the packet, rose with the aid of his staff, and hobbled back to the convent.

In his cell, William lit a candle and opened Baskerville's letter. Following a terse salutation, his mentor had written:

> . . . If ever a place could tempt one to doubt His divine oversight, it is surely the hellhole of Avignon. Thus I pray that the Lord bestows His blessings during your current travails. I remain dismayed, however, by your decision to go there—confirming yet again your unfortunate habit of mistaking hubris for courage. But enough of my reproof, for I write on a matter of far greater urgency.
>
> By now, word has surely reached you that the emperor assigned me to mediate negotiations on the poverty question between the Franciscans and a papal delegation from Avignon. You may *not* know that he did so at Michael of Cesena's urging. As our leader, Michael has long been keen to forge an agreement that will satisfy both Duèze and our Order. He hoped to achieve this at the Benedictine abbey in the Piedmont where the meeting was held.
>
> Alas, the negotiations were doomed from the start owing to Bernard Gui's presence. As the pope's chief emissary, Gui

immediately provoked a dispute over the Scriptures, with each side objecting vehemently to the other's position. A short while later the proceedings collapsed when the abbey's Aedificium was set afire. This occurred in the aftermath of several murders, which the abbot, Abo, asked me to investigate. But I shall spare you the details of those horrific events.

Michael now plans to meet in Avignon with the pope himself. Before the debacle at the abbey, Michael was under extreme pressure to do so but wisely delayed, claiming ill health as an excuse. But now he appears determined despite my strongly advising against it.

If Michael persists in his ill-considered mission, his arguments will almost certainly inflame Duèze and further consolidate his power. Nothing short of the emperor's launching a holy war can protect Michael from him. I therefore ask that you implore Michael in the strongest terms not to become entrapped in the pope's lair. Where I have failed, perhaps you can convince him that our eventual triumph will issue from our *collective* efforts—over more years than we might hope—to cripple Duèze's authority. No single Franciscan, however heroic or wise, can achieve that end.

The advice I urge you to relay to Michael applies with even greater force to you. Unlike Michael's, your temperament—or should I say your irascible temper?—disposes you to fight rather than conciliate. You, William, risk even greater peril should you foolishly wage a solitary battle. Recall my admonishment about mistaking hubris for courage. . . .

When he finished reading, William folded the letter and placed it beneath his cot. His mind buzzed with questions, not only about its contents but also the circumstances of its delivery. He ruminated about these questions as he left the convent, made his way past the palace, and descended a steep serpentine path to the bank of the Rhône. Once there, he soaked his feet in the river's cooling waters.

As he watched the arrival and departure of the barges that supplied the city, he wondered why the secretive young German, rather than another friar, had delivered Baskerville's letter. The German with the imperious bearing, he surmised, was the emperor's courier, which meant that Louis—more likely, one of his agents— had wanted the letter delivered safely no less than Baskerville himself.

What should he make of Baskerville's advice? Was Michael's mission to Avignon that ill-considered? Or, might Michael in fact succeed in resolving the Franciscans' dispute with Duèze? Perhaps Michael's powers of persuasion and conciliation were greater than Baskerville had assumed. William was torn, unsure what to advise Michael when he showed up at Greyfriars convent, perhaps in a matter of days.

And why had his mentor barely mentioned the murders? William already knew some of the grisly details. A week earlier the always well-informed Gerardo told him that five corpses had been found on the abbey's premises, all victims of foul play. Although it was later determined that each was slain by a different hand, the abbey's blind librarian Jorge of Burgos had plotted them all.

Jorge, Gerardo reported, had long been consumed with rooting out heresy, which owing to his messianic passion acquired ever more bizarre connotations. He found the latest evidence of it in Aristotle's newly discovered treatise on comedy, wherein, and to Jorge's horror, the Philosopher dangerously extolled laughter, humor, and irony as virtues. By producing *too much* freedom and knowledge, these "virtues" were instead sins that undermined the authority of the Holy Scriptures.

To arrest the spread of those evils, Jorge contrived the murders of his five Benedictine brothers. All were eager to study the offending tome, which he had hidden in one of the library's darkest recesses. When the abbot, Abo, finally discovered the source of the gruesome deeds, Jorge set the Aedificium's library afire, consuming both himself and the abbot.

How had the famous William of Baskerville deployed his powers of logic and observation in solving the murders? Where was he now, and was he safe? Those questions occupied William's thoughts as he climbed up the path to the palace. He leg still ached and he was late again for Vespers.

Chapter 20

October 15, 1327 — The Pyre

"IF HIS HEAD'S NOT BLOWN to bits first, he could squirm and howl for well-nigh an hour." William and John of Reading overheard this assessment from a voice in the crowd as they trudged behind the executioner's dray. Lashed to the front railing stood a young friar named Guarin, an unrepentant Spiritual from Narbonne. He was shoeless and wore only a thin white shift to shield him from the autumn chill.

"Could take longer," a second voice added. "Last year the other poor bugger lasted *two* hours. The faggots was still damp from the rain, so they had to keep relighting 'em."

He was speaking of Bernard Maury, another Franciscan Spiritual whose burning the previous November was held north of the papal enclave outside Saint Matthews Gate. The sisters at the nearby Carmelite convent complained afterward about the noise from the crowd and the stink of Maury's charred flesh. An alternate site had been constructed amid the debris of the new palace's recently laid foundation.

This morning's trip took longer than planned. A wobbly wheel came loose from the mule-drawn dray's front axle, causing the vehicle to cant sharply to the left and grind to a halt. A tethering rope was all that kept Guarin from pitching headfirst onto the startled mule's back. Onlookers lining the route jeered as the dray's driver dismounted and, on examining the damage, pleaded for assistance. A young carter stepped forth and ten minutes later flexed his muscles triumphantly before the approving crowd upon completing the repair. The mule, however, refused to budge for another ten minutes before continuing its journey.

"Weren't there supposed to be *three* of them?" William asked Reading.

"The two others came to their senses last evening. But Guarin held fast—a martyr to the end." The bitterness in Reading's voice made clear his disapproval of Guarin's intransigence.

"What became of them—the other two?"

"Earlier this morning I was told they were released and left the city. I suspect they're on their way to Sicily to join the twenty who recanted in Marseilles."

William bristled at this mention of the burnings in Marseilles five years earlier. "Four of them *didn't*," he reminded Reading as the crowd's momentum carried them forward.

* * *

A half-hour later the dray descended a slight incline and stopped at an opening to a circular area thirty yards across. Guards in crimson uniforms were there to keep order and prevent the growing crowd from edging too close to the pyre. Someone in the crowd shouted, "Save the powder! Let him burn through and through!" A chorus of catcalls endorsed that recommendation as spectators jostled for an unobstructed view.

The pyre looked much the same as those William had seen before. Standing ten feet high, the stake was ringed by stacked logs, atop which were strewn bundles of small branches, or faggots, to kindle the flames. The palace's executioner stood close by, and William clenched his teeth on hearing him laugh at a remark made by one of the guards.

A dozen palace dignitaries sat in a row beneath a white canopy. Conspicuous by his absence was Pope John, who Reading had told William not to expect. One of the dignitaries was John Lutterell, whose perpetual scowl only partially concealed his satisfaction at being invited. Abbé Thierry sat at the row's far end, fidgeting as he looked away from the dray bearing his errant brother. Perhaps the silver-haired abbot wished he were somewhere else, preferring that his complicity go unnoticed.

Minutes after arriving William tugged on Reading's sleeve and pointed to a bent figure familiar to them both. It was the Dominican inquisitor Bernard Gui, who would preside over today's burning. The pope's enforcer of doctrinal purity was feared and loathed not only by the Franciscans but also by questioning voices among the other orders. Menace glistened in his narrow-set eyes, and his curved spine canted him forward as if he were revealing dark secrets. He gestured toward the pyre as he issued instructions to the executioner.

When two of the guards climbed onto the dray and untethered Guarin from the railing, William saw a small pouch tied around his neck. The pouch was filled with gunpowder that would ignite when the flames reached it, exploding Guarin's skull into bloody fragments. This was a merciful gesture intended to foreshorten the heretic's suffering. It didn't always work, as Bernard Maury learned eleven months earlier when the moist air prevented the powder from igniting.

Guarin scanned the ring of spectators as the guards dragged him toward the pyre. His eyes widened when his gaze fixed on a point in the circle ten yards to the left of where William and Reading watched. William squinted as he traced Guarin's line of sight and spotted Gerardo. He stood next to a young woman, thin and pretty, dressed in a grey and white novice's habit. Her lips parted, she appeared to be in great distress as she stared back at Guarin. William thought he recalled seeing her outside the convent a few days earlier, though he may have mistaken her for someone else. Gerardo grasped her shoulders as if to comfort her or perhaps to restrain her from trying to breach the guards' cordon.

William was puzzled at seeing Gerardo in the young woman's company, but then he remembered Gerardo telling him he had recently begun to hear confessions. Consorting with penitents outside the confessional, however, was considered irregular and would likely raise the older friars' eyebrows. But not William's; more than once he had violated that unwritten rule himself.

"Guarin's sister," Reading said as he had also noticed her. "Named Joyeuse, a novice at the Carmelite convent here in the city. Last evening she was at the jail pleading with one of the sergeants to allow her to see him."

"What were *you* doing there?" William asked in surprise as he watched the guards lift Guarin onto the pyre.

Reading spat a barely audible curse. "Time ill-spent! I hoped to persuade them to reconsider their foolishness, and asked an acquaintance at the palace to get me inside. But when I arrived, the guards hadn't gotten the message. The sergeant who denied Joyeuse's entry also denied mine. I overheard her pleading with the sergeant before some of the older sisters took her away." Still irked by his mission's failure, he exclaimed under his breath, "God's bile! My radical brothers will be the death of me yet."

This had long been a sore point between William, a Spiritual, and Reading, a Conventual. The Greyfriars of Avignon were almost evenly divided between the two factions—those who fully embraced Jesus' example of extreme poverty and those who still balked at doing so. But the Conventuals, including Reading, viewed the burnings of their brother Spirituals with horror—all except Abbé Thierry, who was widely suspected of informing Bernard Gui of the Order's dissident voices.

The execution site grew quiet as the spectators strained to hear Gui's reedy, high-pitched voice. He was addressing Guarin, who was now bound to the stake by ropes around his waist and neck. Unable to hear all of what Gui was saying, William again turned inquiringly toward Reading.

"I assume he's explaining what awaits Brother Guarin's soul if he doesn't recant," Reading said. "I can't make out exactly what he's saying, but that's likely the gist of it."

"Is it too late for Guarin to change his mind?"

"Hard to know," Reading sighed, shaking his head. He now sounded more worried than angry. "It depends on Gui's mood. He can be fickle when it comes to showing mercy."

Gui concluded his brief oration and then nodded to the executioner, signaling him to light his torch. In the dry morning air the sparks from the executioner's flints produced a steady flame a few seconds later. He then edged forward and lit bunches of the faggots on the pyre's periphery. Wisps of smoke rose and then dissipated in the slight breeze that would soon fan the flames. Dry twigs burst, shooting tiny rockets of fire as high as the freshly shaved crown of Guarin's head. William flinched on hearing the faint explosions and turned away. Most of the spectators didn't and instead stared transfixed. Still others shouted encouragement to the flames that crept toward the stake. It took only ten minutes for them to engulf most of the pyre.

William looked across the circle to where Gerardo now hovered over Joyeuse, who had sunk to her knees. She was sobbing as she saw her brother's face contorted in pain.

Another agonizing minute had passed when William heard Guarin's wailing voice. He could make out only a few scattered words above the din of the crowd: ". . . confess my sins," ". . . the Lord's forgiveness," "Praise God!" Guarin then coughed and gasped for air.

Bernard Gui watched and listened impassively. Now feeling the heat from the flames, he delicately wiped his brow and inched back toward the row of dignitaries. After several seconds of contemplation, he gestured to the executioner who, with two assistants, stood close by awaiting further instructions. At Gui's signal, one of the assistants approached the pyre and doused the flames with buckets already filled with water, while another swatted away the burning faggots from Guarin's feet with a staff he held in his gloved hands. The executioner climbed an as yet unlit section of the pyre and with his dagger cut away the ropes that bound Guarin. Once freed, he slumped and started to fall forward onto the smoldering embers but was caught just before landing and quickly dragged to safety. Moments afterward, on his knees at Gui's feet, he reaffirmed his heresy's recantation to make certain there had been no misunderstanding. The pouch of gunpowder still dangled from his neck.

As Guarin knelt before the inquisitor, the crowd groaned in disappointment. Gui gazed down at the now-repentant friar with a thin smile of triumph, although William felt certain he privately shared in the crowd's disappointment.

* * *

Twenty minutes later the crowd had dispersed. Some of the spectators still grumbled on being deprived of their entertainment, but William hoped that others shared his own deep sense of relief. He and Reading lingered at the site until certain Guarin would be released and handed over to his brother friars. Workmen began to dismantle the canopy the palace dignitaries had sat beneath. By now, most of them were gone. Among the first to leave was Abbé Thierry, who slipped away unobtrusively moments after the ropes binding Guarin to the stake were cut loose. Gui had also made a quiet exit.

The palace guards who had cordoned off the crowd relaxed their vigil, allowing Joyeuse to burst through and rush to her brother's side. She threw her arms across his shoulders as he continued to kneel. He was still too shaken to stand without assistance. The hem of his thin white shift was scorched, and William saw him rubbing at his ankles, which had not completely escaped the flames. Cradled in his sister's arms, Guarin also wept. William wondered whether his tears were tears of pain, of blessed relief, or of shame at having betrayed the memory of his fallen brother, Bernard Maury. This question troubled William as he imagined the terrifying possibility, perhaps the likelihood, that one day he would face a similar choice. He had no idea how he would choose.

"Where will they take him?" William asked as he and Reading trailed behind the small procession of friars. Two of Guarin's brothers from the convent braced his arms as others huddled protectively around him. Gerardo and Joyeuse walked a few steps behind.

177

"To the infirmary, I should imagine. His burns will need attention. François can ply him with salves when he gets there."

"And afterward?"

Reading shook his head. "I can't say for certain, but his friends may try to get him out of the city before Gui changes his mind. He could eventually find his way to Sicily or perhaps to . . ."

As the voluble Reading prattled on about Guarin's likely destination, William paid closer attention to Gerardo and Joyeuse walking side by side. Gerardo caught her arm to steady her when she tripped over a rock. Her hand occasionally touched his sleeve, and at least once she brushed something from his shoulder, possibly stray ashes from the pyre.

Chapter 21

November 28, 1327 — Greyfriars Convent

"*MIO DIO*! A HOT POKER up his ass?" Francesco Petrarca exclaimed in mock horror as he glanced in William's direction. "I must say, the English show more imagination than the Caesars in disposing of their annoying rivals. Caligula had nothing on this Mortimer fellow."

"A mere refinement, I assume, of an ancient Italian practice," William said dismissively. His seminar over for the day, he descended the convent stairs with Francesco and Gerardo in tow. The other students had already left for evening prayers. The three peered out the front entrance and saw that an early winter rain had begun to fall. Thunder followed lightning bolts to the west. By unspoken agreement they prudently reversed course, climbed the stairs, and returned to the classroom they had just left.

"In any event," William resumed as he sat on a chair next to the classroom's small window, "I doubt you'll find any mention of a poker in the official account of Edward's death."

"Surely," Gerardo objected, "you don't believe it was—how did they put it?—'an accident destined by fate.'" He was standing, in awkward deference, William suspected, that he still felt in intimate gatherings. Francesco exhibited no such inhibitions as he sprawled on a chair next to the classroom's door.

"Of course not," William said, "only that reports of regicide might be embellished for popular consumption, especially in the case of a king as unloved as Edward II. I've no reason at all to doubt that his death—his *murder*—was Mortimer's doing."

"But what about the queen," Gerardo asked. "Would she have gone along with it? And did she even know about the plan beforehand?

"Unlikely on either count. Remember, Pope John hadn't given up trying to persuade her to reconcile with Edward. Even if she loathed the idea, her complicity in his killing, just a whisper of it, wouldn't sit well with the pope. And she most certainly wouldn't have wanted their son to suspect she'd conspired in his father's murder. She'd be a fool to have had anything to do with it."

"Killing Edward was risky for Mortimer too," Francesco said. "Not by inviting the *pope's* wrath, but the new king's. Assuming young Edward isn't a fool either, he won't be taken in by the canard about the 'fateful accident.' So if I were Mortimer, I'd be nervous. It won't be long before Edward III rules more than in name."

* * *

William gleaned most of what he knew or suspected about Edward's murder from Adam Wodeham's latest letter. After returning from Compline, William read the letter a third time. He was amused by Adam's whimsical dismissal of the hot poker theory, citing the more credible story—told to him by Brother Andrew, the Greyfriars abbot in London—that Edward was suffocated in his sleep. The deed, so it was whispered, was done on September 21, the feast day of Saint

Matthew the Apostle and Evangelist, by two of Mortimer's men, Thomas de Gornay and Simon Bereford.

Afterward, priests, knights, and other dignitaries assembled at Berkeley Castle to stand continuous watch over the former king's embalmed and heavily shrouded corpse before its transport to Gloucester Abbey for burial. Had the onlookers shown up voluntarily, William wondered as he reread Adam's letter, or had Mortimer ordered their attendance under pain of withholding future favors? And why did he arrange the macabre display? Two possibilities came to mind: that he relished gloating over the irony of a public "mourning" for his despised enemy, or that he wanted to erase any lingering doubts that his triumph over Edward was complete.

William still puzzled over an additional item in Adam's letter. Before Edward's murder there were three failed attempts to free him, all of them led by Stephen Dunheved. Supported by a few barons still loyal to the deposed king, Dunheved's band of outlaws included his brother Thomas and a dozen or so of Edward's other fanatical followers.

Most of the conspirators, including both Dunheved brothers, were captured in June after the second abortive foray. This followed shortly after Edward's removal from the Earl of Lancaster's Kenilworth Castle in the Midlands to Mortimer's son-in-law's ostensibly more secure Berkeley Castle, seventy miles to the southwest. Several of those caught met swift and painful ends, including Thomas, who was taken to Newgate Prison in London where within weeks he was either executed or died of a fever while chained in his cell. The elusive Stephen, however, managed to escape his captors in early July. After recruiting a new band of Edward loyalists, he plotted a third and final rescue attempt. Alas, his efforts were dashed in mid-course by de Gornay and Bereford's nocturnal visit to Berkeley Castle on September 21.

William stowed Adam's letter beneath his cot and pinched out his candle. But sleep would not come as he stared into the darkness and formulated questions.

Chapter 22

December 1, 1327 — The Palace Piazza

AMID THE PILGRIMS AND PENITENTS assembled to receive the pontifical blessing, only the white mule John XXII sat astride seemed unimpressed by the pageantry. Those nearest the pope's entourage feared that the brisk wind blowing through the piazza might topple the frail rider from his mount. A bishop William didn't recognize braced the pope's elbow as two young priests scurried after his white zucchetto, his "pumpkin cap," when an errant gust lifted it from his head. As custom required, an almoner from the palace trailed behind and tossed coins to the scrambling supplicants.

A fluffy, ermine-trimmed cushion billowed from beneath the pope's derriere to protect it from the mule's knobby spine. The cushion was a gift from a prosperous local silk merchant whose nerves had calmed on hearing the pope's promise to ask Saint Peter, when the time came, to look the other way as he slinked through heaven's gate. Until then, additional, more generous benefactions would be welcomed.

The pope was clad in his everyday winter attire: a white woolen cassock partly hidden beneath a fur-lined robe shielding him from the afternoon chill. He had shed his liturgical vestments, which he donned that morning to celebrate an early mass at the cathedral of *Notre-Dame des Doms*. It was the feast day of Saint Eligius—the patron saint of goldsmiths.

"Goldsmiths!" Michael of Cesena snorted. "How fitting! Should we assume today's celebration surpasses in holiness the feast of the Resurrection?"

"Thank Christ the avaricious old fart hasn't canceled it," William muttered as they craned for a clearer view.

William and Michael had not entered the piazza hoping to receive the pope's blessing. Both had encountered him before and each time managed to avoid kissing his ring. To his credit, the pope didn't seem to mind, signaling that he, too, would just as soon dispense with the friars' hypocritical displays of obeisance.

Another meeting was imminent as the pope and his attendants turned in their direction. Tugging at the mule's silver-studded bridle was one of the pope's nephews, who on his thirtieth birthday received a cardinal's miter as a reward for his extreme piety. The angular young cardinal halted the mule twenty paces from the two Greyfriars, obliging them to approach his uncle.

"Brother Cesena," Pope John said in a hoarse whisper as he peered down from his perch, "it has been, what, nearly four years since your last visit? I trust the warmer Italian climes have improved your health sufficiently to endure the rigors of Avignon. A harsh winter is coming, or so my astrologer tells me."

"I'm concerned less about the weather, Your Holiness, than other sorts of rigors. Nevertheless, I was most gratified to learn of your eagerness to resolve our differences and pray the Lord might watch over our shared endeavor."

"Time will tell which of our prayers receives His more ardent kblessing," the pope replied with a thin smile, his small blue eyes twinkling in the sunlight.

So much for *sharing* anything, William thought.

"And as perhaps you know," the pope continued as he glanced in William's direction, "I have assigned preliminary discussion of the issues now before us to the commission currently examining the writings of your estimable Brother Occam. A different range of subjects, to be sure, although your appearance here together leads me to wonder about their possible convergence."

"Until we renewed our acquaintance this morning, it had been several years since we spoke," Michael said. He didn't mention the letters they had exchanged, although the pope's minions might have intercepted and read them.

"Ah yes, at the Greyfriars' Assembly in Perugia, I believe." Age hadn't dulled Duèze's memory. "And next May in Bologna, if I'm not misinformed, you expect to stand for reelection as your order's leader. I trust in the meantime you have no plans to leave Avignon."

"Just this morning I received word advising against it," Michael answered in as neutral a tone as he could summon.

Their exchange had already been interrupted three times by penitents entreating the pope for his blessing. As they kissed his ring, he uttered an almost inaudible *Dominus vobiscum* before dismissing them with an airy wave of his hand. On noticing the lengthening queue, the pope's nephew broke into their conversation and signaled the procession to move on. Duèze's hard-eyed expression was replaced by a beatific smile, while his chin lifted imperiously to remind the assembled faithful that God had designated him, and no one else, custodian of their souls. Still unimpressed, the white mule brayed a noisy complaint when prodded to resume its promenade around the piazza.

* * *

"Hardly an auspicious welcome," William said as he and Michael made their way past the cathedral minutes later. Gusts of wind had become more frequent, whipping the hems of their habits. "Are you sure you were wise to ignore Baskerville's warning?"

"You ignored it too," Michael said, eyeing the bell tower atop the cathedral. Construction of the ugly new addition had just begun as he left Avignon four years earlier. "You're still here."

William shrugged dismissively at Michael's comment. "So far, I've been able to sidestep most of the bishops' questions about the poverty issue. I've made only a few corrections to my *Ordinatio*, which appears to have mollified them. All in all, my stay here has been tolerably pleasant."

"Barring any surprises, then, you'll return to England?"

"I've thought about it, but I haven't tempted fate by making firm plans," William said as he eyed Michael warily. "But I assume your asking isn't prompted solely by fraternal solicitude."

"Quite so, and you may not like my reasons." Michael halted as he said this and looked directly at William.

"I'm almost afraid to ask what they are."

"I returned to Avignon," Michael explained, "because I saw no other choice. Baskerville is too optimistic about the 'inevitability' of our defeating Duèze. Which means he's content to wait longer than I am."

"If the emperor and his armies had joined you here, it's possible you wouldn't have had to wait."

186

"Not necessarily. Winning by force, or just the threat of it, would be temporary at best. Someday Louis will die, and new imperial alliances will form, some of which might support us and others oppose us. And Duèze, God willing, won't live forever, so even if he knuckled under to Louis' threats we'd have to contest the poverty question again with his successors."

"So, you believe you can win him over by the eloquence of your arguments?"

"I didn't expect the scales to fall from his eyes at the mere sound of my voice," Michael replied, countering William's sarcasm with some of his own. "In the near term I'd settle for a compromise that could open the way to a better outcome."

"But why would Duèze consider it?"

"I'm not certain he would. But he'd be wise not to offend us unduly or, for that matter, the other orders. Open revolt isn't out of the question if he dug in his heels and conceded nothing."

William's silence betrayed his skepticism, prompting Michael to add, "And placating us could ease tensions between him and the emperor. Otherwise, Louis might contrive an excuse to send his armies here."

"I wish I shared your optimism," William said, shaking his head. "Remember, we haven't yet convinced all our brothers. If we can't claim *their* support, how can you expect to convince Duèze? And if you press him too forcefully, he may take the matter out of the hands of the commission and deposit it in the lap of Bernard Gui. That evil bastard would have you tied to the stake in the blink of an eye."

Michael sighed deeply but recovered in time to nod and intone "May the Lord be with you" to a pair of friars passing from the opposite direction. Michael's arrival in Avignon earlier that morning had stirred much conversation at the convent. No one, including William, knew quite what to expect. "Given your doubts, then, can I still count on you?"

"Of course you can! I just want to be sure you've weighed the consequences."

"I can't see into the future," Michael said, "but I do know that the better we're prepared, the better our chances."

"*Our* chances?"

"None of the friars can match you in argument—which I mention, as I assume you know, because I need your help."

"And, um, what kind of help do you have in mind?"

After a short pause Michael said, "I assume you've studied Duèze's bulls on the matter."

William nodded that he had. The first, he recalled, dated back to the first year of Duèze's papacy and the second, four years ago, around the time he excommunicated the emperor.

"Only a cursory reading. A lot of drivel!" William said as he tossed a pebble at a peacock that had just wandered across their path. He missed, which was just as well in view of the hostile stare he received from one of the pope's guards standing not far from them. William shouldn't have been surprised: Peacocks were the pope's favorite fowl and were granted his official protection.

"Just so, although I hope you'll use more temperate language in your rebuttal."

"I see," William said quietly as the import of his minister general's instruction began to sink in. "Be careful what you ask for, Michael. I warn you: I'll cede no quarter just to help you strike a compromise. And I won't limit my arguments to the poverty question. Once I start, I won't stop there."

"For now I won't argue the point. But I do ask that you consult not only with me but with Bonagratia."

A fellow resident at Greyfriars convent, Bonagratia of Bergamo had also locked horns with the pope over the poverty question. And like William and Michael, he was confined to Avignon under pain of "grave censure" should he try to leave. All three were on the same side, although William struggled to curb his dislike of Bonagratia, a skinny, ferret-faced little man who strutted and bloviated much like the curia's lawyers William had encountered. In fact, Bonagratia *was* a lawyer—of civil and canon law, to be precise—a vocation William deemed a notch or two in respectability below his own.

"I usually try to avoid him. But," William shrugged, "I'll do as you ask. Tell me, though, do you want me to consult him for his 'learned counsel' or because you've instructed him to rein me in when I veer out of control?"

"Only for his wisdom, of course."

"And how much time to do we have?"

"That's hard to know, but I doubt we can try Duèze's patience much beyond, say, the feast of the Annunciation."

"Less than four months, then."

"In time to celebrate the arrival of spring," Michael said with a weak smile.

"Ah yes," William laughed, "and gaze at the blooming of the lavender from the pope's dungeon. Assuming we're locked away in cells with a view."

Chapter 23

February 22, 1328 — Greyfriars Convent and Saint Agricola's Church

A ROYAL DEATH and a royal wedding! The friars had just received word that King Charles IV of France died unexpectedly on February 1. His passing coincided with the long-anticipated marriage in London of the fifteen-year-old English King Edward III to his child bride, Philippa of Hainault. Reports of the two events converged in the palace's hallways and alcoves, spreading to the nearby monasteries and convents. These included the Greyfriars convent where Avignon's four most prominent Franciscans convened in an upper-floor classroom.

Today's conversation among William, Michael of Cesena, John of Reading, and Bonagratia of Bergamo was more than idle chatter about royal politics. The friars were keenly aware of the implications of Charles's death for the Franciscan Order. Without firm backing from the new French king—whoever he might be—Duèze and any Avignon successor faced the possibility of the papacy's forcible return to Rome. This in turn would jeopardize the Church's position on priestly poverty. Any new *Roman* pope, certain to be under the thumb of the emperor Louis the Bavarian, would have to support the Franciscan side as a condition of his selection. Although for the moment the prospect of the papacy's removal from Avignon was unlikely, it was not completely remote.

Michael and Reading sat at a small table in a drafty upper-floor classroom, while Bonagratia paced nervously behind them. William stood, staring out a window overlooking the lane that passed by the convent. He saw Gerardo, his bushy red hair tossed by the breeze, rush down the lane, having just exited the convent. As he disappeared around a corner, William's thoughts drifted while the others spoke.

"First, Edward and now Charles," Michael of Cesena said. "It appears the divine right of kingship confers no assurance of living long enough to savor its pleasures. What was he—thirty-three?"

"I'm trying to conceive of Charles savoring much of anything," the opinionated Reading said with a laugh. "It would be hard to find a duller, more stiff-necked ass in all of France. His own mother, would you believe, nicknamed him 'the Goose' when he was a child."

"Hmm. With 'the Goose' dead, the pope will now be spared the indignity of being called his puppet," Michael speculated, glancing at Reading to confirm his hunch. "Maybe he'll take consolation from that."

"I doubt it crossed his mind," Reading said. "Once it became clear what a pompous ignoramus Charles was, the pope pulled the king's strings rather than the other way about."

"If so, shouldn't he worry about Charles's successor?" Michael asked. "He could be left with no strings to pull."

"Cousin Philip should be next in line. His uncle Valois will see to that," Bonagratia said. He had stopped pacing long enough to explain what was already obvious to the others: Now that the Capet line from Charles's father had ended, his first cousin Philip of Valois would likely take the French crown.

"There's at least one other possibility," Reading said. "If you hadn't heard, Queen Jeanne is pregnant with her second child. If it's a boy this time, *he'll* take the throne, not Philip. In that event, expect a nasty struggle over a very long regency."

William followed only part of the friars' conversation. As he looked out the window, he overheard fragments of what appeared to be a family dispute. Just beneath him in the middle of the lane, a mother guarded her young son as she berated the boy's father (or some other man). The mother had the better of the argument, for the man, his face reddened, managed to inject only a few words in his defense. Rather than appearing frightened or cowed, the boy stood erect with his chin held high, as if fully confident his mother would protect him. A coincidence, perhaps, but William now reentered the friars' discussion about France's likely new king.

"There could be a third claimant," he said as he turned away from the window.

"And who might that be?" Michael asked.

"Edward," William answered in a tone suggesting he was merely stating the obvious.

"Edward? But the Salic law forbids it," Bonagratia objected.

"In fact, it doesn't. It forbids a *woman* from inheriting the throne, but not its inheritance by a male through a female line." Isabella, as all of them knew, was Philip the Fair's daughter and sister to the three kings who succeeded him. This placed her son in a more direct line to the throne than a mere cousin to Charles.

"An English king of France? The French would never tolerate it."

"Perhaps not happily," William said, "but they may not be able to prevent it."

* * *

An hour after the four friars dispersed, William was back at his desk. Scribes, illuminators, and translators chattered noisily, disrupting concentration on his latest missive to the commission. Abbé Thierry's presence felt more oppressive than usual. Recent rumors held that more Greyfriars from distant convents would soon be brought to Avignon to stand trial. If this were true, Thierry must have had a sinister hand in it.

The abbot had other, official duties to attend to, one of which was overseeing the convent's preparations for the Church's feast days. Almost every day of the calendar included at least one canonized name, so he was always busy. Today he was advising an earnest young friar who had arrived from Sweden two years earlier. At a desk near William's, Brother Canute was stymied by his assignment of deciphering and then transcribing into Latin a recently discovered hagiography of his late countryman, King Eric—now *Saint* Eric. The tattered document Canute pored over had been scrawled a century ago in an obscure Norse tongue that Thierry assumed the Swede could translate. Canute couldn't, squinting and scratching his head as he struggled to decipher its words and phrases. The abbot was of no help. Other than Latin, he had mastered only his native vernacular of southern France along with smatterings of Italian and Spanish.

William kept his views about the feast days to himself. The abbot would not be pleased to hear his opinion that the saints' biographies more often revealed ecstatic fantasies than verifiable facts about the saints themselves. And except for the feasts of the Nativity, Resurrection, Annunciation, Ascension, and a very few others, feast days served mainly to solidify papal hegemony in the expanding reaches of Christendom. The recently converted pagans of Finland, for example, would be more inclined to swear fealty to the pope if *their* remote land could boast of a Finnish saint or two. The new Christians would also send their modest, hard-won treasures as proof of their devotion to the Lord Jesus.

William wanted an excuse to escape the scriptorium's noise and Thierry's surveillance. He also wanted to speak with Gerardo, now several days late on his promise to procure more parchment. William hoped to find Gerardo at the Church of Saint Agricola not far from the Greyfriars' parish of Saint Geniès. Because the cramped quarters of Greyfriars convent had no room for confessional booths, the priests at Saint Agricola generously permitted some of the friars to minister the Sacrament of Penance at their church. Gerardo was a frequent presence there, his special talents for spiritual healing now widely sought after.

As he left the convent, William ruminated further about the political economy of feast days. September 2nd, he recalled, was Saint Agricola's designated day, and his name signified "Cultivator of Fields." This prompted his devotees to pray in his name for good weather, especially for rain in times of drought. His portfolio of miracles was copious, for his name was also invoked against the plague and many other calamities. William was astonished to learn that Agricola's prayers thwarted an infestation of *storks* in Avignon a millennium earlier. Surely other factors must have contributed to that success; but having yet to see a single stork during his residency, William found it fun to imagine that the Cultivator's intervention had in fact blessed the city with long-term immunity from the birds' ravages.

His mood sobered as he approached Saint Agricola's church, the oldest church in Avignon. The Gothic Roman structure showed unmistakable signs of age and neglect: only one gargoyle remained where there should have been two above the main entrance's twin doors; streaks of pigeon droppings defaced the southern wall of the squat bell tower; ten crumbling steps led from the street up to the church. Gerardo told him that Pope John was dismayed about the church's state of disrepair and had recently provided funds to restore it to its earlier majesty. He also promised to pay for the construction of two new chapels on either side of the nave, and new bells would soon be installed in the tower when its exterior was scrubbed down and refinished.

William hesitated, wondering if he should enter the church. On a prior visit he had admired its huge baroque altar and might enjoy viewing it again. But he didn't want to intrude on Gerardo, now engaged in an activity more important than running his errands. William was now unsure why he had come at all. Perhaps the parchment was merely an excuse to breathe some fresh air and get some much-needed exercise. But he may have had another motive, one he hadn't admitted to himself—namely, to check on Gerardo, who had been aloof and even secretive during the past few weeks. William worried about him, though he felt slightly guilty about his curiosity. Surely Gerardo did not need his supervision. He was not a child.

William stopped midway up the steps to the church and scanned the small courtyard fronting the entrance. A dozen or so people, including three priests, chatted in small groups. A pretty young woman stood alone next to the entrance. He thought he had seen her before but wasn't certain. She wore a dark blue cape whose hood partly covered the crown of her head, not enough to conceal completely a mass of thick blond hair. She stood with her hands folded, biting her lip as she glanced toward the entrance. William stared like a voyeur, hoping she wouldn't notice.

He saw Gerardo exit the church and stop at the young woman's side. As they spoke, she reached out to caress his sleeve but then abruptly brought her hand to her side. William now recognized her. Gone was the Carmelite's wimple that framed her face and concealed her hair when she and Gerardo walked side-by-side to the infirmary four months earlier. But her large eyes and high cheekbones were unmistakable. It was Joyeuse, Brother Guarin's sister, whom William and Reading first saw with Gerardo at the inquisitor's pyre.

William pulled his hood over his head and descended the steps to the street. As he stalked back toward the convent, he brooded over the scene he had just witnessed. Damnation! At first he felt angry, but his anger soon eased, replaced by worry about the troubles his young friend had brought upon himself. Should he scold Gerardo when they next spoke? Warn him of the danger he faced? Or maybe he would say nothing at all; for the more he reflected on what he had just witnessed, the more certain he became that what he felt was envy. So his thoughts returned to Eleanor, as they often did.

Chapter 24

April 13, 1328 — Greyfriars Convent

SEVEN MONTHS HAD PASSED since Edward II's murder at Berkeley Castle and more than a year since William had heard from Eleanor. If she had survived her captivity in the Tower of London, her fate was now tied to the old king's son. Edward III and Eleanor were first cousins, and William recalled her telling him that when he was a young boy, Edward gave her small gifts of appreciation for her tender attentions. Now that he was England's king, Edward might shield her from Mortimer and Isabella's schemes and perhaps even free her from the Tower. But William couldn't know if the young king, still only fifteen, had the nerve or the power to do so.

William had other worries as well. His sessions before the commission, which now totaled more than forty, had grown more contentious in recent months—hardly a surprise given that his criticism of the pope had become more strident. He had rashly overstepped the brief Michael had given him, ignoring the cautionary advice from his three most trusted confidants: Adam Wodeham, Durand of Saint-Pourçain, and William of Baskerville.

When he returned to the convent after an especially fraught interrogation by his inquisitors—yes, why not call them that!—

William found a sealed packet of parchment on his desk in the scriptorium. He assumed Gerardo had placed it there. The unbroken Greyfriars seal was unmistakable, which meant it must contain another letter from Adam or perhaps, he dared to hope, a letter from Eleanor.

He took it and hurried down the stairway, exiting the building's rear entrance into the convent's vegetable garden. Two older friars paid him no attention as they prepared compost to nourish the recently planted rows of onions and cabbage. He sat on a shaded bench and broke the seal, heaving a grateful sigh on recognizing Eleanor's neat hand.

He scanned the letter and then read it slowly. His sense of relief that she was alive soon gave way to puzzlement, and then alarm, as he reread portions of it.

> . . . A guard still secretly loyal to Edward told me that
> Mortimer has ordered Gerard D'Alspaye to go to Avignon.
> As you may recall, the two of them have been allies ever
> since Mortimer's escape from the Tower five years ago.
> After Edward's capture last year, Mortimer rewarded
> D'Alspaye with an appointment as the Tower's Constable. I
> know nothing about his mission to Avignon, although I was
> glad to see him go. He hated Hugh and, believing me to be a
> grief-stricken widow, seized every opportunity to add to my
> misery. . . .
>
> Shortly before D'Alspaye's departure, Isabella surprised
> me with another visit and immediately began pressing me for
> information. Outwardly, she was relaxed and confident, but I
> could see she was anxious. Isabella can disguise her mood to
> others, perhaps, but not to me. I've known her too long to be

fooled by her pretensions. Among other matters, she asked about my confessors over the years. In particular, she asked about the "severe-looking friar with the limp" who heard my confession in Paris. I told her I recalled your name as Brother William, though I was not certain. I sensed she knew I was lying. . . .

I fear that Edward's fate remains a mystery. I've learned nothing from Isabella to confirm or deny the rumors I mentioned in my last letter, and even she may not know the truth. . . .

God in Heaven! What was she talking about? As he reread each sentence, William recalled their agreement to number their letters in sequence. He felt a surge of bile in his throat when he spotted a tiny numeral *5* barely visible on the lower left corner of the letter's last page. He was now reading the *fifth* letter Eleanor had sent him, but he had received only four! He had also failed to check for the small notch she was supposed to etch on the seal's upper-right corner. But the seal, unbroken before he opened the letter, was smudged, making it impossible to determine if the notch was there. *Shit!*

The mystery Eleanor mentioned almost certainly involved new questions about the identity of Edward II's killers. Was he slain by someone other than Mortimer's henchmen, de Gornay and Bereford, as Adam Wodeham reported to William several months earlier? Or might there have been no killers at all? Perhaps he had taken his own life, succumbing to despair over his ruination. Could he have died from an all-consuming grief—of a broken heart, if indeed there was such a thing? And how might this new mystery bear on Isabella's keen interest in the identity of Eleanor's severe-looking confessor?

* * *

"You seem nervous as a stray cat," William observed as he and Gerardo made their way down the steep, winding alley branching off from the palace's west entrance. It was the same alley where Richard de Bury, young King Edward's tutor, was assaulted more than two years earlier. Now that King Charles's remains were safely interred in the Abbey of Saint-Denis near Paris, William half expected to hear news of de Bury's return to Avignon. He was one of several of Mortimer and Isabella's agents likely to plead Edward III's claim to the French throne should Charles's widow, Jeanne, fail to produce a male heir.

"You have more to be nervous about than I do," Gerardo fumed. "As if you didn't know, the bishops are furious with you. My God, Brother William! Accusing the pope of *heresy*? Not even Durand can defend you."

"Bah! The bishops' 'fury' is sheer posturing. They're probably delighted I made their decision easier."

"Which only makes matters worse. Not just for you, but for Brother Michael and Brother Bonagratia too. Remember, it's not only *your* life at stake. What in the name of all the Saints were you *thinking*?"

Gerardo's barb stung. His brother friars, no less than William himself, would pay the ultimate price for his rashness. He felt irked by Gerardo's reminder of his folly, but he knew the young friar was right. By assuming that his powers of logic could compel Duèze to see the light of reason, William had deluded himself into believing *he* possessed gifts of persuasion that Michael of Cesena and the others lacked. Ah, vanity! He should have listened to Baskerville—if not for his own sake, for theirs.

"As you might recall," William said feebly in his defense, "I warned Michael I'd hold nothing back."

"Hmph. You were certainly true to your word. If seventy errors and seven heresies weren't enough, was it necessary to ridicule Pope John's bulls as, er, let me see," he said, pulling from beneath his tunic his transcription of William's rebuttal, "Ah, here it is: 'erroneous, silly, ridiculous, fantastic, insane, defamatory, *and* contrary to orthodox faith, good morals, natural reason, and'—let us not forget—'fraternal charity!'[ix] On top of *that*, did you really have to call him an *idiot*?"

A thoroughly bad idea, William conceded. His arrogance was again in full bloom, for which today's visit to the Chapel of Saint Nicholas might serve as an antidote—or so he hoped. They were getting close, having just passed a wary toll collector who on a prior occasion demanded proof that the grey-robed William wasn't an imposter trying to avoid paying the pope's exit fee. His pace quickened in anticipation of soon being rid of Gerardo's nagging.

"I have news that might ease your worries," Gerardo said as they approached the chapel. "At least for the moment, Pope John is preoccupied with other matters, including the possibility Queen Jeanne's baby will be a girl. If it is, he'll become entangled in negotiations to name Charles's successor. For the present, your impertinence doesn't rank highest on his list of vital concerns. I've also heard that Pope John is more than a little anxious about reprisals by the emperor if he announces a verdict of heresy against you."

"Nonsense! Louis probably hasn't a clue I exist."

"Far from it; in fact, he already knows from his spies about your battles with the pope. But Pope John has his own spies, so it's safe to assume he knows that the emperor is closely following news of your trial."

Louis the Bavarian was indifferent on theological grounds to breaches of doctrinal purity. But as a politician, the emperor knew that a Franciscan victory on the poverty issue could undermine the Church's influence over secular affairs, further consolidating his own power throughout Christendom. Toward that end, Louis granted protection to such prominent Spiritual Franciscans as Ubertino of Casale and William of Baskerville, artfully deploying their arguments to annoy the French usurper. He was now intent, Gerardo reported, on adding William Occam to his cadre of advisors.

Louis' motives were personal as well as political. He detested the pope—"a consumptive gnome," he had called him on more than one public occasion—for supporting Frederick the Fair, Louis' Habsburg cousin, in their decade-long contest to succeed Henry VII of Luxemburg as Holy Roman Emperor. In 1324, after Louis' election was settled by vote of his fellow Christian monarchs, Pope John refused to ratify the election and then compounded this insult by excommunicating the new emperor. Louis returned the compliment by accusing the *pope* of heresy.

"John is also reluctant to condemn you and Brother Michael without first knowing who will take the French throne," Gerardo continued. "It will most likely be Philip, if only as regent for an infant king, but no one at the palace knows for certain."

"When is Jeanne's baby due?"

"Quite soon," Gerardo said. "Word from Paris should reach here in a matter of days. In the meantime, the pope doesn't know if he can count on Philip's support if the emperor took up arms against him. And he hasn't forgotten that Isabella and Mortimer might try to steal the throne for Edward III. If young Edward became king of *both* England and France, he would probably ally with Louis and try to return the papacy to Rome. Pope John may not have the power to prevent it."

"Power, Gerardo, isn't some sort of essence lying about waiting to be used. You don't *have* power—or not have it. You create it by acting. The cunning old devil knows that as surely as the emperor knows it."

* * *

He was still musing about Gerardo's assessment as he entered the chapel. As usual, Gerardo waited outside the arched entrance so that he might pray in solitude for his Savior's blessing. But today Saint Nicholas's was crowded and annoyingly noisy from the echoing chatter of two Rhône bargemen who had just moored their vessels at the nearby quay.

He was about to rebuke the intruders for violating his retreat's sanctity but held back on overhearing one of the bargemen regale the other: ". . . a pair of fat priests—English, judging from their accents. *Lofty* servants of the Lord, too, with their haughty airs and constant carping about the laggardly pace. Mind you, not that either deigned to lift a pole or tug at an oar. The bigger one said he wouldn't pay a florin if we didn't get a move on. *Mon Dieu*! As if I could speed up the current by barking an order or some such. And the other, the shorter one, forever nattering on about 'urgent business' at the palace."

"Most likely His *Holiness's* distant cousins come beggin' for a cardinal's miter," his companion joked. "I hear he doles 'em out like Communion wafers."

"Hah! Or visiting dignitaries itching to pay their carnal respects to the old sodomite." Both men guffawed at the ribald image of a papal *ménage à trois*.

William's moment of spiritual solace abruptly dissipated on this, the feast day of the martyred Pope Saint Martin. Could the two priests the indignant bargeman complained about be Walter Burley and Richard de Bury? Both were English, both were fat, and both were agents of Queen Isabella and Roger Mortimer. If his hunch was correct, might they have come to Avignon to press Edward III's claim to the French throne? Or could they have come on other business? William pondered these possibilities as he exited the chapel.

He spotted Gerardo leaning against the bridge's balustrade. His apprentice, his friend, was staring at a bank of cumulus clouds that hovered like a giant blue-grey cauliflower low on the northern horizon. He was weeping—over his fractured loyalties or perhaps his *liaison dangereuse*, which the two of them had never spoken about. William now regretted withholding his counsel and sympathy. He had also forgotten, too often, how keenly he prized the bond between them. Gerardo deserved better from him.

He left Gerardo alone a few moments longer, not knowing what to say. He then touched his brother's shoulder, saying quietly, "Perhaps we ought to head back now." His gaze still fixed on the clouds, Gerardo waited before nodding his assent. Neither said anything more as they walked from the chapel toward the guardhouse and, arm in arm, wended their way up the alley.

As they neared the convent, Gerardo nodded a silent adieu and crossed over to the other side of the lane. Thirty yards away Joyeuse stood beneath the awning of a tailor's shop, waiting for Gerardo *there* rather than at Saint Agricola's. This in itself wasn't surprising, for ministering the Sacrament of Penance needn't be restricted to the confines of the confessional booth.

William watched them together, feeling he had intruded on their intimacy. Joyeuse and Gerardo didn't touch, but they didn't need to. As they started to walk down the lane away from the convent, William observed Joyeuse more closely. She looked heavier than when he first saw her six months earlier, and there was also something about the way she walked.

Chapter 25

April 18, 1328 — The Courtyard of the Cathedral of Notre-Dame des Doms

"IF YOU HADN'T HEARD, Queen Jeanne gave birth to another girl—Blanche, after her mother's mother, I believe." John of Reading made the announcement on interrupting his brisk descent of the steps from the piazza. William and Michael of Cesena had just started their upward climb. "The palace is abuzz with news of the blessed event, which took place just over a fortnight ago—on All Fools Day, to be exact."

"Hmph. A fitting testament to the poor child's father," Michael suggested.

"Indeed," Reading laughed, "an assessment I should relish amplifying at length if time permitted. But as usual, I'm running late. Another meeting with the Dominicans, this time to hear their complaints about the library's lending policies. They're keen to borrow some ancient Arab scrolls that will surely crumble into dusty oblivion at the touch of their oily fingers. Before we reconvene, I must craft a polite refusal."

"Godspeed, then, on your delicate mission," Michael said as he bade his colleague adieu. But Reading was already out of earshot as he bounded down the steps. The rheumatism in his knees was not acting up today.

Minutes before their encounter with Reading, William had briefed Michael about the bargeman's harangue he overheard five days earlier. Now, as they strolled across the piazza toward the cathedral, Michael voiced skepticism. "Assuming it *was* de Bury and Burley, how do you explain their early arrival? Obviously, they couldn't have known before they left London that Jeanne's baby would be a girl."

As William mulled over Michael's doubts about the fat priests' identity, he halted on recognizing a familiar stout figure emerge from the cathedral's main entrance. As if materializing from their conversation, Walter Burley was heading in their direction.

They stopped speaking as they watched Burley negotiate the courtyard's cobblestone promenade, his path shaded on either side by rows of groomed cypresses. As he neared the tall poplar tree the two Greyfriars stood beneath, William said, loudly enough for the fat priest to hear, "We might get answers sooner than expected."

Startled by William's familiar voice, Burley jerked his head up and stumbled before regaining his balance.

"Burley!" William exclaimed. "Upon my word, have you been in Avignon long?"

Recovering his composure, Burley replied, "Just recently. And safely, I might note, thanks to our Lord's beneficent protection."

"No doubt an indispensable requirement what with the Rhône's hazardous current." Glancing to his left, William thought he noticed Michael stifling a smile. "I assume you haven't yet made the acquaintance of our Order's revered leader."

"Until the present moment I had been deprived of that signal blessing. Although, Brother Michael," Burley oozed as he turned to face William's companion, "I daresay word of your faithful toil in the Lord's vineyard has spread to every corner of Christendom."

"Hardly the equal of your own," Michael reciprocated. "Which leads me to wonder what vital mission brings you to Avignon."

"I am here as but an insignificant member of His Majesty King Edward's delegation to entreat Pope John to canonize the Earl of Lancaster—the late Lord *Thomas*, that is. Without so much as a trial, as you must recall, the coward Despenser brutally murdered him six years ago, terminating the Earl's valiant struggle against Caernarfon's tyranny. By God's eternal grace, the king showed wisdom and courage belying his brief years by commanding Parliament to reverse Thomas's conviction. Having done that, he now begs the Holy Father's divine sanction of the Earl's martyrdom."[x]

* * *

Burley excused himself minutes later, citing an important matter at the palace that required his counsel. Navigating his way along the promenade, he eyed the cobblestones with caution.

"So, did you believe him?" Michael asked as Burley vanished from view.

"Hmm, yes and no," William replied, pausing to consider his words. "His lavish praise of the late earl was probably meant to hide what he and de Bury are up to. I doubt he'd lie about Lancaster's canonization, but he won't divulge any secrets, either, especially at a chance meeting with a pair of Greyfriars."

"Especially to *you*."

William grinned. "Behind that unctuous smile he appeared to be gritting his teeth."

Michael stood silently for a moment. "But I thought we already knew why they came here: Young Edward wants the French throne and needs Duèze's support to have any chance of getting it. Knowing that, his mother and Mortimer sent Burley and de Bury here to plead Edward's cause."

"Perhaps, but the more I think about it, the more I'm skeptical. Apart from the odd timing of their arrival, how likely is it the pope would risk his standing with the French by supporting Edward's claim? Indeed, why would he even consider it?"

"As I recall," Michael reminded him, "it was you who first raised the possibility. You were quite convinced of it."

"Nothing in the Scriptures forbids me from changing my mind. After hearing what Burley said, I doubt either he or de Bury is clever enough to beguile Duèze with promises or so foolhardy as to try to intimidate him with threats. And young Edward probably wouldn't succeed even *with* the pope's backing. With the throne vacant and the last of the Capets dead, the princes in Paris can resist pressure from Avignon more easily than they once could.

"All of which suggests," William concluded, "that if Edward III does become the king of France, it won't be next month or next year. The reign of *any* English monarch in France would have to follow a protracted war, one that could last a hundred years."

"Then what are they doing here?" Michael asked. But William didn't answer as he retreated into his private thoughts. Perhaps neither explanation told the entire story—perhaps none of it. As he searched for an answer to Michael's question, it occurred to him that it was probably buried in Eleanor's missing letter.

Chapter 26

May 10, 1328 — The Saint Bénézet Bridge

LEPERS APPROACHING THE CITY from the west were permitted to cross the Saint Bénézet Bridge during the morning hours of Monday and Thursday. Other travelers—pilgrims and beggars, merchants and tradesmen, aristocrats, clergy, and prostitutes—could also cross, but many prudently waited until midday for the bridge to clear.

Local monks supervised the crossings, prodding the despised outcasts with long poles to keep them moving in an orderly file alongside the bridge's southern balustrade. Many of the lepers entering Avignon were bound for one of two asylums, or leprosaria, administered by the Order of Saint Benedict. These institutions were located on the city's far outskirts, isolated from the uninfected population. As a condition of taking up residence, new patients took vows of poverty, chastity, and obedience. Flouting them resulted in their immediate expulsion.

Those who kept their vows were treated with the latest remedies and palliatives, consisting chiefly of drinking or bathing in the fresh blood of humans or dogs. One hypothesis held that the blood of virgins could prove especially potent. The supporting evidence was thin, however, owing to difficulties in verifying that immaculate condition. Mysterious reports of cures from Arab lands were also whispered, the most intriguing of which advised vigorously rubbing cobra venom on the skin. Alas, like virgins, the presence of cobras in southern France was also hard to confirm. Over all, morale at the leprosaria was low.[xi]

* * *

The sun shone directly overhead as the last of the day's sad procession passed by the guardhouse at the bridge's Avignon terminus. Toll collectors resumed their stations, bracing for the inevitable haggling over the amounts those entering would have to pay. Many were beggars and pilgrims for whom even a *sou* was too dear a price. A few were averers, tricksters who hid their clothes while posing as robbery victims to cadge money from the gullible and the unsuspecting. Others, with fake boils or tumors stuck on their arms and legs, begged for alms from any who could bear to look at them.

William exited Saint Nicholas's just before noon, having prayed undisturbed beneath the Crucifix of the chapel. He had come there alone, leaving Gerardo behind at the convent to transcribe his latest rebuttal to his accusers. For several minutes he lingered outside the chapel's entrance and watched the passersby, half of them departing Avignon as the others entered the city from the Villeneuve side.

As he watched the streams of travelers, his thoughts turned, as they often did, to Aristotle. The Philosopher was right in reminding that *fortuna*—good luck—was needed for leading a virtuous life. But virtue also obliged the fortunate to admit they hadn't earned or even deserved the gifts nature and circumstance had granted them. Virtue and humility went hand in hand.

William's dour disposition inclined him to brood—more often, he believed, than Aristotle himself—over luck's darker side. Hadn't the sage of Athens known, or cared, that fortune frowned on so many more of God's children than it smiled upon? If only he could witness the souls crossing the Saint Bénézet Bridge: beggars and pilgrims clad in humble attire, vastly outnumbering those wearing silk and furs; the multitudes of tradesmen and artisans trudging laboriously on foot, shoved aside by a privileged few borne in comfort by servants or horses. For each proud, self-satisfied countenance fortune had blessed, he saw a score of the destitute's vacant, downcast stares. Not for the first time he was annoyed by Aristotle's sunny disregard for the many—the unlucky.

William accepted without envy or bitterness what fortune had granted him. He took idle pleasure in imagining how his life might have turned out differently. Had his mother not serenaded him with songs of God's mercy and Father Julian not pressed him to leave Occam for London, he might have ended up a husband and father, a farmer or a merchant or a blacksmith, even the knight of his youthful fantasy. Mindful of fortune's vagaries, William wondered what other fates might have befallen those who now passed by him.

A diminutive Carmelite postulant trailed after a group of older nuns as they proceeded westward toward Villeneuve-lès-Avignon. About fifteen, she appeared timid and modest, but William sensed in her serene expression a profound trust the Lord would protect her from harm.

As his imagination wandered, he saw the girl instead as a novice lady-in-waiting to a queen. She was one of Eleanor's daughters, preparing for a life of genteel servitude. As she gained experience in the ways of the royal court, she would become adept at negotiating its intrigues and wheedling favors from her mistress. In her eighteenth year she would marry a knight, the second son of a wealthy earl, by whom she would bear seven children.

A strapping stonemason approaching middle age toted a large rucksack filled with the tools of his trade: mallets and chisels of odd shapes and sizes, a trowel, and maybe a punch hammer or two. Had he come to Avignon hoping to build a great new cathedral, or were his aspirations humbler—to carve inscriptions, say, on the headstones of the recently departed? His small brown eyes darted about as if on the lookout for footpads poised to steal the means of his livelihood.

Or was he himself a thief, fearful that his victim had tracked him down to kill him and take back his tools? Tomorrow morning would his battered corpse float at the nearby quay, discovered by a river boatman still hung over from last evening's drunken spree?

With two younger, similarly clad women, a prostitute now past her prime marched toward the guardhouse. Her chin was held high in defiance of those who would judge her. She wore a black and white pointed cap and a yellow dress as prescribed by the sumptuary laws requiring her to identify her profession by the clothes she wore. Along with her companions she was probably bound for the southern periphery of the Exchange where bankers, merchants, and an occasional priest, monk, or friar would seek out her officially forbidden favors.

In his mind's eye William washed away the pink rouge that covered her cheeks, exposing the ruddy complexion of his sister's face—of Matilda, whom he hadn't seen in thirty years. The garish yellow dress dissolved into a modest shift made of coarse linen covered by a woolen tunic to keep her warm and dry during the damp English spring. The two younger women were her daughters who, with their mother, were on their way to market to sell the candles they had made. All three were widows, sharing the cottage where William was born.

As he shifted his gaze from the prostitutes passing from view, he noticed a tall, lanky man about his own age easing past the chapel. The man was clad in beggar's rags, and his long, curled locks were matted with sweat and grime. Their eyes met for just a few seconds before the man turned away, looking straight ahead in the direction of the toll collectors' stations. Was he destined for the Exchange to scavenge food and drink from obliging, or careless, street vendors? Or, might he be a leper in search of the mysterious Avignon priest rumored to possess the divine power to cure his malady? Perhaps he was a poor pilgrim, nearing the end of his sojourn to seek the pope's blessing.

As the tall man blended in with the crowd of other travelers, William recalled that his softly feminine blue eyes had shone with fierce intensity, as if daring anyone to stand in his way. He strode with his shoulders confidently thrown back, befitting someone accustomed to wielding power. These impressions evoked a story of the man's mission altogether different from those William first imagined. He then remembered Eleanor's warning that Mortimer had sent his agents to Avignon—one of them, perhaps, disguised in the rags of a beggar, a leper, or a poor pilgrim.

But these were mere flights of fancy William had conjured up to keep his mind off his troubles.

Chapter 27

May 13, 1328 — Greyfriars Convent

HAT WAS KEEPING GERARDO? He should have returned from the chandlery with the fresh supply of candles he had asked for. As the heavy rain pounded the convent's porous roof, William relit the stubby remnant of one candle with the dying flame of another. He was afraid both would flicker out in the draft from the cracked window above him.

Progress on his rebuttal to the commission had been slow even in the best of light and was now slowed even more by nearby distractions. He silently cursed on overhearing two of his elder brethren offer inane advice to the convent's best illuminator on his rendering of Reynard, the sly and vengeful fox of the local folklore.

"Reynard looks too benign," the first friar opined while scratching his chin's greying stubble.

"Indeed," his associate agreed, "perhaps an arched brow would make him more sinister."

They had nothing better to do, which offended William's firm belief in the virtue of hard work. Besides, the young artist needed no assistance. Earlier in the day William admired the graceful sketch of a tiny unicorn that, with the fox and two other exotic beasts already drawn and brilliantly colored, would adorn the margins of a sheet of the convent's finest vellum. A copyist would later inscribe on it a fable inspired by one of the gospels. William preferred the artwork to a silly fable.

He had other reasons to feel annoyed. Some were petty, stemming from flaws in his temperament. Not the least of these was his stubborn refusal to concede that even he, Doctor Invincibilis, could occasionally be wrong. Other annoyances he could rightfully blame on assorted punishments nature had meted out to him: his cursed limp, for one, and now his failing eyesight. Noise irked him too—at the moment, the nattering voices of the younger friars and novitiates echoing in the convent's scriptorium where William perched on his stool. They had assembled a few feet from his desk, having put away their quills, sealed their inkpots, and covered the folios they had labored over throughout the day. The bell had rung for Compline, the last of the day's holy offices, but no one was eager to join the rainy procession. William considered complaining to Abbé Thierry (yet again) but held his tongue lest he appear more querulous than usual.

Voices suddenly reverberated up to the scriptorium from the floor below.

"It can't be!"

"On the steps?"

"God in Heaven! One of us?"

Their smiles had turned to puzzled frowns. First one, then two more friars sprinted toward the stairway. They were followed by others scrambling to the ground level, their sandals clopping on the floor's creaking planks. William heard more cries of alarm as the scriptorium emptied out.

He cast his spectacles aside, knocking over his inkpot. He cursed again as precious black fluid washed over his parchment and obliterated his latest argument. Rather than stopping to clean up the mess, he slid from his stool and hobbled to the lower floor, trailing after his brothers into the lane leading to the piazza steps. Twice he stumbled and had to be steadied by one of the younger friars.

A gust blew his hood from atop his head. Bending into the wind, he felt the heavy rain spatter his face and wash away accumulated sweat; he needed a bath. Low-hanging clouds partially obscured the cathedral, which loomed a quarter-mile beyond the top of the steps. Now silent, its ugly bell tower emitted a faint glow. As he trudged along the crowded lane, a score of more agile friars and monks whisked by him, their feet splashing through the puddles of rainwater and soaking the bottom of his habit.

He jostled with the others for purchase on an iron railing as he climbed the piazza steps. No one begged his pardon or greeted him with a customary "Hail Fellow" or "May the Lord be with you" as they cut in ahead of him. Nor did William offer salutations, as his curiosity was mixed with foreboding.

At the steps' midpoint he was gasping for breath. More than a dozen robed figures, some in grey habits and some in black, pushed and shoved for a clearer view of an outstretched form sprawled halfway up the piazza steps.

Unable to see through the crowded assembly, William glanced to his right toward a narrow passageway, which, he recalled, led to the cistern containing the palace's water supply. Usually blocked to discourage intruders, the entrance was open. A grim-faced uniformed guard emerged, his voice shaking as he informed an associate: "A lot of blood in there!"

A blue-liveried official of the Avignon constabulary and a crimson-clad officer of the papal guard arrived, each demanding in an authoritative voice: "Make way in the name of" his particular jurisdiction. Both wore the plumage of superior rank, and William predicted that control of the investigation would soon be disputed. Three priests descended the steps, carrying torches that flickered precariously in the diminishing rain. The priests were soon ordered to withdraw. As they pulled back, William's eyes adjusted to the faint light of their torches. Then he felt his knees buckle and uttered a silent gasp. It was Gerardo. The young friar—his friend—lay on his back, arms and legs splayed at odd angles, his chin canted upward as if he were craning to admire a lone nighthawk wheeling overhead. Partly covered by the hood of his grey habit, his face seemed frozen in cheerful surprise. A score of new beeswax candles formed a crude semicircle on the steps below him.

* * *

"Blood on the grip," the senior Avignon constable announced as he inspected the staff lying next to Gerardo's body. "Probably the victim's."

"More likely the killer's," the pope's guard countered, signaling his refusal to cede authority to the French Crown. "See, blood here on his tunic but none on his palms. By the looks of it, the poor devil tried to defend himself." He poked delicately with his quarterstaff to lift Gerardo's scapular from his midsection. At the center of his blood-soaked tunic was a gash, and then another, barely visible in the coarse woolen fabric.

As the guards and constables gathered evidence and prepared Gerardo's body for removal, William retreated to a small alcove across from the entrance to the passageway. His hands shook as he wiped raindrops from his bare head. He forced himself to inhale and exhale deeply.

His shaking eased and he surveyed the scene in front of him. A young palace priest and an old friar from the convent knelt near Gerardo's body, offering prayers for the safety of his soul. In the distance William heard one of his brothers—it sounded like Marcel, the Greyfriars' cellarer—chanting the trochaic meter of *Dies irae*: the sacred poem of the Last Judgment in which a trumpet summons the souls of the dead before God's throne. William grimaced on recalling the parodies he secretly composed in his youth to mock the poem's stilted cadences.

Prayers and chants echoed against the walled stairway as a feral white cat darted across the crime scene's perimeter. The cat slowed, prowling around Gerardo's body and sniffing the moist air for clues. It then stopped, crouching on thin haunches to inspect the staff until a guard shooed it away. The startled animal fled down the steps, leaving in its wake a trail of red paw prints that quickly dissolved in the drizzle. As he watched the cat disappear, William imagined Gerardo rising, gathering up his candles, and materializing back at the convent, his errand completed.

On the crowded steps below, Michael of Cesena huddled with two of the pope's guards. Despite his short and wiry stature, Michael's crisp, resonant voice and imperious bearing ratified his authority. As the Greyfriars' minister general, he still commanded the guards' courtesy and deference—even though his own perils were equal to William's. He barked rebukes that cowed the guards into submission as if it were their fault that Gerardo was dead.

The blustery wind obscured their voices, but William assumed the guards were briefing Michael on the murder. After dismissing them, Michael was scowling when he caught sight of William, who was still partly concealed in the alcove.

"Useless, both of them," Michael muttered as he approached.

For a moment William stood motionless, gazing blankly at the candles arrayed on the steps. He felt irked by Michael's failure to offer even a terse condolence.

"You learned nothing?" he then asked as he turned toward Michael.

"Hardly a clue." The inquiring tilt of Michael's chin suggested that William must know something that he didn't.

"I wasn't his confessor!"

"Come now, William. You knew him better than anyone."

"Perhaps he had the wretched luck to cross paths with a footpad," William offered without conviction. "They're more brazen by the day."

"Unlikely. Except for a few candles he had nothing to steal," Michael said as he glanced in the direction of Gerardo's body. One of the guards was on hands and knees probing the area for evidence while another conferred with his superior. Lowering his voice: "Probably an assassin. One of the pope's henchmen, I should think."

"But why Gerardo? And why now?"

"Popes need little provocation for murder. Surely you know that."

"Yes, but in public view," William said with a harsh laugh. "What surer way to inspire awe among the faithful?"

William didn't discount Michael's suspicion, but Gerardo's ties to the palace made him vulnerable from other quarters, including some of the friars from his own order. "Gerardo didn't exactly endear himself to all of the brotherhood."

Michael arched a skeptical eyebrow. "One of *us*?"

"Not all of us share Francis's vision," William said as he looked sharply at Michael. The minister general's own conversion had been belated and reluctant, a contentious issue William decided not to mention.

"Even so, those Pharisees[xii] who sell their souls for a prebend would faint at the mere thought of bloodshed."

William's silence conceded Michael's point. After pausing, he said, "If you're right in assuming Duèze gave the order, might it have been to implicate *me*?"

Michael gave him a puzzled look. "I can't see what he would gain by it."

"Murderers make unconvincing martyrs. What more convenient way for the cunning bastard to rid himself of a nuisance!"

Michael was still dubious. "Why should he care? His *Holiness* answers only to God—or so he says. This isn't Athens!"

Indeed not! As William withdrew into his thoughts, Michael was recalled for questioning by the plumaged officer of the papal guard. From the orders he snapped to his crimson-uniformed subordinates, the stout, square-jawed officer appeared to have taken control of the investigation. The palace was in charge.

* * *

William needed time and space to think and decided to return to the convent. The rain had stopped and the clouds had parted just enough to expose an almost-full moon. Fighting back fatigue, he paused to rest on an unoccupied step, propping his elbows on his knees and clasping his hands beneath his chin as he stared into the distance. The storm had purged the stench of sewage, rubbish, offal, and rotting fish from Avignon's skies, and he breathed in the honeyed scent of wisteria entwined in the arched trellis above him. He scarcely noticed the priests, friars, guards, and constables who passed by him.

Minutes later his thoughts were interrupted by stretcher-bearers carrying Gerardo's body down the steps. He edged to one side to clear a path for them. As Saint Francis had instructed, Gerardo's arms were folded across his breast beneath a white linen shroud. A dozen of his brothers trailed behind in double file, some of them shielding their candles' flames from the slight breeze. William heard one of them—it was Marcel again—intone the final stanza of *Dies irae* as the others keened and wept. The cat perched atop the wall above him—a scrawny white sentinel overseeing Gerardo's transport to the morgue.

As the procession passed, William rose to follow his brothers. When he grasped the railing to join in Gerardo's last journey, he was distracted by the sound of clanking metal. He turned and saw two guards peering down at him from the steps above, the same guards who questioned Michael of Cesena earlier. One carried leg irons and the other, handcuffs.

They had come for him.

Chapter 28

May 13, 1328—The Prison of the Papal Palace

IS WRISTS AND ANKLES chafed against iron shackles as the two guards marched him up the steps toward the palace. He looked about for someone—Michael, Francesco, Reading, even Durand—to protest that his arrest was a preposterous mistake. God in heaven! Gerardo was his *friend*!

The stares of onlookers became a blur as the guards roughly led him across the piazza and then down a steep incline to the rear, north side of the huge rectangular building. At ground level, twenty feet below the palace's main floor, they reached a small gate. Sentries stood at either side, indifferent to the new prisoner's arrival. The shorter of the two guards fumbled with his keys before unlocking a gate behind which was a bolted door. As locks clicked and bolts scraped open, he turned and saw, through a stand of cypress trees, refracted moonlight winking at him from the river's choppy surface. Might the Rhône, rather than the Thames, be his last view of freedom?

Since arriving in Avignon four years earlier William had heard whispers of the small prison concealed somewhere in the palace's nether regions. He knew nothing about it from first-hand accounts, so he could only imagine the configuration of its cells and interrogation chambers. In his grim fantasy he saw instruments of torture for extracting confessions, or perhaps pleas for mercy. And what of the pope's laboratory hidden somewhere in the palace basement? At this moment might Duèze be conducting experiments to turn lead into gold, despite having banned the practice of alchemy years before?

Shoved through the entrance, William found himself in an anteroom about twenty-five-feet square, surrounded by a dozen, perhaps fifteen small cells. Most of their doors were open, allowing the prisoners to move about. A few of them talked quietly while a sergeant-at-arms lounged at a small desk, thumbing through what appeared to be a ledger.

His worst fears eased. No torture devices were visible, and he heard no cries of pain or sobs of anguish. His new quarters, in fact, reminded him of the ground floor of the Franciscan convent where the friars slept. The sergeant at the desk pointed toward a corner cell. After removing his handcuffs and the leg irons from his bloodied ankles, the guards disappeared through the gate. William stood by the entrance to his cell, unsure what to do next. The sergeant at the desk ignored his questions, and no one was there to interrogate him. The six or seven other prisoners in the anteroom also ignored him.

The torches lighting the anteroom provided just enough illumination to see inside his cell. A straw-filled paillasse in one corner would serve as his bed. In the opposite corner a chamber pot reeked of human waste. Outside the cell's door stood a communal barrel of drinking water, apparently monitored by the sergeant. Maybe that was the purpose of his ledger.

William was hungry; he had eaten nothing since his late-morning meal hours earlier. Prisoners relied on friends or family for food, and he wondered if anyone would bring him something. But it was too soon to expect friendly visitors, although he imagined Gerardo, fretting over his mentor's welfare, striding through the prison's entrance with a pot of hot porridge and a jug of the Dominicans' fine Burgundy. As that pleasant thought receded, the shock over his young friend's death returned, soon to be replaced by an overwhelming sadness. Perhaps sleep could banish his grief, or hold it at bay until morning, so he entered his cell and lay down on the paillasse, which barely insulated him from the cold stone floor.

He awoke a few hours later—or was it only minutes?—confused by the shifting images that lingered: the bloodied staff at Gerardo's side; the feminine blue eyes of the tall man on the bridge; Baskerville and Saint Augustine scolding him; a malevolent John XXII, like Boniface before him, brandishing a pair of swords.

Chapter 29

May 14, 1328 — The Palace Prison

"THE STAFF WAS MINE," William said the next morning as he wolfed down the bread and cheese Michael of Cesena brought him.

"What staff?"

"On the steps, next to Gerardo's body. There was blood on the grip."

"Gerardo's?"

"More likely his killer's," William said. "I overheard the guard say he doubted it was Gerardo's."

"But what was he doing with your staff?"

"He fell and turned an ankle on his return to the convent after Vespers. He had errands to run and asked if he could borrow it. I wasn't going anywhere and told him to take it."

"So when the guards learned the staff was yours, they assumed you killed him? That's absurd! Any number of friars can swear you were in the scriptorium."

"They know by now I *couldn't* have killed him. But it's clear I was arrested at the 'suggestion' of someone at the palace. My staff gave them a convenient pretext."

"Which brings us back to the question: Why was Gerardo killed?"

"The possibilities we spoke of earlier. One, to stop him from feeding me information that could jeopardize the heresy case. It was no secret to Fieschi that Gerardo had converted early on. Quite obviously, that would compromise his role as the pope's informant."

"Surely you're not suggesting Fieschi was complicit in his nephew's murder," Michael said. He had lowered his voice on noticing one of the guards refilling the barrel of drinking water.

"Of course not. But events may have spun out of his control. No doubt Fieschi is mortified and furious. In fact, he may fear for his safety."

"If not Fieschi, then *who*? One of the commissioners —Lutterell maybe?"

William shook his head. "Lutterell couldn't have given the order or even been in a position to suggest it. He may be gloating over my arrest, but he has no influence with the pope or anyone else at the palace. They regard him as a joke. And the notion that any of the others on the commission might be involved is almost as far-fetched. Which leaves us with the second explanation."

"You mean, Gerardo was killed to frame you for murder afterward?" Michael asked. "I'm as skeptical now as I was last evening."

"Even so, removing me by 'unofficial' means could make sense if Duèze hoped to avoid a public announcement of the heresy verdict. We both know the problems *that* could cause him with the emperor."

"But Duèze's people would have to contrive a motive for your killing Gerardo," Michael said. He again nervously eyed the cell's door but saw no one near enough to overhear them.

"That would be easy—say, by insinuating some sort of rift between us: that I knew or suspected Gerardo's loyalties had swung back to the pope *or* I discovered his deceit in feigning loyalty to the Spirituals."

"Would anyone believe it?"

"No one would have to believe it. For official purposes any excuse would do."

"But even if that motive, or any alleged motive, were credible, the fact that multiple witnesses can place you at the convent proves your innocence."

"True, but it doesn't prove that framing me wasn't the reason for Gerardo's murder. It could mean that the killer, or killers, simply bungled the job."

"Bungled indeed!" Michael said. "Even the shoddiest plan would have accounted for your whereabouts before the attack. Could the assassin, or his masters, be so stupid as not to have thought of that? And the most meticulous plan couldn't have anticipated that Gerardo would be carrying your staff. You said you gave it to him just before he was killed."

William exhaled audibly, shaking his head.

"I'm surprised you haven't mentioned Burley and de Bury," Michael said. "They've been in Avignon long enough to arrange it."

"Not that I haven't considered them both. But I can't see what connection either of them could have with my trial."

"Burley and Lutterell are longtime allies. I believe you said so yourself."

"But assuming Burley wanted to cause mischief, he couldn't count on any help from Lutterell—for the reasons I gave you. Any part he may have played must have required the aid of someone else."

"De Bury?"

"Less likely even than Lutterell," William shrugged. "De Bury has nothing against me, at least nothing I know of."

Michael sighed and then tried to reassure him. "We still don't know who killed Gerardo, but surely no one can now question your innocence."

The shuffling of feet outside the cell and the guards hovering nearby signaled that Michael had overstayed his visiting privileges. He rose and said loudly enough for the guard could hear, "But first we need to get you out of this pisspot." He made ready to leave, promising to bring fresh provisions of food and drink.

The sergeant-at-arms unlocked the prison's entrance and showed Michael out. As the gate slammed shut, William mused over a faint suspicion, a mere flicker of intuition, he had kept to himself: Gerardo's murder might have nothing to do with his trial. Perhaps it was the sword of the Kingdom, not of the Church, that hovered over him.

Chapter 30

May 17, 1328 — The Palace Prison and the Bank of the Rhône

NEW FIGURES INVADED William's dreams as old ones left. By his final night of captivity the pope had vanished, relinquishing his swords to barons and kings. The soon-to-be-anointed King Philip VI brandished one sword, and Isabella's consort, Roger Mortimer, wielded another. A third sword belonged to Edward II's shrouded corpse. Completing the quartet, the emperor of Christendom held the sharpest weapon of all. Each vied for the honor, perhaps the pleasure, of skewering the meddlesome heretic.

The heretic was granted a reprieve when the swordsmen turned on one another. He stood immobile in their midst as the slashing blades of kingdoms sprayed plumes of blood on his tunic. Or was the tunic someone else's?

Atop a throne safely above the fray an ermine-robed youth watched with amused interest. He was content to wait, indifferent to who won or lost in the mayhem raging at his feet.

Off in the distance loomed the scolds. Baskerville and Augustine had retreated, replaced by two women hectoring the heretic to do something. The deafening clash of steel obliterated the sound of their voices.

A thin, Janus-like figure appeared, disappeared, and then reappeared. One of his faces spewed a stream of invective at the heretic while his other face wept tears of sorrow and sympathy. He was both enemy and friend. But might the same also be said of the others?

William awoke and the cobwebs of his mind cleared. He knew why Gerardo had been slain.

He stumbled from his cell into the prison's anteroom, hoping Michael of Cesena, whom he hadn't seen for three days, had come to take him out. In his stead he had sent a young friar from the convent to bring him food, along with his regrets. William hadn't minded Michael's absence. The minister general had his own tasks to attend to, and whatever it was that consumed Michael's attention would affect him too. But now they needed to talk.

Inmates shuffled about the anteroom, some of them assisting the guards in relighting the torches that had died during the night. It was the only visible sign morning had come in the windowless depths of the pope's small prison. The place continued to reek of human waste, sweat, and tallow, and William wondered if the guards who worked there received extra pay for tolerating the stench.

An hour passed before he heard someone issuing instructions to the guards. The main door to the prison creaked open and then shut, followed by several minutes of silence broken by the muffled voices of other prisoners. Moments later the sergeant-at-arms approached the entrance to his cell. "You're free to go," he said. "Someone's waiting for you outside."

William scanned the cell for possessions to gather up and then realized he had none. He turned and walked toward the opened gate, his pace quickening at the thought the sergeant might change his mind. But the sergeant didn't look up as he made another notation in his ledger.

Squinting into the glare of the mid-morning sunlight, William looked about for Michael to escort him to the safety of the convent. Instead, Manuele Fieschi emerged from the stand of cypresses a few paces from the entrance. Taut lines around his mouth and bloodshot eyes marred his usual aplomb. He looked tired and anxious, even afraid.

Close behind him was the chubby figure of King Edward III's tutor, Richard de Bury. De Bury was heavier but otherwise in better condition than when William saw him two years before, bloodied and battered, at the infirmary. Unlike the worried Fieschi, de Bury's mien was calm, even benign, though William didn't know him well enough to tell if it was merely an affectation honed during his years at the Westminster court.

William's surprise at seeing Fieschi and de Bury together gave way to uncertainty about what to say. Should he protest to Fieschi his innocence of Gerardo's murder, or should he offer his condolences? Suspecting that Fieschi would doubt his sincerity in either case, William held his tongue and waited for Fieschi to speak.

"I'm not at liberty to disclose all the investigators know," Fieschi said after nodding his acknowledgment of William's presence. "I can tell you only that several leads are being pursued. But you may put your mind at ease; it was soon clear you had neither 'opportunity nor motive,' as the constables might say."

"Then *disclose*, if you can, whose idea it was to arrest me and why I was kept in there for four days," he said, gesturing toward the prison's entrance.

"Your release was delayed for various reasons," Fieschi replied, "including considerations of safety."

William saw no point is pressing for an answer to his question. Fieschi was in no position, or perhaps in no mood, to confide his accuser's name. The pope's "messenger," as he called himself when they first met in London, artfully divulged trivial confidences while revealing nothing that might weaken his hand.

"Our interests, Brother Occam, are one and the same. Each of us wants to see my nephew's killer brought to justice. Father de Bury," he said, nodding toward his associate, "has agreed to aid me in that effort."

"No doubt to provide a disinterested viewpoint," William said dryly.

"Nothing of the sort," de Bury said, speaking for the first time. "I offered to assist out of belated gratitude to Brother Gerardo. I don't know if he told you at the time, but after the attempt on my life, he assisted me in countless ways during my recovery. Helping to find and punish his killer is the least I can do to repay his kindness."

Both men were lying, and William assumed they knew that *he* knew. De Bury's explanation sounded contrived and rehearsed, and Fieschi was, well, Fieschi.

As if impatient to move beyond preliminaries, Fieschi asked, "To begin with the obvious question, why should anyone have wanted to kill Gerardo?"

"Because of *me*! You know that as well as I do."

"Perhaps so, but that begs my question. In view of your penchant for creating enemies, your association with Gerardo expands the range of possible killers."

"Don't expect an apology. I didn't ask to come here. I was quite content to remain in England."

"Be that as it may," Fieschi said, "we can agree, I believe, on the need to identify what harm Gerardo's murder might cause you and then discover who could have carried it out. I assume in your own mind you've already eliminated the commission." William nodded but saw no need to elaborate. "But what of others, either here in Avignon or abroad—someone having no interest in your trial? The city is awash with foreign visitors in the aftermath of King Charles's death. Might letters you've received provide a clue?"

"I'm surprised by your question," William laughed sharply. "As a humble preacher of the Lord's gospel, I don't participate in court intrigues and I'm seldom invited into the company of those who do. The only recent exception," William said snidely as he turned back to de Bury, "is your friend Burley. Maybe *he* did it."

"Burley's a fool!" de Bury snapped.

"I believe Father de Bury means that you needn't worry about Walter Burley," Fieschi interrupted. "His fortunes, which he is ever keen to promote, depend entirely on others. We're better advised to look elsewhere—at news, perhaps, you may have gleaned from sources outside Avignon."

"That would take time. And at the moment I have more urgent matters to contend with. The imminent announcement of 'His Holiness's' verdict springs to mind."

"The wheels of the curia turn slowly," Fieschi said as if to soothe William's fears. "In the meantime, I urge you to be cautious. Gerardo's killer may not have completed his mission. And might I advise you to leave the investigation in more experienced hands?"

"I'll consider it."

Fieschi's interrogation continued for several more minutes, prodding William to speculate about possible suspects and their motives. Fieschi affected a tone of grave curiosity, but William sensed he wasn't entirely serious. De Bury kept silent. As their meeting ended, William puzzled over why it had taken place at all.

Fieschi and de Bury walked northward toward the cathedral. When they halted in the shade of a large cypress, their conversation became animated. They were too far away for William to hear, but he could see that de Bury did most of the talking. By his openhanded gestures he seemed to reassure Fieschi about something. Fieschi eventually shrugged his shoulders, and de Bury walked alone back toward William.

De Bury measured his words: "I'm quite aware you have little reason to accept the truth of what I have to say, or even to grasp its full meaning. That said, you might profit from knowing I serve only Edward, England's rightful king and the loving son of his father. Unlike others in Avignon, my loyalties are undivided. So neither you nor Cesena has anything to fear from me so long as you confine your attention to your tribulations before the commission. You would be wise to bear that in mind as you decide what to do next." Before William could think of a response, de Bury turned and walked back to rejoin the waiting Fieschi.

William stood outside the prison gate for a few moments before slowly heading off in the opposite direction. Without his staff, climbing the steep incline next to the palace's western wall was difficult. As he neared the cook's entrance, he saw three Benedictine nuns emerge, each carrying an empty wicker basket. They had delivered their daily supply of eggs from the poultry farm at the river's edge, downstream from the Saint Bénézet Bridge. Perhaps the same sisters who rescued Richard de Bury more than two years earlier.

As the nuns disappeared into a nearby alley, William saw Michael hurrying toward him. He carried a slender loaf of bread in one hand and an unfamiliar staff in the other.

* * *

As they walked, William gnawed at the loaf of bread Michael had brought. The odor of the pope's prison had dampened his appetite, so he ate little during his stay there. The familiar stench of Avignon's atmosphere, however, was hardly an improvement. The relief brought by the powerful storm on the evening of Gerardo's murder had not lasted.

After crossing the crowded piazza and descending the steps, they passed by the infirmary where Gerardo's body had been taken. William detected a faint aroma of incense mingled with the pungent herbs in the infirmary's garden. The incense reminded him that his friend's burial in the convent's small cemetery had proceeded without him. The herbalists and their customers were busily engaged in their ordinary business, oblivious to William's loss. He felt resentful; like him, they ought to be in mourning.

Just beyond the infirmary they turned right to the steep path that would take them toward the bridge. Before reaching the toll collectors at the Avignon terminus, they headed south along the river's bank, a hundred yards beyond the Benedictines' poultry farm. There they would find some privacy and perhaps a refreshing breeze off the Rhône. But on their arrival the river's surface was smooth as glass and the listless current floated barges and debris from the spring rains slowly toward the sea.

Still sorting his thoughts about his puzzling encounter with Fieschi and de Bury, William recounted jumbled fragments.

"Start again," Michael interrupted. "I'm still not clear what they wanted from you."

"Neither am I, not entirely. But I suspect Fieschi's interrogating me was a cover for something else."

"What, that the palace already knows who killed Gerardo?

"Possibly," William said. "And if they do, Fieschi may have wanted to know if *I* knew."

"And de Bury's reasons for joining him?"

William took another bite of the bread, his appetite now fully returned. "I don't know. Although it may be significant that he volunteered that he served only young King Edward. I assume he was telling the truth, but I wonder why he chose to tell me. Obviously, it has something to do with why he came to Avignon."

"Which we still don't know."

"Whatever de Bury's reason, I suspect it was different than Burley's," William said. "When he called Burley a fool, he seemed to mean it. If so, he wasn't trying to shield Burley from suspicion; he was just discounting him as harmless."

Michael paused to gather his thoughts, then asked, "I should have asked earlier, but did you learn why you were arrested and held for four days?"

"Not really. When I asked him, Fieschi was his usual evasive self: 'For considerations of safety' I believe were his words. He didn't say *whose* safety."

"I assume, then, the meeting ended without their learning anything useful from you." Michael munched on a chunk of bread. As William pondered his reply, they watched the crew of a river barge trying to dislodge their vessel from a nearby sandbar. The pilot cursed loud encouragement.

"I can't be sure. I may have revealed something inadvertently. Although it occurs to me that their chief aim may not have been to interrogate me but to give advice. More than once Fieschi urged me—both of us in fact—to be cautious. Then, when I spoke with de Bury alone, he advised me not to pry further into Gerardo's murder. At first I assumed they were both making delicately worded threats. But later they felt more like friendly warnings and in Fieschi's case a reassurance, as if he wanted to protect us."

"From what?"

"True to form, he wouldn't say. Fieschi's power, I've learned, stems from sustaining ambiguity, sending mixed messages to keep his opponent off balance. But it's significant, I think, that he told me not to be concerned about the timing of the pope's announcement of a heresy verdict."

"I suppose he didn't tell you why."

William shook his head and stared at the barge stuck on the sandbar.

For almost a minute Michael was quiet and then asked, "So you learned nothing about *who* killed Gerardo. But did either Fieschi or de Bury reveal anything about *why* someone—anyone—wanted to kill him?"

William paused before answering. "No one did."

"I don't understand."

"No one wanted to kill Gerardo. *I* was the target! The killer mistook Gerardo for me."

Michael sputtered in protest, but William cut him off. "Because of his ankle sprain Gerardo walked with a limp much like mine, which explains why he had my staff. Except for one or two of our frail elders, I'm the only friar who carries one. We're also of similar stature and wore identical habits. The sun had set, and Gerardo pulled his hood over his head for protection against the rain. So the killer couldn't see his face unless he looked directly, *frontally*, at him at close range. An assassin would almost certainly come at his victim from behind. He could have followed Gerardo for several minutes, perhaps longer, mistaking him for me."

"But," Michael objected, "Gerardo could have been the target for the reasons we discussed before your arrest."

"I told you. Gerardo wasn't important in the larger scheme of things."

"But why would anyone risk killing you, especially now? You were already in danger *before* Gerardo was murdered. We both were, and still are. So if someone wanted you dead, why wouldn't he, or *they*, wait a few more days for the pope's executioners to do the deed in public view?"

"Possibly because Duèze wants to dispose of both of us quietly and discreetly. Remember, no verdict has been issued, and we still don't know why Duèze hasn't announced it."

"But how do you square that with what you said earlier about Fieschi's wanting to protect us—unless of course Fieschi is trying to undercut the pope?"

William made no reply but shook his head in puzzlement.

There was little more to discuss, at least for the present, so the two friars rose to begin their hike back to the convent. They felt a sudden, cooling breeze off the Rhône and heard cheers from the barge's crew, who had freed their vessel from the sandbar.

Chapter 31

May 18, 1328 — Greyfriars Convent

ABBÉ THIERRY WAS ESPECIALLY solicitous toward John of Reading. Like many who abused their authority with underlings, Thierry was obsequious toward his superiors and anyone else who could advance his interests. The latter category included Reading, who indulged Thierry's cloying admiration for his latest accomplishment. Or, Thierry would ask his advice on matters of small consequence, advice the astute Reading knew full well the abbot would ignore.

Reading was trapped in yet another trifling conversation with the abbot. Peering sideways from his perch at his desk, William saw Reading glance in his direction, his eyes widened as if imploring William to come to his rescue. William returned his glance with a faint smile and a slight shrug signaling there was really nothing he could do. Still, he wanted to speak with Reading, whom he had not seen since his arrest five days earlier.

Reading finally extracted himself from Thierry's clutches when another friar interrupted to seek the abbot's advice on a housekeeping matter. He slipped away and gestured for William to follow him toward the stairway. William slid from his stool but returned briefly to his desk, having forgotten to leave his spectacles there. Thierry watched them leave.

They exited the convent's rear door, through the vegetable garden and into the Greyfriars' cemetery. Michael was there, gazing at a row of white stone crosses before he turned to face them. The cross at the end of the row marked Gerardo's grave.

Reading got quickly to the point: "After hearing what you told Michael after your release, I must say you're lucky to be alive, though I'm appalled it had to be at Gerardo's expense."

This was the closest Reading would come to a heartfelt condolence, so William simply nodded his acknowledgment. He wanted to hear the well-connected Reading's opinions about Gerardo's murder, but Reading had more questions than opinions.

"Is it possible the pope had nothing to do with it?" he asked. "If he didn't, that could direct suspicion toward Burley and de Bury."

"I told Michael I doubted they could have done it. Can you imagine either of them lurking in a rainy passageway with a dagger?"

"Probably not, but they could have procured the assassin. Burley, especially, might have set aside his scruples to avenge the drubbing you gave him in Paris."

"Unlikely," William said, shaking his head. "If I were killed, he couldn't gloat over my humiliation before the commission. Besides, if he were so much as suspected of complicity in a murder, he could jeopardize his standing at the palace. I'm convinced Burley came to Avignon to ingratiate himself with the pope, probably angling for a cardinal's miter. Serving Mortimer and Isabella is a means to that end."

"Assuming you *were* the intended victim," Reading asked, "does Fieschi know that? If he does, he must have wanted answers to different questions than you've assumed. His interrogation would have had another purpose."

"Possibly," William reflected, "but he may still not know the assassin's motives. He probably suspects, too, that Gerardo's killer is still at large, perhaps here in Avignon. That could explain why he appeared so worried."

"Which brings us back to how Fieschi's and de Bury's interests coincide," Michael said.

William pondered this possibility. "Or whether de Bury has some sort of hold over Fieschi. That could also explain Fieschi's agitation."

William looked expectantly toward Reading, hoping he could shed insights gleaned from his cronies at the palace; but Reading shook his head.

"So we know nothing more about the killer now than we did earlier," Michael said, exasperated.

"I wish I could be more helpful," Reading said. "I can only suggest that you take Fieschi's advice and not travel about alone or leave the convent after dark."

"Sensible advice for both of us," William agreed as he eyed Michael. "It could have been *you* lying dead on the piazza steps."

* * *

Reading left, explaining that business at the palace required his attention—new purchases for the library's collection. William felt dissatisfied with their conversation and was not unhappy to see him go. In addition to Reading's failing to provide any useful information, he seemed too eager to deflect suspicion from Duèze or anyone else at the palace.

Michael sat on a bench next to the row of white crosses, trying to shoo away a pigeon roosting atop one of them. As William took a seat next to him, the bird fluttered to another cross and moments later flew away.

Nearly a minute passed before either friar spoke, with Michael finally breaking the silence. "I'm wondering, William, if you've ever had occasion to ponder the difference between steadfastness and bullheadedness."

"Not recently," William laughed in surprise, "but I assume *you* have."

"When I returned to Avignon," Michael said as he drew in a long breath, "I believed a rapprochement with Duèze might be possible, and I was willing to make concessions to achieve it. I knew the risks, but owing to what I fancied as my talents for conciliation, I set my qualms aside. And though I blush to admit it, I needed his support to secure my reelection."

William said nothing but suspected he knew where Michael's disquisition was headed.

"My 'mistake' was in enlisting *you* as our chief advocate. I should have known you'd concede nothing, and in fact you gave me fair warning. What I hadn't counted on was your convincing me, utterly and completely, of the Spirituals' position. Early on I chided you for your excessive zeal, refusing to concede that you were right and I was wrong—or at least naïve."

"Even if I hadn't convinced you on scriptural grounds, you should have known that compromising with Duèze was politically impossible. I recall telling you that too."

"Be that as it may, once I was 'converted,' it was your steadfastness—which I mistook for bullheadedness—that made my consignment to the pyre feel inevitable. But at least I wouldn't be *alone* at the stake. You would be there with me. For that reason I despair at having goaded you into this."

"Spare me the confession, Michael. I could have said no."

"Still, you *didn't* refuse, and my shame is all the more acute for rebuking you earlier. While I dithered about politics and tactics, you did the right thing."

William permitted himself a smile. The pigeon they shooed away earlier returned to its perch and cooed greetings to the two conspirators. "Might we regard this as a moment of *mutual* confession? As usual, my sin was vanity. For personal gratification more than anything else, I wanted to humiliate and crush the venal bastard. I knew all along I couldn't convince him *or* the commission. Gerardo took me to task for my hubris, and he was right. As a result, I've brought down not just you and Bonagratia but—and may God forgive me!—poor Gerardo too."

Michael sighed. "It appears we both have much to atone for. The question is whether being burned to a crisp before a jeering throng is a just price to pay for our sins."

Chapter 32

May 19, 1328 — Greyfriars Convent

WEEDS, APHIDS, AND ROCKS continued to besiege the neat rows of bean and pea plants William had tended since he arrived in Avignon. Once each week, in early morning to avoid the midday heat of late Spring, he wielded spade and trowel in defense of the brotherhood's sources of sustenance. Though his small victories always had to be re-won, on most days he looked forward to resuming his labors. The Greyfriars' garden was his haven for contemplation.

He continued to worry whether his conscience would allow him to try to escape before Gerardo's killer was brought to justice. But Michael convinced him there was nothing he could do. Had it not been for Gerardo's murder, his decision would have been obvious. Disillusioned with theology and philosophy, William had nothing left to accomplish in Avignon. He had exhausted the reservoir of ideas that energized him earlier and now doubted the power of ideas to make a difference in the higher reaches of the Church.

And would William, Michael, and Bonagratia be arrested and carted off to the pyre if they remained in Avignon? Despite Fieschi's and de Bury's oblique assurances that the pope was in no hurry to act, His Holiness would not postpone indefinitely his revenge against the friars' heresies. Or might they be slain beforehand by Gerardo's assassin, recovered from his wounds and eager to strike again? And were these dire prospects connected to each other? William still did not know if Gerardo's killer was an agent of the pope or of someone else. Did the Sword of the Church or the Sword of the Kingdom pose the greater threat?

* * *

Since his release from the prison, William's thoughts often turned to the Janus figure of his dream. It was Manuele Fieschi, but the appearing and disappearing figure more broadly portrayed his uncertainty about who were his friends, his enemies, and those indifferent to his fate. He knew he could rely on Michael and Francesco, but he still had questions about Reading and the nervous lawyer Bonagratia. Then there was the abbot Thierry of Narbonne, perhaps not as dithering as he sometimes appeared.

He heard a noise behind him and looked up from the fallen beanstalk he had just repaired. Squinting into the morning sunlight, he saw the outlines of two grey-robed figures emerging from the convent's rear door. As planned, Michael and Bonagratia had come to resume discussing their escape plan.

They often disagreed.

"But Francesco reports to Fieschi," Michael warned on hearing William's plan to meet with the young poet the following afternoon. "I've often seen them together."

"You needn't worry about Francesco," William said as he tugged on a clump of weeds he missed earlier. "He despises Duèze, and with Gerardo dead he's our only source inside the palace."

"But he's just a clerk who wastes his time writing lascivious poems to that married woman," Bonagratia said. "The man's a scandal."

"At this point we can't be finicky about his romantic diversions," William said, rankled by the lawyer's prudery. "Francesco's indiscretions pale against some of our own brethren's. And he's preparing for *minor* orders. The last I knew they say nothing about celibacy."

"I'm less concerned about his carnal bliss than whether we can count on him," Bonagratia replied testily. "You yourself said that you've rarely heard his confession since he started work at the palace. Alliances there shift like the winds."

"Unless you have better sources, which I doubt, we haven't much choice." Not alone in his dislike of Bonagratia, William avoided mentioning the lawyer's paucity of friends. "It's a risk we have to take."

As the three of them spoke, William continued with his hoeing, and Michael helped by pulling weeds. Bonagratia stood unmoving, evidently fearful of getting his hands dirty.

"I'm inclined to agree," Michael conceded. "Although, William, I urge you to show more subtlety than usual in broaching the subject with him."

"I'm not as indiscreet as you suppose," William replied in a tone daring Bonagratia to object further about Francesco.

"What about the seal? Can he help get it back?" Michael asked. "You know I can't leave without it."

A small metal object resembling an elaborately carved chess piece, the Franciscans' seal conferred upon the Order's minister general the authority to conduct official business. Michael brought the seal with him on his return to Avignon five months earlier, upon which Arnaud de Trian, Duèze's recently mitered nephew, took possession of it. According to rumor the precious object now lay hidden somewhere in the pope's private chamber.

"Shall we remove our sandals and tiptoe past dozens of palace guards, hoping they won't notice?" William asked. "Or perhaps Brother François can concoct a potion rendering us temporarily invisible. I've heard him boast of more amazing feats than that."

Michael ignored William's sarcasm. "You've said before that Francesco can be resourceful when he puts his mind to it."

"I'll discuss it with him, but what we need most is information. You don't *need* the seal. Your authority won't evaporate if you don't bring it with you to Bologna—if you get there at all. Besides, what if his pet parrot has eaten it?"

"Don't be flippant," Michael snapped. "Our more cautious brothers put greater stock in such things than you do. But setting aside the matter of the seal, we must move quickly. Yesterday Reading hinted that an announcement of a verdict might be imminent."

"Reading *knows* we're leaving?" Bonagratia asked with alarm.

"I didn't have to tell him," Michael said impatiently. "He could easily guess and appears content to turn a blind eye."

William understood Bonagratia's apprehensions but, like Michael, he trusted Reading not to betray them. In addition, William's trove of manuscripts was too heavy to carry on their trek to the Benedictine abbey. He knew he could rely on Reading to keep them safe. In the hands of anyone else in Avignon, all of William's work during the last four years would vanish.

"Back to Francesco," Michael said, "how certain are you he hasn't alerted Fieschi?"

"Francesco is nothing if not discreet," William assured him.

"I assume that in addition to repenting his sins he might be receptive to discussing other matters," Bonagratia injected, unable to resist a final gibe.

William jabbed his trowel at another clump of weeds, pulled them from the ground, and handed them root-first to Bonagratia. "Put these in the compost heap."

Chapter 33

May 20, 1328 — The Celestine Monastery

WILLIAM PREFERRED HIS OLD STAFF to the new one Michael had brought him. He wasn't ungrateful, but he missed the familiar tacky feel of the old one's grip and how, after years of wear, it fit perfectly to his hand. William still felt irritated the palace guards hadn't given it back.

The new staff made a different sound as it tapped on the newly paved streets leading to the Celestine monastery. He kept to heavily traveled routes; the small scar on his neck from his encounter with Stephen Dunheved reminded him to steer clear of deserted lanes. He glanced behind him as he walked and was more than usually attentive to suspicious sights and sounds.

Located just beyond the city's ancient wall, the monastery's tree-lined atrium provided the privacy they would need.

"Avignon has never been a safe place for Englishmen," Francesco said as he edged through a small archway.

"And less by the hour. Which, as you probably guessed, is why I needed to see you."

"I assume you regard the prospect of living to fight another day more tantalizing than the glories of martyrdom," Francesco said with a wry smile. "Although I expected to hear from you before now."

"Since Gerardo's murder, I've hoped to avoid putting you at risk."

Francesco shrugged off William's concern. "Anything to relieve the tedium of my current labors. In truth, I'd like nothing better than spreading confusion among the enemies of Rome."

"I'm surprised you're allowed anywhere near the palace."

"The pope and his minions tolerate my presence as a sop to Cardinal Colonna. I recall telling you the cardinal is an old family friend who sponsors my employment here while I finish my studies. Duèze believes the friendlier his relations with the Italian clergy, the better his chances of discouraging the emperor from doing something rash."

"So you come and go as you please?"

"Not entirely, although my superiors have relaxed their vigil somewhat. I've found it quite easy to vanish into the bowels of the palace while the pope's inner circle deals with important matters. You may not have heard, but Duèze has made overtures to enlist his support for a new crusade to the Holy Land. Whether that's a senile delusion or a ruse to keep Louis' armies at bay I can't say for certain. Though probably the latter, I suspect. Far better for the pope that they march east to Jerusalem than west toward Avignon."

William nodded at this and then changed the subject. "We need to settle on a departure date, a *safe* one. We can't delay much longer, a week at most."

"Hmm, some sort of diversion appears to be in order," Francesco said, scratching his chin as he contemplated possibilities. "Ah! In five—no, six—days from now, on the 26th, the pope will host a wedding celebration at the palace for one of his grandnieces. He has more than a dozen of them. This one—named Robine, I believe—is one of his favorites. Relatives and notables from as far away as Lyon will be flooding the city. Duèze loves these galas and instructed his nephews to spare no expense in arranging the event. They've been giddy with excitement while looting the Camera to pay for it."

The pope's three nephews served as his chief gatekeepers, occupying rooms on the palace's mezzanine between the papal chamber on the second floor and the first floor's great hall. It was whispered, however, that one nephew, Pierre de Via, was really Duèze's bastard son. Those who believed the pope's amorous inclinations tended in another direction were skeptical.

"And how did you come to know this?"

"I've been assigned to assist them. Among my other tasks, I'm in charge of procuring the fowl for the banquet. To be precise," Francesco said, cheerfully reciting the list from memory: "690 chickens, 580 partridges, 50 doves, four cranes, and six peacocks. Although I should think two or three peacocks would be ample."

"It appears you'll be busy."

"I mention it to give you an idea of the scale of the celebration. The nephews want to assure their uncle that the guests will enjoy themselves, but they're also mindful of the problems arising when so many people congregate in the enclave at the same time. Judging from the enormous wine list, rampant drunkenness is a near certainty, which will keep most of the guards and *janitores* busy well into the early hours of the morning."

Just as worrisome to the palace, William suspected, was that bands of brigands might seize the chance to stuff their purses. Scores of them were sure to flock to the city in hopes of snaring easy prey. And a kidnapping or two couldn't be ruled out. It had happened before.

William reflected on another reason Francesco's suggested date might prove auspicious. May 26th, he remembered, was the feast day of Saint Bede—the *Venerable* Bede—the patron saint of scholars: a fitting eve for William, Michael, and Bonagratia to thumb their noses at Duèze as they stole out of Avignon.

For the next hour William and Francesco settled on some of the plan's details. Francesco would procure suitable disguises for their exit from a sympathetic monk at one of the Benedictines' leprosaria. Their anticipated route would take them past the larger of those institutions located on the eastern outskirts of the city. Francesco would also recommend that Pierre de Via instruct the commander of the papal guard to transfer to the Exchange most of the guards who patrolled the enclave's convents and monasteries. The ostensible reason was to ensure the safety of the wedding's visitors, most of whom would lodge at inns and hostels scattered throughout the Exchange. Visitor hospitality, William surmised, was also included in Francesco's portfolio of duties.

Reluctantly, William explained that Michael of Cesena wanted the Order's official seal retrieved from the pope's private chamber. Francesco was dubious about the possibility of getting it but promised to look into the matter as a favor to Michael.

"What about Fieschi?" William asked. "Aren't you worried about raising his suspicions?"

Francesco laughed. "Fieschi doesn't plan weddings."

* * *

As he walked back toward the city's interior, William speculated that the ramparts guarding Avignon's eleven gates were as apt to block his escape as prevent invaders from storming the city. Now in its initial construction stages was a new, outer wall to protect the city's growing population from foreign armies. This second wall was deemed all the more necessary since building began of a new papal palace that promised to surpass in grandiosity the Vatican itself. Another reason to leave.

He stayed alert to unusual sightings, noting pedestrians who seemed out of place. Not for the first time he was struck by the poverty around him. Unlike the Exchange where richly attired merchants and bankers were commonplace, William saw scores of cripples and beggars dressed in rags. He was always appalled by these sights—first in England, then in Paris, and now in Avignon—which led him to reflect upon his own circumstance. He had *chosen* his poverty as a sacred vow; and his reward—that he had taken his vow in emulation of Christ's example—was just and sufficient. As he surveyed the scene around him, he was reminded that the forlorn figures he passed had made no such choice; their wretchedness had been thrust upon them by the corrupt and avaricious Church fathers.

The few exceptions to the cripples and beggars were easy to spot: a wealthy tourist wearing an elaborately embroidered silk-lined surcoat striding briskly along the crowded street, ignoring pleas for alms from the cripples who lined either side; two young women in expensive finery, looking about anxiously for their lost companions.

As William turned to help a lame beggar regain his balance after falling on the unevenly cobblestoned street, he saw a muscular, clean-shaven man of medium height and closely cropped auburn hair pivot away from him, as if to inspect the wares displayed at a shoemaker's stall. The man's dark green knee-length doublet clung tightly to his torso and arms. It was the sort of costume William had rarely seen in Avignon, resembling attire favored by merchants and traders in London. The man's garments were made of finely woven wool and linen. William noticed his calf-length boots and long gloves, sturdy rather than elegant, crafted from highly polished cordovan leather. Odd, he thought, that the man's appearance registered with such clarity.

The hair on the back of his neck bristled. He had seen the man at least twice earlier that morning on his way to meet Francesco.

Chapter 34

May 21, 1328 — Saint Agricola's Church

THE NEXT MORNING an apprehensive William waited for Joyeuse by the altar of Saint Agricola's church. He couldn't refuse her summons and would speak with her for the first time.

She appeared at the main entrance, walking with her head slightly bowed as if to avoid the stares of priests and penitents, and made her way toward the confessional booths. William approached her and pointed toward the large oak door she had entered. It would be best if they spoke outdoors where they couldn't be overheard. She nodded and followed him into the sunlit courtyard fronting onto the street.

They found a bench beneath a locust tree and sat without speaking for several seconds as William rehearsed his apology for the grief he had brought her. But before he could speak, Joyeuse surprised him by saying, "Gerardo wondered if you had ever been in love."

She noticed William's startled expression and continued to speak. "I told him I believed you *had* been in love and probably still were."

"And how would you have known such a thing?"

"Gerardo often spoke of the great Friar Occam," she answered with strained gaiety, "so I felt I knew you. And women know more about these matters than men."

"I shouldn't wonder," William said as he stifled a rueful smile, "but I'm surprised Gerardo would give my amorous sufferings a moment's thought."

"*Au contraire*. He very much wanted to know."

"And why was that?"

"He believed if *you* had loved as he did, you could forgive him. Otherwise, you might not."

"Forgive him for what?"

"Well, for *this*," she said as she patted her protruding belly beneath her loose-fitting gown. "And that we planned to leave Avignon."

"Gerardo did nothing that needed my forgiveness."

"I told him that, but I'm afraid he didn't believe me."

William stared at his staff. "Why didn't you leave earlier?"

"We had hoped to, before the feast of the Nativity, but Gerardo wouldn't leave Avignon without knowing you were safe. He prayed you would leave before it was too late."

William slowly shook his head. "And if not for me, Gerardo would still be alive." He already knew this, but his guilt was now compounded knowing that Joyeuse knew it too.

"Please, Brother William, say no more about it," she said in an almost pleading tone. "I didn't come here to heap scorn on you."

"But why did you send for me?"

"Perhaps seeing and speaking with you would assure me that Gerardo had fulfilled God's purpose and that loving me hadn't diminished his doing so. Knowing that would give me great comfort."

More seconds passed; Joyeuse began to weep quietly as she

inched away from him. He grasped her arm and gently pulled her closer. He imagined that she smelled of lilacs; she had merged with memories of Eleanor. Now, as he recalled their meetings in Paris and London, he wanted to tell Joyeuse that she was right, that he had indeed loved just as Gerardo had. Instead, he asked, "What will become of you?"

"Weeks ago," she said as she struggled to regain her composure, "the good sisters delivered me to the *Repenties* when they discovered my . . . condition. They were kind about it; I'm not the first novice to fall from their favor," she said as she glanced down at her belly. "But the nuns at the *Repenties* aren't as kind. So I'll soon leave and not tell them where I'm going."

There were disturbing stories about the convent for repentant prostitutes. Unwed mothers were considered no less sinful than ladies of the night and were dealt with accordingly.

"And where *will* you go?"

"Gerardo and I planned to find our way to Genoa, hoping his father would take us in. But now," she paused as she again looked away, "I may return to Narbonne if I can find someone, a friend perhaps, to come with me. With our Lord watching over me, I could reach there in a few days."

"You have family there?"

"Mama—God rest her soul—left us two years ago," she said and crossed herself. "Papa is a grain merchant and prosperous enough to provide for me unless he casts me out. Or," she said more cheerfully, "I could go to Sicily. My dear brother Guarin is still there, the last I knew. He would be very glad to see me, and I could have my baby there."

Joyeuse was smiling, but her voice had an eerie, singsong tone. Her talk of traveling beyond Avignon struck William as a wistful fantasy, as if she were in a deep reverie. Narbonne? Possibly. But Sicily was out of the question regardless of her present circumstance. How could she know Guarin would be there and that he would take her in? And how would she find him even if she somehow managed to get there? William had heard enough confessions to know that a penitent's grieving could be softened briefly by fanciful imaginings of better days to come. But he also knew that the happier those imaginings, the more desperate the penitent's postponement of unhappy ends. He had seen it before and was witnessing it again.

Joyeuse rose suddenly from the bench. "I must leave—so much still to do," she said in a quavering voice and then declared, "God has forgiven Gerardo! I'm certain of it."

She didn't look back as she left him and descended the ten crumbling steps from Saint Agricola's church. William remained seated, trying to decipher her parting remark. Had she confused God's forgiveness with his? And why had *she* forgiven *him*? There were many things he had planned to say to Joyeuse but couldn't. Nor could he remember feeling such a deep sadness as he sat alone on the bench and gazed into the distance.

Chapter 35

May 26, 1328 (midmorning) — The Carmelite Convent

SINCE HE LAST SPOKE with Francesco, William seldom left Greyfriars, venturing out only when he had no other choice. They agreed to meet at a different site, this time at the Carmelite convent outside Saint Matthew's Gate, northeast of the papal enclave.

Once there, he breathed easier on finding Francesco waiting for him in the convent's small chapel. Two nuns paid them no attention as they trimmed the dozens of candles illuminating the altar. Only a few candles were lit, flickering precariously. The semi-darkness of the chapel's interior enhanced the familiar aroma of incense.

"It must have been D'Alspaye, one of the young king's men from London," Francesco said on hearing William describe the well-dressed Englishman he saw a week earlier.

"Hmm, more likely *Mortimer's* man than the king's—his accomplice in his escape from the Tower." William now had to discard his earlier theory that the tall beggar he saw on the bridge two weeks earlier was the shorter, muscular D'Alspaye.

"So I recall your telling me. But what interest could he have in you?

"I hoped *you* might know."

"There's little I can tell you. I do know that D'Alspaye and Burley are as thick as thieves and that he and de Bury detest each other. The same for him and Fieschi. The few times I've seen them together they appeared anything but friendly."

William glanced nervously behind him each time the chapel's door creaked open, momentarily brightening the chapel with the midday sunlight. All he saw were fleeting silhouettes framed by the light streaming in. Each visitor stayed a few seconds before closing the door softly on leaving.

Francesco handed William a bundle of old clothing bound with a thin hemp cord. "As promised, here are your disguises. Brother Estienne scrounged them from the leprosarium's undercroft. They reek abominably, but that should work in your favor," he chuckled. "Any of the pope's guards you encounter will want to stay as far away from you as they can."

"How well do you know this Brother Estienne?" William asked as he glanced again toward the chapel door.

"Well enough not to worry. He hates Duèze as much as you do. The pope barely tolerates the leprosaria and threatened to send Bernard Gui to dispose of the poor souls kept there."

"Where will we meet him?"

"Outside the rear entrance to the convent, just before midnight. He'll guide you to the eastern-most leprosarium. The guards posted at the Imbert Gate know him and shouldn't suspect anything. Then, when you reach the leprosarium, he'll bid adieu, and you'll be on your way."

Their business finished, they prepared to leave, each in a different direction. The moment was awkward for them both, especially for William, whose facility for expressing his feelings was no match for the poet's. "Thanking you, Francesco, feels risibly inadequate. You've taken risks far beyond what I could have expected."

"In truth, fewer than you might think, for reasons I suspect you'll understand in time. I do wish you weren't leaving Babylon so soon, though. I fear that confession will never be quite the same."

William smiled weakly, saying nothing.

"One last thing: Earlier you asked me about *this*," Francesco said as he handed William a small metal object.

"How did you get it?" a stunned William asked as he examined the official seal of the Franciscan Order.

Francesco hesitated before replying. "Fieschi," he said so softly William could barely hear him. He thought he detected a slight wink as Francesco turned away, striding briskly past the two nuns and out the Carmelite chapel's entrance.

* * *

Summer's oppressive heat had arrived early. William wiped sweat from his brow and neck as he began his trek back to Greyfriars. Or perhaps it was his nerves, now that his escape that evening grew closer.

The seedy lane he walked along was lined on either side by vendors' stalls, most of them stocked with cheap wares, rotting produce, and tainted meat. None of the stalls appeared busy as the proprietors barked advertisements to indifferent passersby. They competed for customers with a few prostitutes whose songs of seduction attracted just as little interest. Two jugglers and a sword swallower displayed their meager talents, scrambling for small coins strewn along the rutted, unpaved lane.

Gambling inspired greater enthusiasm than commerce. Near the intersection of the lane and an alleyway a game of knucklebones was in noisy progress. Players and onlookers voiced approval or dismay at the end of each betting round. As a child, William played a similar game, though never for money, and was baffled by the arcane scoring rules of the variant played in southern France.

The game was played with four bones of a sheep's ankles, each bone having four sides—flat, concave, sinuous, and convex— representing different point values. After each roll of the bones points were totaled. The winner was the first player to complete a series of rolls in a prescribed sequence.

As William approached the intersection, he sidestepped two onlookers jostling for a clearer view of the action. One of them, a wiry boy barely in his teens, bumped into him, knocking him off balance as his staff skittered a few feet away.

While stooping to retrieve it he heard one of the players shout, "You cheated! That was 'riding the elephant,' not 'frogs in the well.' You rolled out of order!"

Instead of defending his honor against his accuser's charge, the cheater leapt to his feet and tried to run away. He crashed into William, sending him sprawling to the ground. The accuser and his friends sprang after the cheater but found their path blocked by his allies, some of whom had laid side bets on his rolls of the bones. Bystanders jeered as an all-out brawl ensued. A dog barked encouragement to the combatants.

As he crawled on hands and knees to the safety of a vacant stall, William felt his right arm seized by someone behind him. Looking up, he saw that the man's face was hidden beneath the hood of a monk's habit. The man pointing a dagger at him wasn't a monk, which William knew instantly when the man's hood slipped from his head and revealed the scarred brow of Stephen Dunheved.

He heaved frantically to his left as the blade of Dunheved's dagger grazed his right shoulder and parried a second thrust with his forearm. William now lay helplessly on his back, immobilized by Dunheved's full weight.

The attacker then shuddered when a thin scarlet geyser erupted from his throat. His suddenly limp body collapsed atop William. Terrified and confused, William shoved Dunheved aside, but amid the chaos he felt certain he had seen the calf-length cordovan boots of the fleeing Gerard D'Alspaye.

Chapter 36

May 26, 1328 (late afternoon and evening) — Greyfriars Convent

"WHAT DID YOU TELL the constables?" Michael of Cesena's normally calm and resonant voice was an anxious octave higher. They sat together in a corner of the convent's kitchen while William scrubbed his bloodstained tunic.

"That during the melee one of the knucklebones players or the killer himself collided with the victim, who then knocked me to the ground. With bodies flying everywhere I could barely see what was going on."

"Could they have suspected that *you* killed him?"

"Doubtful, but I can't be sure. In any case, one of them ran off to search for a man an onlooker reported fleeing from the scene. I assume *he's* their main suspect."

"They didn't catch him?"

"Evidently not. The constable returned empty-handed."

"So is it safe to assume the constables were satisfied with what you told them?" Michael asked. The tenor of his voice had lowered, but still not to its normal level. "Otherwise, I doubt they'd have released you."

"Perhaps not completely satisfied, but they didn't have strong enough suspicions to justify holding me any longer. The lead constable ordered me not to stray far from Greyfriars, saying they might have more questions."

"Hmm," Michael reflected as he scratched his chin, "I suppose we ought to feel relieved the killing occurred outside the enclave."

William agreed. Had the killing occurred within the papal enclave, the pope's investigators might suspect—or, more likely, *contrive*—a link to William's trial. What easier way to secure a heresy verdict than couple it with a murder charge? Owing to jurisdictional rivalries, however, it could be a day or two before they learned of the killing from the Avignon constabulary.

Finished with his laundering, William casually handed the surprised Michael the Franciscans' official seal, explaining how Francesco had managed to get it.

"Why would Fieschi risk taking it?" Michael demanded.

"Francesco wouldn't say but hinted that I'd soon understand the reason." William noticed the worried look on Michael's face. "You don't seem especially pleased to get it back."

"Ordinarily I would be." The pitch of Michael's voice had risen again. "But if Francesco has involved Fieschi, how many others at the palace know?"

"Fieschi is too discreet to tell anyone else, so stop whipping yourself into a lather," William said with greater assurance than he felt.

Which only riled Michael further. "I'm not! But we now have to worry about Fieschi, not to mention the constables who questioned you. At any moment they could come here looking for you. Also, Reading has been pestering me with questions—just to be 'helpful,' of course, but his curiosity makes me nervous."

"We've known all along there were risks," William said. "Some matters are within our control and others aren't. We won't know if we've succeeded until we reach hailing distance of the abbey."

Unmoved by these calming words, Michael rose to leave, telling William he needed to speak with Bonagratia before sunset.

Alone in the corner of the kitchen, William reviewed his next steps. As the departure hour grew closer, there was still much to do, but one task—a farewell visit to Durand of Saint-Pourçain—nagged at him most. The sessions before the commission had numbered forty-two in all, and Durand stood by his side throughout, except at the end when he was too ill to attend.

Reluctantly, he decided against making the brief trek to the ailing Dominican's monastery. Another assault was possible. Though William had no reason to fear Durand might betray him, his old friend's safety might be compromised if his fellow commissioners later suspected he had known of William's plan. A letter would have to do, which Durand could read after William had gone. But as he stared at a blank sheet of parchment, the expressions of sentiment that clogged his mind felt trite and cloying, as if lifted from a manual on good manners he once read at the seminary. He gave up, vowing to try again later.

* * *

The other friars had been asleep for more than three hours, and the convent's rooms and corridors were dark. As he prepared for his final task before leaving, William lit a candle and climbed the steps to the scriptorium. Once in the upper floor's enormous room, he felt a pang of regret for abandoning his brothers. Many, especially the novitiates and younger friars he had taught and counseled, now shared his passion for Jesus' renunciation of worldly possessions.

He padded over to his desk to retrieve the stack of manuscripts he carefully arranged that morning. He lugged them to Reading's desk, which occupied a privileged, south-facing corner of the room.

For nearly a week William had avoided his amiable rival. Reading would surmise that the sum of William's scholarly efforts during the previous four years was too heavy for the lame friar to take with him. That conclusion would be confirmed the following morning when, untying the parcel stashed beneath his desk, Reading read the message William included:

> Brother John,
> No doubt vanity prompts me to entrust these scribblings to your care. Should anyone ask, would you keep them dry and accessible—at least for a time? When it is clear they are of no longer of any interest, feel at liberty to dispose of them however you see fit.
> In Jesus' Holy name, Occam

Chapter 37

May 26-May 27, 1328 (late evening and early morning) — To the Leprosarium

BROTHER ESTIENNE WAS WAITING at midnight as the friars emerged from the rear door of the convent. They slipped into their disguises and bundled their habits with the few other items they had brought. The disguises were standard leper attire: ragged, loose-fitting tunics with yellow crosses stitched front and back. In England, William recalled, small bells were often sewn to the tunics. The French didn't require bells, but the stink of the garments Brother Estienne supplied would give passersby ample notice of their approach.

Estienne had the foresight to include hats. Three tonsured lepers would attract attention. Michael and Bonagratia donned black woolen coifs resembling oversized zucchettos with earflaps; William selected a floppy, broad-brimmed straw hat.

The others waited while William wended his way through the friars' vegetable garden to the cemetery. At the far end the mound of soil above Gerardo's grave was still fresh. It was also free of weeds, which William made sure of earlier that morning. He removed his hat and knelt to pray again for the safety of his young friend's soul, but he then paused. Surely Gerardo's soul was now safe, and perhaps he would want to know that earthly justice had been done. So William whispered the name of his killer, who just that morning had his throat slit by Roger Mortimer's agent. He knelt a few moments longer and then crossed himself as he rose, donned his hat, and rejoined the others.

Until safely out of hearing distance of the sleeping friars, they communicated by improvised hand signals barely visible in the light of the gibbous moon. They stole into a nearby lane as drunken revelers cavorted in the distance. Most were returning to their hostels after celebrating the pope's grandniece's wedding at the palace. Francesco had evidently succeeded in diverting the pope's guards from the enclave's monasteries and convents to various routes linking the palace with the Exchange.

Estienne spoke for the first time. Without greetings or other preliminaries, he issued instructions: "The guards will become suspicious only if you act suspiciously. So don't whisper or try to hide your faces. Remember, you're harmless lepers, not brigands or cutpurses."

When he stopped to light the torch he carried, the heavy moist air at first prevented his flints from igniting the clump of dried grass he used as kindling. After a dozen tries he finally succeeded, producing a steady flame from the wax-impregnated cattails he had bound to a stick of resinous wood. When lit, the torch revealed little more than Estienne's round, kind face. It was useless for illuminating the route to the Imbert Gate a mile distant to the southeast.

"When we reach the gate," he continued, "stay a few paces back. The guards will know me, but arriving at this hour may raise more questions than usual. And don't be surprised if they wave a torch in your faces to confirm what I tell them. That's part of their routine. The portcullis should already be raised and the drawbridge lowered, so our passage through the gate shouldn't take long."

The next half-hour passed without incident. But when they reached the intersection of rue Philonarde and rue de la Bonneterie, William's throat tightened. Just ahead, the battlements of the city wall—twenty feet high and crowned with spiked grilles—were faintly visible. They loomed menacingly, conjuring the image of boiling oil showering down upon him and his companions as they passed beneath.

Drawing closer, he saw that the portcullis—the latticed metal grating that slid up and down in vertical grooves framing the gate—was lowered! Their passage through the city's ramparts would be restricted to a narrow, well-lit, and closely guarded door. Estienne signaled the friars to halt as he proceeded alone toward the gate.

They watched as Estienne spoke with two of the guards posted there. From his animated gestures, there appeared to be some sort of dispute. Two other men joined the discussion, both clad in the blue uniforms of the Avignon constabulary. In the dark William couldn't see their faces, but he imagined the constables who questioned him that afternoon were less than fifty feet away.

His stomach churned over that possibility, as did the stomach of Michael of Cesena, who lurched into the center of the street and vomited. Panic-stricken, Bonagratia reversed course as if preparing to race back to the convent.

"Don't move!" William hissed. He clutched Bonagratia's arm to prevent him from fleeing. "There's nothing to do but wait."

More minutes passed before the meeting at the gate broke up, after which Estienne left the guards and walked back to the friars. The two constables followed him.

"No cause for alarm," he said reassuringly on his return. "I've just learned that earlier today a man was murdered not far from the Carmelite convent—an Englishman. His killing has stirred some interest at the palace, so they've ordered the portcullis lowered to prevent the killer from escaping. As a precaution, these good officers are obliged to search anyone leaving the city." With forced jocularity Estienne added: "Who knows what sort of disguise the villain might be wearing, eh?"

With huge relief William saw that neither of the constables had been at the murder scene that afternoon. Perhaps fearful of contracting the scourge, they poked the lepers' garments with their quarterstaffs from a safe distance and didn't order the friars to remove their hats. Now satisfied, the senior constable informed Estienne they were free to go. Estienne and the friars slipped through the now-opened door next to the gate and onto the drawbridge spanning the moat. The guards gave them only cursory glances.

Tensions eased as the glow of the Imbert Gate's torches receded from view. The group's pace quickened slightly, making it harder for William to keep up. But he hobbled along gamely, refreshed by a slight breeze at his back. Estienne added to the lighter mood by telling small jokes that made even the nervous Bonagratia utter an occasional chuckle. William had never heard the lawyer laugh before. And Michael made a light humming sound in between Estienne's jokes, as if confident they were clear of danger.

They walked along the Rue des Teinturiers, a wide and neatly groomed avenue adjacent to a canal fed by a branch of the Sorgue River. The river's origin, William had heard, was a huge spring located at the base of the French Alps. Perhaps they would travel close to the river, or *on* it if the current allowed, during the early legs of their trip. William would soon explore unfamiliar terrain and would have to rely on the two Italians, Michael and Bonagratia, to narrate the exotic vistas he would view for the first time. Each of them had traveled that route before.

The rue des Teinturiers ended a half-mile later at a construction site for the outer wall of the city. They passed the church of Sainte Claire where Francesco's inamorata Laura de Noves first "greeted his eyes": the *divine* Laura who William would forever compare to Eleanor. He now wished he had told Francesco about her, but there were lines of intimacy he could not bring himself to cross.

Beyond the site of the new wall, the road narrowed. As they crept eastward, dwellings and shops grew sparser, giving way to small farms and untilled fields. They passed a stable where, Estienne pointed out, the pope's ostlers housed the palace's horses and mules. William could not see the stable, but he smelled it and heard the beasts' nocturnal snorts. In keeping with Saint Francis's admonishment, he had never ridden a horse but had occasionally fancied doing so. But now was clearly not the time to indulge his whim. Among other reasons, he and his companions would have to *steal* the horses, thereby inviting not just Francis's censure but the pope's as well.

They reached the leprosarium more than an hour after their encounter at the gate. From there, William, Michael, and Bonagratia would travel unescorted, leaving Brother Estienne behind. The three friars donned their habits once again and returned the lepers' tunics to their guide. William kept the straw hat.

Estienne waved aside their expressions of thanks. "You had best not delay," he warned. "I didn't want to alarm you, but at the gate I overheard one of the constables tell the guards they were on their way to your convent to question one of the friars about the Englishman's murder. It may not concern you, but I thought you should know."

He turned and dissolved into the darkness.

PART FIVE

TO THE ABBEY

May 27 – June 14, 1328

Chapter 38

May 27 - June 3, 1328 — The Carmelite Convent, Digne

Y THE SECOND DAY the lavender had thinned and by the third day it had disappeared. Its sight and smell reminded William of the city he despised, and so he felt exhilarated by his release not just from Babylon but also from the shimmering fields insulating it from the Lord's vengeance. Awaiting him in the Piedmont were landscapes painted in welcoming colors.

In the afternoon of the third day Michael told William and Bonagratia what they could expect at the abbey. Michael had been there a year earlier and witnessed the burning of the Aedificium in the aftermath of the mad Brother Jorge's mayhem. The abbot, Abo, had died in the flames along with Jorge himself. Some of the monks soon left the abbey, but most had stayed, vowing to restore the giant structure. The emperor Louis paid for the restoration and used his influence with the Italian Benedictines to encourage monks from other abbeys in the region to join them.

"The emperor's nephew, Rupert, will meet us there and act on Louis' behalf," Michael also informed them. "He calls himself a prince, an honorific he's able to get away with, but he's actually the son of the emperor's elder brother Leopold. No doubt he'll annoy us with too many questions, but I'm told he's quite generous in dispensing his uncle's favors to errant friars."

"So Rupert knows of our escape?" William asked.

"We have Louis' agents to thank. While you were basking in the comforts of the pope's prison, I met with two of them. They steal in and out of the city with surprising ease. By God's grace neither of them has been caught, at least so far."

William was surprised by this revelation and sensed Michael was concealing something. "What about other friars? Will any of our own be there?"

"None I know of, although you can expect to see Marsilius. The emperor has asked him to join us."

This was welcome news. Despite their doctrinal differences William was eager to meet Marsilius of Padua, the notorious Italian whose political views so closely matched his own. Like William, Marsilius opposed authoritarian rule in any form, whether by popes or kings. The people themselves were sovereign and were thus the only legitimate source of political authority. He and Marsilius would have a great deal to discuss.

"Anyone else?"

"Just the new abbot, Clario, and the other monks. So don't expect throngs of our supporters to welcome us. Most of them should already have arrived in Bologna." After pausing, Michael added, "Of course, all I've told you assumes we'll reach the abbey before Duèze's men catch up with us."

* * *

As far as William knew, the Carmelite nuns of Digne took their vows of poverty and chastity with utmost seriousness but were selective when it came to obedience. Now, Abbess Véronique was adamantly withholding her consent from a blue-uniformed officer of the French Crown who demanded that she allow his men to search her convent. Murderous cutthroats, likely disguised as mendicant friars, had recently absconded from Avignon and were believed headed her way.

From behind a door to the foyer of the abbess's residence the friars could overhear fragments of the heated exchange. In a voice more commanding than the exasperated officer's, the abbess refused to abide any incursion into her sacred territory and warned of dire punishments in the hereafter should the officer persist. Perhaps knowing her warning might not convince him, she pointedly added that officials at the papal palace would be severely displeased upon learning of this outrage. William took note that the abbess hadn't *denied*, at least in so many words, that she invited the travel-weary friars to lodge in the convent's guesthouse the evening before. Standing firmly on holy principle, she sidestepped the mortal sin of lying to the officer.

The previous afternoon the friars had begun their descent into the small valley where the village of Digne was centrally situated. The convent lay a half-mile to the south, occupying higher ground and providing a clear view of the village as well as the main road running west and east. A dilapidated bridge spanned a wide stream between the village and the convent. Clumps of brilliant blue thistle dotted the otherwise barren stretch of terrain that separated them. The Alps loomed on the eastern horizon.

"Abbess Véronique is accustomed to having her way," Michael told William and Bonagratia. "For years the convent barely subsisted on revenues from tapestries the sisters wove. They were of poor quality, so passing merchants and prosperous villagers would occasionally buy them out of charity in lieu of depositing alms into the convent's collection box. But about ten years ago one of the sisters proclaimed that the hot sulfur spring on their property possessed miraculous healing powers. Ever since, Véronique has shrewdly managed the convent's baths as word of the water's benefits spread. She also honed a talent for fending off the village officials' claims on a share of the profits. Which may explain," he added with a wry chuckle, "why she has little use for civilian authority."

The friars slept soundly in the guesthouse, oblivious to the odor of sulfur seeping through the porous windows. They rose in time for morning prayers, after which they shared with their hosts a hearty meal of dense honey-sweetened porridge and delicious sausages. As with the evening before, Véronique suppressed any curiosity about the reason for the friars' journey. Which made William curious.

After the meal the abbess led them toward her residence where they would thank her for her hospitality before departing. They were about to enter when dogs began to bark in the courtyard while chickens and geese scuttled in all directions. William heard the pounding of horses' hooves approaching the convent gate from beyond a row of trees.

"Quickly!" the abbess ordered as they rushed through the front entrance into the foyer. She gestured toward a small door. "In there!" After quietly shutting the door behind them, the friars found themselves in a pantry cluttered with pots, kitchen utensils, and assorted dried goods. The floor creaked whenever they shifted their weight. At the pantry's far end was the base of a stairway. Standing still as statues, they listened as Véronique berated the officer for his impertinence.

The voices fell silent when the friars heard the residence front door creak open and slam shut. Seconds later one of the sisters beckoned them toward the stairway. At the top they entered the abbess's private parlor where William noticed a small hanging tapestry depicting the Lord Jesus dispensing solace to one of his disciples on the eve of the Crucifixion. The rendering of His countenance was no doubt intended to reveal His serene acceptance of what awaited Him. But the Lord's wide-eyed gaze and parted lips instead struck William as disclosing His alarmed surprise. Perhaps a telling clue as to why the nuns' tapestries had not sold well.

The room was unlit except for a shaft of sunlight streaming in through a narrow opened window fronting onto the courtyard. Thirty yards away the slight, pale-skinned abbess stood erect, chin pulled in and arms folded defiantly across her chest, as the officer continued to plead his case. His outstretched palms suggested he was beseeching rather than ordering, though still without discernible success. The officer's half dozen men milled about. Some of them scanned the convent's grounds and buildings in hope of spotting their quarry.

The scene changed abruptly when three more horsemen appeared at the gate. Their mounts trotted at a slow, deliberate pace as they approached Véronique and the blue-clad officer. After halting, one of the horsemen dismounted and began to speak with them.

"Verdun," Michael whispered to the others.

"Who?" William and Bonagratia asked in unison.

"Verdun," Michael repeated, "the officer of the pope's guard who took charge the night of Gerardo's murder."

As he squinted into the sunny courtyard, William now recognized the burly, square-jawed officer who had wrested control of the investigation from a resentful Avignon constable three weeks earlier. The palace and the French Crown were about to resume their jurisdictional squabbles here in Digne.

While Verdun and the Crown's officer spoke, Véronique's head swiveled back and forth as she listened to their exchange. Verdun said something to her, after which he pulled the officer aside and led him to the shade of a large apple tree, well out of the abbess's earshot. Véronique remained where she was, her arms still folded across her chest.

Ten minutes passed as Verdun and the officer spoke. Verdun appeared to have gotten the upper hand, and the officer ordered his men to round up their horses. Less than a minute later the curious friars saw them pass through the convent gate and onto the main road, turning left—west—toward Avignon.

As Verdun and Véronique resumed speaking, William noticed the abbess point in the direction of the baths. Verdun shook his head, apparently declining an invitation to enjoy the baths' miraculous benefits. Instead, he handed her a small packet she tucked discreetly into a fold of her voluminous black and white habit. Finished with his business, Verdun remounted his horse, signaled to his two associates, and headed out the convent gate. The friars watched as Verdun and his men crossed the dilapidated bridge leading into the village.

"Cutthroats indeed!" Véronique scoffed after stomping up the stairs to the parlor. "You would be well advised to leave as soon as possible," she said firmly as she led them down the stairway and out of the residence into the courtyard. "You may not have seen the last of the Crown's men."

* * *

The friars couldn't be certain of the precise point they crossed from eastern Provence into the duchies of northwestern Italy. National and provincial borders constantly shifted because of ongoing political disputes and as tracts of land changed hands between the region's rich landowners. The clearest marker of their progress to the abbey was the variety of Italian dialects they heard. William had to rely on Michael and Bonagratia to translate, but even they found the local tongues hard to understand. He knew they bore only a faint resemblance to the cultured Tuscan dialect Francesco had tried to teach him.

Since their rushed departure from Digne, William's companions conversed with each other more than with him. He kept his thoughts mainly to himself, preoccupied with solving a mystery—three of them in fact. At night, as he lay beneath the Piedmont's starlit sky, his dreams grew more vivid, causing him to jerk into semi-consciousness before trailing off into fitful sleep. His dreams' vividness was now matched by their simplicity: All the earlier figures, except one, were gone.

Eight days into their journey he found, at last, the key to the intersecting puzzles that had taxed his powers of logic and observation ever since Gerardo's murder. It came to him while he dozed on a mule-drawn cart an obliging peddler invited him to climb onto.

Chapter 39

June 4 - June 5, 1328 — Arriving at the Abbey

ON THE NINTH DAY a dry northerly breeze from the Alpine foothills banished the oppressive moist heat the friars had endured at the lower elevations. Their fears of capture receded, although all three were apprehensive about where they were destined after a week's discussion, rest, and prayer at the abbey. Michael worried that his absence from the Franciscans' chapter meeting held a week earlier in Bologna had jeopardized his reelection as the Greyfriars' minister general. William expressed sympathetic concern but wondered why anyone of sound mind would covet such a position.

The three friars passed some of their time speculating about progress in restoring the burnt-out Aedificium. When might its new library be completed? Would it prove easier to navigate than the labyrinth Brother Jorge had set afire? The rebuilt structure would house a more modest collection of volumes and manuscripts than before. But the monks could find what they were looking for when the new library's shelves were installed and stocked.

On the afternoon of the tenth day, as William waged an imaginary debate with Marsilius of Padua, they cleared the crest of a hill and saw the abbey. The only objects visible beyond its walls were the tip of the abbatial church's spire and, dwarfing everything else, the Aedificium. The huge structure rose from a steep mountainside at the base of which, two hundred yards below, were strewn sharp-edged boulders and dead trees. The abbey's southern and western walls sprang from an undulating plateau extending a half-mile toward them and to the right.

The final brief leg of their journey took them along a curving trail lined on one side by pine trees that occasionally blocked their view of the abbey. As they drew closer to the main gate, they passed a score of peasants and a few monks pushing handcarts brimming with building materials and other supplies.

Once through the gate they plunged into a hive of activity. Abbeys were always busy places, and this was the largest and richest William had ever seen. Apart from the few polite nods and curious glances they received, everyone they saw—monks, workers from the nearby village, and a few tradesmen—went about their business, paying no mind to the friars' arrival.

The abbey's day-to-day operations consumed most of the activity, while repairing and restoring the Aedificium accounted for the rest. A dozen men and boys perched precariously on scaffolding, scrubbing away soot left by the flames that scorched the giant building's exterior a year earlier. Carpenters entered and exited its south entrance carrying hammers, saws, chisels, and lumber. There were scores of animals too. A jittery dog rushed toward them and barked either a warning or a greeting and then ran away. A few goats, frightened by the intruders' sudden appearance, also beat a nervous retreat. A gaggle of brazen geese pecked at their feet before being shooed away.

The compound's disparate smells were positively fragrant in the dry Alpine air—another pleasing contrast to Avignon where those same smells would surely have made the atmosphere even more noxious.

"The abbot, Clario, must be somewhere nearby," Michael said on spotting a stable boy leading a dark-coated horse, at least fifteen hands high. "I doubt he'd travel far from the abbey without Brunellus."

Bonagratia gave him a quizzical look.

"The name of his predecessor's favorite horse, which I've heard the new abbot has grown quite fond of," Michael explained. "A joke I confess I didn't fully appreciate when Baskerville told it to me last year."

William had heard the joke before: The philosopher Buridan had given the name *Brunellus* to a donkey to illustrate a paradox implicit in the idea of free will. According to the joke, the donkey is equally thirsty and hungry, and is standing midway between a bucket of water and a haystack. Unable to decide which of its two needs is greater, Brunellus dies of both hunger and thirst.

He was about to comment on the joke when Michael, seeing no one there to welcome them, announced that he would lead his companions on a tour around the compound's periphery. William and Bonagratia were curious and followed him.

Starting clockwise from their left was the infirmary, which stood behind a botanical garden that supplied the herbs dispensed by the resident healers. Next to it was the balneary, which William eyed with special interest. He craved a long-deferred bath even more than the abundance of wine, meats, fruit, and vegetables they had been led to expect.

They continued, skirting a vegetable garden and then winding through a small cemetery near the Aedicficium's main entrance. William assumed that the remains of Jorge's victims occupied five of the graves. Just beyond were pigsties, stables, and a large smithy. Mills, granaries, oil presses, and either a novices' house or servant quarters lined the southern wall.

As they completed their tour, Michael waved to a thin, stooped figure hobbling energetically toward them. William guessed it was the abbot Clario. Trailing behind were three novices, one carrying a large bowl of water for washing their hands and faces, while the other two brought bowls of fruit, presumably to tide the travelers over until their evening meal.

"What great joy it brings me to welcome three of our Lord's most exemplary servants to our humble sanctuary!" Clario exclaimed with grandiloquent modesty as he kissed Michael in holy welcome. "Pray accept my apology for not meeting you at the gate when you arrived. As you might surmise from the bustle of activity, my duties here are beyond counting."

"May I assure Your Sublimity," Michael reciprocated, "that your joy could not exceed our own on receiving the gracious invitation to revisit this blessed haven. Let us pray the events of the next several days will prove more serene than when I was last here."

William winced at Michael's abrupt mention of the fire and Jorge's murders. As if aware of his gaffe, the minister general made a hasty recovery by introducing Clario to William and Bonagratia. The lawyer's long-winded salutation was graceless even by the lawyer's own low standards. When it was William's turn to greet his host, he intoned a litany of pious pleasantries rehearsed earlier that day but feared he had succeeded only in not appearing rude.

Clario then explained to his visitors the daily schedule of activities they could expect during their stay, in particular the canonical hours.

"Since my arrival here last year, I have taken a few liberties in interpreting Saint Benedict's original Rule," he explained. "Matins is still celebrated well before dawn but begins somewhat later than the hour observed by some of our brethren to the south. Lauds concludes almost precisely at dawn . . ." And so the abbot went on with the list of holy offices—Prime, Terce, Sext, Nomes, Vespers, and Compline—which the monks attended. "If I am not mistaken, *we* begin the day somewhat earlier than you Greyfriars." William thought he detected a sly smile as if Clario were giving his guests fair warning that they would awaken the next morning earlier than they might hope.

He continued his lively disquisition on the abbey's activities while escorting the friars along a pebbled avenue toward the church at the center of the compound. The trees on either side of the avenue were groomed so that their higher branches merged to form a dense canopy—an arboreal cathedral, so William imagined it—that the sunlight barely penetrated.

They veered off to the right into the grassy cloister, enclosed on three sides by the abbey's main structures. The largest of these was the church itself—though miniature compared to the Aedificium, whose southern hexagonal tower rose to more than twice the church's height. Opposite the church were the chapter house, refectory, and abbot's residence, and to the east was the abbey's main dormitory. One end of the dormitory was sealed off to provide a pilgrims hospice where, along with other visitors, the three friars would sleep. Clario now deposited them there, anticipating they would want to rest before sharing their evening meal with the others.

"For your privacy," he said before leaving them, "the chapter house will be available to you between Terce and Compline. Except for servants delivering refreshments and a cat to keep the population of mice to a minimum, no one will intrude on your discussions. The southern exposure allows in more than enough light, and because the space overall is far greater than you will need, might I recommend the alcove as more suitable for intimate conversation?"

"By my count," Michael said, "there should be five of us—no, six, including yourself."

Clario declined the invitation. "I am grateful, but I fear my other obligations will prevent me from joining you."

"Your wise counsel is always welcome, but of course we do understand," Michael acknowledged. "So that would leave Brother Bonagratia, Brother William, and myself, joined by Marsilius and Prince Rupert—neither of whom I've yet seen. I trust each arrived safely."

"The prince, yesterday and Signore Marsilius, the day before," the abbot said. "They are well acquainted, as you may know, and are taking an excursion outside the abbey. You can exchange greetings with them at the refectory an hour from now.

"But," Clario added, "you will no doubt be surprised to learn of an additional member of your party. You couldn't have known, nor in truth had I, that Signore Marsilius traveled here in the company of Brother Baskerville, whom you remember from last year's dismaying events. In the months since the passing of our seven brothers, he has visited the abbey to give counsel on the design of the new library. Other reasons, I daresay, prompted his coming this time. And, Brother Occam," the abbot said as he turned toward William, "your august countryman informed me only yesterday the two of you share much in common—in addition, that is, to the coincidence of bearing the same baptismal name."

"That is indeed so," William quietly confirmed.

Chapter 40

June 6, 1328 — The Chapter House

THEY ASSEMBLED THE NEXT MORNING in an alcove of the chapter house, across from the large rectangular room's only entryway. The room was illuminated by sunlight streaming through the horizontal windows lining the south wall. The windows were positioned high enough that no one could see in.

Unlike the highly ornamented chapter houses of the English monasteries William had seen, the room's overall feel was starkly utilitarian. He approved of this: The chapter house was where the abbey's business was done and required little more than the plain wooden seats, some larger than others, built into the walls. The slightly vaulted ceiling, rather than creating an echo chamber, allowed voices to be heard from anywhere in the room. William noticed the cat Clario had mentioned, the designated mouser of the chapter house, prowling about the alcove in search of prey. William didn't dislike cats, but they made him sneeze.

Prince Rupert stood next to a giant unlit fireplace. His erect posture, outthrust chin, and youthful physique exuded imperial authority, an impression he clearly took pains to cultivate. William took an immediate dislike to him but vowed to himself not to show it.

The others sat on straight-backed wooden chairs. Baskerville, with whom William exchanged warm greetings the evening before, drew his chair back from the irregular circle. Unruly strands of iron-grey hair partially covered his ragged tonsure and narrow forehead, while his hooded hazel eyes scanned left and right, surveying the scene. Baskerville had visibly aged since William saw him in London six years earlier. He also noticed a slight tremor in his mentor's voice. The stresses of serving Louis the Bavarian may have taken their toll.

Marsilius of Padua's appearance surprised William until he remembered that northern Italians were often blond and fair. The compact Marsilius wore his curly hair long in keeping with the current fashion. Or perhaps the philosopher was just indifferent about engaging a barber's services. Radicals, William had heard, didn't care how they looked.

Rupert began by relaying the emperor's compliments on the friars' escape from the Usurper's clutches. His French was fluent, but inflected with a deep, gravelly Bavarian accent. This added to William's instinctive dislike of him.

In deference to the Greyfriars' chain of authority, the emperor's nephew directed his questions to Michael rather than to William or Bonagratia. Michael obliged by recounting the events leading up to their departure from Avignon, followed by vivid details of the escape itself. He noted how, disguised as lepers, they outwitted the guards and constables at the Imbert Gate and expressed special satisfaction at having obtained from Francesco Petrarca the Order's official seal, which he now displayed to the others.

"But how did Petrarca get the seal without Dueze knowing?" Marsilius asked. "He's rumored to be a protégé of an Italian cardinal—and something of a poet, I've heard—surely an unlikely member of the pope's inner circle. Could he have stolen it?"

"Francesco didn't steal it," William said, speaking for the first time. "The pope's aide, Fieschi, gave it to him. When I told Francesco that Michael wanted it back, I expected him to scoff at the suggestion. Instead, he promised to make a few inquiries. When we met a week later, I had almost forgotten my earlier mention of it. So when he gave it to me I was surprised. I asked him why one of the pope's closest confidants would take such a risk. He wouldn't say but hinted I'd soon discover the reason."

Bonagratia had doubts. "But why would Fieschi trust a Vatican loyalist like Petrarca with anything? And how did Fieschi get the seal to begin with? Could *he* have stolen it?"

Baskerville slid his chair forward, and everyone's eyes turned instantly toward the famous detective. Despite its tremor, his voice still resonated his customary self-assurance. "Because we've heard no indication Fieschi might be disloyal, we can safely assume he *didn't* steal the seal. Rather, Dueze *gave* it to him. Ergo," Baskerville paused, gesturing an open-handed invitation to William to complete his thought.

"Ergo," William repeated, grateful that his old mentor hadn't completely stolen his thunder, "Dueze isn't dismayed in the least by our escape. Quite the contrary, he planned it, using Fieschi and Francesco to carry out his plan."

Michael and Bonagratio stared at William with mouths agape, while Marsilius' brow furrowed in contemplation, as if curious but not surprised. Baskerville wore an almost imperceptible smile. Expressionless, Rupert signaled for William to continue.

"Duèze's problem was what to do with us. For weeks we wondered why he hadn't announced the verdict, which surely would have found us guilty. But then he'd have no recourse but to send us to the pyre and invite all and sundry to witness the spectacle."

"So why didn't he?" Marsilius asked.

"It may be that our notoriety saved us," William shrugged. "Consider Duèze's position: His papacy, the *Avignon* papacy, is under threat from several quarters. The emperor, for one, would like nothing better than a pretext to send his armies to Avignon."

"Even so, he could have solved his problem in other ways," Marsilius speculated, "say, by ordering the commission to recommend your conviction on minor charges of doctrinal impurity rather than outright heresy. He could then drag out the debate over the poverty question until everyone tired of hearing about it. Or, he could have quietly disposed of all three of you and spread a story you'd gotten your just desserts at others' hands."

"Which is what we feared," William admitted, "although in hindsight we needn't have worried. Duèze must have known no one would believe such a lie. He might have gotten away with it *before* I accused him, but not afterward. So, when he . . ."

A soft rap on the chapter house door interrupted William's explanation.

"*Kommen*," Rupert barked as he rose and strode across the room, evidently presuming that whoever it was wanted to speak with *him*. William felt mildly irked when the spymaster's presumption proved correct. An aide who accompanied him to the abbey two days earlier beckoned from the open doorway. Rupert left to speak with the aide, closing the door behind him on making his exit.

Further discussion of the friars' escape from Babylon would have to wait. Which was just as well, for the door soon reopened, permitting servants to deposit a tray of fresh fruit and another cask of ale on a small table next to the fireplace. Bonagratia carefully selected a pear, Baskerville exited briskly to the privy, and Michael and Marsilius drifted to the far end of the room, beginning a quiet conversation.

As the servants attended to their tasks, William watched the chapter house's cat toy with a mortally wounded mouse. Earlier that morning he noticed Clario's mouser investigating its prey's hiding place in a small gap between the fireplace's hearth and the stone floor. Now exposed, the smaller creature quivered helplessly between repeated swats of its tormentor's paw. The cat then turned away from the mouse and looked up inquiringly at William. *Do you understand?* William did: He was the mouse and Duèze was the cat, still the master of William's fate.

* * *

A half-hour later the spymaster reentered the chapter house and took his station next to the fireplace as the others took their seats. He offered no explanation of the meeting with his aide. "I believe we were discussing the precarious nature of the pope's authority," he said. Turning toward William, "I assume you haven't forgotten that Pope John also has two new kings to contend with."

"Indeed," William agreed. "When the Capets ruled France, Duèze knew he could count on their support—especially Charles's. But cousin Philip took the crown barely a month ago, so Duèze can't know how firmly he can rely on him."

Baskerville inched his chair forward again. "I should think he ought to be more worried about young King Edward. He hasn't yet assumed control, but he soon will—in two or three years at the outside."

William nodded. "Yes, with his mother's and Mortimer's backing, he's already eyeing the French Crown. Which," glancing toward the better-informed Rupert, "would make the emperor Edward's natural ally in the event of a war between England and France—obviously a bad omen for the pope."

"Perhaps, but war is far from imminent," Marsilius said. "By the time Edward makes his move, Duèze could be dead. He's well past eighty."

"The desiccated old gnome does have his legacy to protect," Michael said. "He doesn't want to be the last Avignon pope."

"Desiccated he might be," Marsilius said, "but shrewd enough to contrive your escape—and with few others at the palace knowing about it. Should we assume no one knew other than Fieschi and Petrarca?"

"I'm not certain, but I believe someone else *did* know," Michael said, "someone in the pope's close orbit who passed word of the plan to the emperor's people."

"What makes you believe that?" an astonished Marsilius asked.

"Just a few inadvertent hints by the emperor's agents I spoke with before we left. They knew more about our plan than they could have learned from me."

"Brother Michael's hunch is correct," Rupert acknowledged, having again risen to his feet. "I suppose there's little risk in divulging who our source was, but I ask you to keep his identity to yourselves." After waiting for nods of consent, he said, "It was John of Reading. Contriving your escape was in fact Reading's idea. He suspected you wouldn't sit on your thumbs, waiting to be carted off to the pyre, and he knew the pope and his minions would suspect it as well. He was also sure they would prevent you from leaving unless he intervened."

"Why would he take such a risk?" Michael asked. He and Bonagratia appeared stunned by Rupert's revelation. William wasn't, but winced at not having suspected Reading's role earlier.

"There *was* no risk to Reading," Rupert replied. "His loyalties may be divided, but here they converged. On the one hand, he wanted to keep you alive, mainly out of affection for his brother Greyfriars. He regards the promiscuous torching of heretics and infidels as supremely distasteful, especially when they're his friends. On the other hand, for self-interested reasons he wouldn't betray the pope. Like Fieschi, Reading's fortunes are tied to him."

"How did Reading convince him?" William asked, impressed once again with Rupert's knowledge of high-level goings-on inside the palace.

"Our agents report that he first broached the idea with Fieschi, who then relayed it to the pope. I doubt Reading spoke with him directly."

"So how did Reading convince Fieschi?"

"His reasoning was apparently the same as yours," Rupert said. "Which accounts for why I haven't been surprised by anything you've told us. Through Fieschi he was able to convince the pope that letting you escape was the prudent thing to do. Reading was able to have it both ways: He could serve Pope John's interests *and* protect his friends."

"What about Petrarca?" Michael asked. "Did Reading deal with *him?*"

"Probably not," Rupert said. "Fieschi coordinated everything, and instructions to Petrarca came from him. Reading knew about Petrarca's part in it, but Petrarca was told nothing of Reading's."

Nodding toward William, "Fieschi used your young friend, and for obvious reasons told him very little."

After tapping a foot in contemplation, Marsilius said, "Duèze may have miscalculated, especially if rumors of his complicity in your escape spread beyond the palace. Once he realizes that, he'll have to do something to lay the rumors to rest. On balance, I think he's now in a weaker position."

"I suspect so," Baskerville agreed. "Now that the three of you are safely out of Babylon you may soon hear reports of Duèze blustering in outrage over your cowardly exit. You could also expect him to send his legions to search for you, promising little short of sainthood to anyone who turns you in."

Baskerville's comment evoked sardonic smiles from everyone except the humorless Bonagratia. But William noticed that his old friend's voice had begun to falter again, as if speaking required strenuous effort.

Chapter 41

June 7, 1328 — The Chapter House

MORE THAN ONE BATH per week was sure to provoke curious asides from the monks, but William had never taken seriously warnings about the perils of frequent bathing. Cleanliness, he recalled from Avicenna's *Canon of Medicine*, was a surer prophylactic against disease than the potions prescribed by the resident shamans. Perhaps exposure of their fraud would force them to find honest work and admit that an ancient infidel knew better than they did.

He was ruminating about this when Michael spotted him exiting the balneary. He was drying himself with a towel one of the monks lent him. It was his second bath in the three days since they arrived at the abbey.

"There you are!" Michael said accusingly. His irritation was evident from the higher pitch of his voice. "The others are wondering what became of you, asking questions I can't answer about Gerardo's murder—that and other matters."

William didn't reply to Michael's semi-rebuke. He finished dressing and nodded his thanks as he handed the towel to the friendly monk. Michael was in a hurry to get back to the chapter house, and William struggled to keep up as they walked across the cloister.

"Baskerville has sent his regrets," Michael said. "He's exhausted from his journey and needs to rest. Perhaps he'll rejoin us tomorrow."

"I'm worried. Yesterday he looked tired, but I fear it may be more than exhaustion." Apart from William's concern about his old friend's health, he was disappointed that Baskerville would not be there to hear his other secrets. He changed the subject.

"I assume you understand that the prince's favors come at a price."

"Most certainly," Michael agreed. "A haven at his uncle's expense, and in return we answer his questions. Although, Rupert seems to know the answers beforehand."

"Many of them, at least. And when he doesn't, he shows an uncanny instinct for asking the right questions. He didn't rise to his position just because he's the emperor's nephew."

It was another fine day, and the sun shone brightly through the high windows. On the table by the fireplace sat a tray brimming with figs, pears, and pomegranates. Marsilius munched on a fig and invited William to try one.

"They're quite excellent, every bit as savory as figs grown farther to the south."

The philosopher was an epicurean, which William most assuredly wasn't. He could learn much from Marsilius in addition to his interesting opinions about Pope John's perfidy.

Bonagratia sat to William's right, making a mess of a pomegranate, its sticky red juice dribbling down his pointed chin onto his scapular. He wiped his face and fingers on a towel as his eyes darted about in embarrassment.

Rupert drummed and tapped his fingers on the fireplace mantle as he waited for the others to settle in their chairs. He had questions.

"In your absence, Brother William, I've learned from Brother Michael that your travails in Avignon ranged far beyond your unhappy experience with the pope and his commission. You must feel doubly grateful on having reached here alive."

"The swords of the Church and the Kingdom cross in myriad ways. I've had the bad luck of being on the wrong end of both at the same time."

Rupert displayed a thin smile. "Bad luck indeed. But my interest extends beyond the vicarious enjoyment of your adventures. I'm certain the emperor will be keen to hear, for example, your opinion about why you were an assassin's target."

William hesitated as he gathered his thoughts. "I have a theory—*only* a theory—that may explain matters. If I appear diffident, it's from not knowing quite where to start."

"Perhaps with the killing of the Englishman after your last meeting with Francesco?" Michael suggested. William had not told him everything at the convent the afternoon before their escape, which Michael apparently suspected.

"In fact, there were *two* Englishmen, in addition to me," William began. "One was Gerard D'Alspaye, one of Mortimer's agents. He killed the second one. Earlier, when I realized I was the intended target when Gerardo was murdered, I assumed the assassin would come after me. I learned from earlier correspondence from London that Mortimer sent D'Alspaye to Avignon, but at first I had no reason to believe he had any interest in me. A week before our escape, however, I noticed someone dressed like a wealthy Englishman following me, a man I'd never seen before. Then, at my final meeting with Petrarca, I described him and without hesitation he said it was D'Alspaye. At that moment I knew—or thought I knew—the identity of Gerardo's killer. But I still had no idea as to his motive."

"What of the second Englishman," Rupert asked, "the man you say D'Alspaye killed? Did you identify him?"

"Not to the constables, but I knew at once it was Stephen Dunheved, the *old* King Edward's bodyguard. In truth, he was far more than that."

"You're certain of it?" Rupert seemed surprised by this revelation, and William felt pleased the spymaster did not know everything. The others appeared confused.

"Oh yes, quite certain," William replied with a harsh laugh. "The two of us had unpleasant encounters before—unpleasant for *me*, I should say."

"I'm baffled," Michael sputtered. "Why were all three of you near the Carmelite convent at the same time? You said D'Alspaye was following you in order to kill you. If so, what was Dunheved, of all people, doing there?"

"No, no," William said. "*Dunheved* killed Gerardo. It wasn't D'Alspaye. And it was Dunheved who was trying to kill *me*."

"But why in Jesus' holy name would D'Alspaye come to your rescue?" the astonished Michael asked, "And how could he have known Dunheved was after you?

"It took me days to answer those very questions, but here is what I concluded: Dunheved killed Gerardo, having mistaken him for me. D'Alspaye *knew* of Dunheved's error and therefore assumed that he—Dunheved, that is—still intended to kill me. For reasons I've yet to explain, D'Alspaye wanted to kill Dunheved. D'Alspaye's problem was how to find him."

"He evidently *did* find him," Michael said. "But why did it take so long? Almost two weeks passed between Gerardo's murder and D'Alspaye's killing Dunheved."

"Two reasons," William explained. "First, Dunheved may have been wounded while killing Gerardo. The palace guard who examined his body noticed blood on the staff he carried—*my* staff, as it happened. The guard speculated, correctly I believe, that the blood on the staff was the killer's, not Gerardo's, and that Gerardo used the staff to defend himself. Depending on the severity of his wounds, Dunheved could have been forced into hiding until he recovered. And second, as a professional assassin Dunheved was no doubt accomplished at disguising his appearance. So D'Alspaye could identify Dunheved only when he exposed himself while trying to kill me."

"So, you were D'Alspaye's Judas goat, leading the unsuspecting Dunheved to slaughter," Marsilius said.

"Which would mean," Rupert said as he raised a skeptical eyebrow, "that D'Alspaye possesses a rare combination of patience, agility, and good fortune."

William twitched nervously on hearing Rupert's doubts. He had doubts of his own. Had D'Alspaye simply been lucky? Or could there be another explanation of his success in tracking William to find and kill Dunheved?

* * *

On that uncertain note the discussion stalled, and by unspoken agreement everyone rose—some to stretch their legs and others to refill their goblets. William wanted to be alone and quietly slipped out of the chapter house and headed across the cloister to the cemetery next to the Aedificium. A stiff breeze had sprung up, causing the giant building's scaffolding to sway back and forth. He worried for the safety of the workmen who continued scrubbing the soot from the outer walls. As he watched them darting about on their precarious perch, he recalled the scaffolding he had walked beneath in the royal palace in Paris after Eleanor de Clare's first confession. That was fourteen years ago, and now four years since he last saw her in London. As far as he knew, she still languished in the Tower of London as Mortimer and Isabella's prisoner, probably pale and thin from her captivity and despairing over the loss of her children. Did she have either the time or the inclination to think about him, or had her memory of him now dimmed? And if ever their paths crossed again, how might she greet him, and how would he greet her? Would their meeting be awkward? Would they touch, if only by accident? Nothing like an embrace, and a kiss was out of the question. He didn't know how to do that anyway.

* * *

William willed these thoughts away as he walked back to the chapter house. His edginess returned as he contemplated a final secret he had not revealed. The others were already seated and looked expectantly as he reentered the circle. As usual, it was Prince Rupert who prompted him.

"I must say, Brother William, you're better informed about English court politics than any mendicant preacher I've come across. But you still haven't told us why Dunheved wanted to kill you *or* his reason for going to Avignon. Or *D'Alspaye's* reason, come to think of it. Why was *he* in Avignon at the same time as Dunheved?"

William paused briefly to consider his words carefully. "Dunheved and D'Alspaye wanted to protect the same secret, but for different reasons. And each believed that *I* knew the secret."

"So tell us what it was." Rupert persisted. "I'm sure I'm not the only one gripped by the suspense of not knowing."

William took a deep breath. "Dunheved brought Edward II to Avignon."

The room turned dead silent. No one could hide his shocked disbelief—except the emperor's spymaster, who William noticed slowly nodding his head in understanding.

A long moment passed before Bonagratia finally spat, "What? That can't be! He's been *dead* for—"

"No. Edward is alive. I saw him on the Saint Bénézet Bridge, entering Avignon. Dunheved must have been close by and saw me looking in Edward's direction. He probably suspected, perhaps believed for a certainty, that I recognized the old king. He was disguised in beggar's rags."

"So why didn't you tell us?" Michael asked angrily as he struggled to digest what he had just heard.

William exhaled deeply before continuing. "At the time I didn't realize the 'beggar' was Edward. One often sees what one *expects* to see. Since, like everyone else, I 'knew' Edward was dead, I dismissed the spark of recognition. I didn't realize it was Edward until the three of us had almost reached the abbey."

"Given your abundance of theories, I assume you can enlighten us with another," Rupert said with mild sarcasm. "Tell us about Edward's amazing rise from the dead and miraculous transport to the south of France. It seems your sources of intelligence are better than the emperor's."

William wasn't sure whether he had received a compliment or a rebuke. "A letter I received from London spoke of the 'mystery' surrounding Edward's death last September. My correspondent raised questions about the generally accepted account: that Edward was slain in his sleep by two of Mortimer's men. At first I assumed the mystery had to do with *who* murdered Edward, but I later realized my correspondent had raised doubts about *whether* he was dead. The letter also mentioned that Mortimer sent D'Alspaye to Avignon but didn't say what his mission was."

"Let me interrupt with another question or two," Rupert said. "How did Edward escape from—where was it—Berkeley castle? Or might he have been released?"

"An 'escape' contrived by his captors, you mean, just as ours was from Avignon?" William asked. "Possibly, but I'm inclined to doubt it."

"Either way, Dunheved must have had a hand in it," Rupert said. "After all, you say he accompanied Edward to Avignon and earlier—correct me if I'm wrong—led three attempts in England to rescue him, all of which reportedly failed. But perhaps the third attempt succeeded. The question, then, is whether Dunheved received help from anyone else."

"Mortimer and Isabella?" Michael asked.

"Or that the barons still loyal to Edward were somehow able to free him," Marsilius suggested.

"Our agents in England," Rupert said, "report there weren't enough of them with the resources to carry it off. As Michael suggests, any help would have come from Mortimer and Isabella." Rupert then immediately reversed himself. "But no, that can't be right! Dunheved and Mortimer *hated* each other. What circumstance could possibly have led them to cooperate?"

Marsilius agreed. "Especially since Mortimer sent his agents—D'Alspaye and perhaps others—to find Edward and kill him before he reached Avignon."

"Which would mean," Rupert conceded after rethinking the matter, "that Dunheved must have received help from his own followers." Rupert was now squinting at the floor, shaking his head, as if he didn't know quite what to believe.

William listened intently to the others' hypotheses as he chewed on another fig. Clario's cat prowled near the fireplace. The first mouse lay in a corner, obviously dead.

"I think it far more likely Isabella and Mortimer have had a serious falling out," he said, "which explains what their agents were up to. Mortimer had no motive for conspiring in Edward's escape. Otherwise, why would he send D'Alspaye to Avignon? Mortimer wanted Edward killed before he could get there. If the pope learned Edward was alive, Mortimer's control over his son—indeed all of England—could collapse, or so he must have feared. Isabella, on the other hand, may have had a *motive* for helping Edward escape but no opportunity to make it happen. She may be cunning, but as a 'mere woman' she would have no allies in England to help her. It's safe to assume Mortimer controlled virtually everyone in her orbit and could easily put a stop to her."

"So, even if she couldn't arrange her husband's escape, she stood to profit from it once it took place," Marsilius concluded as he refilled his goblet. "But what did she have to gain?"

"Her 'gain' in keeping him alive may have been that she still loved him," William replied while refilling his own goblet. "Remember, her alliance with Mortimer sprang from their mutual hatred of Despenser. She and Mortimer may or not have been lovers, as the scandalmongers whispered, but once Edward escaped, the young king would soon learn of it. Knowing of her son's love for his father, Isabella wouldn't conspire with Mortimer in killing Edward, even if she no longer loved him. That fact alone would suggest that a breach occurred between her and Mortimer—assuming it didn't occur earlier."

"I'm still curious about D'Alspaye," Rupert said, changing the subject. "Wouldn't *he* have wanted you dead? Both he and Dunheved wanted Edward's escape from England kept secret. If D'Alspaye thought you knew Edward was alive, he would also have a motive for killing you. If so, why did he come to your rescue?"

"D'Alspaye didn't kill Dunheved for my benefit. And he probably wouldn't have cared if Dunheved *had* killed me before he killed Dunheved. For all I know, D'Alspaye might have slit my throat, too, but didn't because he had to make a hasty escape. Dunheved was his higher priority."

"A good thing you left Avignon when you did," Marsilius observed dryly.

"The thought had occurred to me."

Chapter 42

June 8, 1328   The Chapter House

A LIGHT RAIN HAD BEGUN to fall as they reassembled in the chapter house for a third day. Sunlight no longer streamed through the windows, so a few oil lamps were lit. To William the darker room felt anything but somber. He found it hard to imagine that the abbey, a place so teeming with vibrant energy, could ever seem so. Although a year ago it surely must have when the horror of seven grisly deaths almost destroyed it. The Benedictines, he concluded, were a resilient bunch: Owing to their labors the scrubbed-down and refurbished Aedificium shone again as a giant beacon of welcome and strength.

The abbot Clario beamed with obvious pride (a pardonable sin in William's opinion) at his abbey's phoenix-like renewal, and he made certain his guests shared in its hard-won bounty. Servants and a few novices came and went, depositing fresh fruit and the cellarer's fine cheeses along with ample quantities of ale and excellent wine. Even the nervous Bonagratia appeared relaxed, perhaps because he had given up contending with perilous pomegranates. He settled now for more manageable figs, apples, and pears. The register of Michael's voice had lowered to its normal level, although his occasional frown told William he was still worried about his reelection. He had heard no word from Bologna.

William swapped jokes with Marsilius, including the one about Brunellus, the former abbot's favorite horse Clario had inherited. Marsilius laughed, though he had probably heard it before. William had also heard some of Marsilius' jokes, but it hardly mattered. The engaging banter during their evening walks about the cloister led him to believe he may have acquired a new friend he could both trust and learn from.

As William sat on his chair in the chapter house, his bitter memories of Avignon's stench and corruption receded. He felt safe for the first time since leaving London. Here at the abbey he had solved, or so he believed, three puzzles whose solutions he took pleasure in revealing. All that remained were loose ends to tie together.

Best of all, William's mood was brightened by his mentor's return. "A day of recuperation appears to have sparked a minor miracle," he remarked as a reinvigorated Baskerville settled into the cushioned chair provided by one of the monks.

"So it seems," the old friar agreed. Baskerville's voice no longer quavered as it had two days earlier, and his eyes again gleamed with their usual intensity. "Clario has been most attentive, and some of Brother Guido's herbals may have spurred my recovery. But solicitude soon feels cloying, so might we get on with the business that brought us here? Before retiring last evening, Prince Rupert summarized yesterday's most interesting discussion. I still have a few questions, but they can wait." He glanced at Marsilius' tapping feet and said, "*His* curiosity may exceed even my own."

Marsilius' pale cheeks reddened, but he was undeterred by Baskerville's amiable jibe. "Last evening I was kept awake wondering why Edward went to Avignon following his escape. And wondering also how Mortimer and Isabella could have known."

"Probably from their agents in France," Rupert interrupted before William could reply. The emperor's spymaster had just entered the room. "Even if they weren't certain of his destination, they could easily guess. If Edward remained in England, they would find him within days. His remaining supporters couldn't hide him indefinitely, and he had few friends left on the Continent. Perhaps he could have made his way to Ireland, but it's hardly safer there than in England. And his cousin Robert the Bruce would catch and likely execute him as soon as he set foot on Scottish soil. Seeking the pope's protection in Avignon may have been the only avenue left to him."

"I suspect he had more allies, at least on the Continent, than you might suppose," William suggested. "Though once away from England, he would have had great difficulty in tracking them down. And how could *they* have found *him*—even if they knew of his escape? He could hardly have made his presence widely known."

"Perhaps he had another reason," Baskerville added. "I recall hearing several years ago that Edward believed his many failures as king resulted from not being anointed with the Holy Oil of Saint Thomas at his coronation. By going to Avignon, he could renew his request to redeem himself from his past failures."

William remembered the story too: Edward once wrote to Pope John, who had just been installed in Avignon, asking him to send a cardinal to anoint him. The pope refused but did say that if Edward believed in Thomas Becket's prophecy concerning the oil's benefits, it would not be sinful for him to be anointed by the pope himself. This bothered Edward for years, knowing that his rival Philip the Fair was anointed on *his* coronation.

"Apart from whether Duèze has gotten around to anointing him," the skeptical Marsilius said, "Edward was probably more worried about whether Duèze would protect him."

"Surely he would," Rupert said. "I suspect he already *has*. Assuming they've now met, Duèze must regard the king's visit as a great windfall, especially if he's able to keep it secret."

"If Edward did meet with the pope, where is he now?" Bonagratia asked as he watched Marsilius consume a deftly peeled pomegranate. William leaned forward in his chair, also eager to know the answer.

"Somewhere away from Avignon," Rupert said. "In the Pyrenees or in Italy, maybe not far from here. Duèze would want to spirit Edward out of the city as soon as he could. His remaining there would serve no purpose, and trying to hide a deposed king in the papal enclave could prove awkward. The secret would surely come out if he stayed more than a week or two."

* * *

The discussion halted as four of the others exited the chapter house for a breath of fresh air. Gnawing on an apple, William remained seated next to the fireplace. Rupert drifted to a far corner of the large room and gazed at what William had earlier judged to be a thoroughly uninteresting tapestry. The spymaster appeared to be deep in thought as he idly tapped the toe of an expensive boot against the base of a slightly raised dais. The same dais, William assumed, that Clario stood on when he conducted the abbey's business each afternoon before Compline.

The others straggled in a few minutes later and took their seats. Rupert was the last to reenter the circle and broke the silence.

"Brother William's *speculations*," the emperor's agent carefully intoned, "can't be faulted for lacking coherence or failing to include impressive supporting evidence. But I need not remind him or the rest of you that other explanations may fit the same set of facts. To begin with, unless Brother William's powers of observation were impaired, which I doubt, Edward did leave England and reach Avignon, getting at least as far as the bridge. But we still don't know the circumstances behind his escape—or his release, whichever it was—nor are we entirely certain that after crossing the bridge he met with Duèze. Though it's now unlikely, Edward could be dead, killed by D'Alspaye or other of Mortimer's agents.

"Second, the evidence of a falling out between Mortimer and Isabella is debatable. Absent anything more than Brother William's impressions, a rift appears to be mere surmise, unless he knows something he hasn't confided.

"Also, if the pope met with Edward soon after he arrived, why would Dunheved and D'Alspaye remain in Avignon? With Edward safely under Duèze's protection, Dunheved would no longer have a strong enough reason to protect the king's secret by killing Brother William—unless he wanted to settle an old score. And D'Alspaye, knowing he had failed in his mission to kill Edward, would surely have left for England with his tail between his legs. Except out of sheer spite, he would no longer have a reason to wait around in Avignon, hoping to kill Dunheved.

"Finally, I'm still troubled by Brother William's explanation of D'Alspaye's most remarkable talent, or perhaps luck, in tracking him for more than a week, expecting he would lead him to Dunheved. The 'Judas goat' theory feels a bit contrived.

"That said, I concede that Brother William may be entirely correct. For the present, his is the best theory we have. But we can't know the full truth until all the facts are in."

William resisted the urge to quell Rupert's doubts, in part because it would mean betraying Eleanor's confidences. He had kept her identity as his correspondent to himself and saw no need to reveal it now. He knew, however, that the content of her letters wouldn't, and couldn't, satisfy completely Rupert's lingering curiosity.

After another lengthy silence, Baskerville began to chuckle. "I trust that you won't take umbrage, Brother William, at my suggesting one more reason to question the sum of what you've told us. In other contexts you've lauded the virtue of parsimony: When confronted with more than one explanation of the same phenomenon, the simpler explanation is likely to be the best one. I realize you've amended several qualifiers to that principle, but I'm hard pressed to conceive of a more complicated explanation of the events in Avignon than the one you've given us."

"You may remember," William said as he forced a smile, "that I first learned the nub of that principle from you. So I assume your misgivings at the moment aren't exceedingly strenuous. Still, I've pondered at some length that same irony and can only say in my defense that history seldom honors the canons of logic."

Chapter 43

June 10, 1328 — the Abbey and the Trail to the Alps

T WAS STILL PITCH-DARK an hour before Matins. William had slept deeply until, from the cot next to his in the pilgrims hospice, Michael of Cesena's snoring interrupted a dream. It was a scene somewhere near Oxford: rivercraft gliding on the Thames, sweet violets in bloom, two women—Eleanor and Joyeuse (he realized upon waking)—merged into a single form. He hoped the dream would resume if he could will himself back to sleep.

Shuffling feet and a flickering candle vanquished his hope. He squinted in the faint light and saw that Michael and Baskerville were stirring. Marsilius had already risen from his cot to light a lamp. A few feet away in the semi-darkness Prince Rupert quietly conferred with someone. After rubbing the sleep from his eyes, William recognized the man speaking with Rupert—cropped blond hair, a thick reddish beard, an erect Teutonic posture.

"This is Berengar," Rupert said to William, "I believe you have met."

Berengar gave a brusque nod, a salute more than a greeting.

"Briefly, last summer," William acknowledged as he cleared his throat.

Rupert waited while the others roused fully and began to move about. Bonagratia was the last to be awake and alert.

Rupert then announced to the entire room, "It appears the pope has had second thoughts. Three days ago he dispatched his guards to take you back to Avignon. Berengar will provide more details, though I should tell you his report comes courtesy of our friend Reading."

He held an opened packet of parchment, which Berengar had brought. The aide looked exhausted from his ride—three, perhaps two days on horseback with little rest along the way. His leather breeches were spattered with mud, and his beard was caked with dust and dried sweat.

"I don't know its full significance," Rupert said, "but something Brother William once wrote has been circulating through the palace—spread by someone extremely displeased about your departure." He looked down at the parchment and then at William. "*Gott im Himmel*! Did you really say *women* had the right to overthrow the pope?"

Michael of Cesena let out a weak groan, and Marsilius laughed sharply but then caught himself. Bonagratia exclaimed, "You said *what*?"

Baskerville shook his head, heaved a deep sigh, and said to William, "I trust you recall my advising you to *burn* it."

William's face reddened at his old mentor's reminder.

"Brother Occam's *manifesto*," Baskerville continued, "concocted years ago in a spasm of youthful exuberance."

"It must have been Lutterell, maybe Burley, possibly both," William said. Upon which he recounted a brief history of his intemperate screed, which, with his copy of Lombard's *Book of Sentences*, went missing fourteen years earlier. "And not just women," he concluded his tale, "but the laity as a whole—women *and* men."

No one appeared mollified by that clarification.

Several seconds passed before the puzzled Michael said to William, "Even if Duèze was outraged by your, um, 'manifesto,' surely he couldn't have been surprised. After all, you had already accused him of heresy. So why has he changed his mind?"

Before William could answer, Baskerville provided the explanation. "Duèze would be offended less by its *content* than by how many others have read it. Except for the commission, hardly anyone would have known of Brother William's accusing him of heresy. But if everyone at the palace is now gossiping about his manifesto, Duèze will be livid, especially if he hadn't known of it beforehand. His *Holiness* doesn't like surprises."

Michael shook his head as he pondered another question. "Except out of spite, why would Burley *or* Lutterell have leaked it?"

William was about to venture a guess that would include choice words to describe their stupidity, but the impatient Rupert interrupted his thought.

"What's done is done! We have to move quickly." He looked toward Berengar. "How soon before they arrive?"

Berengar tugged on his beard. "Reading says Verdun was put in charge. From what I know of him, he'll waste little time getting here. He could reach the abbey later today, tomorrow at the latest."

"We can't risk waiting until then," Rupert said as he strapped his sheathed dagger to his thigh. The others began to pack their belongings, which in the case of the four Franciscans were few.

"Where will we go?" Michael asked. His voice had risen to a higher octave.

"The emperor and two battalions of the Imperial Guard are encamped outside Pisa," Rupert said. "We could make it there in four or five days."

"What if we run into Verdun?" asked Michael, who was well acquainted with the region's roads and trails. "From here, the main route—the *only* route—toward Pisa will take us ten miles straight toward them before the road forks to the south."

Rupert nodded his agreement. "The more reason to leave at first light, if not before." He then addressed William. "I recall you saying you've never been on a horse."

The evening before, William, Michael, and Bonagratia had regaled the others with a vivid account of their midnight flight from Babylon. His tongue loosened by libations from the abbey's wine cellar, William had expounded on his whimsical fantasy of stealing horses from the pope's stable.

With strained bravado and a tinge of guilt, he said, "There's always a first time."

The spymaster shook his head. "Too great a risk. Not just for you but for the rest of us, not to mention the horse. Between here and the fork, the route is too dangerous for an inexperienced rider. Even on level terrain, you'd have little chance of surviving a chase."

"So what do you propose?"

Rupert paused to consider his reply. "North—the Alter Hof."

Der Alte Hof: the emperor's castle in Bavaria. William was surprised by Rupert's proposal—his *decision*—but did not object. In Bavaria other errant friars under Louis' protection would be there to welcome him.

Rupert briefly conferred with his aide and then said, "Berengar will take you to the base of the route through the mountains. After that, you'll be on your own."

The spymaster paused and handed William a second packet Berengar had brought. "A message for you from Reading."

* * *

The first rays of sunlight peeked over the Alps. With Clario at his side, William watched his five companions ride out through the abbey's main gate. Moments before, the abbot had effusively conveyed his regrets over their hurried departure. He had also generously provided horses for Michael and Bonagratia. Rupert, Marsilius, and Baskerville had horses of their own, which they rode to the abbey five days earlier.

Weeks would pass before William knew whether they had eluded their pursuers. He worried about this, though he now had a more immediate concern. At the smithy he overheard Berengar having words with Brother Antonio, the abbey's blacksmith. Berengar's horse suffered from an inflammation in the hock of its left hind leg, likely caused by an ill-fitting shoe. Indeed, all four of the shoes needed to be replaced, a task complicated by the size of the animal's hooves. Berengar's steed was even larger than Clario's Brunellis, so Antonio would have to forge new shoes to fit. Adding to the horse's woes (thus Berengar's too), Antonio recommended plying the inflamed hock with heated salves. This would require consulting with one of the infirmary's shamans, Brother Agnolo, who knew the right amount of heat to apply and the correct technique for administering the procedure. Agnolo, however, suffered the aftereffects of his dinner the evening before (which featured tainted goat's meat) and made frequent trips to a nearby privy. This made his consultation sporadic, and Antonio predicted it would be several hours before the horse was reshod and fit to travel. The spymaster's otherwise imperturbable aide was in foul temper, but there was nothing he and William could do but wait.

William spent the next hours exploring the compound. He hadn't yet been inside the Aedificium; so he entered, careful not to get in the way of the carpenters, still weeks from completing the building's restoration. He climbed the stairs to the upper tiers, hoping to investigate the labyrinth where Brother Jorge had hidden his secrets. But as William neared the top, he found that the labyrinth was gone, now replaced by easy-to-negotiate stairways, corridors, and rooms. He felt vaguely disappointed, for he had hoped to experience firsthand the sanctum where the mad librarian had plotted his mayhem.

The uppermost tier consisted of a single enormous room, which William assumed was the new scriptorium. The recently laid floor was barren of shelves, desks, and other furniture, but William was surprised to find a few scraps of parchment that had eluded the workmen's brooms. He sifted through them, fancying he might find scorched remnants of the Bede manuscripts Reading had failed to purchase for the pope a year earlier. Instead, the only item that piqued his interest was a smudged drawing of a fox. It must be Reynard, the sly fox of French folklore the Greyfriars' best illuminator had drawn hours before Gerardo's murder.

Then he remembered he hadn't yet read Reading's message, so he laid the drawing of the fox aside. Sitting cross-legged on the floor, he broke the seal and scanned its two pages, expecting to find more news of Duèze's plans. But Reading's message added nothing to what William already knew from Rupert and Berengar's briefing. He was pleased to learn, however, that Reading had stored his stack of manuscripts for safekeeping.

The message's final item, hastily scrawled as a postscript, made William's heart sink:

. . . No doubt you will recall Friar Guarin's sister

Joyeuse, whom we saw at the pyre with Brother Gerardo last autumn. I was filled with sadness on learning of her death. Two days ago the poor creature was found on the bank downriver from the bridge. May our merciful God rest her soul. . . .

* * *

William exited the Aedificium's south door ten minutes later. It was approaching midday, and an agitated Berengar was listening to one of the monks speak excitedly as he gestured toward the abbey's gate. Other monks and a few workmen scurried about as Clario barked instructions.

Berengar saw William approach and beckoned him closer. His reshod horse stood next to him. "They are here," he said, "a half-mile from the gate, just above the ridge—about a dozen of them."

Berengar had told him earlier that morning they would not leave through the abbey's main gate, which would have taken them west in the same direction as Rupert and the others. Instead, they would exit through a smaller gate by the stables at the compound's east end. From there, William and Berengar would follow a trail eventually merging with the northern route William would take through the mountains. This first leg of his journey to Bavaria would be steep and perilous, but with luck he and Berengar would complete it by dawn the next morning.

His thoughts of poor Joyeuse receded as he and Berengar walked quickly toward the stables. The huge horse barely squeezed through the gate's narrow opening and had to lower its head lest it scrape against the crossbeam. Once outside the abbey's walls, they would travel most of the way on foot, Berengar pulling at his horse's reins and William trailing behind with his staff. The horse's hock needed more time to heal before it could be ridden.

Soon after starting their ascent from the abbey, William said, "Since Verdun has now reached the abbey, I assume the others made it to the fork before he did."

Berengar nodded and said, "In which case he still doesn't know any of you have left."

"How long will he wait to find out?"

"Not long," Berengar said as he turned his attention to the rocky trail.

* * *

From the trail William caught glimpses of the chasm he had seen five days earlier, just north of the abbey's wall, where dead trees and jagged rocks were strewn at the base. Human bones lay scattered among them.

From his present vantage, the abbey lay to the left of the chasm. He saw it occasionally through slight openings in the pine trees that lined the trail. He may have seen a dozen horsemen just inside the main gate, but he wasn't certain of this because the trees mostly obstructed his line of sight. Just as well. If he couldn't see Verdun's men, they couldn't see him and Berengar.

They reached the crest of a hill where the trail leveled out and intersected with another, less-trodden path merging from the left. William paused, panting for breath but grateful at the prospect of the more gradual climb ahead of him. Tree branches rustled in the breeze, pinecones plopped on the ground, and small animals scurried through the underbrush. Unfazed by his own exertions, Berengar steadied the jittery horse as it navigated the trail's sharp turns.

After resting, William started up again and drew even with Berengar, who had stopped to inspect his horse's leg. He knelt to apply more of Brother Agnolo's salve, which he had packed along with other provisions. He unbuckled his sword and laid it aside. The large weapon dangling from his belt interfered with his ministrations. "Go on ahead," he said. "Blitzen and I will catch up with you."

William blanched on hearing the name for the first time but forbore comment. He continued about thirty yards and rounded a bend in the trail. Berengar and Blitzen were now out of sight. He plodded along the path, occasionally looking back to see if they were closing the gap. The sounds he heard earlier had faded. Another minute passed when he heard Blitzen whinnying. The great beast sounded distressed—probably its inflamed hock, which must have been tender to Berengar's touch.

A few steps later he heard muffled voices from the same direction. His heart pounded as he rushed back to the bend in the trail. From behind a tree he saw two armed guards clad in brown uniforms—Verdun's men. Berengar was on hands and knees in a widening of the trail. One of the guards pointed a sword at his neck, while the second stood close by, scanning the area for other quarry. A few feet away, Blitzen pawed at the dirt.

William considered fleeing but quickly rejected the idea. He didn't know the way to the route through the Alps, and the guards would easily catch him if he made a dash for it. But mainly, he couldn't abandon Berengar. That would be an act of cowardice for which he could never forgive himself. Seeing no choice but to surrender, he edged from behind the tree into a clearing.

The second guard spotted him immediately, and William was surprised the guard didn't rush forward to put him in shackles. Perhaps confident he had nothing to fear, the guard laughed at the pathetic, defenseless figure in the shabby grey habit limping toward him.

William's spine stiffened at the sound of the guard's laughter. He heard echoes from his past—the laughter of bullies who taunted him in his youth, the jeering of the two workmen who attacked him on the road to Occam fourteen years earlier. Drawing nearer, he exaggerated his limp for the guard's further amusement and bent forward like a lame old man steadying himself lest he stumble and fall.

Time slowed as his grip on his staff tightened.

The guard winked at his associate and then, smirking as he held out an open hand, said, "Here, allow me to unburden you of your . . ."

At which William jammed his staff into the careless guard's right instep (a lucky blow, he would later admit). The guard howled and fell to the ground, writhing in pain. In the same moment, Berengar sprang from his bent posture and rolled between Blitzen's legs, ending up several feet from where the other guard had held a sword at his neck. Berengar's own sword was out of reach, so he unsheathed the dagger still strapped to his thigh. He was at a disadvantage, but the guard now had to divide his attention between Berengar and the no-longer-limping friar.

Berengar's opponent thrust his sword toward him, but the agile Bavarian stepped aside just in time. In that same moment, William swept his staff across the back of the guard's legs, bringing him to his knees. As his sword skittered away, Berengar leapt forward and plunged his dagger into the disarmed guard's midsection, then withdrew it and thrust it again for good measure. He rose and strode over to the second guard, who was crawling to retrieve the sword he dropped when William drove the staff into his foot. Before he could reach it Berengar grasped the man's hair and slit his throat.

William stared open-mouthed at Berengar, who glared back at

him. "What did you expect me to do?"

William had no reply.

"Their horses must be close by," Berengar said. "They can't have come on foot." He then walked a few yards back to where the path they had seen earlier merged with the trail. Less than a minute later he returned, leading one of the guard's horses by the reins.

"Blitzen's not fit to carry both of us. He'll barely make it with me."

"I thought we were going to walk."

"Not anymore!" Eyeing the slain guards, Berengar said, "Verdun must have divided his force and ordered some of his men to search the abbey's periphery. It's unlikely these are the only two he sent."

William gulped at the prospect of mounting the horse but took the animal's soft snorting as an invitation to try. "You'll have to give me a hand."

As he strained to reach the saddle, he slipped. Berengar caught him and shoved his rump upward onto the horse's back. Satisfied that he wouldn't fall, William took hold of the horse's reins. He canted his body so that his shorter, right leg could reach the stirrup. But now his *left* foot barely touched the other stirrup.

Berenger picked up William's staff and instructed, "You go first and I'll follow." His voice did not brim with confidence.

William knew that to propel his steed forward he should jab its flanks with his heels. He did so, but with greater force than required. As his horse bolted forward, he fell backwards but somehow managed to grasp a clump of the horse's mane and pull himself upright. For a hundred yards he sped helter-skelter in Bavaria's general direction, bouncing up and down on the saddle while leaning precariously to the right. He felt ridiculous and must have *looked* ridiculous to Berengar, who raced at full gallop to overtake him. Once alongside, Berengar grabbed the horse's reins and brought William to a halt.

"We need to adjust the stirrups," Berengar grumbled as he dismounted. "They have to be high enough to bear your weight. Otherwise, you'll fall off or end up with a sore ass."

* * *

They arrived at the main route well before sunset, having ridden most of the way. Blitzen's inflamed hock held up better than Berengar expected and required only occasional applications of Agnolo's salve. To William's surprise, he soon got the hang of riding a horse. He dismounted and walked only when the trail became too steep or narrow. Best of all, there were no further sightings of Verdun's men, though William often glanced behind him to see if they were coming.

William and Berengar shared a final meal of bread, figs, and sausages washed down by the jug of wine Berengar had the foresight to bring with him. After they had eaten and rested, the red-bearded agent inspected Blitzen's leg as well as William's horse, which he would take with him to Pisa. He knew a safe route that would take him well clear of the abbey and any of Verdun's men who might still be searching the area.

While Berengar completed his preparations to leave, William sat on a tree stump, examining a crude map of the route he would take through the Alps. But he probably didn't need it. Mendicant friars were experienced in finding their way through unfamiliar territory.

Berengar had been solicitous ever since William saved him from almost certain death. "How are the stirrups?" "Do you need to rest?" "Are you thirsty?" He didn't ask if William's ass was sore.

He was about to mount Blitzen and head off to Pisa when he

turned and nodded toward William's staff. "Pardon my curiosity, but how did you learn to fight with it?"

William suppressed a grin on recalling the ballads from his youth. "From Friar Tuck."

Berengar gave him a puzzled look and then repeated, *"Frère Toque*. I have not heard of this man. He is French?"

Epilogue

June 14, 1328 — To Bavaria

WITHIN DAYS OF LEAVING the abbey William had to slow his pace. The thin Alpine air shortened his breath, but this allowed him—forced him, even—to gaze and then marvel at wildflowers he had never seen. They bloomed only at "the top of the sky," a phrase he heard uttered by Brother Guido, the dreamy old monk who tended the abbey's botanical garden. William's occasional companions along his route called them gentians, snowbells, larkspur, silvery cranesbill, and scarlet avens—names he soon forgot as each flower acquired new names later in his journey. The name for a single, omnipresent flower changed from one village to the next: "Cat's paws" in the first village were "lion's paws" in the second and "wool flowers" in the third. Weeks later as William neared his destination he learned that the furry white blooms were called "edelweiss" in the harsh German vernacular he would soon struggle to master.

As he negotiated his way between the clumps of edelweiss dotting his path, he imagined his old adversary in London, Walter Chatton, fatuously claiming that each flower must have a correct—a *truthful*—name that represented its essential nature. William knew that the linkage between words and truth was more precarious than Chatton's metaphysical twaddle supposed. Truth was the exclusive province of God, and mere mortals' descriptions of things and events were nothing but fallible opinions, sometimes shared and other times not.

This put him in mind of something the spymaster Rupert said at the abbey. He had noted with a mixture of approval and condescension that William's theories, while consistent with most of the known facts, should be regarded as provisional; perfect solutions could be revealed only when "all the facts are in."

William agreed that new facts might compel him to revise or even reject his theories. His vanity shouldn't beguile him into pretending otherwise. But he also knew there could be no complete account of an event, no perfect solution to a puzzle. Other versions of Edward II's "death," Gerardo's murder, and the Greyfriars' escape from Avignon would be told and retold until people tired of hearing them. One day, perhaps, William would tell a new version of his own.

His analytical temperament at first resisted this conclusion. As a young seminarian he believed that logic, free of superstition and the encumbrance of metaphysics, would aid him in stripping away all that was false and unnecessary so that truth could be revealed. But in the years since, he had learned that logic's chief power lay in exposing its own incompleteness. That very incompleteness, in turn, made room for his faith and freed him to use logic, along with Friar Bacon's experimental method, in solving humbler, practical problems. The Invincible Doctor now embraced his vincibility.

* * *

$\mathfrak{M}$onths earlier William decided he had had enough of metaphysics, natural philosophy, and theology. He no longer cared whether the *existence* of angels was distinct from their *essence*, or if one angel could speak to another, or if God was an efficient cause of things other than Himself.[xiii] He now found such questions, and indeed his answers to them, technical and tedious. Henceforth he would write only about politics.

No doubt he would receive encouragement in that pursuit from Marsilius, who would meet him later at Louis' castle. Together, they were sure to speculate about the war looming between England and France, and whether Louis would wrest the papal throne from Avignon and take it back to the Eternal City. Under the worldly Italian's tutelage William could also learn about food.

Baskerville might join their conversations, although William's aging mentor was known to stay in one place only briefly before heading off on a new mission the emperor assigned him. William had hoped to ask about Baskerville's part in solving the murders at the abbey the year before, but other matters intervened. He would make time for that discussion in Bavaria.

The day before the friars departed the abbey, William learned of Bonagratia's plan to travel south to Naples. Once there, he would partake of the pleasures afforded by the wise King Robert's civilized reign—and annoy the denizens of that happy and peaceful land. Michael would hasten to Bologna and learn if he had been reelected the Franciscans' minister general. In Pisa, Rupert would receive new instructions from Louis and await further reports from his agents in Avignon.

During a private moment earlier in their stay Rupert made what sounded like an offer, although William wasn't sure the spymaster was serious. Might he consider a new vocation, Rupert asked, hinting that the emperor was ever on the lookout for talented agents. Nonplussed at this suggestion, William didn't know whether to feel flattered or horrified. He artfully deflected Rupert's query, saying he couldn't imagine anyone worse suited than himself for such an adventurous life. But he hadn't given him a definite no, and suspected this wasn't the last he would see of Louis the Bavarian's nephew.

William felt homesick but knew he couldn't return to England. Within weeks Duèze's agents would track him down and either quietly dispose of him or haul him back to Avignon to be executed. The pope would never abide the obnoxious Greyfriar roaming free in Albion, spreading his lies and fomenting discord against the unholy church. And if Duèze didn't capture him, Roger Mortimer soon would. Both he and Isabella might know of William's secrets, and besides, he was the confidant and confessor of Eleanor de Clare, widow of the hated Despenser.

This meant that he would never see Eleanor. Was she still imprisoned in the Tower? Could she risk writing to him when he reached his sanctuary in Bavaria? Did she confess to Adam Wodeham and pray each day in the Chapel of Saint Peter *ad Vincula*?

These questions paled before one other: Might she have loved him? Probably not, he had to admit. And if she hadn't, it would no longer tear at his heart. Instead, he could be content knowing that Eleanor felt kindly toward him and wished him well. Not all *he* had wished for, but it was enough—or so William told himself, again, as he inched his way to the top of the sky.

* * * * *

Afterword

Although commentary on William Occam's writings continues to be a thriving philosophical concern, little is known about his life. He was born in late 1287 or early 1288 and died near Munich in 1347 or 1349. If the latter year is correct, he almost certainly succumbed to the Black Death, which killed at least one-third of Europe's population. Until his summons to Avignon in 1324, Occam spent nearly all his years after age eight or nine in London and Oxford, although he may have spent a brief period between 1311 and 1314 in Paris. The date of his escape from Avignon has been reliably documented as May 26, 1328.

The circumstances surrounding Occam's departure from Avignon are mostly matters of conjecture and are unlikely ever to be settled. He and the other dissident friars may have made a daring escape. Or, Pope John's interest in keeping them in Avignon may have waned to the point of indifference, enabling them to leave without risk of being forcibly detained or caught. A third possibility is that the pope permitted or contrived their escape for reasons like those depicted in *Invincibilis*. I make no claim as to the greater likelihood of that explanation other than to note that the pope's power and authority were under continuous threat from the emperor,

Louis the Bavarian, and the various religious orders. John was also known to be cunning, pragmatic, and nervous.

The Fieschi letter: Edward II's fate has been fraught with controversy up to the present day. The nub of the controversy is the so-called "Fieschi letter," written to Edward III, circa 1337, by Manuele Fieschi, a Genoese priest and papal notary serving in Avignon at the time of the events described here. A French official at the Archives Departmentales d'Herault in Montpellier found a copy of the letter in 1878, but its existence didn't receive widespread attention by historians until nearly a century later. Experts examining the letter concluded that it was not a forgery. No one now doubts its authenticity, although the veracity of the story Fieschi told is still disputed.

In his letter to the old king's son, Fieschi claimed that Edward II was not murdered in 1327, but escaped from Berkeley Castle upon being told by a servant that he was about to be murdered by two of Roger Mortimer's henchmen, de Gornay and Bereford. Edward exchanged clothes with the servant, killed one of the castle's porters, and fled accompanied by a friendly guard. He then went into hiding at Corfe Castle near the Dorset coast in southern England where he remained for more than a year. Fearing Mortimer's and the "wicked queen's" wrath for their failure to kill Edward, de Gornay and Bereford had heavily shrouded the corpse of the slain porter, claiming he was Edward. Edward's half-brother Edmund, Earl of Kent, later learned he was alive and plotted to rescue him from Corfe. Upon discovering the plot, Mortimer beheaded Edmund. When Edward learned of his half-brother's execution, he sailed to Ireland where he stayed for several months before crossing the Channel to France and eventually traveling on foot to Avignon disguised as a poor pilgrim. Once there, he met with Pope John, who granted his protection and blessing. Edward spent fifteen days with the pope, after which responsibility for his care was entrusted to Cardinal Luca Fieschi, a distant relative of both Manuele Fieschi and Edward himself. Fieschi's letter claims also that Edward later traveled under an assumed name to various locations throughout Europe and may have met secretly with his son, Edward III. Most of his remaining years (until his death, probably in late 1341) were spent at two monasteries in Italy.

If Edward did escape from Berkeley Castle and go to Corfe Castle and then to Ireland, Fieschi's letter would place his arrival in Avignon nearly three years after his escape from Berkeley Castle in September of 1327. If the letter is generally correct in describing the king's movements, my major breach of the historical record is in having the king leave England just a few months after his departure from Berkeley Castle so that he could arrive in Avignon one month before Occam's escape in late May of 1328.

Some historians, however, still doubt the veracity of the letter, one of their arguments being that the careerist Fieschi, who already held several church appointments in England, hoped to ingratiate himself with Edward III in order to receive royal patronage. His "fake" letter to the young king was thus a ruse to further that end. Or, an impostor highly knowledgeable about the circumstances of Edward's captivity and death may have duped Fieschi into writing his letter.

Those who accept the letter's veracity differ with one another over several questions: What part, if any, did Roger Mortimer play in contriving Edward's escape from Berkeley Castle? Did Isabella collude in it? If Isabella was not a party to her husband's escape, when did she and her son Edward III first learn about it? Finally, what involvement, if any, did Stephen Dunheved have in the third, apparently successful, effort to free Edward?

Historians have long since put to rest the lurid account of Edward's murder by the insertion of a red-hot poker up his fundament by de Gornay and Bereford. That rumor was whispered shortly after the king's purported death at Berkeley Castle and was later dramatized in the 16th century in Christopher Marlowe's play *Edward II* and again, more than four centuries later, in Derek Jarman's film of the same title.

As for Fieschi himself, it is doubtful that his various functions in and around the palace were as significant as I have portrayed them. The position of papal notary, which he held during the four years Occam spent in Avignon, was relatively minor and would have been unlikely to bring him into frequent contact with the pope. He did have a brother in Genoa, Count Gabriele Fieschi. The count was indeed a banker, but Edward II's owing him money is my invention. The king was, however, heavily in debt to various Italian bankers at the time. The count also had three sons, although I was unable to determine if one of them was named Gerardo or if any was a Franciscan friar. The now-famous letter Manuele Fieschi wrote to Edward III prompted me to elevate his stature by including him as a prominent character.

Ian Mortimer's theory: No relation to Lord Roger, the historian Ian Mortimer proposes a theory of Edward's "escape" based on an analysis of the Fieschi letter and other historical documents. Owing to Isabella's still-strong emotional attachment to her husband, Lord Mortimer instructed his nephew Thomas, Earl of Berkeley, to fake Edward's death, sending him to

Corfe Castle to be secretly maintained by Sir John Maltravers while Sir John Pecche was overseas, and embalmed another corpse to be buried in place of the king. Unfortunately for the plotters, Sir John Pecche returned unexpectedly in early 1328 and discovered Edward II at Corfe Castle. Pecche then informed [Edward's half-brother, Edmund Earl of] Kent, who subsequently took action to rescue the king. His plot was discovered by Mortimer's agents. Mortimer's threat to the royal authority—which had been great even before 1330—now became unbearable for Edward III, who saw his uncle condemned to death in parliament for trying to rescue his sadly abused father from Corfe. Having no doubt that his entire dynasty was at risk, Edward III arranged the seizure of Mortimer and eradicated the widespread doubts about his father's fate by finally creating an official, royal version of the "death": that Edward II had been murdered by Gurney [Thomas de Gornay] and Ockley [William Ogle] on Mortimer's orders in Berkeley Castle. This served to destroy Mortimer's support and strengthen Edward III's own status as a ruling king, even though he was still under age. The story of the death of Edward II in Berkeley was thus a political fiction invented by Mortimer and twisted by Edward III into a murder story for reasons of political legitimacy.[xiv]

Ian Mortimer's speculation invites the writing of an entertaining murder mystery, one that would of course be entirely different from *Invincibilis*. Long departed from Avignon by the time Dr. Mortimer places Edward there, the intrepid Greyfriar could not have played any role in solving it. (A sequel to *Invincibilis*, however, might well resolve this problem. Stay tuned.)

Notwithstanding the evident conviction with which Ian Mortimer advances his theory, questions surrounding Edward's fate are still far from settled among other contemporary historians. In her admirably balanced *Long Live the King: The Mysterious Fate of Edward II*, Kathryn Warner examines the evidence and arguments on both sides: that Edward did in fact die in September, 1327 (whether of natural causes, by his own hand, or at the murderous hands of his captors and overseers), *and* that he survived (whether by escaping or being released by his captors) and made his way to Avignon and later to two monasteries in Italy. Warner herself takes pains to remain neutral on these questions until, in her Conclusion, she tips her hand in Mortimer's general direction by invoking the most celebrated idea of none other than Friar William himself.

> After 700 years it is frustratingly impossible to come to any firm conclusions about Edward II's murder or survival, at least based on the evidence that we currently have. Occam's or Ockham's Razor. . . states that "among competing hypotheses, the one with the fewest assumptions should be selected." The theory that Edward II did actually survive after 1327 explains all the evidence we have that he did, whereas the notion that he died in 1327 requires a number of explanations for the later evidence that he was not dead: that the Earl of Kent and his many follows were stupid and gullible; that the Earl of Kent and Archbishop of York were deceived into believing that Edward was still alive so that they would commit treason, as an excuse to arrest them; that Lord Berkeley was incapable of expressing himself properly to parliament; that two popes and a papal notary

were taken in by an impostor; that Manuele Fieschi was a liar and a blackmailer; and so on.[xv]

Eleanor de Clare: Like Queen Isabella and her other attendants, Eleanor de Clare reportedly confessed exclusively to Greyfriars, and her stays in London and possibly Paris overlapped with Occam's long enough that it is conceivable she could have confessed to him. Add to that the fact that Occam was already famously known as the Invincible Doctor and could well have attracted the attention of the nobles of the Westminster court. (In view of his prodigious outpouring of scholarly manuscripts, however, it is hard to imagine how he could have spared the time to serve as *anyone's* confessor.)

The story ends with Occam wondering what had become of Eleanor. Possibly at her cousin Edward III's insistence, Mortimer and Isabella released her from the Tower of London a month or two before Occam escaped from Avignon. In the novel that would (or could) have been while her last letter to him was in transit. Less than a year later, in early 1329, she was abducted from Hanley Castle, in Worcestershire, by Roger Mortimer's distant cousin and then-ally William la Zouche, whom she almost immediately married. It isn't known whether she consented to the marriage, but she later bore a son by la Zouche. Her second husband died in early 1337, followed to the grave by Eleanor herself just a few months later at the age of forty-four.

Eleanor de Clare has appeared in fiction at least twice before. In Maurice Druon's 1960 novel *The She Wolf* (Queen Isabella), Eleanor is portrayed as an enabler of her husband Hugh le Despenser—and every bit as vile as he was. That is saying quite a lot, considering that *BBC History Magazine* once dubbed Despenser "the worst Briton of the 14th century." She received sympathetic treatment in

Susan Higginbotham's more recent (2005) novel *The Traitor's Wife*. In Higginbotham's telling, Eleanor is devoted to her husband and deeply mourns his death, even after she realizes, belatedly, that he and Edward were lovers. I cannot claim my own portrayal of Eleanor as more accurate than either of those novels, but given my development of Occam's character, he wouldn't have been smitten by a harridan nor by a woman so naïve as not to have caught on to her husband's infidelity early on. Thus, a savvy and courageous Eleanor seems a more plausible match for the discerning Occam.

Mortimer and Isabella: Roger Mortimer met almost precisely the gruesome end Occam predicted. Mortimer and Isabella proved to be just as greedy and incompetent as Edward II and his favorite, Despenser. Together they antagonized most of the English barons, including Henry, Earl of Lancaster, who tried to persuade the younger Edward to assert his independence from his two regents. In March 1330, Mortimer ordered the execution of Edward II's half-brother Edmund, Earl of Kent, who Mortimer accused of plotting to free Edward from captivity at Corfe Castle. This was the last straw for the young king, who later that year arrested Mortimer and, after a brief trial, had him hanged for usurping royal power and committing various other high misdemeanors. Not yet eighteen, Edward III thereby assumed effective control over his realm.

Although later maligned by historians and novelists, Isabella was spared Mortimer's ignominious fate, spending the remainder of her life uneventfully and in comfort provided by her son. She was neither imprisoned, sent to a nunnery, nor did she go mad, as some early accounts claimed. Whether she and Mortimer were lovers or merely political allies is still debated, as is whether a breach occurred between them. Evidence of her lingering affection for Edward may be inferred from her burial, in 1358 at the age of sixty-three, at Greyfriars church in London with her husband's heart (though possibly someone else's) placed upon her breast. For a thorough and balanced treatment of her life, I recommend Alison Weir's 2005 biography *Queen Isabella: Treachery, Adultery, and Murder in Medieval England*.

Francesco Petrarca: When I discovered quite by accident that Petrarch, in his early twenties, was in Avignon during the last two to three years of Occam's stay there, the temptation to include him as a character was too tantalizing to resist. I've been unable confirm they knew each other, but it is at least possible they were acquainted. Occam's presence in Avignon was widely known, at least in scholarly circles, and the intellectually precocious Petrarch may have learned of him.

Later known as the "Father of Humanism," Petrarch has been credited with initiating the 14th century Renaissance. As early as 1325 or 1326, however, he was already composing his now-famous sonnets, hundreds of which he sent to his inamorata, the newly married Laura de Noves. Like Occam, though for different reasons, he fiercely opposed the Avignon papacy, which would have given the two of them something in common politically. Petrarch finished minor orders in Avignon in 1330 and spent the rest of his life in the Church's service under the patronage of various, chiefly Italian, bishops and cardinals.

William of Baskerville: Including Baskerville in my cast of characters was even more irresistible. The surname of Umberto Eco's hero in *The Name of the Rose* is an obvious homage to Sherlock Holmes, but less obvious is that the choice of his baptismal name, William, is Eco's homage to Occam himself. Baskerville occasionally mentions Occam explicitly, but much—arguably the core—of Baskerville's philosophical and theological outlook comes straight out of Occam's writings. (In deference to Eco, I have retained the spelling he uses rather than the now more common *Ockham*.)

The murders in *The Name of the Rose* are set in November 1327, just six months before Occam's escape. I took the liberty of placing those murders a few months earlier in order to set the stage for Michael of Cesena's arrival in Avignon on December 1. I took the additional liberties of recruiting a new abbot and permitting the emperor to pay for the Benedictine abbey's restoration. I beg the indulgence of Eco's devoted readers for having done so.

Following the Franciscans' departure from Avignon in late May of the following year, they of course didn't travel to Eco's fictional abbey in the Italian Piedmont. Instead, they made their way farther south to Pisa where the emperor Louis, along with his court and legions, temporarily resided. Louis granted Occam and his comrades protection and patronage, in return for which Occam subsequently wrote treatises arguing in favor of the emperor's supreme control over church and state in the Holy Roman Empire. Upon learning this, John XXII finally excommunicated Occam.

Other supporting characters: The names and titles of the six papal commissioners are historically accurate. I can't say whether Occam had an ally on the commission, but I wanted him to have one and chose Durand of Saint-Pourçain, like Occam a philosophical Nominalist, to perform that role. "Prince" Rupert wasn't really a prince and probably wasn't a spymaster, either. He was the third son of Louis the Bavarian's elder brother Rudolf I, Duke of Bavaria. Assigning Rupert the role of the emperor's spymaster suited my need for an interrogator in the novel's denouement at the Benedictine abbey. Stephen Dunheved, Edward II's bodyguard, may or may not have accompanied the deposed monarch to Avignon (either in 1328 or 1331) and in any case probably wasn't killed there. The last mention I could find of Dunheved placed him in England, in March 1330, on a list of men arrested by Roger Mortimer for aiding the Earl of Kent in his effort to free Edward from Corfe Castle and restore him to the throne. Finally, Pope John XXII—Jacques Duèze—died peacefully in Avignon, in December 1334, at age ninety.

MICHAEL HARMON

Acknowledgments

I have many people to thank for whatever pleasures readers might derive from this, my first novel. By far the most deserving of thanks is my wife and partner in all things good, Annette Beresford, whose support for this project sustained me from my earliest researches to the novel's final polishing. Annette also proved to be a sharp-eyed editor, always—well, *almost* always—right in her criticisms and suggestions for changes.

Many friends, some old and others new, read and commented on various portions of manuscript and provided much-needed encouragement and advice: Dick and Elaine Sullivan, Orion White, Cynthia McSwain, Bill Adams, Roselena Sanders, Rondo Keele, Estelle Raimondo, Jackson Frost, John Thomas, Douglas Beresford, Jody De La Motte Hurst, Gary Watts, and O. D. Hegre. Stalwart members of the Chain Bridge Writers Group—Helen Stine, Paul Bourgeois, Peggy Duffy, and Jesse Galena—were there when I needed them, and I thank them for their helpful critiques and friendship.

My brother Scott Harmon recalled enough from his early training in medieval history to save me from embarrassment on numerous occasions. England, for example, did not have potatoes in the 14th century; a beggar would receive alms deposited in a small wooden bowl, not in a tin cup (too expensive); and Friar Occam would probably have crossed the Channel in a small vessel called a *cog*.

In one of her many books on 14th century England, *Long Live the King*, historian Kathryn Warner provided initial stimulus for *Invincibilis* by invoking "Occam's Razor" to support the controversial claim that Edward II escaped captivity in England and made his way to Avignon. Kathryn has generously answered my many questions with grace and dispatch. I hadn't known, for example, that Queen Isabella wouldn't have been addressed as "Your Highness" or "Your Majesty" (royal appellations not invented until two centuries later) but as "My Lady Queen."

I have also profited greatly from "professional help" given by two gifted novelists. Dana D. Burnell read and critiqued the first draft, recommending among other changes that I include more action and suspense, and delve more deeply into the main characters' relationships. Thierry Sagnier's thorough editing, supplemented by memorable lunches, improved *Invincibilis* beyond measure. At his urging I added two new subplots and enriched the novel's descriptive details of everyday life in Avignon.

ℜotes

[i] Quoted in Stephen Chak Tornay, *Ockham: Studies and Selections*, Chicago: Open Court, 1938, p. 84.

[ii] Franciscans, followers of the thirteenth century Italian friar and preacher Saint Francis of Assisi, were also known as Greyfriars because of the grey habits they wore. Their sometimes rivals, the Dominicans, were for a like reason called Blackfriars.

[iii] At the center of philosophical controversy over the metaphysics of universals in the medieval era was the debate between the Realists and Nominalists. Traceable back to Aristotle (and earlier to Plato in a stronger form), Realism posits that universals (or "essences") are just as real as the physical, or material, objects that are accessible to sensory experience. Aristotle's Realism undergirded the thirteenth-century writings of Thomas Aquinas, perhaps the chief influence on the Dominican philosophers at the Sorbonne in Paris.

Medieval Nominalists, of whom Occam was the most influential exponent, held that universal, abstract concepts do not exist in the same way tangible, physical objects exist. For Occam, universals (and therefore metaphysics more generally) are largely unnecessary. This position is key to understanding what has come to be known as Occam's Razor, the idea that explanations of phenomena should rely on the fewest possible assumptions.

[iv] *Invincibilis* has two English translations: invincible (or unconquerable) and irrefutable. This second meaning is implied in Occam's best-known nickname, *Doctor Invincibilis*. (He also had two other nicknames: *the More Than Subtle Doctor* and *the Venerable Preceptor*.)

[v] The French had long been rankled by England's possession of Gascony in the southwest of France and through devious legal maneuvers had taken back portions of it the English once controlled. Edward II was King of England, but he also held the title of Duke of Aquitaine, which gave him a legal, though shaky, claim on Gascony and other French vassals vital to England's economy. Just as King Philip had done years earlier, his son

Charles IV demanded that Edward go to Paris to swear fealty to him as the price of retaining what lands the English still kept. Edward was galled at the prospect and also feared for his safety if he crossed the Channel to negotiate with the French king. The current situation was in flux, and as events played out in the coming months Edward would have to rely on Isabella to salvage England's interests in France.

vi *O Lord, make speed to save me:*
   O Lord, make haste to help me.
(First verse of the sixty-ninth Psalm)

vii Had Boniface heeded the warning of his fellow countryman, the intelligent Dante Alighieri, he might have avoided this trouble. Just a few years before, the great poet advised the pope not to interfere in secular affairs and instead confine the Church's activities to moral exhortation and prayer. On learning his advice had been ignored, Dante consigned Boniface to one of the lower circles of hell in a long poem he would soon compose.

Occam would later revisit the venerable doctrine of the Two Swords first handed down by the Church fathers in the sixth century. Taking direct aim at the pope, he urged that the temporal and spiritual realms be rigidly separated, presided over by kings and other monarchs in the first instance and by the pope in the second. Neither of the metaphorical swords should hold sway over the other. Because he distrusted authority in any form or guise, Occam doubted either sword would be used justly and competently. Given the strong propensity for incompetence in both realms, it seemed more prudent to divide their powers than unify them.

The powers within each realm should also be checked in order to prevent, or at least minimize, their abuse. Just as Magna Carta set limits on the powers of the English kings, Occam urged that the power of the pope, as well as the clergy generally, be subject to judgments made by the whole body of Christian believers. The laity, including women, were fully equal to the clergy in their spiritual authority and were thus within their moral rights to criticize and even depose the pope for his errors in interpreting divine law or for meddling in secular affairs.

viii Readers of *The Seventh Function of Language*, Laurent Binet's hilarious sendup of twentieth-century French intellectuals, would surely agree on the prescience of Occam's observation. Whether Occam would have been pleased with all of his Nominalist offspring invites speculation.

[ix] This quotation is drawn from Occam's "Letter to the Friars Minor," as quoted in Rondo Keele's excellent introduction to his life and ideas, *Ockham Explained: From Razor to Rebellion*, Chicago: Open Court, 2010, p. 165.

[x] The Despenser and Lancaster clans feuded for more than two generations, punctuated, in 1313, by Thomas's leading role in the trial and execution of Edward II's first court favorite and rumored lover Piers Gaveston. Despenser's father, Hugh the Elder, was Gaveston's sole defender among the barons sitting in judgment at his trial. Despite the futility of the elder Hugh's effort, his steadfast support endeared both him and his son to the grief-stricken Edward. The younger Hugh became the beneficiary of Edward's extravagant favors and soon afterward succeeded Gaveston as the object of his intimate affection.

A year later an emboldened Thomas Earl of Lancaster led a successful rebellion by the barons against the king, after which he ruled England for four years as the humiliated Edward languished impotently in his castles. But Lancaster turned out to be no more popular than Edward himself. Disenchanted by Lancaster's greed and incompetence, most of the barons swung back to Edward's side, enabling him to regain control of his realm. He further solidified his power through Hugh le Despenser's ruthless cooperation, but in doing so provoked whispers among a few of the barons that he was little more than Despenser's puppet.

As Despenser's rapacity intensified, several of the magnates shifted their allegiance once again, with the Earl of Lancaster returning to lead a new rebellion against Edward in what became known as the Despenser Wars. In 1321, Despenser, in league with other Edward loyalists, routed Lancaster's forces at the Battle of Boroughbridge. The defeated earl was taken prisoner and beheaded within days. Owing to his kinship with his first cousin Edward, he was spared the added ignominy of being drawn and quartered. Reports soon proliferated of miracles at Lancaster's tomb at Pontefract, in Yorkshire, leading to his veneration as a martyr to liberty's cause. Into the breach cleaved by his execution strode Roger Mortimer, who bided his time in the Tower of London until his infamous escape.

After Lancaster's execution, his estates were forfeited, most of them reverting to Despenser. Two years later Lancaster's successor as Earl, his younger brother Henry, successfully petitioned to reclaim the earldom of Leicester, a major portion of his family's estates. Then, upon Edward's overthrow and Despenser's celebrated demise in 1326, a victorious Mortimer returned to Henry his remaining earldoms: of Lancaster, Salisbury, and Lincoln.

Mortimer's motives for seeking the canonization of Henry's late brother appeared to be twofold: first, to appease the new earl in order to cement their tenuous bond, and second, to discredit further the memory of the (reportedly) deceased Edward II. Mortimer had reason to worry, however. Within a few short years Edward III would seize his rightful power to rule England by executing Mortimer.

[xi] Lepers had long been feared and stigmatized throughout Europe, but in the spring of 1321, their persecution in France took a new, more draconian turn. Hysterical reports spread throughout the land that Spanish Muslims had bribed the Jews to join with lepers in poisoning the wells of Christians, using rotting bread as a contaminant. King Philip, Charles IV's elder brother and his predecessor on the French throne, instructed the Dominican inquisitor Bernard Gui to investigate. At Gui's recommendation, Philip commanded that all lepers be imprisoned and interrogated under torture. Any found guilty of taking part in the conspiracy were to be executed. The leprosaria, then, were originally intended as venues for incarceration and punishment, protecting the larger populace from the lepers' predations. But under the later, more benign aegis of the Benedictine Order the leprosaria shielded their inmates from fanatical retribution. As a result, tensions eased in the larger Avignon community.

[xii] The poverty controversy raged not only between Pope John XXII and the Franciscans but also within the Franciscan order itself. Franciscans were divided between the "Spirituals," who renounced ownership of anything both individually and collectively, and the "Conventuals," including the "moderate" Conventual Michael of Cesena. In 1316, Cesena was elected minister general of the Franciscans and charged with forging a compromise with Pope John. Like the Dominican and Benedictine orders, Conventual Franciscans were willing to accept communal ownership of property while maintaining their vows of individual poverty. Of the two

Franciscan groups, the Spirituals were more faithful to Saint Francis's original vision, and believed that the Pope—more strictly, the Papacy—"officially" owned and was therefore obliged to manage the various kinds of property (including food and clothing) used by the Franciscans, thus leaving intact both their individual and communal poverty. In 1323, however, Pope John issued a bull rescinding the arrangement by which he would manage the property used by the Franciscans. Cesena tried to change the Pope's mind on this issue, but to no avail. Influenced by William Occam, Cesena eventually converted to the Spirituals' cause.

[xiii] William of Ockham, *Quodlibetal Questions,* Volumes 1 and 2, trans. Alfred J. Freddoso and Francis E. Kelley, New Haven: Yale University Press, 1991.

[xiv] Ian Mortimer, *The Perfect King: The Life of Edward III, Father of the English Nation*, London: Vintage Books, 2008, p. 410.

[xv] Kathryn Warner, *Long Live the King: The Mysterious Fate of Edward II*, Stroud, UK: Amberley Publishing, 2017, p. 213. See also Warner's *Edward II: The Unconventional King*, Stroud, UK: Amberley Publishing, 2014.

MICHAEL HARMON

Made in the USA
Coppell, TX
04 October 2024